DARK SECRETS

RUTH A. MILLIGAN

In memory of my mom, who always saved me a seat next to her on the couch to read; my dad, who gave me the best advice: "Do what makes you happy!" In memory of my bonus mom, who always swapped books with me that inspired me to be the writer I wanted to be.

These wonderful, loving people always encouraged me to finish and publish a novel, and I still hear their words of support coming from heaven.

CHAPTER ONE

They built Juniper Ridge and Black Hills with concrete walls so thick no one could hear the mutants' agonizing cries from the outside. It stood six stories high on the east end of Hill River, murky with pollutants ten miles from the closest town. Built more for stability than style, five small windows on either side donned the office area and the entryway. Wrapped around it was a modest parking lot and a barbed wire fence that almost reached up to the sky, heavy with smog. An American flag flapped in the breeze and the rain.

Adam's full-size Chevy pickup hit every pothole and worn spot on Jefferson Street on his way to work. Led Zeppelin blared out of the radio, drowned out by the pouring rain as it beat against the windshield and the screeching wiper blades.

"I should have had more coffee this morning," Adam muttered as he rubbed his eyes and turned up the heater. The bags under them were so puffy it looked like he packed them for a month-long trip to Peru. Wrinkles around his eyes and mouth were forming well before most other thirty-two-year-olds. He thought of his family at home. "Only a few more years of these long hours."

After scanning his badge and entering his ten-digit code, he passed through the gate and parked on the nearest power pad that would charge his vehicle when he was working. The badge that hung from his neck got him in the front door as he swiped it, a picture of Daniel Freeman framed in gold crooked above the card reader. Daniel was the founder of Juniper Ridge and passed away four years ago. The next two areas included a fingerprint and then a retinal scan. Once he reached the third floor, he could already feel the vibrations from all the noise. The patients, comprising birds, monkeys, cats, and dogs, were feeling rowdy on the new drugs. The doctors kept the animal patients in cages in the rooms upon admission. They strapped the humans down to their beds until proven safe. To anyone else, this noise would deafen, but to Adam, it fell in the back of his mind. His eyes narrowed, and he popped his neck from one side to the other before starting down the hallway to the last two doors, one on either side. He put his hand on the knob of the door on his right and listened before opening it.

Behind the door was complete silence.

He bowed his head. "Please, Christopher, still be alive. Don't make me a failure." He opened the door to find the child sleeping. Christopher had torn his bed to pieces, huddled in the corner with his claws curled up into tight fists where human hands once were.

Monitoring him, Adam grabbed the binder from the wall and opened it up to peruse the notes, reading the transformation from a boy to an animalistic creature. He shook his head, edging toward him at a snail-like pace not to wake him. Adam noticed Christopher's ears were disintegrating and the new scabs covering over them were scaly and red, looking infected. Occasionally, he would scratch at it while he slept. He slapped on some gloves from a nearby cabinet and barely touched the side of Christopher's head, surprised that the boy didn't stir. With downcast eyes, he allowed him to sleep.

Christopher was one of the first human patients. He had run away from home when he was seven, and they found him normal, except for his webbed feet. He was hiding in the sewers, dirty with torn clothes and unwilling to talk to anyone but Adam, the one person at Juniper Ridge that he knew before his discovery. The scientists were concerned about finding him in the worst location, given that the virus that caused the world's decline spread through the water supply. In the sewers, they properly filtered nothing for safety.

A year ago, when Christopher's hands were transforming into claws, Adam studied constantly to reverse his changing. He knew he was doing something right when the next few months there were no adverse changes in the boy after a combination of herbs and medicines were administered. The herbs were rare because of the difficulty of growing things from the damaged soil. They were only effective those few months and the mutant changes began again.

Adam exited the room quietly to avoid waking him. Scooping up the binder, he went to his office on the fourth floor, away from everything, so there would be less chance for someone to disturb him. With all the work that he had been doing, he wondered if it was going to make any difference. The child had already been through so much. *I have to do what I can,* he thought, but some days he wasn't sure if his heart was in it.

"Adam?" he heard behind him as he reached the outside of the door, and Adam jumped, dropping the binder. Jesse apologized as he reached down to retrieve the massive volume.

"So, how's he doing?" Jesse pointed to the files. Jesse's muscular frame overpowered Adam's average build.

"He's changed." Adam motioned for Jesse to follow him and shook his head. "His ears are gone."

"Gone? What do you mean, gone?" Adam opened the door of his dimly lit office after unlocking it. Adam's cerulean eyes had always been sensitive to bright lights.

"I don't know why, or how, but there are just scabs where his ears used to be. If those scabs get infected, he'll need antibiotics."

Jesse sat in a chair opposite Adam. "How are we going to communicate with him now that he can't hear?"

"I didn't think we communicated with him much when he could."

"You have a point there." Jesse stifled a yawn and rolled his right shoulder. "You can get through to him more than anyone."

"The least we can do is get him some antibiotics as a precaution. He has enough problems."

"No thanks to that Jill Freeman over at Black Hills." Adam raised his eyebrows at him, faking shock. Jesse's face hardened. "You know the rumors. She's playing with DNA and test tubes, like the environment hasn't caused enough damage already. Admit, there's been some strange mutants coming in here lately, and I mean stranger than normal."

"I can't say that it hasn't crossed my mind." *Many times. All the time. This world is getting out of control. It has to be more than the environment, because we have all been cleaning up the water supply a little at a time.*

Heavy rainfall intensified, and thunder shook the building. Adam and Jesse glanced upwards, and the next thing they knew, they were both in darkness.

"Just great," Adam moaned. "Hold on. Let me grab a flashlight." He got up and cursed as his shin struck a sharp corner. Opening the bottom drawer of his desk and finding the flashlight, a beam of light filled a small section of the office. "Sometimes I wish this place had more windows."

"You know how the government feels about the whole privacy thing." Jesse paused and glanced around. "There's a danger lurking in the dark. The darkness of my heart..." he sang, quoting the latest song from ZYG8T. Adam groaned, and Jesse halted the lyrics. "Don't tell me the backup power supply isn't working. Sven should be able to hit the backup controls from his lab in the next room. I hope he's okay." Jesse's ears perked up as they both were quiet. "And I hope everything else is okay."

Adam's prior fatigue and worries dissipated, and his heart raced as an eerie feeling of apprehension filled him.

The entire building was an eruption of noise as the mutants barked, cawed, and yelled louder than normal.

"Stick close to me," Adam said, trying to control the tremor in his voice as he exited his office and walked back down the hall, with Jesse right behind him. "The elevators won't be working, so we'll have to take the stairs."

Adam's nerves were so on edge he felt like microscopic bugs were crawling on his skin, and he rolled his shoulders back as he twitched. He swung the flashlight back and forth in front of him until he reached the stairwell. He swore at the impaired retinal scan.

"You mean we're stuck here?" Jesse said as he slid down the wall on his back to sit on the floor, raising his hands. "What are we supposed to do now? I don't know how to fix it."

"Override it." Adam ignored the "I'm useless" muttering underneath Jesse's breath. Adam pulled the keys out of his pocket, using the edge to pry open the case that covered the retinal scan. Jesse leaned in to watch, not saying a word. Adam had Jesse hold the flashlight as he squinted. Adam's hands shook.

From below them, something knocked over and a scream broke the silence as they both jolted. Adam's forehead broke into a sweat as the temperature rose steadily and slow.

"Shit, it's getting hot in here," Jesse spat as he pulled at the collar around his neck.

"We have to get out of here. It sounds like Sven is in trouble." *I must get this to work*, Adam thought, knowing the scream was coming straight from Sven's office. It was faint, but he knew his voice. *If I don't, we'll be stuck on the fourth floor and Sven could be in real trouble. Come on, God, help me out here. Give me the knowledge to fix this.* He eyed the computer chips and wires soldered to perfection. The power came back on with more loud noises. "Thank you," he said to the ceiling, rolling his eyes upward, and slapped the cover back on the retinal scan, looking straight into it, and the door clicked open.

Adam ran down the stairs to the basement, the metal railing almost too hot to touch as if they were traveling down to hell itself.

"Here, this way," Jesse offered, his jacket flying up as he ran, and Adam noted a Glock tucked in a hidden holster he never noticed underneath his bulky lab coat.

The basement door was open, and it reminded Adam of walking toward an oven with the door open to broil. His brow narrowed. "The heat," he panted. "But I don't see any fire and I don't smell any smoke." Sweat gathered around his neckline and dripped from his brow.

He peered down the stairs. Something had a hold of Sven! Adam gripped the railing tighter, leaving a slight burn on the inside of his palm and fingers, wincing at the pain. He narrowed his eyes when he found the direct source of the heat.

If this was a mutant, he thought, what was it originally? It had to be something else that escaped Black Hills when the power went out, but what? A foot shorter than Sven, it was three feet wider and translucent except for the intertwining black and blue vein-like structure. It didn't resemble any human or animal in the faintest way imaginable.

Its head was massive compared to the size of its body, and it moved its head to the noise when Adam stepped, but he didn't see any eyes or any ears. It was just a massive blob. What made it so hot? Excess energy?

"Hold on, Sven!" Jesse screamed, grabbing his gun and aiming it at the thing. He was shaking so badly the gun didn't appear steady. Adam stood speechless. "Stay back," he told Adam. Adam gulped; his eyes steady on the thing in front of him. Why haven't we found a cure? He kept his eyes steady on the creature to prevent the same situation with Sven. Jesse stood, frozen, and backed up from the creature. His shaking intensified, and he almost dropped the gun.

"Oh, for God's sake," said Adam, snatching the gun from Jesse. He aimed toward the center and pulled the trigger, the bullet jetting through the creature and slamming into the wall on the other side. He eased his grip on Sven. It didn't last long, though. In seconds, it gripped Sven with as much force as before. Sven paled and went limp as it threw him to the side. Jesse rushed to Sven, but Adam held his arm out against his chest.

His mind scrambled for a way to destroy this thing. "Search for anything that would set a fire. We have to try something else. The bullets aren't enough. It's already so hot, maybe the damn thing will overheat."

"Let me distract him."

"I don't think that would be a good idea. He's already pissed," Adam warned, but Jesse was far away from Adam, hollering and waving his arms. Jesse found a steel rod that was set up against the wall and haphazardly swung it in front of him. The creature instantly turned toward him. "Hurry, Adam, or we're both goners!"

"Damn it, Jesse. You're going to get yourself killed." Adam frantically scanned the area for anything that would set a fire. He tugged on the lock of the supply closet about five yards from the creature. Adam found a hammer and banged on the lock until it broke, ripping open the mega roll of paper towels. Adam lit it with a lighter he found in the closet and hurled it at the creature that was inches away from Jesse. Fifteen feet from the threat he missed, setting fire to the table behind him near Jesse. Jesse moved from the fire to Adam. The thing came straight at them, and this time it was close enough so he could set the lighter on high and ignite him.

The creature growled and moaned, reaching for the two scientists, its hands now bright flames of light that threatened to burn them. It swiped at them at random as they both moved further back. The creature began to melt, and as it swung at them, a dripping lava-like substance flung toward their faces, causing slight burns from the splatter. They both screamed in pain, but continued to move away from the creature as it continuously became more disoriented. Adam's nerve endings in his face were searing with excruciating pain, making his head pound and eyes water. Its gait staggered, its goo-like hands dripping all over the floor. The intense heat from the creature made Adam blink and scream from his sores that were forming into blisters.

The combined heat from the creature and the fire made it almost unbearable as Adam and Jesse dripped with sweat. Adam almost slipped as he made his way to passed-out Sven. Unaware of how fire could destroy something already so hot, he was just glad that it had worked. Adam scooped his arms under Sven and lifted him as easily as he would his eight-year-old daughter. Veins bulged out of his neck and his eyes watered worse than before, blurring his vision, already limited by the haze made by the flames that were spreading quickly.

"This way," Adam said, finding a break in the fire, but as he started toward it, beams fell. The fire spread toward the ceiling, and he nearly missed a crashing piece of flaming material. He fell into continuous coughing and almost dropped Sven as he knelt on the floor, sputtering and hacking. His eyes watered and burned as everything became even more out of focus. His lungs ached for clean air, his eyes narrowing in determination to make it out of the building when he heard a high-pitched hissing sound. He tried to figure out what it was; he could tell it was all around him, but his eyes and ears were being deceived, and his mind was playing tricks on him. He crawled next to Sven before darkness engulfed him.

CHAPTER TWO

Adam awoke with uncertainty about where he was. A soft surface was underneath him. His bed? Breathing other than his own was close, like he was being watched. He peeked one eye open to Camille, smiling broadly and bouncing up and down, her blonde curls flying. Crouching to his level, she whispered, "Daddy, are you awake?"

"Yes," he whispered back, reaching out to tap her on the nose. "How's my angel?"

"I'm not supposed to be in here. I wanted to make sure you were okay." She looked over at his bandaged arm. "Do you want me to kiss it and make it all better?"

"I think that would be a good idea." She leaned over to kiss his bandages.

"I colored you a picture." Camille proudly pulled out a picture from behind her back ripped out of a Mickey and Minnie Mouse coloring book where the mice were playing on the swings. "This is you and me. When you're all better, we can go to the park and play." Underneath the Mickey in bright red crayon, she wrote "Daddy" and underneath Minnie "Camille". She colored boldly outside the lines in pinks, purples, and vibrant green.

"It's to make you better." Camille scrunched up her face for a moment in thought, then her eyes opened in wide glee. "I want to be an artist when I grow up, like Mommy." She nodded before Adam could say a word. The mural behind her was a panoramic view of a waterfall on a beautiful, cloudless day with sunshine unhidden in smog. The rocks below glisten underneath a pool of water full of tropical fish of golds and reds. "Or maybe on the Monster Squad," she said as her eyes brightened, saying Monster Squad like it was some glamorous thing. The Monster Squad was a street name for MCS (Mutant Containment Services), trained people who arrived at a moment's notice when a sighting or situation occurred with a new mutant, a lot like firefighters. They would bring the mutants to Juniper Ridge for medical treatment, and the overflow would go to Black Hills. Adam thought of all the severe injuries and even deaths of these soldiers.

"Let's leave those 999 calls to someone else. I would stick with the artist," he told her. "Have you been a good girl for Mommy?" Both of their heads turned as they heard footsteps and the door opened. Rachel stood on the other side.

"Now, Camille, I told you to leave Daddy alone."

"It's okay, honey. She's fine."

"Sorry, Mommy." She dropped her head.

"Camille," he heard Rachel say in the doorway. "You need to let your father rest."

"I'll play with you later," he told her. "Go ahead and play," he said. She kissed her daddy and raced off down the hallway.

"Camille," Rachel called, and the little girl came running back, smiling in obvious wonderment of if her mother changed her mind. "Why don't you go to your room and practice what I was teaching you? Remember to always have an adult with you that can help you if you run into trouble. These 'special moves' I taught you are only if something happens and you're in a sticky situation and get separated."

"Okay, Mom," she said, lifting her arms with her hands in front of her. "I'll practice my moves." Rachel gave her a kiss and patted her on the behind, sending her on her way.

"What was that all about?" asked Adam, his neck tensing. He didn't like to be out of the loop, especially when it came to his daughter.

"You would know if you were here more," said Rachel, and Adam let out a deep huff. That was a low blow. "I'm sorry, hun." She rubbed the tension in his neck as he moved it from side to side. "I thought just in case she was in a situation with a mutant and the MCS were on their way, a bit of knowledge and some defense moves would be good for her. At least it makes me feel a little better that she wouldn't be so defenseless."

Adam agreed and sat up to use the bathroom. His head swam from the Percocet that the doctors had given him when he got home from the hospital. He sat on the side of the bed and placed both hands on the edge of the mattress for balance, leaning mostly on his right arm, his left burnt in the fire. His mind felt clouded, his memories of the last couple of days a blur. His bladder interrupted his thought process, and he realized the bathroom was approximately twenty feet away, which felt like an eternity.

"Adam. Wait." Rachel turned and put her hand on his back. "Are you okay? Let me help you." She sat next to him and kissed his shoulder.

"I'm fine," he snapped. "I just have to use the bathroom. Those damn pain pills make me feel dizzy."

"Then let me help you." She sat closer to him in an offer for him to lean on her. "I can be as stubborn as you are, and you know it." He fought the moan that began deep in his throat. "Would you rather pee all over the bed?" He reluctantly leaned in her direction and she put her arms around him to help him up and they began their trip to the bathroom.

As they slowly and steadily approached the door, they heard a baby crying and a phone ringing from across the house.

"I'm fine, go get Henry." He nodded to her. "Could be someone important on the phone, too." She gave him a kiss and promised him she would be right back. He mumbled something back to her about being able to urinate just fine by himself and quit hovering, and after she left stared for a moment at the bathroom door knob having a passing thought to lock it just to get her going and decided against it. After he finished, he made his way back to the bed. The journey had him covered in sweat. He fought for his eyes to stay open.

"I see you found your way back. That was Natalie on the phone. I feel so bad for her, to have a child run away and be found in that condition. I told her I would call her back," Rachel said, referring to her little sister. Adam opened his mouth as if he was going to say something, then shut it. Cradling baby Henry in her arms, she asked Adam, "Are you hungry? Do you want to lay down for a while and take a nap?"

"I want to get back to work." He thought of Juniper Ridge, hoping that there were no other injuries and mutants didn't escape that could harm themselves or others. They had been making such progress. "Have you heard about Jesse and Sven? Are they still in the hospital?"

"I know that Jesse just stayed overnight. Sven might still be there, but he's doing better."

"Good, good. I will have to call the hospital when I get a chance. Okay, call your sister back or she'll keep calling."

"I'm sure your friends will be fine, sweetheart. And remember, the more rest you get, the sooner you can go back to work. I'll call her back later." She let out a long sigh. "It wouldn't be so horrible to be stuck here with your family, now, would it?" Henry reached out for him as he leaned in to give the child a kiss on the forehead, letting him grip one finger with his little fist. "Take care of yourself first, and it would be nice if you put us first sometimes, too."

"You know how important my work is." Her lips pursed together. "You're important, too. I love all of you."

"I know you love me, but sometimes I think you love your work more." The doorbell rang, and right after a persistent knock. "I better get that. Don't go anywhere." Rachel gave him a hard stare before she stomped away.

Adam figured it was probably a neighbor dropping off another dish, so Rachel didn't have to cook when he was on the mend. Everyone brings lasagna, he mused, flipping on the television to *Bachelor Inmate*, seeing if the present bachelor gets time off for good behavior. He turned the volume down low and slid underneath the covers where his head was the only thing peeking out.

"It's all an act. They would never let inmates go out on a date," said Jesse, entering the room. Adam flipped the television off.

"Harmless entertainment. Leave me alone."

"He's grumpy. I would be careful," said Rachel to Jesse, raising her eyebrows. "Do you need anything?" she asked Adam.

"A pain pill, and maybe a piece of toast. I'm not grumpy." She flipped around and made a beeline to the kitchen, a smile escaping. "I love you," he yelled after her.

"Love you," he heard as it faded, and waited until she was out of earshot.

"What's going on, Jesse?"

Jesse limped over to the window, pulling back the drapes. "New window panes, huh? This looks amazing. How could you afford the parlocybonate 10+? This stuff costs a mint and they're so strong you don't have to have bars on the windows with these."

"Those are the new windows that Rachel had to have. She says they make her feel less like a prisoner. She's always painting all the interior walls in this house with all her colors of what the outside used to look like. Those goddamn murals piss me off sometimes. They make me feel like a failure." He tightened his shoulders and his pain intensified, a grimace crossing his face. "I hope we can get back to that again."

"Easy," said Jesse, closing the drapes with a snap. "Maybe we should wait until Rachel comes back with that pain pill and some food. At least with the windows you're safe when you all are sleeping. You don't have those slithery snake-like mutants going through." Jesse flinched.

"That's true. Honestly, I would get more installed but they are always on back order. Someone needs more connections than I have to fill the house," Adam said. "I forgot you had that snake phobia." The mention of snakes made Jesse pale, so Adam changed the subject. "What's with the limp?"

"Nothing big. My leg got caught underneath a piece of wood in the fire. I didn't even break it."

"Good for you." Adam winced as his shoulder throbbed.

"I almost lost my lucky penny."

"Penny?" Adam asked. "Where did you find a penny?"

"It's been in our family for decades, and now I sewed it right into the lining of my lab coat. It's not going anywhere now."

Rachel came into the room with his pill and a small glass of water, along with the toast, and left. Jesse grabbed a chair and sat near Adam. "What really happened before the fire? The details are all a bit fuzzy," said Adam.

As Jesse leaned in, Adam did the same, knowing this was going to be classified information. "I was going to talk to you about this the day of the fire, but I didn't get a chance. I didn't want to tell you now while you're healing, but there's always something. The mutants... well, they are getting worse."

"Why? We've been working so hard." Adam's forehead creased in concern and he shook his head. "I thought we were making progress."

"I guess not enough."

Adam let out the breath that he was holding, trying to process all the information.

"Sven gave me a gun that morning, and he was going to talk to you too, but he didn't have the chance. It's just for emergency purposes. We never know what's going to come around that corner." He paused, taking a deep breath, and looked past Adam.

"What else?" Adam knew there was something he didn't want to tell him. He wouldn't meet his eyes.

"After the fire, they had to move all the mutants from the Juniper Ridge side, well, most of them, over to Black Hills. The fire did not damage that side."

"Damn it. We were making so much progress! The rumors about Jill must be true. Is she trying to end humanity? The normal order of things? What is she thinking?!" Adam stood, then grew dizzy, but he grabbed the corner of the nightstand to balance himself.

"Lie down. You're going to hurt yourself," Jesse said. Adam sat down, but he didn't lie down, waving his hands in front of him. "What about all of our work? What about the mutants that we are trying so hard to cure and save?"

"Well, you will not like this. In fact, I think it's totally ridiculous and they will eventually come to their senses. They want to kill them all. Give up and kill DNA projects and mutants alike."

"That's not right. It's not the patients' fault. We might be able to help them." Adam frantically tapped his fingertips on the nightstand.

"Hey, you don't have to convince me. I'm on your side, remember? You should rest, but at least you have some sort of explanation for what happened. When we all get back to work Sven, you and I will put our heads together and get a plan."

"I have to do something. She will not get away with this." Adam's voice was stern and loud, echoing through the house. His shoulders and arms twitched, and he fought to ignore the excruciating pain that radiated down his burnt arm. "Jesse, help me get out of these sweats. I need my pants." He stood and swayed, leaning his head forward and closing his eyes tight. *Focus. Strength. Lord, help me with this one.* His breath became labored as Jesse reached out for him so he wouldn't fall and helped him back on the bed.

"You're going to need to be one hundred percent before we can do anything."

Rachel stomped into the room, shaking the house. "Jesse, out, now." She rushed to Adam's side. "I'm going to help you get back to bed." Her voice was stern and direct.

"Sleep. I'll be back tomorrow. They haven't even cleared Juniper Ridge yet, Adam. We'll have our time." Rachel glared at him as Jesse rushed out of the room. She handed Adam his toast with some water, then a pain pill.

"This should make you feel better. Now you should get some rest." He nodded and leaned forward until he couldn't see her walk down the hall. Adam pulled out his digital copy of the newspaper and scrolled to the most recent date for Panacea, Oregon: March 1, 2072. To wind down a bit before the drowsiness hit and he fell asleep, the first thing he saw was a screen-filled ad of the MCS hiring more recruits because of the growing concern. With a moan, he switched it off and laid down. If only he could find a place to hide the mutants, just the human ones that had a fighting chance, and make them better, he could prove to everyone that there is a way. There has to be a way.

CHAPTER THREE

"Limping is better, hop along," Adam said to Jesse, running into him in the hall on the way to his office.

"Well, it has been five days. The doctor gave me an injection of Boneflex. It went all the way down to the bone and healed it before I even left the office."

"I am familiar with Boneflex, Jesse. I don't spend that much time here. At least you finally got to that appointment. It takes two minutes."

Jesse cleared his throat. "Actually, I was on my way to find you. We need to go down to the front desk." He grabbed Adam's arm to turn him around, but Adam shook it away.

"Why?"

"Jill is here checking up on things." Adam quickened his step. Heaven knows what she would do to his patients without his presence. It was bad enough they were over in her wing when he was gone.

"Well, she won't be checking up on things without me." When he got to the lobby area, Jill stood there with her arms crossed and foot tapping on the floor.

She looked older than Adam remembered her, and taller, but it could have been the high heels. Her long, dark hair was up in a taut bun. That certainly hadn't changed. She wore her usual pink tourmaline earrings, and the hourglass necklace with her father's ashes.

A young man stood next to her he had never seen before, appearing in his mid-twenties. The lab coat was long on his short stature and his round, boyish face made him appear he was wearing his father's clothes. He consistently looked around the area, occasionally squeezing his hands to pop his knuckles.

"Hello, gentlemen," she greeted them. "I trust that you two have made full recoveries. You both look well." Both men merely nodded. "That fire could have been a lot worse, but at least they are starting on the repairs and adding extra MCS around the perimeter for safety measures."

"Handy, considering the MCS are on our back door," Adam said. Many times, he was thankful that the MCS were close by.

"It is also handy that they have some fire training as well or this whole place would have been rubble before the fire department got here." She made a momentary pause. "I would like to introduce you both to your new intern, Sam Foster."

Sam reached out his hand to shake theirs.

"He was at the top of his class, and we all know we could use the help. You are to teach him everything you know."

"Nice to meet you," Sam said, his gray eyes meeting Adam's, his right eye drifting off to the outer part of the eye. "It's an honor to work with you. I have heard so many things about you. I'm here to learn all that I can and help in any way I can, too."

"Hopefully all good," said Adam with a smile. "Welcome." *This is a surprise, he thought. I love that she always keeps me in the loop. Since I know nothing about this kid, he can help with paperwork. Cleaning the rooms. Some of the lesser inflicted patients.* He didn't want Sam to get hurt and have it blamed on him, and he wasn't about to go near the human patients. Those were his.

"Thank you." He shook Jesse's hand, and they gave each other a nod.

Jill handed Sam his own badge attached to a lanyard with his picture and barcode, showing him how to use the badge to enter the facility. Jill's gaze lingered on the picture of her father. "If I could make that thing pay that killed my father, I would," she said, "but I guess there's no hope in that, is there?" Her eyes narrowed into slits, and her tone grew hard.

"I'm so sorry about your loss. He was a good man," said Adam.

She straightened her blouse and cleared her throat. "He was. He worked a lot and I may not have seen him as much as I wanted to, but he was always there for me when I needed him. I learned how to take care of myself." She opened her arm to the exposed hallway after the door opened from the badge swipe. "He was always here."

There was a long pause, and Adam cleared his throat. "Welcome to the beginning of the tour," he said to Sam. "There are two wings in this hospital, Juniper Ridge that is the original part of the building and Black Hills was added on later after Jill worked here."

"I would love to be in your position someday. Everyone must look up to you. You're the doctor in charge, right?"

"Of the Juniper Ridge wing, yes," Jill interjected.

"It's more than just about prestige, Sam. It's about helping people and animals alike," said Adam.

"Of course," he said with a shrug. "That's what I meant."

Adam sighed inwardly. "But I can only imagine the power that would come with being in charge."

"Why don't we give Sam a tour together?" suggested Jill, stepping forward and starting the tour without waiting for an answer. "I can see how everything is going. I know most of the basement is still closed off because of the repair work in progress, but I understand the rest of the wing didn't have too much damage?"

"Follow me?" Adam said, rolling his eyes when he knew Jill and Sam were well in front of him. Glancing in Jesse's direction, he mouthed, "careful".

"Let's get started, shall we?"

"We have a lot of ground to cover," said Adam, hurrying in front of her so he could try to guide the way. "Four stories and many rooms. There's no way we can get to all of them today. Sam, you might want to take notes."

"I don't need that many notes," said Sam, pulling a notepad from his lab coat pocket. "I have a photographic memory, so it's not that hard."

"Good," said Adam. "This shouldn't take too long before you can get to work." Cocky or confident, Adam hadn't decided yet. Maybe a bit of both? There was something off about him, though. *All this going on is making me paranoid, he thought. If he is as smart as he portrays, he could be a great asset in his own place.*

Adam picked up the binder outside of the nearest room. "This is where we keep all our notes of the progress. We note what's working, what's not, and everything that happens to them when they are in here."

"Do they ever totally recover?" asked Sam.

"We are working on that," said Adam. "But we have made improvements. Are you ready?" Sam nodded, and Adam could hear him swallow twice, Sam's eyes steadfast on the door. "They are all secured inside cages. This one won't hurt you. He can't hurt anyone."

The pungent scent of bleach hung in the air, and the mutant lay in the corner of the cage. It appeared to be just a mass of black and white fur no larger than a house cat rising slowly up and down as the creature breathed until Adam moved closer to the cage and the mutant opened his eyes, a fierce green looking back at them. The animal rolled all over the cage until four webbed feet popped out.

"Does it have a mouth underneath all of that?" asked Sam.

"No, and no ears, either." The creature traveled all over the spacious ten-foot square cage. "We have to feed him by I.V. and we keep all rooms as clean as possible. That's the strong bleach smell. We have a large crew of staff to keep everything as sterile as possible." Adam winced as he gazed at the patient. "Honestly, I'm not sure how he lived before we showed up."

Sam moved closer and crouched down to watch him until the mutant had grown tired and found a corner to lie down.

"They aren't *all* dangerous," explained Adam, "although some are, and you have to use extreme caution. Some are just sick and need our help to get better."

"I understand. And is he doing that? Is he getting better?"

"Because he is a recent admission, we have plans we haven't implemented yet. Surgery is certainly an option."

Sam listened and observed, asking a multitude of questions, until they reached the hall with the human mutants.

"We have only two," Adam explained, "and we will have you concentrating on the animals while you are here."

"Humans are unpredictable, even if they aren't mutants," interjected Jill. "People can be rather savage, so imagine how careful you have to be with the human mutants, if we can save them at all. If the transfers after the fire had turned dangerous, we would kill them instantly."

"The human mutants take a lot of understanding and a lot of care," said Adam with raised eyebrows. "And we can save them. It takes time. These things don't happen overnight."

"The only reason I took this job is because I care, Dr. Davidson," Sam said. "And I have plenty of understanding. I have seen a lot of animal mutants, but haven't observed a person undergoing something so catastrophic. Do you mind if I at least look?"

Adam sighed and looked over at Jill, her eyebrows raised.

"He is here to learn. How is he going to learn if he can't even observe?" She said sharply.

"Careful," said Jesse, creaking the door open to Christopher's room.

"Stay behind me, Sam," instructed Adam as they entered. "And be quiet. He's not used to so many people all at once." Adam paused. "Why don't you two stay in the hall? Maybe he would react better to just us."

"I don't think..." Jill began, but Adam stopped her.

"He's *my* patient, and you may have had him for a while when they were doing some repairs, but I have had him a lot longer than you." His normally bright eyes became dark, burrowing into hers.

"Fine," she replied, lifting her hands in surrender. "I have a lot to do, anyway. He's all yours."

"I'll walk you to the door," said Jesse.

"No need," she said with a smirk, her crimson lips turning up into a smile. "I have the clearance."

"Just the same, you haven't been here in a while. Wouldn't want you to get lost on the way out."

"Just right next door." She pointed to the steel doors that separated the two wings. "I'll be checking up on you, Sam," she said.

"Thank you for this opportunity, Dr. Freeman," Sam said, right before she flipped around to continue down the hall to enter on the other side. Sam's gaze lingered on her backside. The three waited until Adam could swear he heard the faint crash of the steel door open and slam shut.

Adam stood in front of Christopher's door, imagining the two going in together, picturing the look on Christopher's face when he sees yet another unfamiliar face after the fire. *It must have been so scary for him to be relocated, and only God knows what they did to him when he was at Black Hills.* "I think that's enough for today," he decided. "We will have a lot more for you to do when we have this whole building running like always. We just got the patients settled back into their rooms after the fire. It was traumatic for them, too."

"Are you sure?" asked Sam. "I have plenty of time. My day is just beginning, and I promise I will stay right behind you."

Adam remembered the eagerness he had as a young intern, but he still couldn't trust him. *He is new to all of this. Better to introduce him slowly into the field so if he screws up the conse-quences can be handled.*

"You are right about one thing; you have plenty of time. Why don't you let Jesse take you down to the second floor, where you can see some smaller animals? We need to get you better prepared for some of the other rooms. None of us knew that you were coming, so we're not exactly prepared."

"I understand," said Sam, turning to Jesse. "Lead the way."

Jesse opened his mouth, then shut it and shrugged.

"Sure, Sam, follow me." Before he took the lead, he told Adam, "I'll catch you up later."

"I will do the same after seeing Christopher," he said, and took a deep breath before opening the door.

CHAPTER FOUR

On his way home, Adam glanced over at the seat beside him. A sealed box contained the tools he would have given Sam earlier if he had known he was joining them at Juniper Ridge.

Double-checking the address again, he sped down the highway, always keeping an eye out for a deer or something that resembled one. Hitting a straying mutant was something he had only done once and didn't want to repeat. Not only did he injure it enough so it died at Juniper and didn't recover, but it messed up his truck, deeming it undrivable and abandoned in the middle of nowhere with a violent tailless wolf with horns, no eyes, and the most fearsome maw ever imagined. The MCS had arrived in fifteen minutes, finding Adam locked in his truck, a tranquilizer gun at the ready. Adam was fine, his truck was repaired and a battering ram added after many weeks in the garage. He never got that image out of his head or the thump when he hit the wolf.

The street he turned on, where Sam lived, had homes with state-of-the-art security equipped with electric fences, barbed wire, and cameras so someone could watch the perimeter around the clock. He even saw a home in what appeared to be a bubble. The size of most of these houses was the size of the block that Adam lived on, and the perimeter's safety measures made some of them invisible from the road.

He found Sam's address easily enough. The house was five times the size of Adam's, with windows all around.

Must have cost a fortune, he thought. I can only afford my two small windows with the parlocybonate windows 10+, and they surround them. One day I will be there, but at least we are safe while we're sleeping.

No bars at all.

When he got closer, he saw a swimming pool out front, obviously filtered water daily. The swimming pool was in a separate building again surrounded by windows. The air inside the room was clear in contrast to the murky air outside from an air purifier that ran constantly. He wondered how they could make so much money making computer parts. It was true there was a lot of money in it, but the competition was fierce.

"None of my business," he said, before grabbing the box and getting out of the truck. He walked up the long walkway, keenly aware of his surroundings, as he knocked on the door. The time felt like an eternity, even though it was just a couple of minutes before Sam answered the door.

"Doctor Davidson," he said. "What a surprise."

"Can I come in?"

"Yes, of course. So sorry." He opened the door wider so Adam could enter. " I didn't know you were coming over." Sam lifted his Pepsi can up. "Want something to drink?"

"Sure, I'll take one." He followed Sam through the entry-way, a large archway, and paused when he felt tingly all over. Dizziness followed, and when he closed his eyes to regain his equilibrium, he reopened them to find himself standing in the kitchen.

"Why didn't you warn me?" Adam asked, holding onto the counter as nausea hit him in waves. "This is why I don't teleport. It bothers my stomach." Sam tried to hand Adam the soda. "Do you have any Ginger Ale?"

"Yeah, sure." Sam pulled one out of the fridge. "This stuff is great. We just got that installed last year. After a while, it makes me feel a little sick myself, so I don't use it all the time."

Adam instantly opened his Ginger Ale to ease his stomach and dry throat. "So, Sam, anyone else here?"

"My parents and two little sisters are on vacation in 'France' at the back of the house. I wouldn't even want to be included in their package, anyway. The last time we went to Europe, I spent most of the time in the hotel and they forgot about me. It's sad when your family can forget about you on a virtual vacation." Sam rolled his eyes. "Don't worry, they won't be back at the front of the house for a couple of weeks. Why?" He leaned forward with a smile, rubbing his hands together. "Are we getting into some top-secret stuff?"

"I just wanted to drop off some things for safety for you. You probably have most of this, but I noticed today you seemed empty-handed. Jill hasn't given you any protective weapons, has she? Our job is dangerous."

"She probably thought I already had weapons, I guess. Did you know she was in an article in the Science Quarterly last year? With her picture on the cover, I bet it sold a thousand copies."

"I might have missed that one." Adam remembered the lengthy article about how Daniel Freeman's daughter was passionate about her role in changing the world. He grimaced. "Back to why I came here..."

"You missed a good one. She went to the Renault Institute when she was in high school! To start studying about mutants so young. She must know everything about them. With her father being the founder and all, she had a head start. She was the head of the science club. Lucky school. Our head of the science club was a dog." Adam narrowed his eyes and perked up his ears. "Not a mutant dog or anything. She had these thick glasses and acne... Did you know that Jill...I mean, Doctor Freeman...collects knives?"

"That doesn't surprise me," Adam muttered. When Sam gave him a questioning glance, he spoke up. "Speaking of knives..." He pushed the box toward Sam and Adam opened it on the nearby counter, pulling out a tranquilizer gun. "This is your first and probably most used safety precaution, and that's because this won't harm the mutant and it will keep you safe, especially for the little ones. Remember, we want to keep EVERYONE safe. Don't go shooting everything you see with a handgun."

"I know," Sam said. "You think I'm some gun happy psycho?"

"I didn't say that." *This kid is sensitive, he thought. We'll see how he does, but that doesn't look good.* "Some people get frightened, and out of instinct they shoot."

"Okay." Adam pulled out each object, a taser, a pistol, mace, and a spidomed.

"Okay, I can understand a lot of these things, but mace? I wouldn't want to piss them off, right?" Sam grabbed a Pepsi out of the fridge after swigging the first one. "I've never used a spidomed before." He held the injection device by the base, the sharp pieces dangling and covered.

"The mace helps to blind them and gives you an advantage. It buys you just enough time to get out of the room and ask for help. Most of them are in cages, sedated, or shackled, but we need to take them out of the cages to help them, sedations wear off, and shackles can break. We need to be prepared for anything to keep you safe. The spidomed you can throw at a distance if needed. As long as the points hit their skin, it will inject whatever we fill it with: medicine for healing or sedation for protection."

They both grabbed a barstool and sat down in front of the table of weaponry. Sam picked each item up, examined it, and returned it to the table. "I've used most of these tools. I mean, who hasn't? But my question is: where do I keep it all?"

"You don't need to keep all of this on you all the time," Adam said. "That's why it's important you do your homework before you enter a room so you know what you're walking into. The mace can is small enough to fit into any lab coat pocket and the tranquilizer gun I usually have in a holster. Those are the most common. As for the others, I'm sure you can figure it out."

Sam paused, staring at the weapons for a moment without touching them. Then he took a long look at Adam. "Thanks. You didn't have to do all this."

Adam shrugged, amazed at Sam's reaction. He seemed confused that Adam cared. Adam didn't think he was that much of a hardass or left that bad of an impression when Sam was at Juniper Ridge.

"Let me explain something to you before you even begin working. There are two rules. One, everything you see, hear, read, and learn are top secret. If you breathe a word of this to anyone, it could jeopardize our mission. Do you understand me?" Adam looked into his eyes, his voice low and deep, his relaxed stature changed to stiff and direct. Sam nodded, his lazy eye drifting off again. "There are people against us, and sometimes we don't know who."

Sam stiffened and looked around as if the people against them were spying on them. Leaning forward, he whispered, "And the second?"

"Don't get yourself killed." Sam straightened at the reminder of the hazards of his new job.

"I don't intend to."

"Questions?" When Sam shook his head, Adam said, "I have to get home. My family is waiting for me."

"Yeah, I'll see mine when they return," replied Sam. "They may not be the most supportive, but they're still my parents. You know how it goes." Sam walked him to the door.

"Nice place you have here." Adam opened his arms wide to indicate the property.

"It's not mine, it's my parents', but someday I'm going to have a place as beautiful as this one. I will be successful, respected, and live in luxury."

"Success isn't measured by money alone."

"Yeah, that's what the poor usually say."

Adam opened his mouth, about ready to say something, then shut it and shook his head.

"Is that old truck even legal?" Sam asked. "You know they all have to be electric or they're not allowed."

Adam remembered when he was just a teen and he and his dad worked on it to make it electric so it was legal to drive, and it made him smile. "Of course it's electric," said Adam.

"That must have cost a mint or been a lot of work to do a full alteration. Did you do it all yourself?"

"That is none of your business." Adam's voice dropped and grew hard. He didn't wish to talk about his dad with Sam. "I will see you at work tomorrow morning. Don't be late." This kid has a lot to learn, he thought, and just not about the job. As he got into his truck and was about ready to pull away, he looked up at the looming house and he could almost feel the greed.

Is this what I'm fighting for? he thought. Is it even worth it?

CHAPTER FIVE

Adam's office desk was piled high with papers, his wastebasket was full and brimming over, and his coffeemaker was brown stained with coffee that had been sitting there for hours and left a burnt, bitter smell lingering in the air. Adam sat in front of his computer and leaned in to focus, trying to catch up on all the missed work. Notes were made by all the replacements when he was gone. He grumbled at his wasted time recouping at home.

He jumped when the door shook from the hard knocking. "Come in," he replied, and Jesse peeked his head in the door.

"Hey, man, I need to talk to you for a minute." Adam motioned him inside, then waved for Jesse to shut the door behind him.

"You need more lights in here. I can barely see," said Jesse.

"I like it dark. What's so important?" Adam snapped. He noted Jesse's downcast eyes. "I have a lot of work to do. How can I help you?"

"Like I was saying before at your house, Sven didn't get a chance to talk to you about everything. I think it's time that I filled you in." Jesse took a seat across from Adam. "The DNA projects, they are getting numerous and bad…"

"We know this," said Adam.

Jesse put out his hand. "Don't interrupt." Adam's eyes widened. This was so unlike the man, so he stayed quiet. "The DNA projects are getting out of hand, and Jill is up to something. I would keep a close eye on the mutants, especially the human ones. If we don't find a cure soon, they will all die. It makes me nervous that they were on the other side, even if it was only for a few days."

"I know." Adam's eyes narrowed and he could feel the tension across his shoulders and radiate down his body. "Don't worry. I will do something." Visions of the cabin colored his mind.

"We will do something. Adam, it will take all of us. Sven said for this to work we will all have to work together."

"I'm not putting your life in danger. One screw-up, Jesse, that's all you would have to do, and you would die."

"Thanks for the vote of confidence." Jesse slammed a revolver down on the table. "Sven was hell-bent on you having this…"

"I don't need it. Everything else will be more than enough for me. I don't need a gun." Adam took a deep breath, and remembered his father when Adam came to visit from college, his dead body on the floor after he shot himself. *It's all my fault.* He pictured the gun close to his father's hand. He tried to imagine what was happening in his head before he put the muzzle in his mouth and pulled the trigger. Nausea hit him. With a tremor, he pushed the gun back toward Jesse.

"You gave Sam a gun, and you aren't going to give yourself the same protection?"

"That's different. He's not going to be as fast as I'm with any of the other weapons, so a gun makes sense for him. I don't need it."

"What if you end up in the forbidden zone?" he asked, referring to areas with no electrical fences or barbed wire. "Have you seen what those things look like? Do you remember that thing in the basement?"

"I can't believe you made me even try shooting it after you froze. You know how I feel about guns. Besides, a gun didn't kill it, did it?" Jesse stayed silent. "So what good would a gun do me?"

"Not that one, but other times. I know it's harder for you..." Jesse sat up on the edge of the desk, a little closer to Adam. "I get it."

"You don't GET anything." He stood up and pointed to the door. "Get the hell out of my office."

"Fine," he stood to turn, "but I'm leaving that with you." The door slammed shut behind him.

"Damn it!" Adam smashed his fist on the desk. The gun felt cold and heavy in his hands before he slid it in the drawer, praying he wouldn't have to use it. Staring at the door, he stood to run after Jesse, but closed it again and groaned. What would he say to him?

For the next three days Adam worked around the clock trying to catch up on paperwork and fill in for Sven, watching for anything stranger than normal with the mutants. Sometimes that was hard to pinpoint because they were all strange in their own way. Sven was going to be gone a little longer. Just out of the hospital, they ordered him an additional week of bed rest. Adam's coffeemaker in his office got a workout, and he popped energy tablets called Lightning Bugs, the newest on the market. He only used these in drastic situations so he wouldn't fall asleep at the wheel, because he didn't like how jittery they made him feel. Absorbed in his work, he tried to keep his mind off his new-found knowledge. *Why can't they see all the good that we are doing here? What do they think they're doing messing with creating people? Why am I only hearing about this now after four years? How long has it been going on? They did a good job keeping it secret.*

The third day he sat down in the break room on the first floor, eating his double-protein punch peanut butter and bologna sandwich, his favorite since he was fifteen. Having a late lunch the lunchroom was quiet, and his mind roared with thoughts.

If only I could store them somewhere other than here to make them better so Jill and everyone else can see, somewhere where they wouldn't be harmed. Where can they be secure and undetected? Would the cabin be the best place, or somewhere else? Until then, he knew the most important thing was to go right back to work.

As the time neared eight o'clock Adam was one of the five left in the building. His head pulsated and his eyesight became fuzzy. After checking on Christopher, who was the same as when he saw him last, Adam sat down in the chair in his office and laid his head back against the wall falling into a light sleep. As he entered a deeper sleep, the rain slammed more intensely against the building, jolting him awake and he jerked his neck forward. He slammed his bad arm on the wall and let out a cry of pain and cursed, rubbing his eyes. Wind whipped tree branches, thunder boomed, and lightning came dangerously close. "Okay, God," he said out loud, "please, please, not another power outage." The roar of the weather caused the mutants to stir in their rooms louder than normal.

Adam leaned forward in his chair and closed his eyes, squeezing his thumb and index finger lightly on the bridge of his nose. "I need to work. I have to figure this out." After a couple of pages, the words on the page blurred. One dim lamp illuminated the desk surface.

Files and binders were stacked in the darkness up to two feet tall. Information on mutants and medical books were scattered on the floor, the three filing cabinets, and on two corners of the desk. Snickers wrappers and an apple core sat on the top of the wadded-up papers in the garbage can at his feet.

With the absence of windows, sometimes Adam lost track of time, like it didn't exist.

Reopening the file, he read that the mutant that almost killed Sven appeared two months ago, but no paperwork on admittance and where it came from. It was impossible to control, contained in a special cage strong enough to withstand the heat until they could figure out what to do with it. Everything that they had tried to destroy didn't work.

They hadn't tried the fire.

The thought made him shutter that Jill and her scientists were now trying to make a new human race, as if they had given up on actual people and were just starting over.

He turned on the computer to find more information, firing up in seconds when he heard footsteps growing louder from down the hall. He closed the files and grabbed the water bottle sitting on his desk to take a swig, leaning back trying to look casually aloof.

When there was a light knock on the door, he said, "come in," just to see Sven open the door to pop his head in.

"Sven, come in. I didn't think you were supposed to be back so soon." Sven moved slower than usual, and there was a slight rasp in his breath. Even the gray hair on his temples and the wrinkles in his face were more prominent than before the fire.

"I'm not back yet. Just popped in to pick up some things from my office and totally forgot my office was a part of the damn fire. So many of my notes were on that computer."

"You can just upload them from a new computer, can't you?" asked Adam.

"But it's not the same. A new computer, a new office for a while at least...not that the world hasn't changed enough."

"At least you're okay."

Sven paused and gave him a warm smile. "You're so right. Thank God you two showed up when you did, or I may not be here right now."

"You would have done the same for me." Adam shrugged.

"Adam, you need to learn to take a thank you," Sven said. "You two leaped straight to the rescue, and you didn't even know what you were up against. Jesse told me everything. How are you doing with all of this?"

"Well," Adam said, wringing his hands in front of him, "I'm still processing. After all these years, I thought all of my co-workers wanted to change things for the better." His muscles tensed. Just the thought of the deception made his nostrils flare.

"I know it's a lot to take in. I'm shocked, too. When the three of us can get together, we will work out a plan. We need to find a cure and expose all of Jill's crazy experiments. Meanwhile, if you can do any research to get a head start, that would be a good idea."

Adam opened up his file and pointed it at Sven. "I was just getting started."

"Don't work too late," Sven said, taking a glance at the thick file, his face flooded with concern. "I mean it, Adam. We all went through a lot with that fire..." He cleared his throat. "...and all that has been happening. Everything you have discovered. You're right about one thing. It's so much to take in. Is everything all right?"

"Yes, of course." Adam fought a nervous twitch in his left eye unsuccessfully.

"You know it's well past ten. You should go home and see your children before you're attending their high school graduation. Our patients will do a lot better with a doctor in his top condition, physically and mentally," Sven lectured. He stood and picked up the file at the top of his stack. "There's nothing here that can't wait until morning. Remember what we're fighting for."

"I know," Adam agreed. "I won't stay that much longer. You take care of yourself, too. It looks like you need a couple more days to relax. I know you do double duty, even though you have a nurse that comes in for Hannah. How is she doing?"

"She has her good days," he said. "I just wish some days it could all be different. I wish it wouldn't have gotten to this with all this damn smog..."

"I know."

"And now she's paying the price. Her poor lungs. I'm sorry, I shouldn't be troubling you. You should head home."

"I'm here for you anytime. You should take your own advice. Don't worry, we have everything covered here." Adam stared at the door to hint at an exit from Sven so Adam could go back to work.

"I'm not worried about trusting you with this place. I just worry about you," said Sven.

Adam was beginning to think it would be a great idea to wrap everything up and go home for the night. His head hurt along with a slight ringing in his ears. "Fifteen minutes," Adam said, "and then I'll head home." With the computer on, he wanted to at least scan the notes to give him a general idea.

"Okay," Sven said, satisfied, and turned to walk out the door. "I'll tell Hannah you said hello." Adam stood still and listened to Sven's boots click down the hall, echoing on the slick tile until they faded into nothing.

Now that Sven was gone, the institution seemed the quietest it had ever been. Even the mutants were hushed into silence. Adam wondered if they were all right.

Maybe Sven had a point. He couldn't fight his eerie feeling and jumped on the phone to call Rachel, and it rang only twice.

"Adam?" After hearing her groggy voice muffled from sleep, he felt reassured and he let out his breath that he'd been holding. "Are you okay?" She was alert and her voice flooded with worry.

"Yes, sweetheart. I just called to check on you and the kids. You know I love you, right?"

"I love you, too. When are you coming home?"

"I'm just leaving." *Just after I check on someone, he thought. Maybe Christopher will be awake this time.*

"Drive safe," she said before hanging up.

He squinted in the bright hallway before his eyes adjusted and entered Christopher's room. Christopher sat on the edge of the bed, his head in his claws, his elbows on his knees, staring at the floor. Even though Christopher couldn't hear Adam, he looked over his way. Christopher let out a sniff.

Adam sat next to him, putting his hand on the child's shoulder to offer comfort through the metamorphosis he was going through. It felt like just yesterday Christopher was a baby. Rachel and he visited Natalie in the hospital when he was only a few hours old.

Adam never would have thought his own nephew would be in this place.

Christopher wrapped his arms around Adam and Christopher gradually tightened his hug the longer he held on. Adam felt the child's tears as they splashed against the collar of his lab coat. Adam's body hung heavy, clinging to the boy with a tightness in his chest. The only people that existed were Christopher and him.

Adam pulled away and looked Christopher straight in the eye. "I will make you better," Adam stammered, shaken from the jolt of emotion. Adam was hoping Christopher could read his lips, and Christopher nodded as if he understood.

"I need to go to work." He gripped the boy's "hand" before he left and could already feel the stinging on his back where the claws scratched him, but he didn't care. It just reminded him of what he needed to do.

Sven showed no surprise after seeing Adam's back and asked, "What happened?" Sven asked, coming out of a room and pointing to Adam's back. 'Hazards of the job' they called it.

He could understand why Sven might mistake his tears for physical pain.

"I thought you would have been home by now," Adam told him. When Sven shrugged, he understood. Sven, like him, would stop by and check on a patient on his way out, especially after being gone for a few days. "Nothing too bad happened, Sven," he said. "We'll be okay," referring to Christopher and himself.

"Of course, you'll be okay." Adam tried to muster up a smile, but it was beyond his grasp. "If you ever need to talk, you know I'm here."

"Thanks," Adam said.

"At least let me patch you up before you destroy a perfectly good lab coat." Adam could feel the rips across the back of his ruined lab coat, but he went along with it and followed Sven down the hall into one of the examining rooms.

The room was small and sterile, everything a shiny silver and smelled of alcohol and bleach. Sven patted the seat without a back, and Adam sat, peeling off his lab coat and unbuttoning his shirt. Sven washed his hands, gloved up, opened up a drawer and opened a gauze packet, getting ready to dab it in alcohol.

"I feel bad. You should be home, resting," Adam told him. "You just got home from the hospital."

"Oh, I think I can handle this. It won't take very long." Adam got ready to take off his shirt, but the back stuck to his wounds, the cuts still oozing blood.

Adam winced.

"I got it," Sven said, slowly peeling the shirt off his torn-up back. "Sorry."

"It's okay." He could feel Sven clean the cuts with alcohol and put some sticky salve on his cuts to keep them from bleeding. Adam let Sven bandage the cuts; meanwhile, Adam thought of Christopher, and was wondering if there were any other medicines that he could administer or other procedures that would help him. Glad that the research and action they were doing to improve the quality of the water was working, the partial reason that Christopher was "wrong" in the first place, didn't help him much now.

"Is he growing more violent?" Sven asked Adam.

"No," Adam said, shaking his head. "He was just trying to give me a hug."

"Oh." Sven worked quietly for a few minutes. "Adam, we've made progress with him before. I'm doing everything I can and I know that you are, too. We've just got to retrace our steps to figure out what we did right. You need to hang in there. I know you two are close..."

Adam's voice tightened. "I know, don't get too close to the patients..."

"That's incredibly difficult sometimes, and it's different for you in this case. A lot of things people wouldn't understand until they go through them. Your whole family has been through so much." Sven grew quiet and worked in silence.

"Sven, is everything okay?"

"Not really. I'm just worried. Everything is going to change when Hannah... it will be just me." Sven took off his gloves and threw them in the garbage, washing his hands. "I'm 71 years old with no children and I've outlived all of my siblings. My parents have been gone for a long time. Honestly, what will be left? I have a few nieces and nephews around the globe that I don't talk to."

"You have me, and Jesse, and the mission." Adam turned to face Sven, who had been washing his hands in water so hot steam rose. "We can't do it without you, Sven. A lot of the progress we've made is because of the work you've been doing in the lab. It's more than just that, Sven. We're friends."

"Everything is changing," Sven said, "just when I was getting used to how everything was."

"Are you having second thoughts about the plan?" asked Adam. "It's change, but it's for the better."

"I know. Of course," he said flatly. "I'm sorry, Adam. I'm just tired." Sven came closer to Adam's back, examining the bandages without touching them. "How does that feel?"

"Not bad. I've had worse." Adam shook his head at his rough week. A burnt arm and now a scratched-up back, but when he thought about it, both injuries were worth it. "Get home and relax," Adam told Sven. "Spend some time with Hannah. I'll be fine. I'll see you in a few days."

"All right. I'm feeling a little tired," said Sven. He pointed to Adam's back. "And you take care of those scratches. Maybe there's a way we can file those claws down."

"Sven, go home and take a break from all this. Take your own advice. We've got it covered, okay?"

"I'm going." He chuckled. "I know when I'm not wanted."

"Thanks for the patchwork."

Sven shrugged and headed out the door.

Adam took a moment to sit on the chair and just relax, letting the stinging subside before he started walking.

I must do everything to stop Jill from bringing a halt to this program for the mutants. For the broken ones. I made far too much progress to have it all go down the toilet.

He thought of what he had told Christopher.

I made a promise.

CHAPTER SIX

After his rounds, Adam clicked on the main file for Black Hills on his computer. The cursor behind the word password taunted him, knowing that too many wrong answers would block him. Continuously rapping a pen against his desk, he attempted to start.

JILL2142020.

"Incorrect Password" ran across the screen in bold red letters. *Not her name and father's birthdate. No, she wouldn't use something so obvious, but maybe she would use something more personal.*

DANIEL5162068DAD.

The date that he died. Incorrect password did not appear, and the whole screen turned white. Adam leaned in, gripping the sides of the computer in hopes that it was about ready to load something right before the screen went black.

"Damn it," he said, plopping the pen in an old coffee cup. A pounding shook his door, and he flipped off his computer before opening it to see Jesse on the other side, wide-eyed and disheveled.

"You have to come downstairs." Jesse tugged on Adam's coat. "We have a new patient, and I don't think it's a run-of-the-mill mutant, if you know what I mean." Adam followed him down the hall close by his heels, hardly able to keep up with Jesse. He had never seen him in such a state of panic. Jesse spoke urgently as the two of them sped-walked. The admit area was on the main floor at the back of the building, so they had a lot of ground to cover.

"I like that your office is closer to the ground floor so you can tell me things ahead of time."

"I heard Sam is already there."

"Sam, the new intern? Hope the new patient isn't too much for him to handle just starting out. So what makes this mutant so unique?"

"Gruesome, and get this, another human. This would only be our third one, or maybe fourth in all this time. A little boy that looks at you like he wants you for dinner. Sounds like another project we are going to have to clean up. Did you bring your gun?" Adam patted his side, but grimaced. "Good, but he might be fine."

"Maybe even fixable?" Adam said.

"Maybe, by some small miracle." They were on the ground floor and headed to the back. Down the long hallway, they could hear the familiar voices of the MCS.

"Get a good hold on him, Timothy! I have the paralyzer gun."

"I'm trying!" Timothy squeaked, out of breath. "Now, Becky, hurry!"

Sam stood near the door, well out of the way and several feet from the action at hand. Adam and Jesse entered the room just in time to see Timothy lying on top of a boy who appeared to be around ten years old, and they were both shocked at the description Sam gave them. The boy didn't seem all that strange. Scrawny and pale, his mouth twisted into a snarl. Against appearances, he was brutally strong. Timothy was six-foot four and three hundred pounds of muscle that twitched with effort to hold the admit. Becky shot the boy with the paralyzer gun right before he reached over to bite Timothy on the leg. It was a good thing they were wearing their protective suits. The boy might as well have bitten into concrete.

The boy went limp instantly. Becky and Timothy smiled at gave each other. "Let's go to lunch," Timothy said. "After that, I'm starving."

"After we secure him," Becky replied, looking over at the three doctors, "he's all yours. The paralysis only lasts five minutes."

"Thanks, Becky," Adam said.

"I guess they will keep him sedated by keeping drugs in his food, but I'm not sure how they are going to do that, considering his food choice." Becky let out a shudder.

"We will administer an I.V. I'm almost afraid to ask about the food choice," Jesse remarked.

"Let's put it this way, he sure wanted to take a bite out of Timothy, and not just to escape. He can't live on the food you and I live on. They don't usually give us the details," Becky said when she saw Adam's surprised face that she had so much information. "We usually just bag them, but this was for our own protection."

"He's strong," Timothy warned all three of them. "Be careful."

"Thanks," Sam said. He turned toward Jesse and Adam. "They mentioned they have a free room on the third floor near the other human mutants."

"Good," Adam said. "They can be close together so I can keep a good eye on them." He couldn't keep his eyes off the mutant as Becky and Timothy lifted him onto a stretcher and his hands and ankles were in restraints. He didn't understand the gruesome factor, just appearing like a thin little boy. "As soon as he's up there, we need to do labs."

Sam raised his eyebrows and shook his head. "You go right ahead. I'm not going to do them."

"Thanks for the heads up." Sam followed the men, Adam pushing the gurney and Jesse right next to him. "I'll do them since Sven isn't back yet, if you want to start the binder after we get him up to his room," Adam said to Jesse. "This one is definitely not a folder."

"I'll grab a big one." The wheels from the gurney rattled down the hallway with Adam and Jesse moving swiftly, stepping aside to let the MCS go past them and Adam gave them a smile. For a moment, he remembered Camille saying she wanted to be a part of the team. Artist is a much better choice, he thought, but he respected the bravery and importance of the team. He just didn't want his daughter to have any part of it.

The next thing he knew, the mutant had pulled off his left arm restraint and grabbed Jesse by the throat, pulling Jesse down toward the mutant's face. They were seeing eye to eye, and Jesse tried to reach for his gun, but he was off balance. Adam went to grab his gun when they heard someone shoot through the air and the creature went limp again. Sam stood there, stunned.

"So much for the five minutes," said Adam.

Adam stared straight ahead, panting at the shaken Timothy, who was holding his paralyzer gun in his hands. Jesse stood up, coughing and gasping for air.

"Are you okay?" Adam asked Jesse, and Jesse nodded yes.

"I think we should accompany you on the way up," Becky said, "just to make sure you make it there safely."

They all nodded in agreement, and as Adam pushed the gurney, he kept a watchful eye on the boy. Jesse and Sam kept at least an arm's distance away.

—·—

CHAPTER SEVEN

After snapping on some latex gloves, Adam grabbed his scanner, wishing he didn't have to be in contact with the skin to do labs. He pressed the scanner against the mutant's skin and a multitude of numbers ran across the screen that were being transferred to the main computer and analyzed. If he could find a cure for this mutant, a person forced to eat human flesh to survive, it would be a major breakthrough. They would have to listen. It would prove to her that anything is possible.

Adam's heart pounded, but he tried to ease his mind, easier than he supposed at the appearance of the mutant. Children always seemed less threatening.

Focus.

"I know you, Adam." The voice was so quiet he could barely hear, and he looked up to see the new patient staring down the bed at him with half-open eyes. "They talked about you. We are going to be great friends."

The patient laid back with a smile on his face and closed his eyes. After checking all the restraints, Adam went next door to

Christopher's room. He grabbed the binder outside the door, which seemed to be lighter as he lifted it. He flipped through the pages. Something was missing, but there were so many notes he couldn't tell what. He returned the book to its place and entered the room.

Blood splatter covered half the room, and Adam fought back tears. He tried to breathe through a rock that formed in his chest. "What the hell?" His feet, no longer frozen to the floor, enabled him to look for Christopher, or his body, he thought with a shudder.

In the corner, not making a sound, he saw the back of the creature that appeared to be staring at something on the wall. Fury welled up inside of him, wondering what happened to Christopher. Did the giant thing eat him? The thing flipped around.

Christopher.

His sorrow transformed to rage, but he knew he wasn't mad at the boy, but the monster. The reformed Christopher was five times the size of the boy, and he wasn't sure if it was bravery, stupidity, or unexpected grief when he sobbed and yelled, making an enraged sound of a mixture of conflicting emotions that resembled the cry of a dying wolf.

Christopher looked more animal than human, like his claws were the beginning of a transformation that was almost complete. Hair grew on his body right before his eyes, and horns sprouted on the top of his wolflike head, which he had to bend down to not hit the ceiling. Raw sores covered his back, trickling blood.

When Adam looked into Christopher's eyes, he saw an uncontrollable and unharnessed anger that he had never seen in another creature, and it scared him. But when Adam looked deeper, he could still see Christopher, like something evil had a hold on the boy and he couldn't control it. *Christopher's emotions are driving him insane, Adam thought.*

Adam felt a chill, afraid of the creature before him, sad for the child trapped inside, and mad at himself for not being able to cure him when he had a feeling he was so close that he could touch it. It was hard for Adam to tell what emotion was the strongest, but the answer became evident when Christopher opened his mouth to a set of teeth that were just as sharp as the claws that dug into Adam's back days before.

He reached for his gun and pointed it at him, a gnawing voice in the back of his mind reminding him of the promise he made to heal him. There had to be another way. His heart quickened along with his breathing, and his hands trembled so horribly he could barely hold the gun steady. Christopher reached out and Adam felt a searing pain as claws from one "hand" embedded deep in Adam's skin. They latched onto his side as his other claw took a chunk out of his right ear, almost ripping it off. Searing pain stung the side of his head as blood ran down the side of Adam's neck and spread on his face. This brought Adam out of his shock. *Screw it. If I have to injure him, at least there's still a chance to heal him.* Adam shot Christopher in the foot, and Christopher stumbled to buy Adam enough time so he could get a few feet away. Blood gushed from the gunshot wound, and Christopher pulled back his foot, howling. He stepped away from Adam, and for a moment Adam thought Christopher was going to retreat into the corner where Adam could take care of his wound. Adam went to the supply closet to grab some gauze to put pressure on his foot to stop the bleeding. The room boomed as Christopher stomped toward Adam.

"Damn it!" *Why are bullets never enough anymore?* He was just too close, too dangerous.

Focus.

"This is for your own good, Christopher," he said. Using his badge to get access to the supply closet in one swipe, drawers opened, spilling microneedle patches, vials of miscellaneous medicines and bandages on the floor, until he found a spidomed he used for injections. He found one filled with Hyperdrizen, a heavy sedation drug with barbs as large as a meat thermometer. Adam fumbled as his hands sweated from anxiety and heat. Adam caught his breath, clutching the spidomed in a tight fist high above his head, praying it would work. "Where are you when I need you?" he said, speaking of the absent Jesse and Sven.

Adam looked up to a mouth full of teeth and black saliva as it dripped from his mouth onto Adam's face. He embedded the needle in Christopher's right arm with all of his strength.

Christopher staggered back, reaching for the spidomed to pull it out, but by the time he did, Christopher lay in a heap in the middle of the floor.

Adam thought of Christopher and his eyes narrowed, his jaw clenching as his throat tightened.

He's not dead, he thought. He's going to be okay. Leaning closer to him, he couldn't hear his breath. He laid his head on his chest, and there was a faint heartbeat. Adam began CPR, the wild animal disappearing, only seeing the boy that he rescued from the sewer.

He continued to do CPR for a full minute and leaned down to listen with still no success. Christopher's heartbeat was continuing to grow fainter, and Adam pounded on his chest with compressions, tears flowing, and veins sticking out of Adam's neck. He looked down at the empty spidomed and knew the combination of the gunshot and high dose of Hyperdrizen were too much. The gunshot slowed him down, but too much of the drug. Oh, God, I gave him too much.

Christopher, as a small child when he arrived at the institution, flashed through Adam's mind. He recalled Christopher in Jesse's arms, the child lightly sedated, blonde hair and blue eyes just like Rachel's. If Christopher had spoken at first, would he have called out to Uncle Adam? He remembered his toes forming into webbed feet. A normal, cheerful kid that he saw just a week before he had run away.

Adam yelled for help, but when no one arrived, he knew Christopher was gone.

— · —

CHAPTER EIGHT

Adam sank to the floor, crouched down with his hand over his mouth. Shaking and looking over the room full of chaos, he couldn't bring himself to believe it. The walls were spotted with Christopher's blood and his own. After all that research, all the time. The recovery of this sweet boy was in his grasp to have it yanked from him in a sudden blow.

"I will cure mutants," he muttered through shaky tears, "Or find a way where this won't happen to anyone anymore. This world may not be perfect, but it's still mine. Christopher, I'm sorry I couldn't save you."

After a couple of deep breaths, he wiped away his tears and knew he had to get to work if he wanted to make it home anytime soon. Home. He would have to tell Rachel, and he knew he should be the one to call Natalie. He couldn't think of all of that. One thing at a time, or nothing would be done.

Adam made a phone call for someone to come and pick up Christopher, but meanwhile he thought he would start the clean-up. He couldn't leave the room like this, and he knew he couldn't sit still. In the supply closet, he grabbed the strongest garbage bags after putting gloves on, beginning to clean up, trying to turn off his emotions and focus on the task at hand. He heard footsteps down the hall and peeked out, figuring he could use some help.

"Hey, Sam, how are you?"

"I'm fine. Are you okay?" Sam asked. Adam had temporarily forgotten how the recent fight had probably torn him up pretty badly. He was sure he would feel it later.

"Rough night. Could you give me a hand? If you could help me with the clean-up, I could get a head start on the paper-work."

"Sure." Sam walked into the room, his eyes growing when he saw the bloody room and his attention shifted back to Adam. Adam's bloody face was tear-streaked, his eyes bloodshot, and his skin was a paler hue than normal. "What happened here? Are you sure you're all right?" He put his hand on Adam's shoulder. "Are you sure you don't need to sit down?"

"Thank you." Adam pushed his hand aside, wanting to finish what he had to do. He couldn't look at it anymore. "I'm fine. What I really need is some help to clean up so I can finish the paperwork and go home to my family."

Sam took another look around the room, examining it entirely, and looked at Adam, and his face twitched, his eye wandering. His gaze held steady on the empty bed. "Christopher? Oh, I'm so sorry."

Adam handed him a set of gloves and Sam gathered the broken pieces from the bed. When he bent over what was left of Christopher Adam clinched Sam's arm.

"DO NOT put him in a garbage bag, you understand?!"

Sam instantly put his hands up and stepped away. "Got it," he said. "I'll just clean over here."

They both continued cleaning the mess until a man from the "clean up" crew came in and took the body. Meanwhile, Adam explained to Sam everything that had happened. Adam left Sam to clean up so he could start the paperwork.

Adam sat in his office and opened up the bottom file cabinet drawer with the special paperwork for incidents when something happened to a mutant. The paperwork for when a mutant died, especially a human one, was massive. They were all trying to learn from their mistakes. He wondered how many people actually looked at these. Sent to the people that were funding the program, Adam was sure that Jill got her hands on these, too. He pushed papers, books, and files on his desk off in one big sweep with his arm. They all crashed on the floor with a bang. Pens gathered in a gray cylinder were in the far right corner. He reached over to grab a pen and began the process. Adam tried to distance himself from what had just happened, but he didn't want to believe it. He let out a deep breath and gripped the edge of his desk, dropping his head into his lap, shutting his eyes, and letting everything disappear. If only he could make it all disappear. *Why do I do this day in and day out? I didn't react fast enough. I couldn't save him, and it is all my fault. What the hell did that bitch do to him when he was over there? He was fine the last time I saw him, but maybe it took time for the effects to surface. God, oh God, this is all my fault. I have to fix it. I have to fix them all.*

There was a knock on the door.

"Such bad timing," Adam groaned, waiting for a moment. *It could be Sam. He could have some questions. You were there at one time.*

The kid knows nothing, and I want to keep it that way.

"Adam?" Jesse's voice bellowed on the other side of the door.

"Come in," Adam said, figuring he had better get this over with. He didn't want to talk about it, especially since it was so fresh, but might as well pull off the Band-Aid.

Jesse walked in slowly, his brow creased in a concerned look. "I just passed by Christopher's room and saw..." He stopped when he saw the pile of papers and files on the floor and Adam was a bloody mess. "Are you okay?"

"I'm fine, Jesse. I have a lot to do now, if you don't mind."

"I'm just glad that you're not hurt?" Jesse pointed to Adam's cheek, where a trickle of blood dripped again. Adam swiped it away with his hand, rubbing it on his pants. He placed his hand on his face to apply a bit of pressure. "You could have died."

"I'm fully aware, but I wasn't the one that was..." Adam stopped, unable to say it so freely. "I don't know how I'm going to tell Natalie, and I will be the one to tell her." He let out a pent-up breath. "Maybe Rachel should tell her. Oh, God, how am I going to tell Rachel?" Adam's head pulsed, and the tension in his body grew.

"You'll find a way. I know this is going to be hard. You've lost patients before—"

Adam interrupted him, "But he was my nephew, Jesse. This is different. This is so different."

"I get that," said Jesse, stepping away from Adam as Adam got up from his desk. "Your cheek is bleeding."

"I told you, I'm fine, but now I have a lot of work to do. Leave me alone."

"Okay, I get it." Jesse went to leave, then turned. "If you need to talk, find me," and disappeared down the hall.

"Damn it." Adam opened another drawer to grab a bandage and tape it to the side of his face. "This cut is a pain in the ass, and so is Jesse. He just doesn't understand." He picked up the piles of papers that fell off his desk and opened the top drawer of his file cabinet, throwing them in the back. "Maybe I will talk to him later." He put his hand on his forehead as a throbbing headache intensified. He grabbed some painkillers, swigging them down with a glass of water. Adam inspected the water after he drank with a grimace. How long had that been sitting there? It was warm and tasted off, or that could have been the pills. He finished up the paperwork, placing it in a sealed envelope to drop off downstairs and grabbed his coat, ready to go home. He felt so drained, mentally and physically. Every muscle ached as he moved. Locking up, he passed Christopher's room to see everything almost perfectly clean and figured Sam must have had some help. No one cleans that fast.

He stared at the empty room and the fact that Christopher was no longer in that room stared back at him. Coming out of his daze, he dropped off the paperwork in a slot by the entrance and headed home.

CHAPTER NINE

The road felt long as Adam drove home. He pulled into the garage and almost fell out of his truck, trying to step down. His head bumped the side of the truck, but he was too tired to care. He just wanted to crawl into bed, curl up with Rachel, and fall asleep.

He went through the kitchen and noticed the door was heavier than before and sealed air-tight, needing to put some muscle into it to open it. It pulled on his tired body. Opening up the fridge for some ice cold water, he felt the warm trickle of blood run down his face. He held onto the bandage for a minute and hoped it wasn't a situation where he needed stitches. With the sound of footsteps, he turned toward the fridge, trying to mask his obvious injury, the others hidden underneath his clothes.

"Hey, honey," Rachel said. "You're home late. Rough day?"

"Yeah, you could say that. I noticed the new door attached to the garage. That's a heavy-duty one. Could barely open the thing."

"I had them all replaced. They are so much safer for this house, especially the children."

"Well, good." His shoulders slumped as he turned around.

"What happened to you?" She put her hand on his cheek where his hand was, and he turned away. "Here, why don't you let me bandage you up in the bathroom and you can tell me all about it?" She put her hand on his shoulder and tried to ease him out of the kitchen.

"I got it," he said, turning away from her. "I know where the damn bandages are."

"That's not the point. I'm trying to help you, Adam. You need to talk to me." Her tone changed from soothing to strained. "It will make you feel better."

"I know I need to talk to you. There's something I need to tell you." He sat at the kitchen table, then stood up. He tapped the kitchen counter repeatedly with his fingers, his gaze steady on the floor.

She put her hand on his back until he gained eye contact. "Just tell me what you need to tell me."

"Christopher's gone." He spoke so low that he could barely hear it himself.

"What?"

"Christopher's gone!" he yelled, shaking and sobbing, grabbing the kitchen counter so he wouldn't fall. She held onto him and cried.

"I don't understand. What happened?"

"You know I can't tell you the specifics. Really, honey, you don't want to know."

"Yes, I do. I want to know what happened to him. Has anyone called Natalie?"

"Not yet. I thought it would be best coming from you."

"You're probably right." She picked up the phone, then turned to him, her hands shaking so much she could barely hold the phone. "So what do I tell her when she asks me what happened?"

"Tell her the truth, that he died."

"She deserves more than that."

"You know we have a strict policy, and I can't tell you exactly what happened. I could put you in real danger."

"What danger? I won't tell anyone except for Natalie. It's her son."

"What if she tells other people? She doesn't need the gory details, Rachel. It won't help her deal with any of this. Think about this. Don't be an idiot."

"An idiot? Is that what you think I am?" He paused, mad at himself for not watching his words. Damn, it had been a long day.

"Of course not. I'm sorry, I'm tired, I'm sore. Why don't you let me take a shower and then I can meet you in the bedroom? What I wouldn't give for some sleep."

"I'm sorry you've had a bad day. You don't have to let it all out on me. Think about what I'm going through. You may have lost a nephew, but he was *my* sister's kid. You don't understand what impact that will have on her, or me, you selfish prick." She crossed her arms and her feet were wide apart. When he didn't return, she followed him. "And you don't call me an idiot and get away with it. Just because I'm not some brilliant scientist like you doesn't mean I'm stupid. I have a college education, you know. I was a damn fine phlebotomist by the way. That was before I quit so I could raise our children by myself, I guess, because you are never here."

Adam rubbed his temples and his ears were ringing. "You don't think the work that I'm doing isn't for our children, for the entire world?!" His voice escalated to screaming.

"I'm not concerned about the entire world; I'm just concerned about this family!" He turned the water on in the sink and rinsed his face, letting the blood run into the sink. Henry wailed from the other room. "And look what you did. I will be back," she spat, stomping out of the bathroom. "After I take care of our child and call my sister. I will tell her what the brilliant scientist thinks I can understand."

"Look, I'm sorry," he said. *What the hell? I can't do anything right. Now she's really pissed at me, and she has every right.* He grabbed some antiseptic to put on his cut. At least now it looked like it was clotting. After bandaging it up, he set the toilet seat cover down and sat, his legs weak underneath him. His eyelids felt so heavy he struggled to keep them open just because he wanted a quick shower to get everything off. He felt gooey and smelled like sweat and blood. Besides, it would give Rachel some time to calm down, take care of the baby, and call Natalie. Gathering all the energy he could muster; he unbuttoned his shirt and his shoulders screamed at him as he pulled it off. He refused to yell, but just suffered in shallow breaths as he removed the rest of his clothes and turned on the shower.

The soap and water stung at his lacerations, but the steam and warmth relaxed his muscles. Letting the water run down the drain, he turned the shower head all the way to pulsating right before he almost slipped, wishing he could wake up from this nightmare. Too tired to make it a long shower, he dried off and went to get into some pajamas. About ready to button up the top, Rachel had come back into the bedroom.

"Henry's asleep," she said, "and I called Natalie. I couldn't tell her much, but I don't think the poor thing would have heard me, anyway. I still can't believe it." Adam heard sniffling from her side of the bed as she faced away from him, then she flipped around to face him. Her eyes were bloodshot and her face red from crying. "I'm worried about you, Adam. You are such a different man than the one I met when we were in school. When we got married after graduation, I never pictured our life like this. You're always working. You're so tired and grumpy."

"Yes, I'm exhausted. I just want to go to bed." He crawled underneath the covers, wrapping himself around Rachel.

"Adam?"

"Yes?"

"Why don't you tell me what happened today? I'm your wife. I won't tell anyone, I swear, not even Natalie. Do you think someone might have bugged our house?"

"Of course not. What's done is done. You knowing about it won't make it any better, and it won't make it go away, so why don't you just leave me alone?"

"You know you can talk to me. I love you."

"I love you, too. And I loved Christopher, and now he's gone." Adam fluffed his pillow so aggressively he almost put a hole in it. He wasn't supposed to say anything. "Damn it, just go to damn sleep!"

Rachel laid there quietly and turned toward him, putting her hand on his shoulder. "I loved him, too." A long pause followed. "I'm sorry, I shouldn't have pushed."

"No, you shouldn't have." He got out of bed, putting as much distance as possible. "And now you've done it. Do you think you can make things better? Putting on new doors and teaching our children karate moves while you paint these pictures of a better world?" He thumped his palm against her painting that filled the wall behind the headboard. "This will never happen." She jumped at the thump, her eyes beginning to water. "And you don't get to do that. Don't cry." She pushed the covers off the bed, stomped to the bathroom, and slammed the door.

Adam stared at the mural, noticing all the intricate detail and work that she had put into it. He yearned for it to come true and twinged as he heard Rachel sobbing in the bathroom.

"I'm sorry," he said through the door. "Why don't we just sleep on it, okay?" The sobbing turned to sniffles as she blew her nose. He tried the locked door. A stone sat in his stomach as he thought of how he had hurt her. She loved Christopher, too, and was grieving. Giving her some time, he crawled into bed after rearranging the covers and struggled to stay awake, but ended up falling asleep alone.

Chapter Ten

A dam turned away from the corner of the bed that he had pulled himself in, the rancid smell of his breath making his nose crinkle. Blinking his eyes, he wiped away the goop that formed in the corners and around the edges. As he sat up, his head stopped spinning and his stomach growled. Camille's laughter trailed from the kitchen. He smiled. The smell of coffee, maple syrup, and bacon teased his nose, and his stomach grumbled again.

"Feeling better?" Rachel asked him as he entered the kitchen, turning from the coffeemaker with robotic movements to give him a kiss. "You look a lot better."

"Hi, Dad!" Camille squealed as she ran to him, wrapping her arms around his legs, almost knocking him over. He reached down to pat her head.

"Well, hi, Princess," he said. "How would you like your dad to sit and have breakfast with you?"

"Yeah!" She looked up at him, taking one of his hands and leading him to the table, where she pulled out a chair for him and promptly told him to sit down so she could take care of her daddy. Rachel watched in the kitchen's corner with a shaky grin, then served up a plate of three pieces of French toast and two pieces of bacon and handed it to her daughter. When she was sure Camille had a good hold on it, she let go and Camille placed it in front of Adam.

"This looks delicious. Thank you."

"You're welcome." She gave him another toothy grin as her eyes squinted shut. "Would you like something to drink?"

"I got it," Rachel said as she put a cup of coffee next to his plate. Camille gave her mother an evil glare. "You did a great job, Camille."

"I know how to pour coffee," she said with a pout and stuck her lower lip out.

"Can you pass me the syrup, please?" Adam asked her, distracting her as she leaned across the table, passing him the slightly warmed bottle. It delighted Camille that Daddy was paying attention to her.

"Are you going to work today? Maybe we could go to the park!" Camille smiled at her dad.

"I think your daddy needs to stay at home. He has been working a lot lately and needs to relax. We don't want Daddy to get sick, do we?" Rachel said, narrowing her eyes at Adam.

"Another time," he said to Camille. Camille stared down at her breakfast, munching on her bacon as Rachel fed Henry in his high chair, eagerly awaiting his next bite of baby food.

"What do you say I take you to the park today so Daddy can rest? We'll bring a picnic." Camille came back with a slow smile.

"I guess." She shrugged.

Adam nibbled at his breakfast and sipped his coffee. *How can I save these mutants? How could I ... Damn it, Christopher ...* He couldn't handle seeing any more death. He thought of his family cabin miles away in the woods. No one would suspect it because it was a forbidden zone so long ago, and it would be far enough from the house that there wouldn't be a problem.

After he was done with half of his breakfast gone, he pulled Rachel aside. "I'm sorry." He wrapped his arms around her. "I've been so stressed and pulled in every direction. I was tired last night and didn't mean it. Your paintings are beautiful, and so are you."

"I'm sorry, too," she said, kissing him firmly on the lips. "You caught me off guard last night. I guess I was just too hopeful. You relax today and when we return, maybe you and I can have some time alone after we put the kids to bed."

"That would be nice." He gave each of his loved ones a kiss and told Rachel to have fun at the park. He would just kick it around the house and talk to her when she got back.

Peering out the window until the car was out of sight, he pulled back the drapes and was ready to leave. He had work to do. It didn't look too wet outside today, but he still wanted to be ready for anything. He first took a long, hot shower to loosen all his muscles before the work at hand had to be done. He found a comfortable pair of jeans and a light sweater, and grabbed a knapsack from his college days. Unzipping it, he scourged around the room as he filled it with things that he would need. First, protection. A knife, tranquilizer gun, and last of all, the gun that Jesse had given him. He put it gingerly in the bag like it was a bomb and some bullets, knowing if things continued how they were, he would need the practice. It would be more realistic on something alive.

After finishing his packing with some snacks and water, he went into the garage, always taking a full sweep to make sure everything was safe before he pulled out, and watching the garage door shut behind him to make sure nothing was waiting for his family when he returned. He took a long drink of water before he drove down the road toward the cabin, hoping he would make it home before Rachel and the kids got home. Otherwise, he would have a lot of explaining to do.

He let the radio blare so loud the truck almost shook, and sang along to AC/DC's TNT. He didn't care if the music was one hundred years old. According to him, they didn't know how to make decent music anymore. *I wonder what Jesse sounds like when he plays his music?*

Nearly an hour later, he was pulling into the gravel drive next to the cabin. Yes, this would work. The cabin was hidden by tall trees that seemed to be untouched by the destruction of the times, the house in disrepair. The porch was warped, the roof needed fixing, but unlike the homes in town there were no bars on the windows, no covered garage, and no tall barriers of fencing and barbed wire. Primitive, yet Adam saw the future. Someday, if this all worked out, every home could be this simple, and it would be safe, but not yet. Conscious of his surroundings, he was jumpy and moved with haste.

Grabbing his bag, he headed into the cabin, careful to be alert in case there were any mysterious animals hidden inside. He looked around the cabin, making mental notes of everything that he would have to bring to make it a better place to hide the mutants. More security would be number one. They would all have to be safe before he could help anyone. The second would be cleaning. The cabin had been dormant and the thick layer of dust tickled his nose.

Wanting to put it off, he knew he had to practice with his new gun, so after a long drink of water, he headed out into the woods. He heard plenty of rumors that a lot of the mutants hid here because people didn't come out in the area. If they did, they would be in a lot of trouble. He listened with each step, and as he entered the woods the atmosphere changed. It was cooler and so dark that even though it was daytime, Adam had to let his eyes adjust to the darkness of the trees as they hid the sun. They weren't as full and bushy as they would have been years ago, but clustered together made almost a blanket from the sky.

Even though he had a flashlight, he kept it on dim to not disrupt any wildlife, and relied on sound and instinct. When he was a boy allowed in the woods he knew the area. It was such a long time ago he couldn't rely totally on memory, and as he knew, things change all the time. In fifteen minutes, he came to a clearing where there was a small opening in the trees and he could see.

A deer coming out of the bundle of trees onto the edge of the clearing startled him. It stood still and stared at him, unmoving. Adam jumped at first, then stayed still. He stared at the beautiful fawn, flawless and untouched by humans or anything evil. If only this utopia could exist ...

Adam stayed completely still for a full half minute before tightening the grip on his Glock. His hands were shaking, his palms sweating against the cold firearm as he took a succession of quick breaths and raised his gun. *What am I doing? I'm supposed to save lives.* He thought of all the animals he was trying to save, but knew he had to practice on something living. He bit his bottom lip, causing a trickle of warm blood on his chin.

Wiping the blood from his chin with the side of his hand, he smeared it on his jeans and leaned down, tears beginning to fall. *Christopher was gone after everything the kid went through. I was so close, Adam thought. If only I had a little more time.* Flashes of Christopher changed into a monster filled his mind, and the pit in his stomach went from sorrow to rage, his eyes darkened almost to black, and he grabbed the gun from the ground through blurred vision pointed toward the deer, and let out a shot.

And the deer ran off.

He dropped the gun, leaning down into a crouch, trying to figure out what happened. He clutched his head. Was he going crazy?

The woods seemed silent once more, and Adam didn't move a muscle. With the climbing temperature, he downed more water, but didn't look down for a second. Scooping up the gun, his eyes darted in all directions as he stayed alert. With the sun setting, he turned to go back to the truck, prepared to return with cleaning supplies and equipment.

Before he pulled out of the driveway, he glanced at the cabin and thought of all the work that he was going to have to do, and fast before anything drastic happened.

He looked back at the woods.

CHAPTER ELEVEN

It was another busy day at Juniper Ridge, and Adam, Jesse, and Sven were all working fourteen-hour days with the mutant number rising. Adam was rushing to see his next patient when he heard Jill's voice coming from down the hall.

"Father, I know. He was getting better. I'm not sure what happened. Now he's gone." Adam dared to move closer to the door and he could see through the crack. Jill had Christopher's stack of papers in one hand. She was pacing the floor, and put the papers down on a nearby rolling cart. Jill gripped her hourglass necklace tight and continued to talk. "He was improving before he had gotten worse. Maybe something was done right." She ran her hand through her hair. "Sometimes I don't know. Is this the right thing to do? I'm doing it all for you, Father. It's all for you." She picked up the paperwork again, sliding it into a file folder. "He was just a boy when he came to us. I remember it like it was yesterday. He didn't deserve to change like that. Am I changing, too? Am I changing for the worse?" Jill bit her bottom lip, her eyebrows dropping. She blinked quickly as her eyes watered.

Adam couldn't move from the door, but looked around once in a while to make sure no one was coming to interrupt his eavesdropping.

"No, Father, I'm not!" Jill's lips pressed together and eyes narrowed. Adam jumped back and almost hit the door. He paid attention to his quiet breathing. "I'm changing for the better, making the world a better place. I'm sure if you were in my place, you would understand. If something had happened to me, you would do the same thing. You were all I ever had. Growing up, it was just school and you, and now you're gone, but I'm going to make you so proud."

Jill exhaled deep, grabbing the file folder and straightening her lab coat, loosening her grip on the necklace until it hung free.

Adam hurried down the hall to his next mutant to visit for the day. He thought of everything he had just seen and heard, and although he knew Jill was his rival, a part of him felt bad for her. Adam knew how hard it was to lose a dad. He studied the notes he had written about Julia, the girl that had been at the institute for almost three years. Sven had created a medication that might help slow the progression of her medical abnormalities in the hopes of reversing it. He shut the folder and left his office, taking the folder with him. He went down and as soon as he opened the door to the lower floor, all the mutants' hollering hit him. By the time he got to the end of the hallway, his head felt like it was going to explode. He found it strange how he could tune it out before and now it affected him so much.

Until he got down to Julia's, where he saw Sam enter the room. Adam knew he wasn't quite qualified yet to deal with his human patients and his special cases, especially on his own.

"Dr. Davidson," he greeted him as he came in. "I was just—"

"Leaving?" Adam interrupted him. He didn't want to be an ass, but he still needed to make a point. "And in the future, me, Dr. Olander, or Dr. Stein only see Julia, unless we say otherwise, and always in our presence. Understood?"

"Sorry, sir. Yes, Sir." The next thing he knew, Adam was standing in front of the door all by himself.

He eased open the door and found Julia sitting on the edge of her bed, arms loose on either side, and staring straight ahead. Julia had fluorescent green eyes where they were trying to correct her blindness and ended up giving them an eerie glow. The result of the surgery was a partial success. She could see not only normal, but she saw things that no one else saw. They entered her dreams and sometimes Adam heard her scream when he was working late. Sores swelled the left side of her deformed face that never healed properly. When Daniel was in charge, they shaved a part of her head and the hair never grew back, leaving a patch on her top right side where they had installed a chip in her brain. The chip was an effort to figure out why she experienced what she did, and they threatened to take it out, knowing it would probably kill her.

Adam wouldn't allow it. Not until he knew it was safe.

She was the most reachable patient, and possibly rehabilitated mutant there. Adam was determined to help her.

"Hey, Julia. How are you feeling today?" She barely moved as he spoke to her and came in to sit beside her. She looked at him, still playing with her hands in her lap.

"Tired," she said. Her stomach grumbled.

"Maybe I could get you something to eat. Are you hungry?"

"I think so." Her right hand went out to touch his face. She jumped back, and her eyes glowed an even brighter green, like two emeralds deep in a cave. He couldn't tear his gaze from her eyes, and tears spilled from the green depths. "I want to go. I want to get out of here. This place scares me."

Adam took her hand in his, pulling it away from his face. "It's okay, Julia."

"I hear him. He whispers to me through the walls." Adam could believe this. She had amazing hearing after so many of her other senses faded.

"What does he say?"

"That I'm going to die. That we are all going to die."

"I will do everything in my power to prevent that from happening." He swallowed the lump that formed deep in his throat. He was determined to win.

"That's what I'm afraid of." Her face went white, and she jumped from him, pressing herself against the wall as if she was trying to escape, turning toward the wall and clawing at it, trying to burrow a way out of the room. "It's coming. It's coming." He hugged her close to him to prevent her from hurting herself when she clawed at him. "Doctor, you need to stop!" She screamed. "He will change everything." Exhausted, she crumbled down to a pile on the floor. "The monsters, they will end you."

His eyes grew wide, and he promised her he would get her something to eat after he administered a microneedle patch full of drugs to calm her down. He picked her up and laid her on the bed, stroking her hair away from her face. *What kind of chip did they really put in your head?* He picked up the file folder that had fallen on the floor with the strewn papers. He took a moment to write a note, but he wasn't sure what to write. *How did she sense what was happening? Did it happen when she put her hand on his face? Did the thing next door whisper it to her?* He just left the file blank for the day and went to find something for her to eat when she came to.

He always tried to keep his promises.

The hallway was loud again, and he was thankful that he gave her the medication, wondering how she slept without it, believing most of the time she was in her own world. He heard banging from one room, and stopped right outside of it, looking at the notes on the door.

A monkey that had been there for two years with a disorder that kept some parts of him growing past his adult years, and some parts stopped too early. His head was twice the size of a normal monkey, but the arms were only a foot each in length. There were round hairless spots all over his body, his exposed skin sensitive to everything around him. He grew two extra eyes on his head. The mutant was so tall he barely fit in the cage that took up most of the room. He was never that much of a problem. He had been meaning to get him a bigger cage.

When Adam opened the door, he entered a room that was in total shambles. The scent of feces and blood permeated his nostrils as he pinched them closed. The monkey's body was on the floor of his cage in a pool of blood. He could see where the monkey had torn out all his fur and left it all over the cage. He wondered how the animal had reached with his stubby arms. His hands still gripped those shreds of fur. It appeared he was slamming himself into the bars of the cage. Bloody marks were all over the iron, and Adam leaned against the wall, shaking his head. He wrapped his fingers around the back of his neck, sighing. *When was it going to get any better? I'm afraid to enter any more of the rooms.* He made a phone call from his cell phone to have someone come in and clean up the mess and continued down the hall to the stairs to get something for Julia to eat.

Many of the doctors were doing their last rounds before leaving for the night, and by the time Adam got to the cafeteria, most of them were gone. There were just a couple that remained for the night shift. Many of the lights in the building were off. He headed to the kitchen and found some leftover spaghetti in the fridge, popping half of it into the thermo bag for a quick bite for himself, and it was steamy in seconds. He grabbed himself a Pepsi and took a long drink after cracking open the top, leaning on the counter and trying to think of his next move.

He tried to shrug off his bad feelings, but they were usually true to form. Before he even reached the door, he was hot and took a long drink of his soda, placing the almost empty can on the table. The first worry that came to mind was Julia. He was still hungry, but too tired to finish the rest, anyway. Adam had too many other things to do. After heating her spaghetti in the thermo bag that he brought up to her room, which she readily ate, he headed to his office, convinced she was better for now.

Sven and Jesse were waiting for him at the door. He unlocked the door and waved his hand for them to follow him in.

Sven closed the door behind him, leaning on it. Adam pulled out two chairs and motioned for them to sit. Sven sat in the chair while Jesse picked a corner of the desk. Adam cleared his throat and remarked how good Sven was looking, asking how he was feeling.

"I'm fine. Let's get down to business," Sven said. "I need to update you two that everything is getting stranger and more frequent. I just found this out, and we have to be careful. We can't trust anyone. I used to think everyone working here had the mutant's best interests at heart. We were here to cure them, to improve their lives, to do research and brainstorm ideas to speed up the process to improve the world. Now so many are giving up and they want all this destroyed."

Jesse stared at the ground. "They think they're so perfect." Jesse's voice was a deep whisper, and Adam wondered for a moment if he was talking to himself. He lifted his head and stared at Adam and Sven. "Creating people from DNA that they gather from donors that don't even know what they are donating to. It's wrong on so many levels. They even gave this new 'person' a name, Seth. Such a human name."

"It is wrong, and that's why we're going to do something about it. They want us to think of him as a regular human mutant that we're trying to help. It doesn't change the fact that he's not." Sven paused and stood to stretch. "Is there any way we can stop them from creating more? We need to buy time. After they started filtering the water when they found the virus, we've made even more changes from electric cars to pollution from the factories. The atmosphere is healing itself and soon the virus will be nonexistent, but this will take time. It took time to almost destroy everything. It will take probably twice as long to reverse it. If we could make them better in the meantime, that would be a plus." Sven was brainstorming out loud, trying to throw out any possibility.

"We don't have a lot of time, though," Adam said. "And I thought of a way maybe we could buy some more time. Tell me if I'm totally off base here, or if anyone has any other suggestions." Both of the men leaned in. "What if there was a place where we could hide them? We would do the same thing there that we are here, but we wouldn't have to worry about them being killed or taken from us before we can help them."

They both were silent, and Adam tried to read their expressions, but had no luck.

"Any ideas where?" Sven asked.

"We have a family cabin many miles out in the woods and no one goes there anymore. It's secluded enough, it just might work."

"We're going to need all the supplies that we have here," Sven said. "It would take a lot of planning."

"We might need some extra help," Jesse added, standing up and rubbing his chin with his fingers. "I think you might be onto something. How are we going to explain all the disappearing mutants?"

Adam let out a sigh. "Don't worry, I can get all the supplies, and I can do the planning. There's no time to take. Everything has to be done now or it'll be too late. I'll go out and clean up the place, add the security measures, and I will definitely need a medical van. I haven't figured out all the details yet."

"There's no way you can do all of this yourself," said Sven. "I'm the youngest of five brothers and sisters. Believe me, I know how important it is to work together. Besides, it's dangerous enough without you being there all by yourself. It's against the law for good reason. There aren't any fences, traps, or MCS anywhere near there. You are going to need some backup. It will be a handful enough with the mutants *we* are sneaking out of here, and there might be other mutants that come out of those woods. Isn't that the reason your family doesn't go out there anymore? The lack of safety measures?"

"All valid points, but I know I can handle it. I have to do what's right and help them NOW." He raised his shoulders and turned to Jesse. "Back me up, will you?"

Jesse pressed his lips together. "I'm sorry, Adam, but I'm with Sven on this one."

"This has to all be figured out. We need a definite plan and we need to work together. This is going to take some time, but we need to figure all of this out if this is even going to work. A lot of lives are at stake, including our own."

"We don't have that kind of time. Don't worry, I will take care of everything," said Adam, his voice strong and authoritative. *This needs to be done NOW. More like yesterday.* "You two can just keep an eye on things here to make sure no one is suspicious of what I'm doing."

"This may take a bit of time," said Sven, "but it will all be worth it in the end. We need a solid plan."

Adam clenched his fist as he banged them on the table. "We don't need a plan. I have a plan. I'm going to sneak Seth and Julia out of here, take them to my cabin so they won't be messed with and sent over to Black Hills. Meanwhile I will be working on a cure, as you two will be, here."

"That temper isn't working on me this time." Sven waved his hands in front of him. "It will be dangerous enough out there with the mutants. Julia won't be too much of a problem. It's Seth I am worried about."

"That's right. Seth is batshit crazy. You can't just go off on a whim," said Jesse. "Everything will fall apart. Don't you get that?"

"Okay." Adam raised his hands at them. "What do you suppose we do?"

"First, we will do everything you were talking about, but we can split up the tasks, and we can all work together. If you are in such a hurry, Adam, you should know it will cut back on time and increase our chance of success. I can work on creating a cover for why they are leaving Juniper, but I'll leave the rest of it up to you two. You two are the master planners."

"Okay," agreed Adam. *I will go along with the help for now. We shall see how all of this plays out.* "But we shouldn't be gathering in my office too long with the three of us. We might look suspicious. In off hours, we should meet. How about when we go to clean the cabin and set it up?"

"Great idea," said Sven, and Jesse agreed.

Chapter Twelve

Adam entered the room, noticing that the fox was sleeping comfortably. He moved closer to the animal, but left him still in the cage for now while he was observing. His alabaster, furry coat had thickened where it was once more like a scaly lizard skin, and the muscle tone had improved. One of his ears was in the middle, where a snout would normally go, the other closer to the back of his head. But still, it used to be so hyperactive, and he knew it wasn't just because of the knock-out drugs. They were doing something right.

Adam smiled. Glancing at the chart, he read they were giving him an oil mineral from the soil by rubbing it on his skin. He wondered if it was because the earth was improving, if even a little, it was benefitting him.

The fox stirred, as if he was dreaming something good, and Adam's concentration broke when the door flew open in a whoosh.

Adam stood straight up from where he'd knelt and had seen someone he had never seen before.

"Who are you? You're not allowed to be in here!" he bellowed, right before Jill walked in behind him.

"We have information that this mutant isn't making enough improvement over here. We're taking him to Black Hills." Jill didn't so much as crack a smile, but the edges of her mouth twitched as if she was fighting it.

"Your information is wrong," said Adam. "I can show you. I have the notes right here." Shaking the paperwork, he said, "Look how much better he's doing. He came in here with lizard skin, for crying out loud, that's almost back to normal!"

"He could never make it out there on his own. He's too abnormal, Adam. Don't worry, we will take good care of him." It took every ounce of energy to not hit her, or the man that was with her. He was MCS, which was obvious by his tactical armor and weapons. The cage that he was carrying was so small for a fox, making him feel claustrophobic and flip out. Adam was sure they would put that in their notes, not his advancements.

"Give us some more time, and we will show you even more improvements. Besides, there is the proper paperwork that has to be done. Jill, you know the procedure." Adam looked over at the animal and then stood between the cage opening and the strange man. "I won't let you take him, at least until I see proper documentation." Not even then, he thought, and clenched his jaw when she handed him the transfer papers. He wanted to crumple them, but knew she had more copies.

"Excuse me, Sir," the man said, his voice deep, taking a step, so he was standing directly in front of Adam. "It's my order. I have to take the mutant." He was two feet taller than Adam, so he had to crane his neck to look into his face.

"Can't you see that this is wrong?" He didn't know why he said it. There was no reasoning with the man.

"I have my orders. They must have their reasons." The powerhouse shrugged his shoulders.

"Just let the man do his job," Jill said, her hands on her hips. "It's for the best. He will get excellent care."

Sven entered the doorway. "What's going on here? What's all this?"

"Just a standard transfer," said Jill. "This mutant is making no improvements, and so we are transferring him to Black Hills for further testing so we can help him, or at least try."

"You're wrong." Sven shook his head at her. "This is one of our star patients. He is almost recovered. We just have to figure out how to keep him going in the right direction. If we keep improving the environment, the animals will have a drastic chance of success."

"He will have proper care at our facility. We have new ideas and we can try them out on him."

"Aren't we on the same team?" asked Adam. "Shouldn't we be sharing these ideas?"

"They are still experimental," she said, "and I'm not ready to divulge them until I know the results. Don't worry, if the results are non-favorable, we will take care of the matter." She brushed the palms of her hands together like she was dusting them off.

"Take care of the matter?" asked Sven.

"What does that mean?" Adam demanded an answer. "You aren't giving him a fair chance. We could find a cure here. Like I told you, we are on the right track."

"No listening to reason." Jill pointed to the fox. "Johnathan, contain the mutant. Don't let them get in the way." She took three steps back, but Adam stood his ground. Johnathan wrapped his hands around each of Adam's arms, and lifted. Adam winced, but he wouldn't give the satisfaction of anything more. The guy embedded his fingers into Adam's flesh and caught him off guard, and set Adam against one wall out of the way like he was some discarded item or he was just cleaning up, and put in the combination to open the cage.

The fox stirred, not knowing what was happening, and clawed at the stranger. Adam knew with his MCS suit, Johnathan would be unharmed. Johnathan shoved the fox in the traveling cage and slammed it shut, securing the lock. The fox pushed against the outside of the cage to get out, extending his claws as far as they would go.

"I would stay away," said Jill. "This one obviously isn't doing well. Hopefully, we can do something for him."

"This isn't right, Jill, and you know it." Sven's face turned red with a scowl.

"You can't get away with this," said Adam.

"Watch me." She flipped around and walked away, Johnathan and the fox right behind her.

"You're going to pay for this!" Adam yelled behind her, lifting his right arm in a fist, his biceps achy from the tight squeeze earlier. She dismissed him with a flip of the wrist, not even looking behind her.

"We are going to take care of this," said Sven. "You have to keep a level head if we are going to catch them off guard."

"I know, I'm trying," pleaded Adam, staring at the empty room with only an open cage and a locked cabinet in the corner. "I don't trust her, not one bit." He hurried down the hall, watching her in the distance turn the corner toward the Black Hills side. "It's not fair that she has access to this side and we can't go over there."

"It's all in family history," said Sven. "It isn't fair, but that's the way it is."

Adam felt the need to do a walk-through of the entire wing, checking on all the patients. Who knew if he wasn't in the room, he wouldn't have known about the stolen animal?

To confirm his suspicions, he said, "Do you think she has taken any others without our knowledge?"

"I wouldn't put it past her," said Sven.

Adam systematically went through every single room in a flash, going door to door and peeking in to see if the registered mutant was still in their room. Two hours later, exhausted and sweaty, he opened the last door to find it empty.

He concluded she had taken the smaller ones easier to transport, and the ones that had been making the most progress. This mutant was a squirrel, except for the webbed feet and gills, so he had to live underwater. They had almost had it so he could make it out of the water by developing his respiratory system the way a squirrel is supposed to, much like a human.

He was gone, and Adam was sure that Jill didn't handle him properly. She didn't take the water tank. He would be dead by now.

Fury welled up inside of him. A churning began deep in his gut, and an urgency to do something. He was going to have to step it up on moving these mutants. His greatest fear was walking into a human mutant's room to find them gone.

"That won't happen," he said. "Not as long as I'm here." He immediately made plans to clean up the cabin as early as the next day.

— • —

Chapter Thirteen

"So, what do you think of my plan?" asked Adam as he, Jesse, and Sven headed up to the cabin.

"It's worth checking out," Jesse said. "No one has been out to your cabin in a long time, and it's secluded enough. No one should poke around up there."

"It's a nice thought to think we will use the family cabin for good. And you're right about one thing. No one has been up here in ages," said Adam. Sven pulled into the driveway and the steps up to the porch creaked. "I guess I should get that fixed."

"We'll work together," said Sven. "We have to get this done before it's too late and there's nothing to save." Adam unlocked the door and noticed the cabin was dusty and a little musky, that was something he could handle, and fix. A two-bedroom with just a kitchen, dining room, and living room made it easy to heat with the wood stove that was in the center of the house.

"We'll have to clean it to make it more sterile," Jesse said. "Do you want me to grab the cleaning supplies from the car?"

Sven threw him the keys, and it gave Sven and Adam time to look around the cabin.

"It is small, but we don't need a lot of room if we're only bringing two mutants to start." Sven opened the bedroom door, leaning down to check on the knob. "And we're definitely going to need better locks than these."

"I'll start a list." Adam opened the blinds to the window without bars. It made him feel free and uneasy, knowing anything could leap through. He tried not to think about it. These are things they could all fix. Adam stopped to listen to what could lurk outside. "I'm glad the solar panels are in good shape. They've been converting the little sunlight through the smog for all these years to energy. We should be good." He pulled out a piece of paper from the bureau drawer and a pen in a cup holder on the dresser. "At least this works," he commented, talking about the pen.

"How much vacation time do you have left?" Sven asked Adam.

"A couple months, I think. The days just kept accumulating. I guess I was waiting for something I would need them for. We need someone to hold the fort at work to keep an eye on everything."

"I'm sure you'll be stopping by Juniper Ridge within the next couple of months," Sven said.

Jesse returned with the cleaners and they began in the kitchen, Adam scrubbing the range, Sven and Jesse cleaning the walls. Jesse sang as he scrubbed the walls with the disinfectant. "Scrub down the walls...scrub down the walls of my heart..." Adam chuckled under his breath, and Jesse cleared his throat. "I've been researching why the mutant population is growing, too, while we have all this in the works. I figure if we could find out why it's getting worse while the environment is getting better, we might be closer to being able to stop the growth and have it decrease the admits, at least of the actual mutants. I can't say anything for other man-made creatures out there." Jesse continued to scrub, and the more he talked, the more vigorous he cleaned.

"If we could find an animal that had never been a mutant at all before, that might be a cure," said Sven.

"We've been saying that for a while," agreed Adam, "but good luck finding one. It seems as if every mutant has at least one characteristic from an existing animal."

"Still, I think I will delve into that."

"Field work? Be careful, Sven. Sounds dangerous," said Jesse.

"I will be. Promise," Sven held his hand up as if taking an oath. "I have seen so many animals in my time that no longer exist. All kinds of insects, frogs..."

"You've seen frogs?" asked Adam. "No way."

"I've never even seen a photo of a frog," argued Jesse.

"I didn't say it was recent." They continued to scrub and clean.

"We should have this place ready by the end of the week," Jesse said, taking a step back to look at the wall. "It won't take that long, and we can work a little before and after work. I think I found a way to remove Julia's chip where it won't be life-threatening. It might help her heal and become more human."

"We don't want to do anything drastic until we are absolutely sure. I wouldn't want to put that poor girl in harm's way. She's been through so much," said Sven. "Taking our time and doing it right is the best route."

"What I don't get is why they installed the chip. It was to gather information about her brain waves and control her, I suppose, but I never saw the information that it gave about her. How were they trying to control her? Whatever they want her to do, it's not working." Adam grabbed his second scouring pad and began scrubbing again, his shoulders already aching. *Geez...how long will it take for my shoulder to heal after that fire?* He knew he was going to have to strengthen himself for the task at hand.

"That's what the intent was, but the reason you found nothing is that it never worked. She always had control."

"It's like her senses are heightened to the brink of driving someone mad. I stop in at least once a day to look over her notes and check on her. I've been scanning her for bloodwork to examine the changes, but I'm not sure if it's good or bad." Sven paused and rubbed his chin. "If she could handle it, it could be a significant benefit to her."

"They can't kill Julia." Adam put down his scrubber and turned around to look at the two men. "And if they realize they can no longer control her, I know they will. We have to hurry and get them out of there."

"We're working on it," Jesse said, "but we have to be smart about this. If we get caught, it could mean jail time. You have a family to worry about, Adam. Sven, what about your wife? With me, it's just me. I will use my vacation time and spend the most time here. I don't have any other responsibilities. Besides, would it really be worth it?"

"Saving them when it's not their fault? Of course it's worth it." Adam scoffed.

"I'm just saying, maybe not every person on this planet is worth saving. Nothing to do with them being a mutant or not, just..." He paused as if trying to find the right words. "There's evil in a lot of people. Maybe not everyone is worth saving."

"I can't believe I'm hearing this from you," said Sven, eyes widening, shaking his hands in front of him. "Are you with us or not?"

"Of course I'm with you. I care about our patients, but we have to be careful." He raised his eyebrows.

Adam scrubbed harder on the stove, the grime long gone, almost wiping off the top layer of paint. "Did you feel that way about Christopher? That he wasn't worth saving?" Adam remembered what Jesse had said to him afterward in his office. "That we were trying to help him?"

"No, of course not." Jesse let out a long sigh. "It has nothing to do with him. I would never talk bad about him, Adam. He was your family and someone you loved very much. I was just glad that you weren't hurt." Adam raised his eyebrows in warning Jesse to watch his words. "Someone broke into our house when I was a kid, and I hid. Lily was visiting Grandma. My parents were both killed that night, and we were left to watch out for each other. So, no, I don't think everyone is good. It may be wrong to think that way, but that's the way I see it."

"I'm sorry for what happened to you, but you can't compare everyone to that. It's not fair to them. So you don't think they're worth saving, so why don't you just go home?" Adam had stopped scrubbing the stove and was right up in Jesse's face. "I don't want anyone here that I can't trust."

"That's not what I'm saying." Jesse took a step back, letting out an exasperated sigh. "I want an end to all of this. If I didn't want them to be cured, I wouldn't work at Juniper."

"In or out?" asked Sven. "We can't have any halfway."

"I'm in." Jesse raised his hands in surrender. "Look, let's just get this place cleaned, okay?"

Adam watched Jesse clean, wondering if he could truly trust the man.

"So, how are we going to do this?" asked Sven. "I can take the weekends. I have someone to take care of Hannah."

"How is she doing?" asked Adam.

"Not well. All of this has taken a toll on her. I'm afraid that our efforts to make this world a better place is a little too late for her." Sven cast his eyes downward. "After she's gone, I won't have anything left." He paused and stared off into nothing. "I will have my work, and that will just have to be enough."

"You should be with your wife. I can be here," said Adam.

"What are you going to tell yours?" asked Sven.

"I don't think she's going to believe you are working that much overtime," said Jesse. "She probably thinks you're at work right now, am I right?"

"It will be fine. I will figure something out." Adam was growing agitated again, and glad Jesse was changing the subject.

"We do need to figure out a schedule, and what are we going to tell them at work? They are going to think it's suspicious that we are taking such a long vacation," said Jesse.

"Especially you," said Sven to Adam. "You never take a vacation. I remember when my family and I went on this huge vacation right before I went off to college. My parents were a little nervous about me going off to school at sixteen, and so was I. I didn't fit in as well with any of my older peers, at least at first, until lab class. I played some of the best practical jokes..." Sven gave a sideways grin and a chuckle. "Let me tell you, things were different in the good old days of 2017. I was just a boy then, ready to take on the world."

"Why don't you tell us some of your pranks?" Adam asked to lighten the mood. Besides, he was curious.

"I liked to switch chemicals and make things blow up when they were supposed to bubble, things like that." He shrugged.

"If you don't want to tell us, that's fine," said Adam.

"Okay, okay. There was this professor who was just plain mean. He wasn't just hard on the students, but he would make fun of the ones that took longer to understand. He opened his desk drawer, and there was a little explosion of pink smoke. It's not like he lost any limbs or anything, but it scared him enough to pee his pants." Sven chuckled.

"Somehow that doesn't surprise me about you," Adam laughed.

"It surprises me, a little," said Jesse. "I decided to be a scientist thanks to my neighbor who was always there to help me with Lily. He was a volunteer at the local clinic with all the sick kids that didn't have money, and he would always look so sad when he couldn't help them. I wanted to be the one to do something about it. Not sure if I'm doing any good, but I have to try." He raised his hands palm up on either side of his body.

"Of course you are. We're working together. Look how fast we're getting this kitchen cleaned," said Adam. He leaned into the wall where Jesse was scrubbing. "You missed a spot."

"I'm not done." Jesse laughed and threw the sponge at him. "Did you find anything when you scanned the bloodwork on Seth?" he asked Sven.

"Not yet. Still doing tests." He shook his head. "Something should have been obvious in that bloodwork. It makes little sense."

"It's okay, Sven, it all takes time," said Jesse. "We'll figure it out. We just have to move them here before Jill gets to them."

Adam put extra energy into scrubbing the range. "I have to get this thing done. We have a house to clean. If only I could have clued Rachel into helping us. She would have this done in no time. I can't tell anyone, though."

"No," agreed Sven. "We can't tell anyone."

"And I have to be so careful with her. I feel like she's always listening right behind me. If I talked in my sleep, I would be in serious trouble."

"If you're sleeping, how would you know?" asked Jesse.

"I don't talk in my sleep. Let's finish so I won't have to think of another lie. Could you scrub any faster?" With Adam's agitation lately, he wondered if he remembered how to relax. His muscles were constantly tight. He wanted to get those security measures up, not just for protection from the mutants they were bringing in, but from the ones that could be outside.

"Did you hear that?" asked Sven before he went to the window and glanced out. Adam could hear a rustling of the trees in the woods, and was hoping it was the wind. All three were still and their ears were perked. Adam had turned to shut off the lights, hoping not to attract any attention from outside predators of any sort, mutants or wild animals. Mostly the mutants.

Adam stood behind Sven and he could see a shadow underneath the glow of the moonlight. The silhouette wasn't much to go on, but it was over 20 feet tall and moved fast, especially for something so large. It had horns that were shaped almost like antlers and a projected snout. It made rasping noises, as if it had trouble breathing.

"I don't like the looks of that thing," said Sven, rushing to their box that they brought in supplies, pulling out the binoculars, his gun clutched in his other hand. He passed the binoculars to Adam.

The night binoculars made it clear what they were up against. It had the skin of a hairless cat, pink and dry, flakey like it was shedding. Its eyes were exceptionally large for its massive frame, and it appeared as if it was looking right at them.

"Right now would be a good time to call the MCS," said Jesse, and Adam could feel his heavy breath on his neck.

"If we do that, we risk exposure, and our entire plan is for nothing."

"Our plan won't happen if we're dead," said Sven, "but I have faith in us. The house might slow him down..." He took another look around, "... a little, but not by much. There has to be something here that would slow him down without killing him, although if it's him or us, I'm going on us."

Sven went over to their cleaners and walked right by the weapons.

"Sven, what are you doing? We need to fight!"

"Yes, but maybe if I find the right combination of chemicals, we can make something that would harm him. I have seen mutants with that skin before, and they were sensitive to everything. This bleach is already making my hands itch. You two get ready with whatever weapons you can get together and cover me."

"Cover you from that?!" Jesse pointed outside.

"Come on, Jesse, no time." Adam began digging into his duffle bag and had his tranquilizer gun, a knife that he hoped he wouldn't have to get close enough to use, and his gun he had for the last resort, although this thing was so large that's what it might take. He caught Jesse grabbing microneedle patches as well.

"Do you know how close you will have to get to that thing to use those?" Adam asked with wide eyes.

"Hey, I'm grabbing everything," said Jesse.

Meanwhile, Sven had a large bucket with some containers of bleach, window cleaner, and rat poison. "I can't do this inside. It's too dangerous."

"Oh, for God's sake, do it here," said Adam. "I'm NOT having any of us going out there willingly." The creature had gained ground and they no longer had to use binoculars to get a good view of the mutant.

Sven dumped the chemicals in the bucket using a painting stir stick to mix it up, urging the other two to step back and cover their mouths and noses with surgical masks. He did the same so he wouldn't breathe in as many fumes. The mutant punched out the window, glass flying everywhere. Sven stuck the bucket underneath the new opening, the smoke rising and the vapors hitting the fragile skin of the mutant. The mutant cried out, but continued to push through the window, not realizing that he couldn't fit. The framework of the window cracked and splintered with every movement. His skin grew boils, and he burst through the wall.

So not only was he in, but he was howling in pain and not happy.

Adam shot him with a tranquilizer dart in the arm, but it only seemed to slow him down a little, and he was back on the move.

"Did you see what that did to his skin?" asked Sven.

"Busy now," said Adam. He was reloading the tranquilizer gun when Jesse fired two shots, one in the creature's hip and one in his foot. The mutant lost his balance and leaned back, falling. The substance that Sven used still hissed at the mutant's skin, and blisters continued to form. He let out a cry that shook the house, slowing down from the tranquilizer setting in and the gunshots. Sven stooped behind the two scientists, mixing up more of the mixture in case he needed it for another round.

"I have made nothing like this in so many years!" said Sven. "I didn't know I had it in me."

The creature was about ready to come at them again, regaining his balance as he stood, and Jesse ran over to Sven's bucket, grabbed both sides in a firm grip, and let the mutant get closer to him before he flung the acid into those huge, staring eyes.

The mutant wailed again and stepped back. The creature was retreating, to retrace the steps that it came, but it couldn't see. It kept tripping over things as it tried to crawl away. It clawed aimlessly in front of itself, not knowing that it was clawing at thin air. Maybe it thought it saw fake images that played with light and shadow.

Right outside where it had broken through the window, it had collapsed in a heap on the side of the cabin.

Adam stayed still, shocked. Inching toward the mutant, he still had a knife and gun ready. "I'm sure it will now be blind. No hope of finding a cure for that." He hated to admit it, even to himself, but this mutant was a lost cause. He was lucky if he would live through the night. "We should put it out of its misery."

Sven and Jesse nodded, and Jesse crept closer, firing five more times at the creature's head. Jesse walked away, staring at it as if it could stand up and attack from all of that.

"Jesse, we're done." Adam leaned forward, trying to catch his breath. He threw down his weapons and wished he would have been more prepared. He should have known something like this would happen out in these woods. Well, this would not happen again.

"We need to take care of him," said Sven.

"Yes, and we need to do it safely," said Adam. "From now on, someone has to have an eye on those woods with whatever we need to do to make it safe. Cameras, binoculars, or whatever tools we can get, especially until we fix this place to make it safer."

"Totally agreed," Sven said, and he didn't hear any arguments from Jesse, shaking, wiping the sweat from his brow. Adam saw the burns that overtook over half of his body, the bleeding gunshot wounds, and the injuries from breaking through a wall, and knew that Jesse was right.

"I guess we are going to bury him," Adam said, going out to the shed to grab the two shovels that he owned. With every exhausted step to the shed, he felt keenly aware of his surroundings. And now they were going to have to dig. It was getting late, and the sun had already set hours ago. How were they going to do this in the dark?

He returned without the shovels. "It's getting late. It won't hurt to leave him out here. No one comes up here, and he is no threat to anyone. He's dead. If someone found him, they would just think that he stumbled on the cabin and broke in through the wall. I'm tired, and to be honest, I don't know if I can come up with that many excuses."

"What about the gunshots in him? That definitely doesn't happen from breaking through a wall," asked Sven.

"Well, we just have to hope and pray that no one comes up here," said Adam.

They spent the next hour gathering up things from the house and called it a day.

For the next week, they spent a few hours each day working on the house, after disposing of the mutant body. One of them was always on the lookout. After building the wall, they set up outside cameras for security. For the inspiration of a brighter tomorrow, Sven told them more stories about when he was a young man, when the world was different. It was safer and care-free. They strengthened the doors with stronger locks, installed stronger windows with bars, fixed the steps on the porch, and moved medical supplies they knew they would need. Some of them they bought from the local medical shop because they were afraid if they took too much from the hospital, someone would notice.

Like they weren't going to notice two missing mutants, the only human patients, Adam thought.

When it was all prepared, Adam had rented a medical transport van and picked up Jesse before heading to work. He told Rachel he was going in early to catch up on some paperwork. He hoped she wouldn't be up to notice it was three in the morning.

CHAPTER FOURTEEN

It was four o'clock in the morning when Adam and Jesse scanned themselves in. The building was still loud from all the mutants, but the halls were mostly void of people except for the occasional janitor or the few scientists that were ending their shifts. While Adam went to his office and grabbed some paperwork on the mutants, which he dropped twice, Jesse and Sven were shutting off the security cameras and making the monitors run old footage.

Adam met Jesse and Sven in front of Julia's room.

"Did you give Julia and Seth a hearty dose of anesthesia?" Adam asked Sven. "I don't know how they're going to react away from here, especially Julia, who's been here so long."

"An hour ago. Both are knocked out." Adam glanced behind Sven, and a slight tremor overcame him. "Don't worry if anyone suspects anything." Sven patted Adam's shoulder. "I will handle it." Adam pursed his lips together and nodded.

"Wish us luck," Jesse said, pushing the gurney into Julia's room as the two men followed. Adam moved quietly and quickly to not attract attention. As Jesse and he lifted Julia to place her on the gurney, he noted how light she was. "She must be losing weight again," he said, not wasting any time, moving with agility and speed. Sven stayed in the hall with Julia as Jesse and Adam moved Seth to a gurney as well. They heard movement outside the hall. Adam leaned out to see if Sven needed some help with anything and turned right into Sam.

"Sam," he said, his eyes widening. "You are here early this morning."

"What, don't you find it impressive?" Sam grinned at him. "Thought I would get a head start on the day. The road to learning and all of that. Actually, it was my father's idea to get a head start. Can't wait to see me start to succeed and follow in his footsteps."

"So he was a doctor? I thought he owned his own business." Adam kept one eye on Jesse, letting him know he was trying to distract Sam.

"Oh, he does, but being wealthy and having a certain place in this world isn't down to one profession, am I right?" Adam nodded in urgent agreement, turning his focus outside of the hall out of the room. "Dr. Davidson, why is Julia on a gurney?" He looked past Adam's shoulder and tried to move around him, but Adam blocked him.

"She's just going down to the first floor for some tests," he said.

"Very early in the morning for tests. Can I come? Maybe I can learn something." *What can I say? No? So it will take a little longer to get them out of here. We have to make this quick. Jill is usually here by seven, and it might take some time to get down the road...Oh, shit, this is not good at all.*

"Dr. Davidson?" Sam broke his train of thought. "Can I go or not?"

"That's fine. I've got this," he told Jesse. "Why don't you check in and see how Sven is doing with the new admit?"

"I just saw him down the hall," said Sam. "Is he going down to the testing room, too? It's not my place or anything, but considering how dangerous Seth is, is it wise to have them both down there together? Wouldn't it make more sense to do the tests in the room, anyway?"

Adam's voice turned deep. "We know what we're doing, Sam."

"I didn't mean..." His words were apologizing, but his smug smile said otherwise.

"You have a point," he said, thinking if he could move Julia down to the testing room with Sam, it would give Sven and Jesse a chance to at least move Seth to the van. It might be easier one at a time, although not as time effective. He worried about the sedative. It wouldn't matter what it would do to the tests. Sam would not see the results.

Adam sped down the hallway on the way to the elevators, with Sam trailing behind him. "Trying to lose me or something?" Sam asked.

"Just have a lot to do today," said Adam. "This place gets busy, and you aren't the only one trying to get a head start."

They were the only ones in the testing area, and Adam could tell it had just been cleaned. Everything was pristine and gleaming white. He rushed over to turn on the micro-ometer, an enormous archway of white metal with computer screens on each side that a doctor could just push the patient through to measure brain waves. Being sedated was going to make this so much easier and faster, which was what he was hoping for. Julia kept asleep as he aligned her with the machine.

"Is she okay?" Sam asked.

"Just tired, but she's fine." Adam pushed her through the archway, but nothing was on yet.

"At least her eyes are closed. Those green eyes are creepy. It's like she can see right through you, but not." Sam let out a shiver.

"Better get used to it," said Adam, "because there is a lot of 'creepy' around here. I'll just take care of this later."

"Oh, I can handle it," boasted Sam. "I know how to run one of these machines." Sam reached out to touch the power button on the panel, but Adam blocked him.

"I will take care of it," Adam snapped, his deep voice forceful. If they ever did tests on that, they would find the sedative effects and he would be as good as caught.

"Fine, I was just trying to help. I'm hitting the break room for a Pepsi. Looks like I'm going to need it for today."

And Sam was gone.

Adam was about ready to get the hell out of there until he heard Jill's voice in the hallway. "Well, hello, Sam, and how is everything going?" After that he could hear only muffled conversation, and flipped around to turn off the light, pulling Julia out of the machine and hiding both of them behind a curtain. "You are the best intern and smartest I have ever had," she cooed. Adam narrowed his eyes in confusion as he listened. "You are going to do great things here. I can tell." Standing perfectly still, he waited and listened until he heard the door open. He gripped the scanner, afraid that even the slightest movement of placing it in his pocket would move the curtain. Damn, I should have found a better hiding spot.

"Sam, I thought you said Dr. Davidson was in here. I don't see anyone."

"I just saw him, I swear."

"Just remember, Sam," she said, "we are a team, and you and I are partners. We help each other out. You help me out, I help the situation with your parents."

"You could do that, couldn't you?"

"Certainly." The light flipped on. Adam had both hands on the metal railing of the gurney, squeezing it so hard in fear it was going to break. Her heels clanked on the tiled floor and he could hear her moving things around like she was looking for something, he supposed. Sam's footsteps were close to her as well. *There's no way she knows I'm hiding, does she?* The clicking stopped in front of the curtain, and he was grateful the curtain reached the floor so as not to expose his shoes. "Strange," Jill said, and continued to look around the room and close the door, shutting off the light.

Adam let out the breath that he had been holding, listening to the footsteps as they faded away. He looked down at Julia and prayed that she would be out longer than they expected. Now they were going to need more time.

Adam kept a watchful eye, feeling that someone was watching him as he rushed Julia back up to the front of the building. The atmosphere heightened Adam's awareness; the patients, the staff, and even the smell of the cleaners they used regularly. He could hear Jill behind him demanding what he was doing, although he knew she wasn't there. While he was speeding along, the low rumble of the animals in the rooms and the squeaking wheels of the gurney were the only sounds in the building. The hallways felt like never-ending white tunnels to Adam.

At the end of the hallway stood Juniper Ridge's nighttime security, Tom Blanchfield, a man in his fifties with a receding hairline and a set of teeth so white they didn't look real. "Hey, Adam, where are you going with the patient?" Adam wondered where Seth was. He assumed he was in the van already, but for now, he had to play it cool.

Adam cleared his throat and said to Tom as he leaned in, "I'm not supposed to tell you. It's top secret, but you do work here, and I know I can trust you not to tell anyone."

"Okay." Tom leaned in, barely a whisper, and said, "What's going on?"

"They're building a new top-notch facility, and we're moving the human patients first. The rest will come along soon after." Adam knew how much Tom trusted him, and as much as he hated to do it, he was using this to his advantage. Tom had worked at Juniper Ridge almost as long as Adam. "And don't mention it to anyone."

"Why not?"

"Especially Doctor Freeman. It's supposed to be a surprise."

"I won't tell anyone," Tom said, grinning with excitement. "It's going to be a great surprise. I'm looking forward to seeing her reaction. They should really get a new roof-it leaks some-times." Tom nodded and waved at them. Adam could hear him talk behind him. "They don't tell me anything. Isn't there another one? I don't see him in the room. I have been watching all the patients closely, just like you always ask me to."

"Yes, Tom, he's coming next."

"I'm so glad they are getting a new facility," said Tom as he shook his head. "I could surely use new monitors. They have been a little snowy lately."

"Must be hard on the eyes. Talk to you later, Tom," he said with a wave and was out the door, just to see Sven and Jesse out by the van.

"Back door," said Sven, as if reading his mind. Adam noted Sven was out of breath and thought of the long trek they must have had to make around the building quickly before being discovered. They were lucky in the absence of rain, but there was a freezing wind that picked up as they left the facility. The patients remained still as Sven opened the back of the van, and Jesse and Adam loaded them in, strapping down the gurneys.

"Good luck. I'll let you know if anything happens here you need to know about," said Sven.

"Thanks," Adam said, smiling. "Everything is going to be fine. Watch our new intern, will you? He's ambitious, but I don't want him hurting any of the patients while we're not around as much." Sven gave him a sideways glance. "On accident, of course, but sometimes I'm not so sure of his intentions."

"Oh, he's harmless. I can do that. Meanwhile, I'll be at the lab, still working on a solution. I'll let you know if I find something new."

"I'm sure we'll hear from you soon," Jesse said. Adam jumped into the driver's seat and they both rode away, waving at Sven. Adam took a deep breath and hoped the transfer would go smoothly. He gripped the steering wheel and peered in the rear-view mirror, pointing it toward the passengers to get a glimpse. They were both quiet, and he tilted the mirror back toward the street, his foot heavy on the accelerator.

Jesse turned on the radio and began scanning through the stations when a news bulletin came up. He was about ready to keep dialing until Adam said, "Hey, one second. Turn that up."

"Okay, but I thought we would listen to something that would keep us awake." The station clear, the reporter spoke of an electronics company, Foster Electronics, cited for breaking many environmentally crucial codes by doing illegal dumping of garbage and polluting the water with toxins. The authorities are currently conducting further investigations and will press charges in the future.

"Do you know who that is?" asked Adam. "FOSTER Electronics?"

Jesse shrugged. "Any relation to Sam Foster?"

"Only his parents. That explained how they could afford their lap of luxury, messing up the environment like that. That's wrong on so many levels."

"Well, it sounds like they are going to pay for it."

"I hope they do and don't have fancy lawyers to get them off."

"You know how everyone feels about bettering the environment. I don't even think fancy lawyers can do much." After the news, the station played rock music. Jesse sang along. "What, you don't know the words?" Jesse asked Adam.

"Never heard of it. Who are these guys, anyway?"

"Rat Bomb has been around for the last five years, Adam. You should take a listen. They aren't bad." Jesse took a drink of his coffee and put it down before turning a sharp corner. They had been in the middle of nowhere for the last fifteen miles. "There's something about music that keeps me going. I can't imagine life without it. Maybe it's because it's one thing in this world that we don't have to fix."

Adam laughed. "Well, that's a matter of opinion."

"You can act old for your age, ya know? You need to listen to the radio once in a while. When I was in high school, I got into music to impress a girl, of all things."

"How pathetic. Did you get the girl?"

"Something better. I learned how to play the guitar and I love it. And write music. My teacher was amazing. If only Mr. Finkelsteen could see me now."

"Any good? I should hear you play sometime."

"Nah," said Jesse. "It's just for fun." He became quiet and focused on the road, his singing so low that Adam could barely hear him.

Two miles later, Jesse nudged Adam, shaking his head. "Do you hear that?" Jesse asked. Adam took a moment, and he heard a movement in the back of the van. He glanced back to see Julia's eyes flutter.

"Shit," Adam muttered, pulling over to the side of the road. There wasn't much room, and the right side was close to the ditch, so he put his hazards on and warned Jesse to be careful getting out. "You have knock-out drugs?" he asked Jesse.

"Right here," he said, pulling out a microneedle patch he had kept handy. "Just in case I keep it real close."

Jesse squeezed in between the seats to go to the back just in time to see Julia look up at him with her eyes narrowed, her lids not fully opening. "Where am I?"

"It's going to be okay."

He was about ready to inject her when her neon green eyes opened wide and she sucked in a quick breath, looking past Jesse. "Oh, God, what is he doing here? Where am I?"

"It's okay, Julia." Adam had made his way to the back, the four of them crammed in the tight space. "We're here to protect you."

She sat up from her bed, and Jesse injected her hip, but it took a minute to take effect. Trying to get away, she moved to undo the straps that held her in place. Jesse went to stop her, but she pushed him, and he fell on Adam, which bumped Seth.

Seth opened his eyes, popping off his restraints and grabbing Adam. Seth was gaunt and pale, red rims around his eyes and he garbled "hungry" as he seized the closest human flesh he could find, Adam's arm. Adam pulled back just in time before Jesse threw a microneedle patch in Seth's neck. His hold weakened, and he collapsed.

Julia screamed right before falling back asleep.

"That was too close," Jesse breathed. "Are you okay?"

Adam nodded, unable to talk, trying to slow his breathing.

"No one said this was going to be easy." Adam refastened the restraints extra tight, rubbing his left arm. "That's going to leave a beaut of a bruise."

"Hey, do you want me to drive?" Jesse asked after making sure that Julia was good.

"Yeah." Adam climbed in the passenger seat, putting on his seat belt with some difficulty because of his trembling hands. He tried to tell himself he knew it was going to happen. Doing good, evil things sometimes happens. You just need to be prepared the best you can.

Main objective: stay alive. Second objective: save the mutants. Find a cure.

This kept running through his head as he watched the road blur by. There were no other cars to be seen. He fidgeted in his seat, every couple of minutes looking behind him at the mutants they were transporting. Both mutants seemed to be out for another long while.

"Hey, man, are you okay?" Jesse asked. "How's your arm? You had to yank it back fast."

"It could be worse, considering someone tried to eat it and it got burned," Adam said, shaking his head. "You know what, Jesse? It's time. My bad luck is going to turn around. I can feel it."

"I hope so. You're due, that's for sure." Jesse made a right turn and began the long road up to the cabin. Adam reached underneath the seat for the thermos of coffee he had placed there. He was running on very little sleep and wanted to make sure he kept his wits about him. The sun started rising, and he put on his sunglasses.

"Want some?" he asked, pouring a cup of coffee from the lid. Jesse nodded, and Adam passed it to him. "No creamer though."

"It's okay. I have a feeling I'm going to need it." Adam figured it was the combination of the fear that the tranquilizer would wear off before they got there and the urgency to get the transfer finished when Jesse sped up another fifteen miles an hour.

"Who knew there would be a time limit on curing them? After all this is done, I swear I'm going to take Rachel and the kids and go on a long vacation."

Jesse let out a chuckle as Adam handed him the coffee. "No, you won't. I know you, Adam. You'll find another project that will have to be done. You've been talking about a vacation for years."

"I'm serious this time." He rolled his shoulders, taking another look behind him. "I think my body needs a break, too. My body and my mind, or else I'm going to go crazy."

"Hey, sounds good to me," Jesse said. "The vacation, not the crazy part, although I think we're already there. If we don't get thrown in jail."

"We've got to try." They almost reached the cabin, and Adam put the lid back on his coffee, happy when the patients were still out cold. They pulled into the driveway and jumped out in a frenzy, the icy wind whipping all around them."It's freezing out here. Let's get this done," Adam said, and Jesse agreed as they opened the back of the van. Jesse crawled in the back and undid the straps that held the gurneys so they wouldn't slide all over the back of the van and slid them out, where Adam helped him from the ground below. Both of the patients were still out of it, the only movement was the slow rise and fall of their chest as they breathed. Adam and Jesse got Julia and Seth in the house and into their rooms, the doors locked firmly behind them.

"Let's fire up the video footage," said Adam, going into the dining room that had three monitors set up connected to the cameras in the bedrooms. They could watch every move from the comforts of the dining room, and had the cameras set up to their watches. Any time they could check on them, but they still agreed someone would be there at all times, two if possible. Jesse glanced at his watch to check it, happy when the picture of the rooms in the cabin was nice and clear. Adam grabbed a glass of water from the kitchen, thirsty from all the day's work. He downed half of it in three gulps. Adam's picture was clear as well, and as he was flipping through all the angles on his watch, it rang.

"Rachel," he said with a deep breath, and crossed his fingers. It rang three times before he answered. "Hi, honey," he replied. "This is a surprise. You don't usually call me at work. Is every-thing okay?" *Lots to do today. I have got to get her off of this phone.*

"It isn't," she snapped, and he heard the cupboard door slam shut. *Oh shit, she's pissed. Whenever she gets furious, she eats.* "What the hell is going on?" He could hear the chomping of potato chips on the other end of the line. "Why are their mutants in our cabin? I recognize it, ya know, even though it looks different. Nice clear picture you have on your watch phone."

Adam shifted his eyes from side to side, lifting his eyebrows. "Why would there be mutants at the cabin? It's a new room at the Ridge. We're trying a new experiment." Jesse jumped up and moved to sit next to Adam, leaning in closer to the phone. Adam pushed him away.

"Will you quit lying to me? I'm watching it right now on my phone, which is connected to yours. I had to keep an eye on you somehow."

"I really think it is best that you get off the phone and we can talk in person. You never know who could be listening. This experiment is confidential." Adam leaned forward in his chair, grasping the phone tight, and whispered, "I will talk about this when I get home."

"No, not on your life. I will see you in a couple of hours." And the phone line went dead.

"Rachel...Rachel...it's not safe..." He stood up, about ready to yank his watch off, but slammed his fist down on the table instead. "Damn it! Not another problem!" His head throbbed and his hands trembled. He was sure his blood pressure was through the roof.

From across the room, Jesse said, "She's not coming here, is she?"

"I'm calling her back, and she better listen to me, or we have some bigger problems coming up." When Adam called, he ignored the crack that was beginning in the screen's corner. It went straight to voicemail. "Listen, honey, it's best if you stay home and wait for me to explain what I can to you tonight. I love you. I will talk to you this evening." As he hung up, he prayed she would listen to his advice, but this time figured his prayers would fall on deaf ears. "I have to make something up when she shows up, or she will screw up our plans."

"Why don't you just tell her she can't come in?"

"You don't know my wife." Adam turned his attention back to the monitors after taking aspirin for his pounding headache. With no bottled water in the fridge, he used the tap. "You don't tell that woman to do anything." Julia's eyes fluttered up on the screen and she sat up, looking around. She walked around the room in a daze until she found the window. The three men had installed unbreakable glass so they wouldn't escape. Julia stared at the window, placing her palms on the glass, and grinned. In Juniper Ridge, she never had a window and was always cooped up in her room.

She stared out at the trees, the raindrops that just fell, and she cried. Adam had almost forgotten how long it had been since she had even seen outside. He immediately felt stronger pity for the girl.

"Don't worry. We'll figure out something," Jesse said to him. "These cameras are better than I thought. This picture is amazing."

"It looks like it still knocked Seth out," said Adam. "This reminds me, did you turn the cameras back on at the Ridge?"

"Yeah, we're good to go. I did it all on the phone. Look at her," Jesse said, referring to Julia. "It's like she's never seen outside before."

"Imagine when we make her better. She can have a normal life. Then she can go outside whenever she wants. I have a feeling she will appreciate it more than any of us do. We have to keep making 'outside' better, too, or she'll revert right back, I'm afraid."

Jesse went into the kitchen and opened the refrigerator, grabbed a couple of sodas, and gave one to Adam. They both sat in front of the monitors and observed.

"Changing the world. We just can't pull ourselves away from a challenge." The soda felt nice and cold as it ran down Adam's throat and he gulped down the first half. "If only everyone would have known this was going to happen years ago, we could have stopped it from getting this bad. Do you remember the day you decided you were going to work at Juniper?"

"Do you think if Daniel Freeman was still alive, this whole idea of DNA testing and doing away with the projects would happen?" Jesse asked Adam.

"No way." Adam remembered talking to Daniel. "He had big plans. I'm sure he's rolling in his grave right now."

Adam's attention shifted to the monitors when Jesse tapped on the screen, monitoring Seth urgently. "It looks like he's coming to, and he doesn't look happy."

Both of them watched Seth, and they knew if he wasn't so sickly, he would be more dangerous. His hunger was their worst enemy.

"I tried to give him animals to eat instead of people," Adam said. "It made him gag, and he couldn't keep it down. I knew anything else was out of the question."

"I guess for now we just watch him and make sure he doesn't escape until we hear from Sven."

"But meanwhile, how are we going to keep him alive? If he doesn't have human flesh to eat, he'll die." Adam looked away from the monitors, deep in thought, and knew he didn't hate anyone in the world so much he'd want to feed him to Seth.

"Well, he can't have me for dinner," Jesse interjected. "We should call Sven to let him know we made it here."

"I got it." Adam tapped on his watch phone, running his fingertip along the crack in the corner, mad at his inability to control his temper. He knew if the crack spread, the picture wouldn't be as good and this is where they were watching the mutants. It rang four times before Sven answered. "We're here," he said. "Any problems?"

"None here. It seems the three of us were the primary doctors for Seth and Julia, so they'll believe anything I tell them. I told them they were downstairs for testing, twice. I don't know how long I can keep this up."

"You're doing fine, Sven. We'll think of something. Everything is okay here. I'll let you know if we have any problems."

"I know curing these mutants will take time, and we need to take all the time that we need. When we do something, we need to do it right, so when we find the cure, there will be no question about our findings." Sven paused. "I think I may have found a lead, though. An animal that hasn't been affected. I'm working on it. For now, just make them as comfortable as they can and improve their lives, but keep them safe with us."

"We don't have all the time in the world, Sven. We need to take care of this as quickly as possible, remember?"

"I don't know if that's the right solution."

"It's the only way. I will call you later to check on you, okay?" After hanging up the phone, he said, "Jesse, I think you should go check on Sven. Something just doesn't feel right to me. Sven may have second thoughts about this whole thing, although he would be the last to admit it."

"I'm not leaving you here alone," Jesse said. "He may be in a building with more mutants, but they're better contained with better staff. Besides, what if Rachel shows up? Not that I can help much, but at least you won't be dealing with this all by yourself."

"Julia is peaceful. It looks like she's going to go back to sleep and look at Seth. He doesn't even have the strength to open the door. You'll only be gone a short time. I can handle my wife. I got this."

Jesse shook his head. "No way. It's a two-hour drive up here. If anything were to happen to you, I couldn't get up here in time to help. You said so yourself that Seth doesn't look happy. If he escaped..."

"I set it up like a pro. I'll probably just sit here and watch them stew in their own juices, trying to figure out a solution until you come back."

"I have a bad feeling about it. Maybe after a while, when they've been up here and we know they're secure." Jesse couldn't take his eyes off the screen. "I'll *call* Sven. It will be fine."

"That's going to look suspicious. Get up there, and I'll be fine. If there's any problem that I can't handle, I'll know to call 999, and then call you. If we bust the plan or not, okay?"

"The MCS are still human, and they can only get up here so fast." Jesse stood up and rinsed out his can, setting it in a bag for recycling. Adam took this as stalling. "You're no good to us dead."

Adam picked up his revolver. "I have protection. I'll be fine."

"No, Adam, and that's final. It won't look fishy to call Sven. We call each other all the time. Besides, I doubt they are monitoring us. We'll figure out a way for Sven to cover the fact that they're gone. Create paperwork that they were terminated because of them being a dangerous threat."

"They will love that. What are we going to do about producing bodies?" Adam's veins pulsated down his neck.

"One thing at a time," Jesse said, nodding to the left monitor where Seth was growing more agitated and pulling on the doorknob. "I think we have a problem to take care of." Jesse gave Adam a smile. "You need me here."

"Get that smug smile off your face and let's take care of it." Adam opened a cabinet to the right of the stove where they had stashed extra medical tools, including tranquilizer guns strong enough to knock Seth out until next week. At least, Adam hoped. He loaded two up and gave one to Jesse. "I'll unlock the door while you shoot the dart. When it comes to life and death, I will be the first to admit you're a better shot than me. I don't understand how he could pull on the doorknob like that. He was so weak."

"I don't know. Maybe I should unlock the door. What if I miss?" asked Jesse.

"You won't miss." Adam put his hand on his shoulder. "You're the one that said I needed you here."

"Okay, fine." Jesse muttered. "He must have gotten his second wind. Who knows how he works?" Jesse's eyes narrowed as they both rushed to the door. Adam pulled the keys out of his pocket, jingling as he reached for the door.

"Are you ready?" Adam asked, his back against the wall, his hand on the knob. Jesse stood a few feet from the door so he could have some space between him and Seth before he shot the poison. By now, the door was shaking from the other side, and Adam knew they had little time before the element of surprise wouldn't be on their side. He unlocked the door and flung it open, staying between the door and the wall for protection while Jesse aimed and shot the arrow, whizzing through the air, and slammed into Seth's right arm. Seth screamed and stumbled to the ground. He stood, slamming the door against the wall, trapping Adam. Seth's stare never left Jesse. Adam kept a tight grasp on his gun, so his knuckles turned white. With one swoop, Seth smashed the side of Jesse's head with his fist and Jesse hit the floor, unconscious. A fine trickle of blood escaped his temple.

Adam's eyes narrowed at Seth, and he shot another tranquilizer dart, hitting him in the forearm before Seth could go after Jesse. Adam felt stronger than he ever did in his life. He threw down the gun and ran toward Seth, pinning him against the wall with his hands around his throat.

Adam looked into Seth's eyes and for one moment saw a trace of humanity, just a child stuck in between a person and a monster, right before Seth's eyes turned dark and he reached up to bite Adam in the left shoulder. Adam let go just enough to hit him repeatedly, first in the stomach, where Seth doubled over. The second blow was to the jaw. He wasn't giving him the easy way out. Death. He was hoping there was something inside that was still a person he could save, and he hoped he wasn't wrong. Blood squirted out of Seth's nose and his eyes watered so he couldn't see. Adam tied him back to his bed with strong restraints even though Seth was limp from what Adam guessed was exhaustion. He knew anything could change in one second. He rushed to the kitchen to retrieve the knock-out drugs they administered on the way up there and loaded Seth up on the drug.

As soon as he knew Seth was secure, he rushed to Jesse to get him out of there, returning to give Seth another dose of knock-out drugs via dart. He was thinking about how one more might just kill him, but remembered what Jesse had said, "you're no good to us dead." If it was Seth's life or his, he would need to protect himself.

Jesse was regaining consciousness once Adam got over to him. Adam helped lift him up, Jesse leaning on him until they got to the other room. Seth's room was secure, tightly locked, and under heavy surveillance. He was worried more about Jesse. They sat at the table; the closest chair available. With a towel pressed tight against the source of the wound, Adam asked Jesse, "What's your name? Where are we?"

Jesse's eyes got big, and he put his hand in front of him to steady him. Jesse shook his head as his eyes narrowed. "Why are you bleeding? Is that blood mine?"

"Answer the question," Adam asked.

"Jesse Stein. We live in Panacea, Oregon. Now answer my question. Are you okay?"

"Oh, a mere flesh wound." Now that Jesse mentioned it, Adam's shoulder stung, and it was creating a spot of blood pooling under his sleeve. "Seth just tried to take a nibble. The boy certainly is persistent." Adam reached to take off his shirt to get a better look at the wound after Jesse continued to put pressure on his head and the blood was slowly clotting. Adam found he had to press the shirt against the deep teeth marks in his shoulder to stop the bleeding. He heard thumping against the wall and at first thought it was from Seth's room, but wondered how that was possible until he realized it was Julia. She must have heard all the fighting and was freaking out, he reasoned.

"If you're okay, I should check on Julia before she hurts herself. I can explain what happened here. She'll understand." Jesse gave him a smile and a nod before Adam got up and immediately sat back down. He leaned his head over his toes, trying to catch his breath as drops of sweat beaded on his forehead. It felt his chest tighten and his stomach felt hollowed out. "One minute, Julia," he murmured.

Jesse's watch phone rang. "I'm on my way," Sven said on the other end. "I'll get there as fast as I can."

"Sven, how did you know?" asked Jesse.

He heard the long sigh through the line. "I can see all the video footage on my phone, remember? Don't pass out or bleed all over the place before I get there. Remember, pressure on those wounds." And he hung up. Jesse wasn't sure if Sven was more concerned or annoyed.

Adam let out a long, pent-up breath as his head swam. He opened his eyes wide and blinked. "I don't feel so good." Glancing at his shoulder, it looked like the bleeding was slowing down. "I feel funny."

"It sounds like a good thing that Sven is on his way. We're not in the best shape." He let out a snort. "What a first day up here. This better not be a sign…" He paused. "No, I'm not even going to think that way. Looks like you need to lie down. You look so pale."

"I think that's my normal color. You might be right about me having to take a breather. I felt like I just finished a bottle of tequila."

"You feel that good, huh? I will have a killer migraine until next week," Jesse said.

"I think I might be catching the flu." Adam's gut ached as his stomach muscles convulsed. He leaned back, rubbing his abdomen with his right hand, a burning pain seizing his left shoulder. "How could all of this happen? We had this planned out. We built this cabin like a damn fortress." Adam could feel the blood pump through his veins at an accelerated rate. His breathing was becoming rapid and his dizziness intensified. He pounded his fist on the coffee table.

"Relax," Jesse grumbled. "We'll fix it. Both the mutants are contained."

"You sound like the MCS." Adam raised his nose in the air and took a deep sniff, pausing in contemplation.

"What's up with you?" Jesse asked.

"I need to get out of here." Adam clutched his stomach again, and the room was spinning. Visions of blood and destruction filled his mind. His hands were shaking uncontrollably, but somehow he found strength in his legs...

Adam bolted into the woods, feet flying, not sure what he was even running from. His heart was pounding so hard it made everything shake. The sun was setting, giving the sky a hue of pinks and oranges. As he progressed through the woods, the trees blanketed the sky and he felt like he was entering a black hole, and something was so very wrong.

Distance was the only thing that he could think of. He had to maintain some distance until he figured out what was going on with him. With all the excitement, it was really hard to tell, but he felt a little sick to his stomach. It was no wonder, with the stress that he had been under. His immune system will take a toll and he was more than likely ill.

He paused underneath a tree and took a deep breath, clutching his stomach. "Okay, God, help me out," he said as he looked up at the sky, trying to find a crack within the trees as if God could hear the message clearer. "I'm so confused. It wasn't supposed to work out like this. What am I supposed to do?" Adam doubled over in pain, clutching his stomach. The pine scent was so strong it played with his nose from the recent rain. The mud was slick underneath his feet and he slid haphazardly down the side of a tree to the ground. His eyelids were heavy, but knew that he had to fight through it. Staying where he was, someone could find him. He wasn't sure exactly what was going on with him. He felt feverishly hot, like he was on fire, even as the cool air whipped through the trees. "This is certainly the worst flu I have ever gone through," he gasped out loud, although the weakness he felt wasn't like a flu-like weakness, but stronger, like it overtook every part of his body. He stumbled through the woods, his feet slabs of concrete, his eyes watery and out of focus. He didn't want to move fast and step into a hole and twist an ankle or... worse. So many things could happen out in the woods like this.

So he kept moving, and his eyes became clear, sharper than he had ever experienced before. Even though the wooded area was pitch black, he could make out the outline of the trees and debris that covered the forest floor. Blinking, there was no change. It was clearing up as if the sun was rising underneath the tall tree, leaving the hue like dusk.

His weakness was fading away as well, his energy seeping back into his body. Adam swore he could feel his muscles expand and tighten with each second. He needed excess fuel. The pain in his stomach as it growled urged him to find food. Ravenous hunger ate at him as he continued through the forest, on a hunt for food, while still trying to distance himself from the current situation.

Yes, he thought. "I'll think more clearly with something in my stomach. His mouth salivated from hunger, his muscles twitched, and his keen sense of sight helped him as he spotted red berries in the woods. He wasn't sure if they were poisonous or not, unfamiliar as they appeared, and wondered if he was just seeing things. He was too hungry to care.

Keeping an eye out for people after him and mutants that may be in these woods so open and unpatrolled, he took a handful of berries and ripped them off the bushes, shoving them in his mouth.

He bit so hard he almost put a hole through his lip. His teeth were so much stronger than before. Adam ran his tongue over them and his canines were most definitely sharp!

What? Panic set in. The berries tasted rotten! He spit them out. Anything that tasted so foul *must* be poisonous.

Heightened sight, sharp teeth, stomach pain, strength...this didn't sound like any illness that he had ever heard of. No, I couldn't be...He thought back to when Seth showed up at Juniper. Images of the creature in the basement flashed through his mind like flashes of light.

He heard something in the brush in the distance. Narrowing his eyes, he leaned forward to focus and see what was rustling. A small figure stood before him about 15 feet away, and from what he could tell it was the appearance of a little man.

This wasn't a normal dwarf, he could tell. The man was stocky and short with oddly shaped ears, the lobes pointed at the bottom. His face was crinkly with deep crevices, worse than anything Adam had ever seen. Wild hair sprang from different facets of his head, and it appeared that all of the bugs in the forest were attracted to him, perhaps his putrid scent, for they were crawling all over his body. When Adam crept closer, he noticed the bugs were crawling underneath its clear skin, and when the creature opened up his mouth, he displayed two rows of razor-sharp teeth.

Breath caught in Adam's throat, and anger filled him. It was as if his legs were trees with the roots anchoring him to the ground. Adam bent his knees and held a defensive stance, taking a deep breath and clenching his fists as the creature lunged at him.

Adam clamped on, his prior weakness and pain suddenly absent. In its place, a fury took over. He pulled the thing away as it tried to claw at his face, and Adam kicked him as hard as he could. The thing went sprawling against a tree, and moments later headed toward Adam again.

The thing gouged Adam's cheek, and Adam grabbed its arm and twisted as hard as he could. It howled as Adam clawed at the thing's face, releasing the insects that were inhabited there. Ants, beetles, and gnats covered both of them. Adam smashed them with his fingers and stepped on them, but the number was staggering.

A rumble began in Adam's stomach even after the berries, and he continued to claw at the mutant's face, the bugs all around him he didn't even notice anymore. The anger faded, as did the mutant's life.

When the mutant's face was gone and beaten down to the bone, Adam stopped. *What the hell did I just do?* Most of the insects he had already ground into the dirt, the rest had traveled to the rest of the forest. His hands and face were covered in blood, and his teeth had made wounds in his lips. His skin was coated in insect bites.

"Why?" he asked himself, as if the forest had an answer. "What happened to me?" He shook as he remembered the blood-hungry Seth that showed up at Juniper Ridge. He was strong and driven.

Adam looked down at the sore from when Seth had bitten him, the sore swollen and fresh, but barely hurt anymore. "Ah, shit," he said, his brow narrowing as he stared at the dead mutant before him. "He must have been part human." He looked down at the mess that was left of the mutant. Bones and flesh with the smell of blood disgusted him, as he had to travel away just not to look at the remains. Even when he squeezed his eyes shut, he could still see the mutant attacking him, and he could still see the remains over the forest floor. His heart accelerated at the excitement of the kill. He hid the remains in a nearby bush.

"This isn't me," he said, gathering as much distance as he could from the evidence of his savagery. *What have I done? What would cause me to do this? The world is improving because of the water supply being purified from the virus...*

Staying still underneath a dark corner of a Douglas Fir, memories of the cabin flashed at him. "The water. Oh my God, why the hell did I drink the water? Those pipes haven't been used in ages! It hasn't been purified at all. No one else even knew we were out there!" Punching the tree, splinters flew in all directions. The skin on his knuckles tore open and bled.

In a fit of energy, he tore off into a sprint through the opening in the wood. He listened intently as he traveled out of fear that he would hurt someone else.

He had gotten a glimpse of his father's thinking, and a different type of anger washed over him. "I could have helped him somehow," he bellowed through the trees, and quieted down to remember that he was in hiding. *Maybe I could have done something, if I had known. If I was already in this program, if I had studied this earlier and taken an interest in it, taken an interest in what was happening in our world and how it was so fucked up...*

He stopped for a moment and watched, bending down almost to his belly underneath the brush. With his new supersonic sight, he saw people in the distance, like looking through a pair of binoculars without the binoculars, and the first person he saw was Rachel.

His heart dropped. She can't see me like this. "Go away," he muttered. "I'm not myself. I might hurt you, too." The thought ate at him as he scanned the rest of the area and saw others fully armed in MCS gear. Blood sped through his veins, expanding the flow to his brain as thoughts became clearer and energy heightened. They surrounded her to protect her as she lingered behind them. He could hear them arguing. She wasn't leaving. One offered to take her back home. He wished she would listen to them.

When they were at a slightly further distance, after they had changed course and were going away from him, he ran again. His full strides were gaining ground, but he knew that if he kept going, they were going to find him, anyway. He needed a place to hide, and he needed supplies. Not liking the filthy feeling of dirt, blood, and dead bugs, he found a cavern covered in moss. He covered the opening with fallen tree limbs. Here he could do some thinking and try to get some rest, figuring out his next move.

As he laid on the hard dirt floor of the cave, exhaustion took him, but he didn't rest soundly. Dark images filled his mind before sleep, and during, they consumed his nightmares.

— • —

CHAPTER FIFTEEN

Adam awoke, his mind a fog as he tried to remember what happened the day before. The inside of the cavern was so dark it was impossible to tell what time of day it was, much like his office. He stretched and yawned from the fitful sleep that he had.

As much as he wished it was all some crazy dream, traveling again through the woods, he knew it was a living nightmare. He decided his next plan would be to go back to the cabin in hopes he could get some necessary supplies without anyone lurking around. He wished he had some kind of weapon.

The cabin was in view, Adam masked far away behind a cluster of trees. He couldn't see any vehicles, but he considered the possibility that they parked on the other side. The sun warmed his back, and he perspired. *Just slip in and out of the back door. There's no way they would still have those mutants in there. They would have moved them already.* He didn't like the idea of the open space between where he was hiding to the back door, but that was a risk he had to take. Needing nourishment, basic medical supplies, and a damn bar of soap, he felt grimy all over and could smell the blood from the recent fight with the mutant in the woods. He wanted to wash it all away. The reminder gnawed at his gut and angered him, and he was tired of being angry.

Adam crouched down and spread out his feet, looking from one side to the other before sprinting across the open area of grass. His strides were pulling so far he could feel the stretch in his thighs. Sweat formed on his forehead and ran down his back. He focused on the cabin in front of him and prayed no one was watching.

Adam, back flat against the outside of the cabin behind the back door, stopped and listened. Even his breathing stopped for a moment as if someone would hear his breath and jump out of the cabin, clutching him in an instant capture. All he could hear were the birds chirping and a slight breeze that made the grass sway. Convinced that the coast was clear, he turned to open the door.

The locked door. He reached into his empty pocket. The key must have fallen out and was somewhere in the woods. Damn, he hadn't expected this as he looked around for anything that would jimmy the lock. He was trying not to leave evidence that he was there. That would be one more clue... and he knew he was already in enough trouble. Or maybe another way in? An open window or perhaps another door? He stayed in the shadows as he moved around the perimeter of the cabin, and along the side he heard a vehicle coming down the gravel road from a distance. With a quick intake of breath, he hid behind the bushes against the building, waiting and listening.

"Take it easy, Sven. You're going to hurt yourself." He heard Jesse's voice.

"Good Lord, quit mothering me. Take your own advice. You're the one that's hurt. What do you think happened to him?"

Jesse's voice dropped in volume and he said, "I don't know. I just hope wherever he is, he's okay. If anything is going to ever be okay. This is such a mess."

"And what if we don't find him? What if he disappears forever? What if a wild animal or mutant ate him? Nothing will ever be the same." There was a catch in Sven's voice, a pause of contemplation.

"We'll find him." Jesse patted Sven's shoulder.

"I'm right here," said Adam. "Just go already." He heard them walk into the cabin. He tried to turn the corner to get a look, but he was afraid that they would see him. He wouldn't dare take a peek until the door slammed shut behind them. He tried to look in the windows, but they were hard to get to without being detected. At least if he got close enough, he might hear what they were talking about so he knew what was going on outside of the woods.

"They haven't found the mutants yet?" Sven asked Jesse.

"No, not even Seth. They could still be in the woods, but who knows where they are by now? At least no one will be hurt out there if they are, it being against the law to even be out there. It's deemed unsafe and all."

"In my opinion, no electric fencing and distance from MCS headquarters doesn't make it that much more unsafe than anywhere else. It's getting so bad everywhere." Adam heard a thump that sounded like something dropping, like a fist on a table. "Damn it, we shouldn't have done it. We shouldn't have gone through with Adam's stupid plan. We aren't any better off than we were before."

"We had to do something. If we knew all this was going to happen..."

"Just grab what we need and let's get out of here."

Yes! Get out. Please. I'm sorry, guys. It was all my fault. My damn desperation. He clenched his fists as fury grew inside of him, his jaw clenching together in a straight line, and the pollen tickled his nose. He plugged it, ducking as to not be seen, but getting deeper in the bushes just enhanced the tickle. His hands flew off his nose as he sneezed.

All was quiet. The men inside had stopped talking and Adam stayed as still as he could, trying not to make any more noise to arouse suspicion. Almost out of the woods.

"Did you hear something?" Jesse asked.

"Shhh...I think it was from outside," said Sven. Even though he couldn't see them, he knew what they were doing. They were grabbing whatever weapons they had handy, assuming there was a mutant from the woods outside, perhaps one as familiar as Seth or Julia. Adam looked for an area where he could return to the woods for another hiding spot, but there was no way he could get away without going through the clearing. The other direction was to the vehicles where he knew he would get caught.

He heard them go out the back door and the screen door slam behind them. "We should be quiet," Jesse whispered, and Adam was amazed at his improved hearing. Adam eased against the house, keeping his back flat against the cabin, wishing he could melt in against the wall or blend in like a chameleon. There was a small opening through the bushes that he could see out of, and he peeked through, hanging back when he spotted Jesse. Sven came into view.

Adam caught their scent, something aside from Jesse's stinky aftershave and Sven's chocolate breath. A human smell that he never noticed before, different from anything else, animal or otherwise. His stomach growled, and he hoped the men couldn't hear it from where they were.

Sven had a tranquilizer gun close to his side, ready to aim, and Jesse had a revolver in one hand, and a knife in a sheath of his belt at the ready. But something else was there, and Adam could sense it. He heard something close to where he was. A growl that was not his own. Adam's eyes narrowed, and he leaned into the thick of the bush, trying to see beyond it, wishing he wasn't in such a predicament. Adam saw a break in the bushes, and stayed close by, ready to help if need be. His hiding would all be for nothing if anything happened to his friends.

It came out of the woods, a mutant grizzly bear that loomed over Jesse and Sven. Adam wanted to help them, but he didn't know how. He didn't have any weapons, but his newly sharpened skills, and he was ready to use them. It looked like they were well prepared, but still...

Adam extended his claws and neared the opening. The two scientists didn't notice, as they were focusing on the mutant in front of them.

The bear stood over fifteen feet standing on his hind legs, and his fur was matted and spotted with dried blood. The mutant only had one eye that was centered in the middle of his face. There was no nose, and his mouth was microscopic. Adam wondered how it breathed and concluded not very well. No wonder the animal was angry. There were no claws on its absent paws, but slimy stubs at the end of his arms. Adam concluded the only way this creature could hurt them was by trampling them until the bear opened his mouth and a forked tongue flicked out, reaching two feet. Wings of enormous proportion were on his back, making him more like a furry dragon than a bear.

The bear stood twenty feet from the scientists and was gaining ground, but not quickly because of the stubbed feet. Adam rushed toward the mutant at an incredible speed, slashing the back of its legs as he catapulted by, ending up on the other side of the clearing deep into the woods. They had a chance, Adam thought, until the bear took flight.

Jesse and Sven looked up in shock. "Did you see that other mutant?" said Sven. "I think it was trying to help us."

"I saw him, but I don't understand it." They both tried to shoot at the bear-mutant. Sven got it in the arm while it knocked Jesse's gun out of his hand, but the creature couldn't grasp it for himself because of missing hands. The creature swayed a bit, but kept flying.

Adam bit his lip and watched intently from the woods, his heart quickening. He was ready to assist again, but didn't want to distract them. They thought he was a mutant? What if they thought he was dangerous and didn't focus on the real threat? "Come on, guys," he said to himself, and looked over at the back door in the distance, beginning to grasp at his middle as he sweated. They were totally occupied and wouldn't notice if he had slipped in the back door at his amazing speed. At this point, he assumed, they wouldn't notice if the cabin was on fire. Just to make sure that they are okay, he reasoned, and then it would be fine to go through the back door. The MCS are going to be all over this place, he thought, in just a few minutes. I'm sure that Jesse will make a quick call after they are all safe, and then I'm in real trouble. Someone will detect me then.

Jesse reached over to grab the gun where the creature had sent it flying, but the creature was going for it at the same time. Sven got up to help Jesse, but tripped on an unlevel surface on the ground. He got his bearings just fast enough to get another shot off on the tranquilizer gun, hitting the bear in its enormous eye.

The bear howled and blood shot out his eye, dripping the blood on the two men struggling to protect themselves. Jesse got the gun and shot the bear three more times, twice in the chest and once in the head.

The bear dropped to the ground with an earth-shattering thud and didn't move.

Adam just realized that he had been holding his breath, and he let it go. They did it. They were going to be all right, but it still left the problem of him sneaking into the cabin without getting caught. This was going to be close to impossible. The MCS are going to be there to pick up the mutant and make sure it was disposed of properly, for it was surely dead, especially after Jesse shot it two more times in the head for assurance.

"I'll call it in," said Jesse, rushing back into the cabin to use the phone while Sven kept an eye on the bear, tranquilizer gun at the ready and keeping a distance if by chance the animal somehow came to. He returned minutes later letting Sven know that the MCS were on their way.

Adam eyed the nearest door, hoping that they would be so preoccupied by the bear, they wouldn't notice a slight opening and shutting. Hey, at least now he knew it wasn't locked.

He spurted to the door when they were staring at the bear to make sure it would not reawaken, barely opening it to enter.

The men continued to keep their eye on the mutant, but the door shut behind Adam with a tap.

He headed to the kitchen first, stuffing an apple in his mouth as he continued to grab food and filled up a canvas bag underneath the counter. He spit the apple out immediately as he grimaced at the foul taste. No time to eat, he told himself. Grab and go.

In the bathroom, Adam scavenged for soap and cleaners, and hid behind the shower curtain when he heard voices. They didn't sound like Jesse or Sven's. Must be the MCS, he thought, listening to them talk about how they were going to transport the bear. He heard someone announce to give him a minute, he just had to use the bathroom.

Adam froze, clutching his bag to his chest, and bit his bottom lip. He looked up to the sky and said a silent prayer that no one would see him. He held his breath as the man relieved himself, sorry for his heightened sense of smell and afraid the man would hear him breathe. The water was running, the door was opening, and the man shut it again. Adam could hear him in the bathroom still. "Something is not right," he said. Adam closed his eyes and waited, his knees buckling underneath him. "They don't even keep soap in here. Disgusting. And they call themselves doctors?" He closed the door behind him. "Hey, Steve, did you call Rachel Davidson back? You promised to keep her informed of any more information about her husband, remember? I feel so bad for everything she's gone through. That poor woman."

"Why would I call her back?" Adam heard. "We have no news, good or bad. They humored her and let her join them in the search for Dr. Davidson for a short time, then gave her a ride home. You know they won't keep her informed on every step. I told her I would. I would want someone to do the same for me." He recognized the voice. Steve Fob? The Doctor Steve Fob that worked at Juniper Ridge on opposite shifts of Adam?

"True." There were footsteps going to the front of the cabin, and the front door slammed shut.

Grasping his bag of treasures, he tenderly walked across the wood floor. How long had Rachel been in contact with Steve? How long had she been spying on him, and why? He felt her distrust burn at him. All the questions he was planning to ask her when he saw her again. He shoved the idea that he may never see her again from his mind. That wasn't an option.

It appeared the coast was clear. They had hauled off the mutant in record time, and Adam didn't see anyone in sight. He didn't dare grab anything else, exhausted from the anxiety and tension. He bolted out the door and blindly into the woods.

CHAPTER SIXTEEN

E ven with the murky water, Adam enjoyed lathering up to get as much blood and sweat off of him as possible. In between scrubs, his mind raced. *What is going on with Sven and Jesse? How are they doing without me? How could I make all these stupid mistakes? And now look what happened.* A part of him didn't even know why he contained this furious rage deep inside of him. He scrubbed harder and harder until his own blood was dripping into the water.

He could feel every little thing that was going on in his body, how it was morphing into something that he didn't recognize. His blood quickened; he could feel it rushing throughout his entire body. What he had just gone through should have left him exhausted, but he didn't feel any fatigue. In fact, he felt almost hyper and keenly aware of everything. The birds, the insects, every single muscle he used with every movement he made.

His hunger had not improved at all, but was just one more thing that added to his frustration.

He heard footsteps in the distance and grabbed his clothes, pulling them behind a bush as he dressed at lightning speed. Unable to see in between the shrubbery, he used his keen hearing and noticed there was another sense that he had gained besides the normal five senses. He knew someone was out there, three in fact, but he couldn't see them. The MCS were searching while they were in the area. The strange thing was, he didn't know how he knew, he just felt it. He could almost delve into their minds. Not where he knew exactly what they were thinking, but he could see without specifics. Even when he was this far away, he knew one was tired. It had been a long day, and it was time to go home. Adam focused on him and had a connection, being physically able to feel his tiredness. One was learning and paying attention to every detail that the others did with enthusiasm. The third was determined to find him. He always got his mutant. And they were coming closer.

He stayed still and listened.

"What do you say we give it a rest?"

"We will, after we find him. He hasn't been gone long. He couldn't have gone far." His voice was deep, his step heavy on the forest floor. Adam pictured him as a burly guy, but didn't dare look.

"Wouldn't it make more sense for there to be more of us to find him?" the younger man sounded. Adam hoped he just sounded young. Just a child to join the MCS. They really were desperate. He leaned to the right just a little to see, and that's when he heard a yell from a few yards away.

"Open your eyes, guys, he's right there to your left!" Adam took off in a sprint.

Sure, if it wasn't three against one, he might stay and fight, but he felt the odds weren't in his favor. He couldn't believe how fast he could run, and how good it felt.

He reached one of the tallest trees in the woods in the thicket where it was the darkest, even in the middle of the day, and he attached himself to it and climbed it like a squirrel. Finding a limb on the very top that was sturdy, he held on, looking down. He could smell them and see them, but they couldn't see him. He stayed still so nothing on the tree would drop, not that he thought they would notice in this condition. His heart beat fast in his chest, and his breathing was heavy, but he was still steady, waiting. He felt like a predator.

He didn't like the feeling, but he couldn't shake it. Not wanting to hurt them, he just wanted them to leave him alone. He had to figure things out, and he didn't need any help there. They would just get in the way.

"Where the hell did he go?" one asked.

"You go that way, I will go the other," one said, and he stayed in the tree, watching them all split up. He didn't move long enough for his arms and legs to start and ache, and his stomach growled again. He couldn't remember the last time that he had eaten, except for the apple, and it must have been old because it tasted rancid.

The coast seemed clear; they wouldn't repeat where they had been, but made a complete circle back to where they began. He dropped from the tree and landed on all fours, figuring that was the safest bet.

"I'm in better shape than I thought," he told himself, standing up and looking around. He heard something again approaching him from a distance and focused through the brush to see a figure that he knew wasn't MCS. It was entirely too small. He moved in closer as the figure rushed toward him, and surprised himself that his instincts this time weren't to run, but fight. He would have a definite size advantage, anyway.

Seth.

The boy went straight at him in a full run, and Adam wasn't afraid. He rushed toward him as well, and they clawed at each other. His head was trying to wrap around the actions his body was doing, but it couldn't catch up. All of the anger that he had been holding in for everything now had exploded and surfaced at one time, and he just wanted to destroy.

Seth pushed at Adam where Adam attached to his shoulder, burying his claws in Adam's knee. Adam howled, not in pain, but in the fight's thrill. Seth went to crouch down and bite on Adam's neck, but in one swoop, Adam pushed him away and threw him into a nearby Sequoia. The smaller body made a hard, thumping sound as he struck the tree. There was blood everywhere as they both bled from their wounds.

Adam's teeth extended and sharpened almost to the point of making his tongue bleed. He learned quickly to keep it out of the way. Echoes of "kill or be killed" rang through Adam's mind, but he didn't know their source.

It was coming from Seth. He could see it in his eyes.

This time Adam went for Seth, a welcome change that he was no longer afraid of him. He wasn't afraid of anything.

Adam held down Seth's head as he sat on him, taking his right index finger and burying it in his right eye socket. Seth howled in pain as Adam pulled his finger out, his eyeball stuck to the two-inch claw that now extended from his finger.

They were extensions on all his fingers.

Seth was bleeding all over the ground, swatting blindly at Adam, but Adam shoved his knee into Seth's stomach, and it wasn't hard to keep him from moving. He was so much smaller. Adam endured the slight cuts that resulted from him squatting there, waiting for all Seth's energy to be depleted, until he went limp.

Adam bent down and listened, not hearing any breath out of Seth. He looked down at his clawed hand, and stuck the claw in his mouth, chewing the eyeball until dissolved, and swallowed it.

His eyes widened at what he had just done, but the hunger in his stomach was feeling better. His hesitation lasted only a moment, and he continued with his razor-sharp teeth and claws, cutting up the parts until they were more bite-size, and ate. Ravenous with hunger, he barely tasted what was going down his throat. Most were slick, but some pieces were tough. Blood ran down his chin and soaked his clothes, but he barely noticed.

When his hunger was satisfied, he stopped and looked down at himself. He shook from the shock and horror of what he had just done.

Seth was a mutant, and a mutant that looked like a child. Deep inside, that's probably what he really was, a child, and Adam had just eaten him like he was at a Christmas feast.

How could I do this? I'm...holy shit, I'm a monster. He pushed the rest of the unfinished body pieces off of him and scampered away until he found a burrow underneath the brush. He crawled into the darkest, dankest hole he could find and shook.

What have I done? What is happening to me? Am I even me anymore? Thoughts swam through his mind as he clawed at his own body, trying to punish himself for his actions. He knew he could not control himself, but somehow that had made it all worse. What would be next? For the first time, he wasn't afraid of the world at large and all the changes that had been happening. He was afraid of himself.

I'm capable of anything now, and that is not a good thing. I'm not safe to be around anything or anyone. I can't help anyone, not even myself. Everything is so screwed up, and now there is no turning back.

His arms stung, his body was a little stiff, but he felt so much healthier than he was before. That just reminded him of the result of what he did. He couldn't even think of it, let alone say it out loud.

This time he didn't want to wash up, but left the blood and pieces of Seth on him to remind himself of what he had done. This is it.

I can't do anything for anyone anymore. He contemplated finishing it all. All he would have to do was slit his own throat with one of his talons and it would all be over, but that was too merciful. He would go quickly and he deserved to suffer. He remembered how he felt when he was hungry and was sure it would get worse with time.

I refuse to hurt anyone else, and I won't risk finding a cure because that's exactly what might happen. He wrapped himself in a fetal position in the darkest place and cried, tension and fear welling out of every sob, thinking of his family and his friends. He would never see them again. It would be too dangerous. He refused to risk them.

He loved them too much.

As he laid in the dirt, his senses had heightened to their brink. The smell of the pines was potent, as the coppery smell of the blood on himself, the taste on his tongue, and he tried to block it all out with no success. He grasped at his head, threading his fingers through his hair, wanting to rip it all out, wanting to rip himself apart.

Shaking and torn, he eventually fell asleep on the forest floor.

CHAPTER SEVENTEEN

Heavy footsteps through the woods woke Adam, and he slowly opened his eyes to peer out of the brush to see if it was a mutant or an animal going by.

Then he heard his name being called. "Adam!"

"Shit," he spat, trying to recoil himself into a ball so no one would find him. With the movement, the brush shook. He knew it was Jesse, and he could hear Sven not far behind.

"I think he's close," said Sven. "He had to be here somewhere, but these woods are so dense..."

"We'll find him," assured Jesse. "We just need to keep looking. He was freaking out. He may be hurt or in serious trouble, especially if a mutant got a hold of him out here."

"I know. He could be bleeding to death somewhere, or..." He paused, then shivered.

"Let's just keep looking." Jesse put his hand on Sven's shoulder. "Think maybe we should split up?"

"Bad idea. Too dangerous. You saw that thing when we were at the cabin. Neither one of us could handle something like that alone." Jesse nodded in agreement as he surveyed the area, pulling out his binoculars, which stopped when he pointed them at the shrubbery Adam was hiding behind.

Adam froze, even stopping his breath.

"I thought I saw something in this direction," said Jesse, and he walked toward Adam, Sven right behind him. They both had weapons at the ready. Jesse had a Glock, and Sven had a tranquilizer gun hanging at his side. Sven nodded, and Jesse pulled aside the bushes to see Adam pulling away from them.

They both stopped and stared. Adam tried to get up, then tripped and fell.

"Stop! Adam? It's okay," stammered Jesse, a slow realization coming across his face.

"Take it easy, son," said Sven. "We're here to help you." His fangs hung over his bottom lip, cracked and slick with blood. Regaining balance without fingers to claw the ground was a challenge. His tattered clothes were blood-soaked in many spots. He felt like a savage.

"You need to stay away from me," he said, pulling away more. He opened his mouth wide to scare them, but they just both looked amazed. "How are you not afraid?"

"It's you, in there somewhere," said Jesse. "What the hell happened?"

"Can't you tell? I'm done. This was all a joke, thinking we could change things. Now I told you once and I will tell you again, leave me alone. The world will never change." Adam turned and ran.

"Not going to happen," said Sven. "I hate to do this, but you give me no choice." Adam felt the wiz of a tranquilizer dart go past his ear, and he changed course. He could hear the crunch of the leaves behind him as they ran, could smell their fragrant humanity; the salty and sweet combination made his stomach churn. Both of the men were chasing him, and he ran away, fighting his new instinct to run to them and attack. He maneuvered around every familiar tree and woodland debris until he felt the sting of the tranquilizer dart in his shoulder, and he pulled it out, staggering away. *No, not the loss of control. Not again.* Hunched over on the ground, he stood up with all the energy he had remaining and turned, his claws slicing into Sven's abdomen right before he hit the forest floor.

Adam's view was hazy as he gathered all the energy he could muster to open his eyes. When he went to rub one of them, he noticed he was unable. Both of his restrained wrists were against a cold, metal surface that smelled of rust, chilling his body. *Where am I? How did I get here? What are they going to do to me?*

"What the hell?" he exclaimed, pulling tightly at the restraints until they almost broke. He relaxed when he saw Jesse and Sven, one on either side of him.

"It's okay, Adam. We're here to help you." Adam could lift his head and he saw he was in an open space, and it was definitely not a hospital. Jesse said, "Sorry about the cuffs, but we didn't want you to hurt yourself when you came to."

"I told you two to leave me alone," he growled.

"And you know how well we listen," said Sven. He could see Sven's eyes widen at his new appearance, his eyes especially steady on his claws and sharpened teeth that had elongated enough to overlap his lips. "We need to do something now. Serious action has to be taken until you can't come back from this. Starting with me. I need to work harder and focus on this. I won't lose any more mutants, Adam. I won't lose you."

"I'm just trying to keep you safe," said Adam. "I already hurt you out there in the woods." He thought of clawing Sven and his fingers burned with the memory. He tapped his claws on the table in such rapid succession and so fiercely the edges wore down with each tap, leaving a powder residue on the surface. "I can handle this myself. It would just be better if I didn't exist." Adam closed his eyes and wished himself to disappear and hoped when he opened his eyes that they would be gone. He was done. He wasn't going to help anyone the way that he was; he wasn't going to help anyone ever again.

"I can't believe I'm hearing this," said Sven. "This is not the Adam I know, the man that is determined to make a difference."

"Take a good look," said Adam. "I'm no longer a man." He could feel one of the restraints loosening. "I think you should go. These won't hold me much longer."

"Then break through them, and we can work together," said Sven, but Adam noticed he moved back a few steps and had his pistol at the ready. "Adam, do you realize this is the perfect opportunity? We will know how well the cure is working if one of our own is experiencing it, especially you. You are the very top in your field. Don't you see how important you are? I'm not talking about the world, but I'm talking about how important you are to me."

"Come on," said Jesse. "Give us a chance. Give yourself a chance. Jill has been moving more mutants over to Black Hills since all of this has been happening, and it's easier than ever for her now. Time to take action."

"I miss the days when it was just Juniper Ridge and we didn't have to worry about Black Hills. We have enough problems just figuring out how to fix this mess without them interfering," said Sven.

Adam's anger grew when he thought of all the mutants that he had been working with over the years, but felt totally helpless. In his current state, he wasn't helping anyone. He was glad that he didn't wake up at Juniper Ridge, even more glad that he wasn't in Black Hills, took a deep sigh and thought he should take advantage of his good fortune there. Still afraid that he would hurt his friends, his family away from home, he shared his thoughts.

"I don't think it would be best if we worked on this together," he said. "Someone could get hurt, and I don't want to be the one to cause it. I don't think I could live with myself…" He was about ready to say mutant or not, but he couldn't say it out loud. It was as if saying it would make it any more true than it was. "No excuses," was all he could muster. "You're not in my position. You don't understand."

But while he argued with them, he thought about what they were saying. He now knew what it was like on the other side. Would that be an advantage for finding a cure? Would that help him out? And, as much as he hated to admit it, now it would almost be impossible to do it alone. Everyone was looking for him, and if he ended up in the wrong hands, they might really prove their point that this could happen to anyone, even one of their own, and people could get hurt. He tried to focus and think about what would be right, but his mind was all over the place, and he got frustrated.

Frustration was not good for him right now. It just fueled his anger and hunger.

"Leave me alone," said Adam, yanking on the restraints until he got the right arm loose, then loosened the left. Both of the men raised their weapons.

"Don't make me knock you out again," said Sven, a tranquilizer gun at the ready.

"Okay." Adam jumped off the table in one instantaneous motion, knocking the tranquilizer gun to the floor.

Sven reached down to scramble for it, and Jesse yelled, "Stop!"

"You won't shoot me," said Adam after grabbing the tranquilizer gun before Sven could get to it. Adam pushed the table at Jesse, knocking him over. As Jesse fell backward, the gun went off, missing Adam's head by millimeters.

"I'm going to the woods, and that's where I need to stay. There's no one there that I can hurt. Don't follow me." Jesse was a little wobbly getting up, but didn't seem to be horribly hurt. Adam doubled over in pain, but fought the urge to cry out. I have to be tough. I can't hurt anyone else. But now, I have had the taste for it, and it will be hard to stop.

Either I die, or I find a cure. Or Jill finds me, and I die. I have to find it soon, because I will die before I hurt anyone else.

"We will keep looking for a cure, and when we do, we will find you again."

"Same spot," said Adam, turning away from them to block their scent. "I have to go." By instinct, he left the abandoned warehouse, out in the middle of nowhere with no safety precautions, so he knew there wouldn't be many people, and traveled back to the woods. He found a new spot besides where Jesse and Sven found him, and again hid behind a tangle of greenery, careful to be still, and laid in agony until he finally passed out.

CHAPTER EIGHTEEN

Adam crawled out of the bushes. The pain in his side subsided. "Maybe I'm just getting accustomed to the ache. Something to eat," he said to himself. "I just need to find something. A cure, I need to find a cure. I will not rest until I do." He thought of Rachel and his kids, and not seeing them grow up. He thought of Jesse and Sven, his two friends that would have to face all of this all alone, and he wouldn't allow it. *Enough feeling sorry for myself, he thought. This isn't the time.* He thought of Seth and what he did to him. He thought of Christopher and what he couldn't do for him. This was the time to fix it all.

Adam was growing accustomed to the pain in his stomach, and he worked through it as he traveled through the forest, trying to think of a cure for everything that he was going through. The crunch of the leaves underneath his feet grew louder than they had always been. He felt in tune with nature. He looked up at the birds overhead, their bodies different. One flew right over him with missing feet and he watched the bird land, slowing his wings until it gently hit the ground and ate the bugs on the forest floor, resting on its belly. Even the birds had learned to adapt.

Oh, God, I don't want to hurt anyone. I'm not going to eat people to live. The poor little thing. He went to pick it up, grateful that he didn't feel hunger around other animals, and the bird flew away.

He remembered when Seth was a patient. They were looking for a way the boy could survive on normal food instead of human flesh, and now he had the same goal. It was more urgent.

He traveled farther into the forest, slowing down as his energy was depleting. Adam stayed sharp in case any more people were searching for him here, but he had a feeling they had moved on. He wondered how his family was doing. Rachel was surely flipping out, demanding answers. Praying she wasn't getting herself in trouble with the institution, he imagined what Jill would do to her, and it made his anger flare up again. His body grew warm, his muscles tensed, and he tried to calm himself down again. *It's time to find a cure.* He found a place underneath a tree and sat, doing some deep breathing. His eyes closed, and he pictured himself back home, sitting at the breakfast table with his wife and kids, and the picture turned violent as he grabbed onto Camille with his talons.

He opened his eyes and screamed into the empty forest to no one.

An unfamiliar sound echoed through the tree. A frog? He had heard frog sounds on an old recording once recorded years before he had even been born. It sounded distinctly like what he was hearing.

No way could it be a frog! Only fabricated fairy tales. Frogs don't exist. He always thought Sven told a good story and had a creative mind. *My mind is playing tricks on me. I'm tired, I'm stressed...* Yet when he looked again, he saw something move, and the next thing he knew, he held a tree frog in his hand.

The tree frog was the only animal that had never been a mutant... EVER.

His eyes grew wide, and he grasped the animal in his hand so it wouldn't escape. Maybe they shouldn't have been so distant from this forest for so long, full of mutants but perhaps full of animals totally unaffected. He heard somewhere in the past of people using frog skin for medicinal purposes, but frogs disappeared decades ago.

Or so he thought.

Adam stood perfectly still, not moving a muscle, and focused entirely on what he could hear. He closed his eyes and heard more frogs, perhaps even in the same tree. It could be possible. Now he wished he had access to Jesse and Sven. How was he going to contain these creatures and test them to see if it would work? He had nothing.

He held onto the wiggling frog that tried to escape, looking up at the tree and hearing all the other frogs croak. The sound was almost deafening to his ears. It reminded him of Juniper Ridge, where he was trying to save the world.

He was hungry. In one sense, it disgusted him to think of eating a frog raw, but he had eaten a... no, he couldn't even think of that. Desperate times call for... oh, what the hell. He took one of his talons, peeling off the skin and throwing it in his mouth, and beginning to chew. The frog squirmed more in protest.

With his old teeth, this might have been more work, but with his new set, it was like knives were chopping it up before he was digesting. It reminded him of the skin of a chicken, but tougher and way undercooked. More like flakes of something bad.

His stomach churned.

Keep it down, he thought, trying to think of something else it could be. He thought of Seth and how delicious he was, and his stomach seemed to settle. He kept eating until the skin was all gone, and he started on the meat. By now, the frog had stopped moving. This was the first thing that he had eaten that wasn't human that wasn't making him ill.

Sometimes it took some time for it to have an adverse effect on him, so he tried not to get too excited. Meanwhile, he turned back to where he had put all of the supplies that he had stolen from the cabin just to see what he had hidden there. He had to have something to store the frogs where it wouldn't hurt them. He couldn't hurt them. They were the most natural, untouched by human stupidity thing that he had ever seen. They were the only things on this earth that didn't need fixing.

They might be a cure.

Adam smiled then, leaning back against the tree, and he wasn't sure if his relief was from hope for a cure or that his belly was full and he wasn't feeling so primal. He figured hunger had something to do with it.

He heard another sound in the distance, and sat straight up, standing up and staying still to hear what was coming. It sounded like another animal. A beastly cry spread across the forest, and the first thing that Adam thought was, "I'm going to do anything possible to protect these frogs. They may be my last hope." Adam had his claws outstretched in front of him, his feet set apart for balance, and waited in silence.

Something slithered across the forest floor that blended in with its surroundings. The only thing that Adam saw was a pair of red eyes the size of dimes that reflected off any bit of light and could hear the rustling of the leaves as they moved.

He saw a three-headed snake at his feet in a matter of seconds and reached for it, but the snake was fast. The mutant was twelve feet, some parts slimy and some smooth, all covered in tiny spikes that retracted and extended in tandem. Adam swung at it, and as he cut off a part of it with his claws, it would rejuvenate at an alarming speed. The snake was just so fast.

Adam screamed as it wrapped around his leg, the spikes digging into his skin and letting go so it could move upward. Blood ran down Adam's leg and he howled in pain that fueled his fury.

He tried to pull free of the snake's hold on him, but it wrapped around him and pulled tight, biting him with its three heads on the way up. It reached his neck in minutes.

The snake wrapped around his throat and Adam took all of his strength and pulled the snake off of him, the spikes leaving wounds all over his body. *This would not be it. After all that I have been through, he thought, this mutant is not going to get the best of me.*

With all of his strength and anger, he attacked the snake, sliced it up into pieces before it could rejuvenate, and cut off its heads one by one with his sharp claws. He stared at the pieces: the three heads, spikes skins both smooth and sticky, and the long rattler. This one was a new one. Hoping there wasn't any more like it in the woods, but he had already seen enough. It was time to find a cure and get the hell out of the forest after collecting all the frogs that he could find. He wasn't even sure if it was a cure yet, but he had a feeling.

He had never seen a mutant resemble a frog of any sort. Nothing with any frog parts, and he had seen hundreds of mutants throughout the years. For the first time since he had entered this God-forsaken forest, he was feeling something he hadn't felt.

Hope.

Now, he was tired, which was surprising because after the transformation, being tired wasn't an issue, especially after he had eaten. Maybe it was the anxiety from killing the snake, maybe cutting up the mutant, but whatever it was, he took a rest underneath the very tree that held the tree frogs and listened to them croak. It was one of the most wonderful sounds that he had ever heard.

He looked up in between where there was a crack in the trees, and said, "oh, please, let this one be it. I don't want to die. I don't want Black Hills to win. This has to work."

The opening of the sky turned black as clouds overhead hung over. He could hear the thunder and see the flash of lightning right before the rain fell.

Chapter Nineteen

Adam stretched, listening all around him to make sure he was safe. Now he knew he had to return to where he stashed everything from the cabin earlier. He found a spot in the woods and put the soap, food, and other items that he might need. Placing them all in a box when he left the cabin, and that's what he needed. The box.

This is where he could store the frogs, or at least a couple, until he knew if they had a positive effect on him. He had a good feeling when his rage began fading. He hoped it wasn't just wishful thinking.

He missed his lab and all his equipment, but he figured this was the time he was learning to use what he had. As he went to retrieve the box, he was hyper-aware of everything that was going on around him, using his new sixth sense to heighten his awareness. He wiped the corner of his mouth where he was salivating, his teeth still a mouthful of knives and his claws still extending from his fingers. God, he was hoping he could reverse all the effects.

The anger returned, along with the hunger. Instead of protection being the key reason for his awareness, it turned into something more predatory. Hunting. Filling the empty spot in his stomach and something deeper than that. Trying to distract himself from the despair that clouded his mind, he continued to roam the woods until he came upon a deer.

Memories came flooding back when he was practicing with his gun and he couldn't shoot, and now he wanted to attack and rip the animal into pieces. The deer scurried off, and he continued on his way to find the stash of items, fighting off the urge to run after the deer, knowing he could catch it. He clutched his hands into fists until his palms bled from the claws, and he instinctively licked the blood from his hands. He stopped when he realized what he was doing, shaking his head at himself.

"When is this all going to stop?" he asked. "At least my tongue hasn't changed." He went through the box of things he got from the cabin, putting some salve on his cuts and remembering Sven doing this for him with Christopher's cuts.

Everything comes full circle.

He took the box, but before he could return to the tree that he nicknamed the tree of life he had to stop and rest. He wasn't sure if anything was to come of his discovery, but he attempted to be hopeful. There had to be a reason for him still being alive. After resting, collecting two of the frogs and making special notice of exactly where the tree was, he wondered the best way to administer the tree frog skin. Eating it was one thing, but if he could condense it and inject it directly into his bloodstream, it would work that much faster, but before any such drastic measures happened, he had to make sure it was working.

But then again, he had little time. If he didn't do something drastic, and soon, he would be gone, and what would happen then?

His mind went back to his family, and he reasoned he was feeling a little better. Maybe he wasn't totally free of bloodlust, but he was improving. He dreamed of getting a glance at them just to make sure they were okay. He knew Rachel would flip out, but would put a strong face in front of the children. And his Camille. What would he think of him if she saw him like this? The monster that she always wanted to capture?

Adam reasoned he could safely take a quick look if he stayed out of view. Far from home for so long, things were different now. He was stronger, and maybe he could find a way, but how was he going to go such a distance undetected? He had lived there all his life, knowing the area and all of its shortcuts. Nighttime would be the best time to travel, and most people kept inside because of all the dangers.

He missed his link to Sven and Jesse. They could get him to his family, but he knew even if he could talk to them, they wouldn't agree to it. At least they could tell him that his family was doing okay. *But I won't risk them doing anything stupid. I made this mess, and now I have to fix it.*

CHAPTER TWENTY

The night was one of the darkest nights Adam had seen, and he was so glad because it would hide him better from what he was about to do. The heavy smog and absence of the moon helped, along with the clouds that had rolled in with the heavy rain.

Meanwhile, he was getting soaked and not caring. He just wanted one glimpse of his family to know that everyone was okay. He just wanted to see his daughter's smile or hear his son laugh. Now, out in the elements, dirty and feeling like a family dog that had been left out in the rain, he would do anything to be at home, wrapped up in Rachel's arms in front of one of those bright murals that she had painted throughout the house that he once hated so much. He couldn't get into the backyard with the high fence wrapped around and the security cameras set up, and he knew he couldn't get into the house through a window, but with his new traits he could at least get a glimpse of someone that he loved.

He assumed it was getting close to bedtime, and he looked through one of the windows where the light was on. Adam watched Rachel tuck Camille in and give her her stuffed bunny, Lopso. Camille was not smiling.

"I want Daddy to tuck me in," she whined.

Adam was thankful for his new super-hearing, and as he focused, it sharpened. "Daddy's right here," Adam said, his heart dropping. He had to fix this.

"When Daddy comes home, he will spend a lot of time with you," said Rachel, her voice shaking. "It's all going to be okay. Give Mommy a kiss and go to sleep."

Camille slipped back into the covers, kissing Rachel good night, and Rachel left her room, leaving the door cracked open. Adam expected her to go to their bedroom at this hour, but she went to her studio and sat across from an easel. Straddling a stool, she stared at the piece for a second before reaching down and grabbing some paint. She mixed it on the easel and painted broad strokes. Adam strained to see what she was working on, but his eyesight wasn't that enhanced.

Adam yearned to be in the house with his family. He pictured cuddling up with Camille, reading her a bedtime story with the voices and throwing Henry in the air. His heart dropped as he thought of kissing Rachel and holding her until he fell asleep. He missed ice cream and late-night movies after the kids had gone to bed, even though he usually fell asleep.

"I'm right here," he said again, although this time to Rachel as she struggled to paint. Leaning down, gripping his hair, he wept.

He could feel eyes on him, and wondered how long they were watching. Concentrating on something else, his focus wasn't on his surroundings like they should be. He was mesmerized as Rachel painted. She painted slow and deliberate strokes, and he could see her slumped shoulders and bowed head.

He had done this, and he had to fix it.

It was time to leave. Just one more minute...

He heard something wiz past him, and turned to see silhouettes in the distance surrounding him. Adam knew he had stayed too long, but he couldn't leave with no opening in sight. Rachel stood up and looked out the window. At first, he wasn't sure if she was looking at the circle of men near her backyard or him, but she leaned forward to make out the figures. He saw her bring her hand to her mouth as she saw the men circle in and capture him with their paralyzing guns that made him totally immobile. He couldn't even move his eyes to watch his family anymore. They moved swiftly all around him, five of them picking him up and putting him in the back of the MCS unit. They laid him on a gurney, restraining his wrists and ankles. Even if he could move, he wouldn't have fought them. There were way too many and his chances were slim. He reasoned if his inner rage were to surface...

He could hear one of the MCS talking to him, and he recognized her as Becky, remembering when she brought Seth in. Becky sunk her brow in puzzlement, then asked with wandering eyes, "Dr. Davidson?" The look of pity that crossed her face just then ate at his gut, and he turned his head, closing his eyes. He didn't want pity. He wanted solutions. "First Dr. Freeman almost being killed, and then this?"

"I know, Becky," the man beside her said. "It's been a weird week. And the mutant that attacked her was the strangest thing I have ever seen, and that is saying a lot. At least she's okay. It looks like he didn't get so lucky."

"They took one of the human mutants found at the cabin back to Juniper, but they didn't take that 'boy'. Hope he's not out there hurting someone."

His shoulders jerked. "That's a scary thought."

It didn't surprise him that Jill got attacked. He was so glad that Julia was okay, and at Juniper instead of under Jill's control.

Adam wanted to punch the guy. He was still him, somewhere inside of him. Without his experimental cure, he was afraid that he was going to get worse fast, and the very thought of that angered him.

The doors behind him slammed shut and the vehicle moved, the tires rough over the gravel. He was wondering what Rachel was thinking just then, wondered how his daughter would look at him if she ever had the chance...

No, she wouldn't see him like this. *I will be cured... I have to be cured.*

"Adam Davidson, the one and only," he heard from someone behind him, but had a hard time craning his neck to see the speaker. He knew that voice anywhere.

Sam Foster.

What was Sam doing in the back of the MCS unit with him? He wasn't MCS. This was his last thought before they injected him with something and faded off into nothing.

—·—

Chapter Twenty-One

Adam still felt groggy as he opened his eyes to a strange smell. It wasn't a smell of wet pine or scurrying insects or animals that he had become so familiar with. It was the coppery smell of blood and a stench that he couldn't quite place.

He discovered his shackled wrists when he pulled up his hands to rub his eyes to focus. Pulling on them harder proved that they were cinched down tight. His wrists burned from the pulling and he thought he could almost feel one loosen a bit, but he couldn't move them enough to make a difference.

He could turn his head enough to see a corner of the dimly lit room. Blood and grime covered one wall and the floor had missing tiles showing the black floor underneath with torn-up grooves in the foundation. This was a time he wished his heightened senses weren't in overdrive right now. *Where the hell am I? Why would the MCS bring me here?*

He heard a door open with light footsteps, and close behind the person. He tried to lift his head, but it was still hard to see until the person came into the light.

188

"How are you feeling?" Sam's face was slightly illuminated, casting a shadow on the wall. "Don't worry, we will take good care of you over here at Black Hills."

Adam pulled again at his restraints, both the ankles and wrists, and yelled, "What the hell, Sam? What are you doing over here? What happened?" he asked, but he had figured it all out seeing the smirk that spread across the bastard's face. He always figured that Black Hills didn't take care of the mutants nearly as well as Juniper Ridge, but he didn't know what kind of filthy conditions the poor patients had to live in. No wonder they came back needing special care after the fire.

"We know everything that has been going on at Juniper Ridge. I know that you've been trying, but the progress has just been too... Well, what progress, right? We can take over and make it happen."

"You know that's not true. What have you been telling Jill? What lies have you told?"

"No lies," said Sam with a little laugh. "I would just call them fibs. If she took some information wrong, it really isn't my fault. She's going to be so busy over here with all the mutant uprising, and you're in no shape to take over. Who knows how long it will take you to recover, if you do? You know, we are all still looking for a cure."

"Yes, and I can help with that. I think I might have found one," said Adam, "but I need to talk to someone. You need to let me out of these." Sam didn't make a move. "Don't you want to help? I thought you were all on board with the mission to save the mutants and finding a cure, just like I am. I thought you looked up to me."

"Finding a cure would be cool." Sam shrugged with a crooked grin. "I want to be the one to find it."

"Look, I know deep down you know that this is wrong. I saw you after Christopher died when you were cleaning up. You didn't think I did, but you looked so sad... I saw you." Sam didn't say a word and showed no emotion or reaction whatsoever. "Please...Sam. Please." Adam yanked on his restraints without any give. "A part of you gives a shit, so let me out of these!" He pulled harder and almost flipped the bed over. He could feel the conflict that inhabited Sam's mind. He could feel his conflicting emotions that were almost as conflicted as his own. "I can't help anyone like this. You disappoint me. I thought better of you. You could have had such a bright future."

"You're right about one thing," said Sam. "You can't help anyone. Now who's in charge?" And he walked out the door.

"Sam!" he yelled behind him as the door made a loud clunk. "Someone, help me!" He could hear his voice echo in the room that was no larger than ten feet by ten feet. He felt like he was in a box and he couldn't breathe.

Time to relax, he thought. Time to figure out a plan, but first, you have to breathe.

He let his eyes, now adjusted to the lack of light, trail around the room. There was still a dark corner, but he noticed the room was very basic, except for a camera in the corner so small the average man would have missed it. Not surprised they had such a thing; of course, they had the same security at Juniper Ridge, but the fact that someone was watching him when he was trying to figure all of this out agitated him. He stared at the camera lens, watching the red light almost hypnotized, and in an instant it went off.

He blinked to make sure he wasn't seeing things, but the power button was definitely off. He had seen that kind of camera many times before, and it was always the same thing. Listening, he didn't hear any commotion going on outside of his room, so he thought nothing of it. *They probably don't keep up on such things over here, he thought. Look at the damn walls. It looks like they don't keep up much on anything.*

Adam felt nauseated and cold, his skin the color of alabaster, and he had the light case of the shakes. He needed something to eat. Either the frog skin wasn't the cure at all or it wasn't enough and was wearing off fast. His breathing became shallow as everything came in and out of focus. His frustration and anger grew, but he had little energy to express it.

He was exhausted, but afraid to sleep in fear of what they would do to him. They would have more control when he was sleeping, even though now he felt totally helpless in the straps that tied him down like a dangerous mutant.

I couldn't hurt anyone right now, he thought. I don't have the strength.

He fought the urge to fall asleep with all of his will, trying to slow down his breathing and take deep, long breaths. He opened his eyes wide to keep them open, stifling a yawn when it threatened to surface. "Stay awake," he told himself. "This is no time to fall asleep." He couldn't fight against the restraints any longer, and wished he wouldn't have earlier. That was the energy he could have saved. The red button on the camera had turned back on. A temporary power outage somewhere?

He fought it as long as possible, but fell into a deep sleep.

CHAPTER TWENTY-TWO

Adam woke up to movement in his room as the door closed with a quiet thumped echo. Jesse and Sven leaned down, Sven whispering to Adam, "We don't have a lot of time. The cameras will only stay off for about half an hour."

"What's going on?" asked Adam, his hallucination swimming all around him. Oh, God, how he wished it was real. He had no idea why he was talking to his imagination, but it was reflex, he supposed.

"We're here to save you," said Sven. "Now you have to stay quiet so we can get you out of here."

"Adam being quiet isn't the problem," said Jesse. "He doesn't look at all well. I don't like moving him in his condition. What if we run into someone and I can't get us past them? What if we..."

Adam's complexion was completely white, his lips pale, and he still had tremors.

"We can't keep him here," said Sven.

"Yes, yes, of course," said Jesse, shaking his head. "It makes sense, but I don't like it. I have a bad feeling about this after screwing up in the woods, letting Adam take off. You take the lead, Sven."

"I can't do this all on my own. You're not having cold feet on me, are you now? We need you."

"Okay." Jesse gripped the gurney. "Let's just go before I lose my nerve." The two men wheeled Adam down the hall, and Adam had a flashback of when they were sneaking Julia and Seth out. He thought of what he did to Seth and closed his eyes. With the movement of the bed, this was a bad idea. Nausea hit him like a slow leak of burning acid in his gut, and he would reach for his stomach, but it was an impossibility. He gagged.

"Sorry," said Jesse. "We'll go slower." But they didn't go slower, and Adam tried to concentrate on something else. They made it down the hallway when they heard an alarm go off. Red lights on the walls, once dormant, lit up and spun. The walls turned a crimson of light.

"Oh, crap!" yelled Jesse, turning Adam to go down another hallway. Sven looked in all directions, pointing to an open door of a vacant room.

"In here," he said, and they pulled into the darkness and shut the door. Pulling the bed as far away from the door as they could, they all stayed quiet. Adam was glad to be out of the light and the red pulsing alarm as it played with his equilibrium. The darkness was nice. The sound of the alarm he could deal with. Working at Juniper Ridge, he was used to noise.

"What are we going to…" said Jesse before Sven shushed him. They waited in the darkness and listened. Adam heard footsteps running down the hall and passed his door, and he could swear it was the clicking of high heels. Moments later he heard another set of footsteps walking slower and with purpose. With the pace Adam could imagine this mysterious person searching the area, examining the rooms, emptying the closets as he heard things falling in the distance, and the sound stopped right in front of his door.

His shaking had grown worse, but not from his condition. He felt like he was on fire and flash-backed to the basement, where they saved Sven. Lately, he hated the heat. As his two friends held onto the bed, he could feel them tense up as well. He tasted the bile that came up his throat and swallowed it back down again, trying not to imagine what they would do to the three of them if caught, or when caught, rather. It wasn't looking good.

The door flung open along with a flood of bright light. Adam squinted and closed his eyes before reopening them. Jill loomed in the doorway, arms crossed, eyes dark with anger. The neat bun that usually perched on the top of her head was in disarray and her cheeks were bright red, matching her lipstick.

"What the hell is going on here?!" As Jesse made a move toward the door, she held onto the door frame with both hands, blocking the exit. "No one is going anywhere. How did you two get in here?" She pointed her index finger at Jesse and Sven. Before they could say a word, she said, "If you care about him at all, you will let us do our job."

"We're here to help," said Jesse. "All of this can be reversed. We have cases where mutants are getting better. Just give us a chance."

"He's right," Sven added. "Some mutants were getting better. We had a hard time getting the medicinal elements for the cure because of the soil, but the soil is improving as the virus is filtered out of the water. We are on the right track."

Adam's mind was swimming. *I should mention the frogs, he thought,* but it scared him. *What if Jill went out into the woods and destroyed us all, leaving all the mutants, including me, like this? She is already on the destruction path. What would stop her now?*

"I can't trust any of you," she said right before Sven and Jesse bent at the knees, pushing the gurney as hard as they could with all of their strength, knocking Jill off balance.

Jill fell backward. "Get them!" she screamed behind them, and Adam could hear her scrambling to get back up. The halls echoed with people running, but it was hard to know where it was coming from.

"This way," Sven said as he jolted down the hallway to the left.

"No, the right," Adam urged, feeling the presence of someone nearing from the left side. "Fewer people." Jesse flipped the gurney around to go the other direction, and Adam's stomach tightened. "Just get us out of here!" Adam groaned.

Rushing down the hallway to the right, Adam shut his eyes and felt like everything was closing in on him. The ceiling was collapsing; the walls were crumbling all around him, and he would be buried forever, trapped for all eternity.

The gurney's abrupt stop made him open his eyes. "Oh, shit," said Jesse. The hallway ended with a door that Jesse and Sven desperately tried to open.

"Let me help," Adam suggested, and he willed the door to open with all of his might. It wouldn't budge.

People were running toward them, and Adam hated the hopeless feeling of being trapped, not only strapped to the bed, but at the end of the hallway. *Damn, I had led us here. I didn't know. I shouldn't have said turn right. Another damn fuck up.*

"Stop right there." Men with guns pointed at their heads blocked their retreat from where they came. Jesse and Sven raised their hands in surrender.

Jill stood behind the group of guards and made her way to the front. "Take them." The demand sizzled off her tongue as two of the largest men seized Jesse and Sven by the arm. "They are working against the cause. Teach them a lesson."

The taller of the two smiled then that raised Adam's uneasiness, yanking Jesse hard enough that he winced and glanced at his shoulder. Both of the men were dragged out of the room. Sven said, "hey, let's talk about this. We can work together."

"We are all on the same side, right?" asked Jesse. They were both ignored, along with Adam's protests.

"You can have me. Just let them go. They had nothing to do with this. This escape was all my idea."

Jill shook his head. "I'm smarter than that, Adam. Don't worry, we'll take good care of you and make sure you stay safe and sound. I'll give you some medication to make you feel much better."

"Yeah, I bet," he said as Jill navigated him out of the room and back down the hall. Her color had returned to its creamy white and her hands were steady as she pushed him down the hall.

Now is the time, Adam thought. She won't know what's coming.

— · —

CHAPTER TWENTY-THREE

Adam stared at the ceiling in his new room, dark and musky like the other one. A monitor hung in the corner where he could watch himself if he lifted his head far enough, but if he did that for a while, it made his neck sore and he was already sore enough everywhere. A guard stood right outside his door. With the heightened senses after the transformation still there, he could hear everything from the man's breathing to the shuffling of his feet until he got into a comfortable stance. When someone else walked by, the guard became still. Adam imagined him watching everyone that came down the halls.

Adam slammed his head back against the bed, the pillow hard and flat. A little more lift and he could see better, even though there wasn't much to see.

But there was something about that monitor that captured his attention. He kept staring at it, and kept thinking about Jill, mad as hell that she seemed to win. There had to be something that he could do. He pictured her with her smug little smile, her hair in disarray, blocking the door. No way was she going to control him. No way was he going to... his anger was growing, and he pulled on the restraints. But they were even tighter than the last time.

The monitor went to snow.

He wasn't sure if it was a power failure in the building somewhere or if Jesse and Sven had gotten away and had another plan, but somehow he doubted the latter.

The monitor came back on again, but it wasn't him any longer. Jill was in what he guessed was her laboratory, and his eyes widened. Was this possible because he had just willed it? Ever since he had started the change, he was more in tune to others, but he figured that was because of an animalistic thing, like how animals can sense when people are afraid of them. This was new. It reminded him of Julia and how she could almost read minds. Fascinating. He hoped she was doing okay.

And there was Jill, standing in her lab, and Adam's mouth was agape at the scene. Her face was hard from frustration as she loomed over the table in front of her, a dead gi-raffe/hawk/mouse thoroughly dismembered by the act of a blade that she clutched in her right hand. She threw down the blade, covering her face with her blood-soaked hands, smearing the blood all over her face.

Jill clutched her hourglass necklace and spoke out loud to her dead father. Adam leaned as close as he could, being so restrained and was glad his ears were sharp because the volume was so low it was almost nonexistent.

"Dad, I'm doing the right thing. These things hurt you. They took you away from me forever and I can't have that." She turned away from the massacre in front of her. "I will have to fix everything." She looked across the room as if talking to someone that was there. "I know Adam was one of your first. I know he's an amazing scientist, but he's not a scientist anymore. Don't you understand? He turned into one of THEM." Jill clenched her fists, then swiped at a table of instruments as they clinked to the floor like tiny pieces of broken glass. "It wasn't your job to cure everybody. Not to risk your life like that. What about me!? I miss you, and now I'm all alone."

Adam laid back down, thinking about what he had just seen. He felt sorry for her and everything that she had been through. Jill never had a mother, dying giving birth to her, and Daniel had never re-married. It had only been the two of them when she was growing up, but that didn't change the fact of what he had to do.

Adam wasn't watching, but he was still listening. "I don't trust how this world is going, Dad, and I'm just stepping in to make it all better. If I don't fix this, I can never be close to anyone again, not like I was with you. There is only one solution, and that is to start over. I can do better than this mess. I can do better than God."

He heard the door open to her lab and Sam's voice. "You wanted to see me?" he asked.

"I wanted to show you something." Adam lifted his head up again, watching as Jill directed Sam to a cage in the corner. A lizard hunkered down in the cage's corner. Adam tried to focus on the animal. He found no deformities and wondered why she would capture such a creature. It couldn't have been a mutant. Nothing was wrong with it. "I created this with my own two hands. A few DNA samples from other animals, and there you go."

"Woah.." Sam leaned in close to the cage right before the lizard leaped from the back to the front bars, his mouth opened fully and wrapped around the bars, and when he flapped his tail, which instantly fell off. The lizard bled from the open wound and collapsed to the bottom of the cage.

"It needs some work," she shrugged, "but it's the closest I have gotten to getting it right."

Sam's face scrunched up in a scowl. "It looks like he was in pain."

"Not for long, and it's all for the sake of progress. We are improving the world, Sam, and you are going to be a big part of it. I'm sure that won't go unnoticed, not by me or the rest of the world." She clicked some keys on the computer at a desk in the corner and leaned back to show him the monitor contents. "It's all here. This is our discovery."

"And I helped," he said, standing tall after looking at the computer.

"Yes, you did." Adam leaned back and clenched his teeth, his fingers rapidly tapping on the bed.

His fingers? Some of his talons were transforming again into fingers! *The frog skin must have been it. It must have worked. Sometimes things just take time. More! I need more.*

Adam took a deep breath, grinning so big his face hurt. On the monitor, Jill was smiling, a different type of smile than his own. Not a smile of accomplishment, but her face all twisted up as if she was experiencing joy and sadness and they were fighting with one another.

"What am I up against?" Adam said, his eyes drifting to fight sleep. He did not trust anyone in the facility except for the two men captured. Weakness filled his entire being: physically, mentally, and emotionally. He wondered how that happened with the monitor and what else he could do.

The hunger for human meat still gnawed at him, but he held onto the hope of recovery after the beginning of his hand transformation. As he fell asleep, he wished for dreams of happier times.

CHAPTER TWENTY-FOUR

Adam jumped as the heavy thud of the door opened, scraping the bottom of the floor. He was hoping for something that would make him feel better. Adam was clammy and exhausted, but unable to sleep. His stomach grumbled.

"Don't worry, Doctor. We are going to make you feel so much better." A tall man wearing a lab coat with the name Dr. Soren embroidered on the pocket came in, wheeling an I.V. stand with two units of a clear liquid.

"What are you giving me?" Adam asked him.

"Something that will make your life a lot better," Dr. Soren said, his dimples flashing as he talked. "After a couple of units of this wonder drug, you won't even have to wear the shackles anymore. We can take all the restraints off. Doesn't that sound nice?" When he didn't get an answer, he said, "Are you going to make me put it in the hand where it hurts more? Or are you going to cooperate and let me insert it in the nook of your arm?" Adam groaned in protest and went to flip his arm over, but the restraints were too tight.

"You're going to cut off my circulation," he complained. "If you loosen them up a little, at least it will make it easier on both of us." Adam tried to work his way into the man's mind, trying to relax his mood.

The doctor paused and looked at the I.V., then at Adam as if assessing the situation.

"Well, I guess you have a point. Just a little," he interjected, raising his index finger. "And don't you try any funny stuff." Adam wished he could think of something more to do, but he didn't have the strength. Dr. Soren went to loosen the strap one notch, and as soon as the pin slid out to slide to the next spot, Adam yanked up.

The doctor tightened it in one jerky motion, giving Adam an evil glare. Adam didn't yank up far. He didn't have as much energy or strength as he thought he had.

"There goes your chance," said the doctor, getting ready to swab the top of his hand. "I tried to warn you. You're going to get it either way." The needle slipped in, stinging and burning, but he wouldn't allow it to show. He gritted his teeth and wanted to just lean over and take a bite out of this man, but he fought it.

Adam glanced up at the monitor again, and this time he didn't think of Jill, although that would have been an advantage. His friends were on his mind. He wondered what they were doing to them and where they were in the building. He was certain they wouldn't let them out. Jill was slipping into somewhere where she could never return, and there was going to be a lot of collateral damage. Not if he could help it. Not his friends.

He saw Sven, but it was hard to see because where Sven was, the area was dark and small like Adam's, but worse somehow. He couldn't tell. The picture was hazy. Adam was relaxing and falling into a mysterious place. His breathing slowed and he could feel his blood pressure dropping. He looked over at the doctor swaying next to him. If only he would stay still. He squeezed his eyes shut and reopened them in an effort for better results.

Sweat moistened his brow and he could smell the sickness on the sheets he laid on.

"I can see it's already working," said the doctor, but Adam only heard pieces. He tried to focus on connecting with Sven, so Sven knew he was okay. Concentration was almost impossible. "I will return when this bag is done and give you one more. And then, Doctor Davidson, it will be fine to take off your restraints. You will do no harm to anyone." Dr. Soren patted Adam on the shoulder, and as Adam turned his head to take a bite, the swaying continued, and his mind became a bigger blur. "No harm at all."

Adam waited until he heard the door shut behind him. "Sven..." he whispered, thinking himself absurd. There was no way Sven was going to hear him from a monitor. Must be whatever they are giving me. But then again, I saw Jill out of my demand. "Sven," he said louder, but still soft enough no one was going to hear. Of course, no one was going to hear.

He could see Sven's silhouette on the monitor, still looking at his room. There was no way that Jill would let him see Sven on his screen, unless she wanted to show him what would happen to him if he didn't cooperate. He tried to make sense of it all and laid his head back for a moment. Looking back up, he swore he heard Sven's voice. "Adam?"

It's the drugs, Adam thought. I'm hearing things. Adam looked up at the monitor, and he swore Sven was looking back at him. "Adam, are you okay? We need another plan. That was our mistake. Always have a backup plan. That's what I should have learned the first time."

Sven was barely audible, and the picture was blurring. Adam tried to focus, tapping into all of his energy. Jesse popped into his mind.

Another figure showed on the monitor, taller and more brawny, but still only a silhouette. Jesse? The figure stood in the center of the room examining the area and went to the door to pull on the knob with no luck. The man paused, then looked around again and said, "Adam, are you in here? I can't see much. It's so dark."

"I can see you," said Adam in a slurred voice, "but I'm not there, but in my room. Trying to talk to Sven, I lost contact."

"Contact? Like a telephone? Is there a speaker or something like that in there?"

"No. I don't know how this is happening, but I just think of you, and... none of this is probably real. Must be the drugs. I'm probably hallucinating this entire conversation." As the I.V. continued to drip into his body, Jesse faded. It was like he was talking through a tunnel and stepping backward on the screen.

Adam went to lift his head, and he could barely move it without extreme effort, so he just lay there and stared at the ceiling. Even speaking had become a challenge. "I don't think these are helping. They are just making me so...sleepy... Hey, if I don't...wake...up..."

"We'll find you," said Jesse in a voice that was so low Adam could barely hear until Jesse's voice faded away into nothing.

Adam strained to contact Jesse or Sven through the monitor before he drifted off with everything that he had, focusing all his energy he had left, and the screen exploded into tiny pieces with a spark and a pop.

CHAPTER TWENTY-FIVE

The next time Adam opened his eyes, it took a few minutes for everything to come into focus and he heard voices, familiar and new. Surrounded by white lab coats, the cloud of white made him wonder if he had left this world and continued his journey into heaven. The beeping of the I.V. and his view sharpening as he awoke brought him back to his room.

The room in Black Hills.

"I have no idea how that happened. I swear the restraints are on tight. Besides, look at him. There's no way he could have reached up to that monitor with anything in this room and thrown it," Dr. Soren explained.

"Well, something is going on here," said another doctor, he assumed with the lab coat and hazy name stitched on it. His world was not in view yet.

"I have seen nothing like it. We must tell Dr. Freeman," said a third voice, a woman with a high-pitched squeal. Her tone made his skin crawl. It was like fingernails on a chalkboard.

They all stopped talking when they saw Adam's eyes open, and he felt like he was on display. Silence filled the room until another figure entered.

"Tell me what?" Jill came in to check the I.V. fluids and glanced around the room, peering at Adam. "Why is everyone in here? Does he need another bag? How are you feeling?" she asked Adam.

"A little groggy," he admitted, knowing this would not harm the situation any.

"Well, just relax. It will help you heal until we can figure something out for you." She followed everyone's gaze up in the corner and noticed the monitor with the cracked screen, pointing to it and the debris on the floor. "What happened here?"

"We don't know," said Dr. Soren. "I just came in and it was like this."

"Who else has been in here?" She narrowed her eyes, and when she didn't get any answers from the doctors, turned to Adam. "Who else has been here?"

"I couldn't tell you," said Adam. "I don't know what happened to the screen." If it wouldn't have broken, I might have communicated with Jesse and Sven, he thought. If only there was another way... He stared at the screen and the mess, back at the broken monitor, as if willing it to repair itself, and sparks flew out of the broken mess on the wall.

Jill held up her hand to the doctors, telling them to just stay where they were and be quiet. "Did you?" She paused, pointing at the screen and back at Adam. "Did you do this?"

"No," he said, not wanting to give her any more ammunition to deem him dangerous.

"Maybe..." She rubbed her chin with her fingertips, "you did, but you just don't realize it." Adam faked shock, and she pressed her lips together and narrowed her brow in contemplation. Dr. Soren went to hook up Adam to a new I.V. when Jill waved her hand at him. "Not yet. No more sedatives. I think this is something that may be worth exploring. We're going to need to move him to a bigger room."

"But Dr. Freeman..." said the woman, but stopped with one icy stare from Jill. "Of course, whatever you say, Doctor."

"Transfer him to 206," she instructed, and they all stopped as if they wanted to say something, but continued. Dr. Soren removed Adam's I.V. line and the other doctor with the hazy name offered to take care of paperwork. "Start with bloodwork," she said, "and I will be in to check on him after you get him all set up. We are going to do ALL the tests."

What does that entail? Was the first thing that came to Adam's mind. Or do I really want to know? Where the hell are Jesse and Sven, and what are they doing to them?

He was on the move and understood the vastness of the wing of Black Hills. He was on his way to the third room he had been in and traveled down many hallways covering a lot of distance, and he thought of what use they could make of all of this room and equipment on the other side. Juniper Ridge could clean this place up...

His thoughts were interrupted when wheeled into his new room, five times the size of the one he had just departed. It may have been larger, but the feeling of being closed in was the same. The walls were dark green, and the lighting was dismal. Usually Adam preferred the dark, but now he wished he could see better to plan. The sedative was wearing off, and he imagined eating everyone in the room.

He needed some of that frog skin. In his heart, he knew that was the reason for him feeling more like himself after the transformation began. If they could liquify it, inject it, it would work so much faster than just eating the frog, which tasted vile.

And humans taste so much better. *Whoa. What? I really need to fix this.*

He stared at Dr. Soren, and the doctor couldn't meet his gaze, looking around uneasily. It seemed his new power had made them all a little uneasy.

"What else do you think he can do?" asked Dr. Soren.

"Oh, you don't think he actually did that to the monitor?" asked the other male doctor, whose name was previously hazy but now he could read. Dr. Hamly.

"How else would it have gotten broken?"

"Well, I'm not afraid of him." Dr. Hamly opened up a drawer of a metal cart after putting in a code, and removing a scanner.

"To start, I think we should scan his skin to get his blood work so we get a better idea of what we're dealing with here, and then move on to a CAT scan and move up to more invasive steps."

His icy hands made Adam jump. He waited for the scanner to come in contact with his skin, already turning over and in the restraint but the thought of the doctor getting near him repulsed him. Adam closed his eyes and wished he would just leave, imagined pushing him out the door, and when he opened them, the doctor was millimeters from his skin. The doctor's hand was shaking. He was wheezing and panting.

"What's wrong with you?" asked Dr. Soren, and the young woman grabbed the scanner out of his hand.

"If you're too afraid to touch him, I think I can handle it."

"I'm not afraid... it just wasn't working. It was like something was holding my hand back physically." He shook his head with narrowed brows. "I'm going to talk to Dr. Freeman." Dr. Hamly kept both eyes on Adam as he backed up toward the door. The door flew open on its own, the hinges shaking, threatening to rip off.

Oh, Lord, he just wanted to be left alone. He wasn't up to any tests, and the suggestion of invasive testing pissed him off. His anger grew, and if they moved any closer, he was going to take a bite out of someone's arm.

No, he couldn't do that. He must fight it. He couldn't hurt anyone else. Adam kept his eye on the scanner, so angry, and the doctor's hand went from Adam's arm and she flung it into her own.

The doctor screamed, standing up and getting as far away from Adam as she could. Adam struggled to get his restraints off, but they held fast.

"Out!" he yelled, yanking at the restraints, his blood pressure mounting, and his temperature rising and his frustration grew. An overhead light fell and landed right behind him, almost hitting him in the head. "Damn it," he said, unable to control himself. The doctors ran out.

With an empty room, Adam laid back and breathed deep, trying to relax before he brought the whole damn ceiling down on his head. *First the monitor and now this? What the hell is going on with me?* He tried again to work against the restraints, but he was so weak he could barely lift his arms and legs. He closed his eyes and welcomed the darkness and his solitude.

A sound from far off down the hall caught his attention. The clinking of high heels, Jill's or the female doctor that was just there, he wasn't sure. He wouldn't assume it was the doctor that just left him with the expression she had when she left.

"Adam, I heard you are causing problems." Jill's voice was cold and even. "These recent developments are interesting, but I don't think it's safe to continue any further investigation."

"So, you are just going to admit me as a regular patient?" Adam asked, trying to pry the information out of her.

"The chance of you coming back from this is slim." She walked around his bed, examining him from afar at first, but then grew closer when she saw the straps were still tight. "I'm afraid I have no choice."

The door opened again. "You wanted to see me, Jill?" asked Sam. He stood by the bed even closer than Jill dared. "How are you feeling, Doctor Davidson?" Adam heard no concern in his voice. Just a doctor's medical analysis of a patient. It angered him Sam tricked him after he misjudged him. He was ready to teach him everything he knew, but Adam still saw something good in Sam that he refused to believe he imagined, and he hoped he wasn't wrong.

"I've been better," Adam croaked.

"Sam was telling me about Juniper Ridge and how the mutants are getting worse. I have the paperwork right in my office. All this time, you're wasting the funding and working against the mission statement to cure mutants." She clicked her tongue against the roof of her mouth. "I never expected this of you, of all people."

"It's a lie." Adam stood his ground as weak and tired as he was. "He changed all the documentation. He had to." *I was so wrong about him.*

"I don't believe he would do that. He is new to all of this, uncorrupt. It's amazing. Most people are corrupt, don't you think? Mutant or otherwise, humankind isn't worth it." Jill looked down at him and shook her head.

"What are you saying?" said Adam.

"Let me tell you one thing: it doesn't look good for you. Don't worry, Doctor. You won't have to worry about anything much longer." Before he could reply, she flipped around and headed out the door. Sam still stood next to Adam, watching him until Jill reached the doorway. "Sam, are you coming? You have things to do."

"Of course," said Sam, his trance broken, and followed her.

Chapter Twenty-Six

Adam refused to lie there and wait for Jill's plan to unravel before his eyes. He concentrated as much as he could to control his new power, yanking on the straps until he got one loose. The sedative was wearing off to his advantage. As the damn door opened again, he laid still to look weak and incoherent.

Jesse and Sven entered the room, with Sam right behind him. They didn't have anyone else with them. They didn't look to be held by force, so Adam said, "This is our chance. Tie the kid up or something so we can get out of here. How did you two get loose?"

"Look, Adam, I'm sorry. I didn't know," Sam pleaded. Adam waited for more, and when Sam saw he didn't understand, said, "I didn't know that she was planning on killing you. I'm not for that. You're Adam Davidson, the one and only. I only played along with her game so she wouldn't kill me. The bitch is clearly psychotic. I had to say all that stuff earlier. She has cameras, you know."

Adam gave an inquisitive look to the other two scientists.

"He freed us so that we could help you," said Jesse.

"That has to count for something," said Sven. "He's putting his own neck on the line."

"I know the ways to get out of here," said Sam, "undetected. You think she has cameras everywhere? She hasn't thought of everything. Although she thinks she is, she's not perfect. After what my parents did, I learned never to trust anyone totally. All you have is yourself."

Adam remembered listening to the radio when they were talking about Sam's parents on the news and was too preoccupied to think of how it would affect Sam. It would crush Adam if he found out such a thing about his parents, back when they were around, that is.

"We don't have a lot of time," Sam said. "Do you think you can stand up? It might be easier to get where we're going if you're not strapped to a gurney."

"I think so." Adam was feeling stronger, and the three of them worked fast to untie the restraints. Blood flow worked its way around again, but the extremities were still a little tingly from being tied down for so long. "Those things were tight!" He could walk, but not quickly at first, until he regained his footing. His balance was unsteady, but they all worked together and let him lean on them. They had stolen a lab coat Adam could wear, and he draped it over his patient gown, and when Adam remarked he looked ridiculous and obvious, Sam remarked they would not go far and probably wouldn't run into anyone, anyway. They may be in a far-off shot of some cameras, though, and the lab coat would disguise him.

They had gotten as far as the elevator, with no one in sight. Adam wasn't sure if it was a stroke of luck or with his new sense, he could just make people stay away. He was hoping it was luck, because he yearned to get back to normal. He hated having to escape and be in a weakened state, still having the new cravings, but he admitted they were nothing as strong as when he had just changed, and as weak as after he had eaten the frog.

Sam hit the button to go one floor underneath the main floor. "Secret passageways will take you all the way to the outside," he explained. "I will lead you to the last tunnel, and all you have to do is go the rest of the distance and you will be on your own." They dropped to one floor, then another, and Adam waited for the door to stop and open to see one of Jill's minions on the other side, and even worse, Jill. He looked up at the ceiling and prayed to God that they could get out of this. He prayed and hoped that this was what they were waiting for. Away from Black Hills, they could regroup and find a way to bust Jill.

The elevator stopped, and the doors opened. They had reached the last floor with no stops along the way. Sam explained this was one of the lesser-used elevators, so their chances were better, and this is the one that took them on the way out.

The atmosphere was different when they stepped out of the elevator. The air smelled stale, and it was obvious the air purifiers in the main part of the institute did not continue to the underground floor, the outside air making it hazy. Passageway walls made from stones instead of the smooth walls of the upper floors, the lighting so dim it was hard to see each other. The slick floor was cool underneath Adam's bare feet as he shuffled down the way, following Sam. He lost his footing, but Jesse was there to catch him. His knees were tired and weak, barely being able to hold him up.

"Just the end of this passageway, and you'll see a light," said Sam. "There's a little alcove, and beyond that is the way out."

The way out sounded great to Adam, and he tried to hurry without slipping and falling. The thought of him injuring himself and slowing them down when they were so close to freedom made him incredibly cautious, but still moving at a steady pace.

"It's okay, I got you," reassured Jesse, almost lifting Adam up to help him move. Adam had forgotten how strong Jesse was, and as Adam leaned on him, Jesse supported almost all his body weight.

They had made it to the end when Adam swore he heard something. Not anyone speaking, but more like a hiss or a growl. His uneasiness grew and he put his feet down more solidly on the ground so Jesse couldn't assist. "What was that?"

"What was what?" Sam asked, and the other two men did the same.

"I heard something."

"I can't hear anything but us moving," said Sven, but motioned them to be quiet. His ears perked up to listen as well.

"There's nothing," Sam said. "Let's get moving. This is your chance. Come on."

The tunnel grew darker as they continued to move, and Adam swore he heard other noises but no one else heard them, so he chalked it up to his imagination and fear. He knew it was amazing how your mind could play tricks on you.

Sam was slowing down, and when Adam looked around, he saw Sam behind them instead of leading the way. "This is where I draw the line. Good luck. I better get back upstairs and iron everything out before Dr. Freeman flips out. I can slow her down for you."

"Thanks for everything," said Adam, and they kept going a few feet, Sam about twenty feet behind them. There was a loud thud as a gate closed between the three scientists and Sam, and he could hear Sam laughing.

"Good luck," he said. "Dr. Freeman promised to get my parents out of jail if I did this little favor for her. Nothing personal." And Sam was gone.

Another gate opened further down the passageway, and the sounds that Adam heard became more prominent. He leaned against a wall to catch his breath and stood on his own two feet.

"That little shit," Jesse spat. "Right into a trap. I should have seen it coming. I'm such an idiot."

"You're not an idiot. We all fell for it," said Sven. "We just went from one trapped room to another, but why would they put us somewhere together?"

They all stopped when they noticed there was a strange stench that permeated their nostrils. Adam's nostrils flared as he picked up on Seth's scent.

"What is it?" Jesse asked.

"Seth spent a lot of time down here," said Adam.

"Why?" asked Sven. Adam turned and his eyes had adjusted to the dim light, but there was still a trace of light for him to see by. He moved the wall of the room and put his hand out, feeling the side of the wall until he felt slime, and then pulled his hand away when it hit something sharp.

A claw.

He focused closer and saw a whole appendage. It appeared to be a wing with claws at the end, still dried blood splattered on the remains. When he continued to examine the room, he found more animal parts, strangely formed parts, and blood covered most of everything except the ones that were rotting with decay and decomposition.

"Is this what I think it is?" asked Sven, stammering as he spoke. "This appears to be some sort of underground graveyard, a dumping site for mutant parts. Why would she put us down here?"

"To let us rot down here with the rest of her mistakes," Adam said, shaking his head as he thought of all the mutants that he could have helped that ended up at Black Hills. All for Jill to destroy them.

"Ummm... guys?" Jesse questioned, and they all turned to where he was pointing. "I think I figured out where they found Seth's food." Jesse moved away from the wall he was examining and they heard a crack as a mutant rose from the corner of the wall where he once had blended in so well. He was once human, or the basic part of him was.

A part of his head was missing, leaving his skull exposed at one side. Covered in scales and misplaced eyes, the right one where a normal one would be, the left hanging below his chin, it didn't move. Adam assumed it wasn't functioning. His mouth opened to a forked tongue that lashed out at them. Legs and arms were not malformed, but the hands and feet were eagle talons and it didn't speak.

"I think we need to find an escape fast," said Jesse, and Adam looked around for anything to protect them from this creature and anything else they might encounter while down in the secret room.

"We found where she keeps the darkest secrets, that's for sure," said Adam. The only thing he could find quickly was a brick that had come loose from the wall, and he gripped it, holding it in front of him.

"You're weak, Adam. Get behind me, both of you," said Jesse, looking for an exit but hardly being able to see.

"What are you going to do?" asked Adam.

"Protect us." The disoriented creature came after Jesse because he was the closest target. Jesse spread his feet apart and put his fists up in front of him. Jesse hit it in the face when it came closer and it swiped at Jesse with its right claw. The creature held one claw to his own face, dripping with Jesse's blood as a cut ran across Jesse's cheek.

Adam threw the brick at the thing, but it just moved and Adam couldn't throw it very hard. Sven grabbed Jesse's arm. "Run while it's disoriented. Come on." They ran down the darkened area, not knowing if there was an exit or what else they might run into. Adam felt something brush up against his leg and kicked it away. He felt it smoosh underneath his bare feet and grimaced.

This was no time for the old Adam to be here. He forgot about holding back his animal tendencies and let them loose, hoping no one would get caught in the crossfire. Every movement he felt, every sound he heard, he would attack. He was not afraid. That part of him was gone. He gave way entirely to survival instinct.

"You two okay?" he asked, his weakness forgotten as he ran off adrenaline. He didn't get a reply, but heard them moving behind him, satisfied. Adam would not have it end like this. She would not win by trapping them with a bunch of mutants. He could feel the emotions all around him of the mutants as well, and some were just as afraid as he was.

He was more than afraid. He was mad, and he used that. Adam tried to take in the room. As he focused on the walls piled with something he didn't detect at first, he moved closer and felt around, picking up a human foot.

"Check this out. She must have dismembered some mutants and placed their parts down here to hide them. You realize what this means?" Adam asked.

"We're in deep shit," said Jesse, "because some of them aren't dead?"

"We are about ready to blow this thing wide open. She never should have led us down here. This is all the proof we need."

"She never thought we were going to survive," said Sven with a shiver. "We have to find a way out of here." Adam could see Sven's sudden movements to the other side of the room, and Adam saw something in the shadows chase after him.

Adam attacked, not knowing what it was. He heard a snarl and Adam dug his claws from his left hand deep into the mutant's neck. He could feel the warm blood spray all over his hands, but the thing kept going. It whimpered but was resilient. It knocked Adam to the ground, and when it came at him again, Adam kicked it in the feet, knocking it off balance as it went splaying. He stepped on its neck where the wound was, soaking his feet in more blood. The thing was unmoving, and he looked away for just a second, keeping his foot on the mutant's neck so if it moved, he could feel it, and saw both Jesse and Sven fighting creatures with him as well. Mutants or DNA experiments gone wrong. He wasn't sure what, but either way, they were danger-ous.

He found a hand with razor-sharp nails that reminded him of the creature that he had fought in the woods attached to a hairy arm and threw it at Jesse to use as a weapon. It took a second for Jesse to comprehend what it was. His eyes weren't as good in the dark, but he grabbed it when Adam said, "Use this. The sharp nails might help." Jesse took the arm and with all of his force slapped the hand in the creature's face, the five "daggers" making five bloody wounds on his face resembling a pentagram. It slowed down the creature, but he still kept at Jesse, his face bleeding and he kept blinking from the blood dripping in his five eyes.

"You may see better than me," said Jesse, "but I'm strong." He shoved at it hard enough to throw it up against the wall, more body parts falling from the walls that were embedded there. The creature went at Jesse again, hitting him in the head, and Jesse went sprawling backward.

When Adam knew the creature was dead beneath his feet, he attacked the beast that was going after Sven, a sasquatch type that came out of the shadows. Most of these creatures were dying, so they weren't at their full potential, but they were desperate with nothing to lose, and that's what made them the most dangerous. Sven looked around for something to fight with, the room full of creature parts, when he backed up against the wall. He threw himself into a fit as the creature leaned close to him, and Sven began kicking and punching, his view not the best in the darkness, just hoping he was injuring the creature.

The creature cried but continued to go after Sven, Sven only suffering from scratches and bruises, but Sven didn't stop. "This won't happen again," he said. The creature, being preoccupied with Sven, didn't notice Adam coming close to him, and Adam bit him on the leg and latched on with his razor-sharp teeth. The creature tried to shake him off, to no avail. Adam latched on.

The thing tasted rotten but for Sven, Adam didn't move, his body hurting from the jolting. Sven used the opportunity to kick the creature in the head, hard, when it was down on its knees from the pain. Jesse stabbed it on its side, embedding sharp spikes that were covering a mutant's head.

The mutant collapsed and Adam let go of his bite, spitting and hacking, praying the bite wouldn't affect him negatively like when he bit Seth. He had to do it. Anything for his friends.

The three sat on the floor of the room, panting and trying to catch their breath, bloody and sore from the fight. "Thanks, again," said Sven.

"Hey, we're a team," said Adam.

"Damn straight," confirmed Jesse.

The room smelled worse than before, and Adam's stomach cramped. He could barely move, so exhausted, hoping nothing else was going to spring up from the shadows. He spit out a few more chunks of the creature that got stuck on his teeth, and pulled hair from his mouth. "I don't know about you two, but I'm tired of this. We are going to have to end this."

"This all should have ended a long time ago," said Sven. "This never should have started. What the hell has she been doing? I knew she was experimenting and killing mutants, but to put them down here to die? Throwing their dismembered bodies down here? She's more deranged than I thought."

"No more talking." Adam took a few deep breaths. "Time to take care of this." He stood up, a little wobbly on his feet. He clenched his hands and shut his eyes, trying to concentrate on his breathing. "You two stay here. I got this."

"What!?" Jesse stood up, as well as Sven. "You're leaving us down HERE?"

"I don't feel any life down here anymore. You should be safe. I'll come back for you."

"No way," said Sven. "You can't do this alone. Adam, you can barely stand."

"I'm not risking you two. You both almost just died."

"So did you," said Sven. "If you have learned anything from all of this...Adam, we have to work together. We are stronger together."

"But I have an advantage. She thinks I'm dead. She won't see this coming. I'm not risking either of you." He would not have something happen to one or both of them and have that death hanging over his head as well.

"She thinks we're all dead," argued Sven, and Jesse agreed. "Let us help you." The thought gnawed at Adam. "You're weak right now from... lack of food consumption, and we haven't found the cure yet, not for sure."

"But I think I have. Not that they have any of that here. No time." Adam paused and leaned against the wall. He hated the fact that he was so tired, and might have to admit that they were right. The prime goal was success, and if he was to pull this off... if they were to pull this off... they would have to work together. His head swam. Jesse wiped away the blood from his face and Sven stretched and moaned from sore muscles, maybe even more injuries. What if anything happened to them? It would be all his fault. They both didn't look in the best shape either.

He would not be responsible for any more deaths.

"Adam?" Jesse asked, and Sven was looking concerned at him as well. Lost in his own thoughts, he paused for the longest time. He didn't realize he was thinking out loud.

"What deaths are you talking about?" asked Sven. "None of these are your fault. You can blame these all on Jill. She's the one that's standing in our way."

"Before Jill." He pictured coming home from college. His Dad sounded so weird on the phone and Adam was scared, so he came home from school. He remembered the hug that he got from his father when he showed up, and then his father was hiding most of the time. Adam didn't understand until he came downstairs and found him dead, a gun in his hand, and brain matter scattered all over the living room. He heard his mother's scream and could never forget what she had told him.

It was all your fault.

He never should have come. He should have stayed at school, and maybe his dad would have still been alive.

"Adam?" Sven asked. "We need to do something fast." Adam felt something creep up behind him and jabbed his elbow into the thing's torso before he turned around to see a man with no face walking toward him. Even as he fought it, his constant scientist was at work. How does this thing breathe?

Jesse and Sven didn't have to do anything. Adam had the man pinned down in seconds, which surprised them after he had seemed so weakened moments before.

"Now, that felt good," he said. "Look, guys, I know you mean well, but really, I don't want anyone else hurt on my watch."

"At least let us help," said Jesse. "If you want to kill the bitch, go ahead."

"I don't want to kill her," said Adam. "If we do that, what makes us any better than her? I'm tired of all the killing. Let's just end this."

"We know where she is," said Sven. "We had to break in to save you, or try to save you, so we know our way around. We did our homework, and you can bet she will be in her lab. She's usually in her lab. Just to prepare you..."

"I can imagine," said Adam. "But we are losing time. If we wait too long, she will figure out that we are still alive, and we won't have the surprise factor on our hands."

"Follow us." Jesse waved them in the right direction moments before Adam crushed the mutant's larynx.

First, they had to get through the door.

"Step back." Adam feebly kicked the door to have it not budge. Jesse tried it as well, but it stayed steadfast. They looked for something in the room to pry it open, and Sven found a talon that was slightly curved at the end and jiggled it through the lock hole.

"Those things are sturdy," remarked Jesse. "Where did you learn that?"

"Probably a juvenile delinquent," said Adam. "I can see that." Sven put up his hand for silence, and wiggled that talon until he heard a click.

The talon had broken off in the lock.

"I have an idea. Cover me." Adam concentrated on the door, remembering there could be things coming to life. He stood two feet away and used all of his energy to open it, along with his mind, remembering what happened with the monitor. Picturing the door opening and the three running down the passageway, he mentally pushed the heavy iron door with his mind, and he could hear a squeal.

It was the hinges. The pins were dropping out a millimeter at a time.

"Stand back!" he said and did the same as the six-foot door crashed right in front of them with a heavy thud. He couldn't think about what was being unleashed down there. Someone could recapture and take care of the released ones properly. The three men ran down the narrow passageway, their new weapons in tow. Jesse still had the taloned hand, and Sven a leg of spikes that belonged to a creature down there at one time. Adam had his fangs, and with his current mood, he figured that was enough. They were almost tripping over each other with urgency. The air felt thinner down there so it was difficult for Adam to breathe, or maybe it was because of all the effort he had to take to open the door, or fight the mutants that were attacking them. Or the healing process that never got to be completed.

He wished it did. He still had to fight off the hunger, but it helped to focus on something else. Sweat poured off his body and his limbs shook. Despite his blood and grime-covered feet, he kept going, trying not to slip.

He reached the elevator. Standing in one place for a minute felt heavenly, but he was also eager to get this taken care of. He was done with this and wanted it solved.

When they reached the proper floor, two scientists were walking down the hall, and the three men ran past them. The two scientists chased after them.

"Be careful," one of them said. "They're dangerous."

"Yes, we are." Jesse one man catch him and punched him in the face before he could react. "Just down this way." He left the man on the floor, the other knelt to see if he was okay.

"Go, get them!" the hurt man urged him, but they had already reached the door.

"You can't go in there!" the follower screamed. Adam yanked hard on the door; his eyes wide that it was unlocked. *This has got to be a trap. No way would Jill have kept this door open to such a horrific place.*

CHAPTER TWENTY-SEVEN

The walls were covered in blood, and a table stood in the middle resembling a hospital bed with open restraints on each corner and others on the side. Adam could imagine what creatures and people she had hurt there. He was certain at one time it was meant for him, until she learned of his powers and was afraid of him. The table was covered in blood as well, black and red, and bright overhead lights hung from the ceiling, the fluorescents shining off the red and black. The smell of death filled the room.

Pieces of mutants, human and animal, were spread around the room. Half of the room was filled with cages with alive animals, altered by the environment, or more than likely, her. A cat growled in the corner with webbed feet and a forked tongue. A hummingbird with bat wings and feelers perched on top of its head flew around a cage in the corner.

But the one that caught Adam's eye was the toddler appearing to be about three years old. Chestnut brown braids hung on either side of her head, and big brown eyes looked up at him.

Sadness radiated from her, but she didn't hide in the corner or shake, but masked it and leaned against the front of the cage. He knelt in front of her, feeling a connection with her when he put his hand on one bar of her cage, and she snatched his arm.

And she wouldn't let go. The child was super strong, and the sadness changed as she gave him a grin, yellow stained teeth looking back with three or four missing. "We're the same," she whispered.

Adam yanked back, almost falling over, when he heard Jesse yell his name and looked up.

Jill.

She had emerged from the shadows, but she wasn't the Jill that he remembered. She looked more like the creatures in the cages. Her long hair hung well below her waist in straggly strands. One eye had begun to puss and gleam over with a white goo, and the other had grown twice in size. She opened her hands to expose razor-sharp fingernails that extended many inches and her body had a stench to it like something that Adam had smelled many times.

Like death.

It jolted him backward, and he remembered the screen just recently where he had seen Jill and her arguing with her father, and stared ahead, wondering what had happened to her. Had she accidentally ingested something like what happened to him? Had it exposed her to something? In one action, she grabbed a microneedle patch and injected herself, saying, "my last dose, and I'm now one of them. I'm of my creation, and I can never turn mutant if I'm never truly human. I have all the control," she hissed.

"You don't look like you're in control," said Jesse. "You look like shit."

She looked over at Jesse with barely a glance, her gaze fixated on Adam. "You may think I'm like you, Adam, but I'm something better. Not an environmental mistake, but a man-made solution. If I don't fix this, if I don't kill all the mutants, I can never be close to anyone again, not like I was with my father. There is only one solution, and that is to start over. I can do better than this mess. I can do better than God." *How did she do this?* It felt like she was squirming around in his mind. He didn't like the invasion, not to mention the headache it had ensued. His brain pounded and his weakness from lack of food and energy spent was taking a toll on him.

Focus.

"Jill, this won't bring your father back." He thought of Daniel and filled his mind with all the splendid memories that he could conjure up, knowing she could see them, too. Adam remembered how Daniel smiled when he got hired and Daniel reassured him they all would make a difference. When he and Daniel had lunch together in the cafeteria, they talked about their families. When Daniel talked about Jill and he boasted about how well she was doing in school and how proud he was of her.

Whatever new power Adam had to connect with people and read them, Jill had tenfold.

"I know that." He could almost see a tear in her eye, but it was hard to tell from all the gooping it was doing. "It is my job to avenge my father. I'm keeping the world safe. That's what he would have wanted. If only you had the courage to do what your father did when he started turning mutant. He was afraid to harm you, Adam." Adam's hands clenched in and out of fists in rapid succession as his nostrils flared. Of course she would know this, but hearing it out loud quickened his breath, and he ground his teeth.

She stopped, and a bewilderment filled her face. Turning to the right, she stared. Adam couldn't see what she was looking at except for a dark corner where there was nothing. "Yes, Dad, I know, but it's for the best. You don't understand." She stopped, and Adam wondered what her departed father was saying to her, or what she was imagining. *I know she's off the deep end, but I didn't realize the extent.* Hallucinations from grief. *What would have happened if the shoe had been on the other foot? How would I have reacted?*

If he would have lost his father to a mutant that he was trying to save instead of his father developing into a mutant and killing himself out of fear that he would hurt his family. He tried to suppress these thoughts. He knew she was in his brain and wondered if she was dragging the unwanted thoughts to the surface.

But he doubted it. She was too busy talking to her dad.

"I'm doing this for you! I'm doing this for the world!" There was no doubt now that tears were falling from her eyes, and she crunched a wrangled fist into a nearby table, cracking the table. "Damn you for always fighting with me. You should have been more careful and took precautions instead of just leaving me, forgetting your daughter at home. You were all I had, and now you're gone." Another pause, and then she yelled, "Don't go, Dad! I'm sorry! Please don't go!"

Adam stared at Jill, but in his mind he saw Camille, and a pang of guilt and uncertainty filled his thoughts. What if she was to resent him for all the missed trips to the park, time playing with her toys, and story time? He knew the bedtime kisses were getting more and more infrequent as he grew more and more fatigued. He admired Daniel, but it may be better to not be exactly like him.

Jill's lips turned into a snarl and he knew she could read his emotions just as he could. "She could hate you now." Adam's face hardened from fury and emotional pain. She flipped around, taking a step toward the three. Adam could hear sounds out in the hall of people trying to get in from the locked door with something that they couldn't undo. Adam's guess was her mind.

"Aren't you a resourceful bunch?" she remarked, noting the dead DNA projects behind Adam. Sven and Jesse used the time well when Adam was preoccupying her. The door shook harder with people trying to get in. "So many will help me because you know that I'm right, but they aren't in this fight. This is between you and me, and although I thought it would be fun to see my hard work demolish two more lowly humans that can go through my mutant change, I suppose the plan backfired. You, Adam, are no longer fully human. You're just a mutant. I won't have you tread on my earth and risk me and everyone else." She took three steps toward him and reached over to grab Adam, but he moved out of the way and she grabbed empty air.

Jill stumbled, then regained her balance, making dented footprints with every step. She seemed to get stronger.

But slower.

She went after Adam again, and he tried to avoid her, and she reached close to him. More puss poured out of her eye, impeding her view. This didn't stop her from clawing in front of her, even though her vision wasn't totally clear. She swiped twice and missed, but the third time clawed Adam in the side.

Sven lifted an instant scan reader, a block weighing 20 pounds of steel, and rammed it into her head. Jill screamed, clutching the side of her head, now dripping with blood, the flow increasing as the wound opened further. Sven had a moment of surprise at himself, where he stood speechless. She paused, clawing at Adam, and grasped the side of her head, applying pressure on the wound. When the blood continued to seep through her fingers, she kept clawing at Adam, her growl twisted into a snarl, letting the blood run freely down the side of her face. She missed several times until clawing his leg. He tried to stay out of arm's reach and back up, but she had him against the wall.

She was about ready to give him a life-threatening blow, but she stopped and screamed, clutching behind her and ended up on all fours on the ground, trying to reach the weapon that was in her back.

"Nice work, Jesse," Adam said with a smile and a pant. Jesse had used a clawed hand from the underground room to embed in her back, the very thing that she was trying to hide stopping her.

She lost consciousness.

Jesse reached down to press his fingers to her neck, checking her pulse. "Don't worry, she's still breathing. It went just like we planned."

"Good." Adam's eyes drifted to a mangled corpse in the room's corner, which looked a bit like a leopard. "No one deserves that. Not even her." Adam clinched at his wounds, trying to stay steady as he leaned against the wall for support.

"Are you okay?" asked Jesse, rushing to him as he leaned on Jesse on one side and Sven on the other.

"I'm good. It's all going to be okay."

Jesse reached into his lab coat pocket to rub his lucky penny through the fabric of the lining, but his finger went right through a hole. "My lucky penny! It's missing! The fabric must have had a flaw."

"You don't need a lucky penny," said Adam. "It was all you. It was all us."

Adam's thoughts transformed into wonderful memories. The hug from Christopher and Sven bandaging his wounds. Jesse promised he had his back even after he started turning mutant. Of his father when they did things together, like working on his truck out in the garage with the music blaring, passing around tools and laughing. These are the things, he thought, that make the fight all worth it.

Adam slapped him on the back. "I'm really proud of you."

"So am I," said Sven, and the once-locked doors opened wide. The gathering of scientists stood at the opening of the door, each trickling in with mouths agape at the bloody sight of the lab, Sam in the front.

"What happened?" he asked, rushing toward Jill, and his eyes opened wide when he saw the changes in her. "I thought she was just kidding. Why would she do this to herself? Testing me to see what I would say? To make sure that I was on her side? Is she alive?"

"Just passed out," said Adam.

"I'm tired of people disappointing me," he admitted. "First my parents, and then... she promised me I would be in charge of Juniper Ridge, but I didn't know she would change herself. I thought she was against all this." The murmurs around Jill were similar as the scientists talked amongst themselves. He placed his palm behind the base of his neck. "I'm sorry. I want to be in charge, but not drag the rest of the world down for it."

"Apology not accepted," said Adam, and walked off, fully ready to make the kid pay. With the scientists working together, they attached Jill to a bed and wheeled out of the horrific room.

Adam would be fine if he never went in there again.

Chapter Twenty-Eight

The road that led to Black Hills was loud and bright, with sirens and flashing lights as emergency vehicles flooded the scene. Detectives were on site to assess the situation, MCS to handle any unsafe conflict, and EMT to take any normal humans injured to the Panacea Hospital. Any humans without mutant problems were patients there.

Adam had answered a multitude of questions. They kept a watchful eye on him, even though he was on his way to recovery. This recovery situation was new to everyone. They had never been on this good of a track.

"Well, I guess Sven and I are back on community service," Jesse told Adam. "I'm sure you will be in the same boat with us."

"What's the job?"

"Litter patrol, in only designated areas, of course." Jesse rolled his eyes. "That was a lecture and a half."

Sven pulled himself out of the crowd. "Adam, can I talk to you for a minute?" Adam nodded, and they took a short walk away from the commotion, but still well within the safe perimeter.

"What's on your mind?" asked Adam.

"I have a confession to make. I had the idea of a tree frog weighing on my mind as a cure. Since they hadn't seen them since I was a boy, I honestly thought they didn't exist anymore, but if they did... I should have told you my idea, but I didn't want to get anyone's hopes up."

"You should have brought it up," Adam spat. *We could have been exploring this idea all along and he didn't think to bring it up?* Sven's downcast eyes and tremor made him think back to how disagreeable he had been, and it had all turned out okay in the end. "But I can see why you didn't. I know I've been difficult lately."

Sven looked up at Adam, shrugging his shoulders. "Besides, I thought that if we cured the mutants for good, no one would need me anymore. With Hannah as sick as she is, when she... no one would need me if it wasn't for this hospital."

Adam took a deep breath. *I have been such an ass.* "I'm sorry, Sven. There's something that you have to understand. You will always be needed."

"I know. I've been thinking..." he began, "and even after we find a cure, for sure, we will all still need to implement it, and deal with the supply issue, and take care of the ones that can't have it..."

"Exactly. You'll always be needed," said Adam, "because there are always problems. Let's get back. I don't like being this far from everyone, fences or not."

They headed back to the crowd and Adam saw Rachel appear out of nowhere, the two kids next to her. He could feel the sigh of relief that she expunged as she rushed toward him and held on as well as she did after teleportation. She saw past the claws, jagged teeth, and stench.

She pulled away and held him at arm's length, not letting go for anything. "Adam? What happened to you? How could you do that to me? I thought you were dead. Don't you ever..."

He kissed her, instantly stopping her in mid-sentence. Her stance relaxed and he pulled away. "Don't you think you are off the hook..."

"Wouldn't dream of it." He looked her straight in the eye and said, "I'm sorry. I'm so sorry."

Camille hid behind Rachel, rubbing her stomach. The teleportation took a lot out of the average person, and children were worse. Henry looked at him as if he was trying to figure him out.

"It's Daddy," Rachel coaxed Camille. "Want me to rub your tummy?" Camille ferociously shook her head and closed her eyes.

"It's okay. Give her time. About all this, everything that has happened, it's a long story," said Adam.

"You don't have to tell me," she said. "Only if you really want me to know." Adam smiled in relief. "I'm proud of you,

Sweetheart. You make a big difference in this world and it will make it safer for everyone, including this family." He reached down to kiss her again, careful that his fangs wouldn't nick her fragile skin.

Sam came up to them, head hung low. "I don't want to interrupt anything," he said, seeing his family there. "Sorry, I didn't know," he said, and he could tell Sam was taking his advice with the secrecy pact. "That she was going to go to such an extreme and do THAT. I heard she's going to be in your wing until healed, and then spend a very long time in jail." He kicked at some dirt on the ground. "I know I have no right to ask this, but do you still think I can work for you? I mean, I know I asked before, but I'm REALLY SORRY."

"Sam, I said no." *You led me to death and you expect me to forgive you?*

Two detectives pulled Sam aside. "We're going to need to speak with you," the taller one said, the other about ready to pull out handcuffs. *I don't think you'd be able to work for me, anyway.*

Adam put his arms around his family as a mist of rain began.

Epilogue

Adam entered Jill's room, looking behind him before he closed the door. Her puss-filled eye healing and her claws were beginning their transformation back to human. He stood next to the head of the bed, turning just right to block the camera that pointed to her face. Someone shackled her hands and ankles, not only because of her condition, but she was also a prisoner.

He slipped a syringe out of his pocket, ready to administer the cure to her, just so she could go to jail and pay for her crimes. They didn't use syringes for decades, but why save her pain?

"You're healing well," he remarked to her.

"As have you," she said. In fact, he had felt better than he ever did. He finished his medication and a week later, took two weeks off to spend with his family.

"It might take you a little more time. That's where we're different. I may have been a mutant, but you have done this to yourself, and for that, I have no sympathy."

She said nothing, but gave him a little smirk that made him uneasy. He injected her in the upper arm, knowing that the coarse skin would leave no mark. She grimaced, and he smiled.

"Someday soon, we may not have these types of hospitals. They might not even be necessary." Before she could reply, he turned away from her, and closed the door, locking it behind him with his code.

As he listened, the loud noises of the hospital had reduced to a low hum, and he wondered if he would ever get used to the change. It made him apprehensive to wish for a better tomorrow. He hurried to the entrance to go home. His workday was done.

A man entered the lobby that Adam had never seen before. "Adam Davidson?" He reached out to shake his hand, but pulled it back after Adam gave him an inquisitive look. "They've notified me of everything that has been going on here that I will look into. Meanwhile, we are going to shut the whole Black Hills wing down. I know you will have a lot going on with extra mutants to cure, but rumor has it you have a lead."

"News travels fast. A lead that's helping me so far." Adam waited to divulge any more until he found out who exactly he was talking to.

"Yes, and eventually it will all be opened up as Juniper Ridge. I will trust you that you can make all the difference. My brother spoke highly of you."

Adam's brow narrowed as he shook his head. "Sorry, I didn't catch your name."

"Oh, how silly of me. Josh Freeman." Adam's eyes widened. The Josh Freeman that Daniel said disappeared three years before he died? "I will talk to you later, Adam. It looks like you're on your way out."

Adam turned to glance toward the door, and Josh was gone.

ACKNOWLEDGMENTS

Before I took on this project, I didn't realize all of the people that it took to create a novel. I pictured sitting in the corner on my little desk typing away at my computer, but it was a lot more than just me.

For years, I plugged away at my rough draft, and re-wrote, and re-wrote some more, but I just wasn't happy with it each time. Then, one Christmas, I opened up a package from my parents only 6 inches square in bright penguin Christmas paper. In it, all rolled up in a box, were dollar bills. Inside read a note in my mom's bubbly cursive: "I have been collecting all of my dollar bills for the past while to give to you to open an account for your editor fees. I thought it would give you a kick start. Love, Mom and Dad." So I took that $84 and put it in a special savings account, and put my own money in whenever I got the chance.

So down the road, I joined a writing group on Facebook, and found a writing coach that could help me where I was stuck and get some feedback. Max and Ben from First Book Coaching were just the people I needed to help me figure out what was missing and how to fix the mess I had made. They taught me all the tools I needed to write a novel and were the best to brainstorm with! Thanks! I couldn't have done it without you.

After I had finished the rough draft, and edited as best as I could, I sent it out to Beta Readers. While being supportive and telling me what worked, they had a sharp eye to find things that I was missing or ideas that made the novel better, especially Sarah who took plenty of time to chat with me about not only this novel, but the sequel.

Through all of this work, I made a lot of new writing friends, too. We would chat about our struggles and victories, lifting each other up, especially Victoria and Lauren. Thanks, ladies!

Most of all, I would like to thank my family and friends. Rachel, my bestie since middle school, who always made sure we made it home early from errands so I could have my writing time. My boyfriend, Peter, who even put the television on mute and read subtitles so I could write, but we could still "hang out". I couldn't have done it without all the love and support from both of you.

Last, but not least, thank you, dear readers, for picking up my novel. Enjoy!

—·—

About the Author

R uth A. Milligan lives in Oregon. When she's not writing, she likes to hit the beach, go to ice hockey games, or curl up with a good book and a hot cup of coffee. This is her first novel.

Yatoa frowned. "You knew facts about the case and you didn't tell me?"

"Yup," Arlicia admitted guiltlessly. "I didn't want to taint how you viewed your own case with my perceptions of it. It'd be best if you heard the details straight from the client's mouth." Yatoa turned to face her mentor's smug smirk.

"But you're not supposed to keep this stuff from me. You're my mentor and this is my first case. I need all the help I can get!"

Arlicia shrugged. "I hope for your sake, Toa, that last part isn't true, because you will receive next to no assistance from me. You'll be standing in court by yourself after all."

"*What?* But this is my first trial, you're *supposed* to assist me!" Yatoa was yelling much too loud at this point. The guards in the hall outside could probably hear her, but fear gripped her too tight in its fist for her to care.

"I'm not *supposed* to do anything. The only one who's supposed to do anything here is you. Now are you going to defend your client or are you going to give up on becoming an attorney?" Arlicia's playful tone fell away and something harder replaced it. This was a tone she rarely used outside of court and almost never with Yatoa. The sudden change in her mentor's demeanor shocked away all Yatoa's anxiety. A stubborn determination filled the empty space.

"Of course I'll defend my client!" She snapped more savagely than she had meant to. She never took that tone with her mentor, and she immediately felt bad for the blatant disrespect. Arlicia grinned.

"Good, because your client is here." The door opened.

2

Gob'Alondis' Story

Dal Gob'Alondis was unceremoniously shoved into the small room and the door slammed shut behind him. Gob'Alondis was only a head taller than the table which made Yatoa realize for the first time how strange it was that the furniture in this room was human sized. Dal had red skin; one of the three colors a Goblin could be. His ears were pointy and they had a slight droop to them at the ends which added to the forlorn expression on his face. He had a slight under-bite with a fang that protruded upward out of his mouth. He looked up at them with cautious, big green eyes.

Yatoa stood and held her hand out to the man. "It's a pleasure to meet you Mr. Gob'Alondis. I am Yatoa Hu'Dectalaciumina, and I will be representing you in court."

Gob'Alondis stared at her for a long moment. He didn't take her hand.

"I knew they was goin' to assign me a free lawyer because I can't afford one of my own, but I wasn't expectin' an apprentice and a human to boot," he said dejectedly, then turned to

Arlicia and said, "That can't be legal, right? You gotta be the real lawyer, yeah? This is all a joke, isn't it?"

"I assure you it is most certainly legal Mr. Gob'Alondis," Yatoa said, forcing down her annoyance. "I am perfectly capable of defending you in court. My mentor, Arlicia Sa'Krieglund, is one of the most renowned Lawyers in the world. She taught me everything she knows. I graduated from-"

"You're the God Lawyer!" Gob'Alondis said excitedly cutting Yatoa off and pointing at her mentor. Another spike of annoyance impaled her, but with effort she maintained her mask of control.

"In the flesh. Luckily for you, my Goblin friend, I've decided to take on your case pro-bono. My best apprentice will be handling it personally," Arlicia said. She neglected to mention that Yatoa was also her *only* apprentice.

"Well, I'd really rather have you defend me ma'am if it's not too much of a bother," Gob'Alondis said with a sheepish grin that showed off his fangs. Yatoa noted he was missing one in the top row.

"I'm sure you also wish you weren't in jail, yet here we both are in a small room mutually dreading ever having to set foot in Goblin Court," Yatoa snapped. Gob'Alondis' eyes bulged at that remark. So much for containing her annoyance. She needed to recover from this. "But I will do everything in my power to defend you Mr. Gob'Alondis, that's a promise, and you won't find more genuine conviction from any public defender. Now, if you would, sit in the chair across the table. The sooner we can get started the better prepared I'll be for the trial."

This seemed to satisfy the Goblin. He rounded the table and climbed bodily up into the human-sized chair, then crossed his arms on the tabletop in front of him. Yatoa took a deep breath to settle her nerves. This was it. Her first case. This was exactly what she had wanted. Despite the odd circumstances she felt eager to get to work and finally use everything she had learned over the past four years.

However, before she could retake her seat a knock came at the door. It was Freeda. She brought in a tray with two tall glasses of juice. Arlicia eyed the orange juice hungrily.

Yatoa finally took her seat and did as her mentor wished. "Mr. Gob'Alondis, would you care for a beverage? The drink on the left is orange, the other apple. You may take whichever suits your fancy," she said much to Arlicia's satisfaction.

Gob'Alondis licked his lips and, after Freeda exited the room, he grabbed the glass of orange juice. Arlicia leaned back in her chair smiling triumphantly. "Don't mind if I do," he said casually. "Oh, and the name's Dal by the way. Nobody goes around callin' me my family name, and I'd prefer you didn't either."

"Alright Dal," Yatoa said in a less formal tone. "Please know that anything you say to us will remain strictly confidential, and we will not discuss any of it with anyone without your consent. So, I'll get right to the point. Did you commit this crime?"

Dal held his glass in both hands. He stared down into the juice for a moment, then his big eyes met hers and Yatoa could see concern in them as clearly as she could see their color. "Yes."

Yatoa nodded to herself. "Very well. I will do everything I can to lighten your sentence. Now if you would-"

Arlicia smacked her hand down on the table, jolting some of the apple juice out of its glass. Yatoa nearly jumped out of her seat in fright. Her heart thundered in her chest as Arlicia raised a disapproving finger.

"You will do nothing of the sort, Yatoa."

"Excuse me?"

"You will not do everything in your power to lighten his sentence. Instead, you will do everything in your power to win this Goblin a complete acquittal. That is the assignment. I expect nothing less."

Yatoa stared dumbfounded at her mentor for a time. "But he committed the crime! If we don't fight for a lighter sentence, then he could lose everything! Goblin law states that the punishment for theft under article 225b is-"

"Death by marble crushing. I'm aware, Yatoa. But this man doesn't deserve *any* punishment for his crime let alone death. Which is why you will see him acquitted."

"Um, excuse me," Dal said, trying to cut in.

"But he *did* commit the crime! Don't criminals always deserve some kind of punishment for their crimes?" Yatoa shot back completely baffled.

"I'm fine with a lighter sentence, I-" Dal tried interjecting.

Arlicia shrugged while the Goblin spoke, then cut him off mid-sentence. "Criminals do not always deserve punishment for their crimes. It depends on the circumstances. In this case I can assure you Dal does not deserve death or even imprisonment. I'll explain why later. Now continue."

"But-"

"*Continue, Yatoa.* Do as I say."

Yatoa let out an exasperated sigh. An acquittal? This was only her first case! Nevertheless, she continued.

"Well, um, sorry about that little display Dal. Now, if you would, tell us in your own words what happened." Yatoa sat back with full expectation that he would follow her command. His silence filled the air between them, but Yatoa didn't break it. Long silences were uncomfortable for everyone involved, and the longer they went on the more everybody wanted to break it.

Dal took a long gulp of his orange juice, polishing off the glass. "Well, I suppose it started about two weeks ago. I was runnin' across some financial troubles, and I needed some more dough for my family, but my job wasn't cuttin' it. I needed something more lucrative."

"And what is your job?"

"I'm a cobbler. I make boots. I don't take much pride in my work. It doesn't bring in any high-rollers, but my boots are affordable and they're good enough for most of the folk down in the Saern District," Dal said with a shrug.

"I suppose the Saern District is where you live?" Yatoa said.

"Yup. Born and raised. In the Saern District you'll mostly find folk down on their luck who can't keep their heads above the water, but not for lack of trying mind you. It's a little hard to come up for air when someone in a boat is holding your head down, if you know what I mean." Yatoa nodded thinking of her home island in the Geltian Archipelago and her ancient life there. She could relate with that sentiment.

"Anyway," Dal continued with a wave of his hand. "So, I got my crew together. I have a theivin' crew see, and occasionally we do a little theivin'. We were more active when I was young. We're all older now, I'm thirty-nine myself, and we only get together and do a little thievin' about fifteen times a year." Yatoa raised an eyebrow. Fifteen thefts a year didn't seem as big a deal to him as it was to her. "Though I wanna be clear, I only get half a share of the dough. You see I'm an upstandin' guy. Real moral. I don't take more than I need. That way everyone else on the crew gets more – and they need it more than I do too so it's a real good thing I'm doin' here."

"Right…" Yatoa said with a mental sigh. "May I ask the names of the members of this crew?" Dal's eyes widened and he flashed his fangs.

"Not a chance apprentice. I'm no rat. I'd never tell that to anybody – not even my wife!" he snapped. "If you wanna help me, you gotta do it without that info. Got it?"

Yatoa gritted her teeth, but she nodded. The identities of his fellow crew members may be useful, though she understood why he didn't want to tell her. No one would trust someone they just met, and she'd bet Dal didn't want to get any of his crewmembers in trouble.

"Good. Now as I was sayin', I needed some money for my family real bad. My daughter is sick and she needs treatment. Now I don't know what it's like where you're from, but they practically charge us our lives for proper treatment around here. I'm sure you understand I had my hands tied. I needed money fast and I wasn't gonna make it sellin' cheap boots to folks poorer than I am.

"So, we made a plan. There's a mansion we'd been wantin' to hit for ages. Belongs to this rich fella who owns a bunch of real estate in the workin'-class part of town. Makes money off people's need to stay alive, so he's a real leech. A fella like that oughtta be on trial not a upstandin' citizen like me. Now If I were in charge-"

"Dal," Yatoa cut in carefully. "I would appreciate it if you would stay on the topic of the crime rather than philosophizing."

Dal waved his hand in dismissal. "Yeah, yeah I get ya." He turned to Arlicia. "Kids these days always wanna rush into things. They don't take the time to stop and play a game of 'here's a Goblin there's a Goblin', if you know what I mean."

Arlicia chuckled, a light and crystalline sound. "Trust me I know," she said with a smile. Yatoa bristled at that.

"Dal, if you would, please continue," Yatoa said more firmly than she had meant to. The Goblin flicked his empty glass, then leaned back in his chair.

"The fella's name is Cartaneal Gob'Franat. Seemed like a good target and an easy one too. He has a large jewelry collection and we was planning on theivin' at least some of it. We're courteous see, we don't take a lot of things if we don't need to."

"Of course," Arlicia said with a nod. Yatoa however was growing impatient with the man's long-winded recounting.

"So, you made a plan and carried it out," she said, trying to speed things along. "But something went wrong." A forlorn expression passed over Dal's face. Yatoa's awareness of the chains on his wrists sharpened. When Dal had first entered the room all she had seen was a client. Now she saw something else there in front of her. A prisoner. One that was facing down a death sentence. She mentally scolded herself and decided she needed to be a little more empathetic.

"Yeah, something went wrong alright. Everything was going fine at first – all according to plan. We got into his jewelry display room and we had bags stocked up and ready to go. The only thing left was to hit his study. See there was some documents in there that a certain fella – who I won't name because I'm a Goblin not a rat – said he'd pay good money for 'em. There shoulda been a lookout while I rummaged in his study to try and find them, but a pair of house guards came burstin' through the doorway right when I found 'em. I tell you I never jumped so high in my life. I was at least three-feet off the ground. They almost gave me a heart attack. I thought my lookout would at least give me a warnin', but nothin'."

"I'm assuming they caught your lookout as well?"

Dal shook his head. "Nope. My lookout got away. The only member of the crew that got caught was me. Far as I know they're spendin' their new money in bar somewhere."

At first that seemed strange to Yatoa, but it didn't take her long to come to the only conclusion. "Your lookout ditched you," She thought aloud.

"She would never!" Dal snapped back almost too fast. From his reaction and that vicious desperation on his face Yatoa figured the thought had crossed his mind before. He didn't want to accept it. "No member of the crew would ever turn their back on the others. We've been pals all our lives. Somethin' important must've happened."

"Yes of course. I'm sorry for even considering it," she said to diffuse him.

"That's the end of my story I suppose. There isn't much more to tell. Got caught, now I'm here."

Yatoa rested her elbow on her knee and her chin on her fist to think for a moment. It *was* pretty cut and dry, though the story left her with some questions. Who was in his crew, and what were their stories? Who was the lookout and why did she abandon Dal? It bothered her that there were multiple witnesses to this crime, yet she had access to none of them. Those questions she couldn't answer for now. Instead, she asked the most pressing question.

"What were those documents that you tried to steal?"

Dal didn't seem bothered by this.

"They were some documents about some plan to buy up property in the Saern District and build some sort of fancy market. Didn't seem especially important to me but I didn't give 'em a thorough read neither."

"Interesting," Yatoa said to herself. "Well Dal if you remember any other details about what happened be sure to let me know. Every detail in this case is vital." Yatoa stood, signaling the end of the meeting. "Sorry for the rocky introduction, but I assure you I will handle this case. You'll live through this, one way or another." She eyed Arlicia as she said that though her mentor remained silent. Aiming for a full acquittal seemed silly given the circumstances. There was no way to pull that off. The City Watch had caught Dal in the act, so there was little debate as to whether he committed the crime or not. If she played her cards right, she could at the very least earn the Goblin a lighter sentence and spare him a premature trip to the city cemetery.

Dal hopped down from his chair and scampered around to their side of the table to stand before Yatoa. "I'll be in touch," Yatoa said. "We'll discuss more tomorrow. For now, it's getting late and to be honest with you I'm starving."

"Don't worry about it. I have faith in you, Yatoa," Dal said. She figured he wanted to believe those words, though he didn't sound entirely sincere.

"Oh, and before I go, there's still one vital piece of information I need to ask you about. When is your trial taking place? Do we have over a month? A few weeks?"

Dal blinked in surprise. "You… you don't know that already? You don't get weeks, Yatoa. Try four days." Dread. She opened her mouth to respond but nothing came out.

"You'll be fine, Toa," Arlicia said, placing a hand on her shoulder. "I wouldn't have picked this case for you if I didn't think you could handle it."

Yatoa shut her eyes and submersed herself in darkness, trying to escape it all. "After this case is over, I'm going to kill you," she groaned. Silence. She cracked her eyes open to peek at Arlicia's face. A smirk greeted her

"That's only fair. If you win this case, then I won't even put up a fight. Just make sure you win, alright?"

3

The Shatter

Arlicia threw a wet rag on Yatoa's sleeping face.

"You're a monster," Yatoa mumbled through the damp cloth.

"Guilty," Arlicia said.

They slept in a small room with two beds, a full body mirror, and a washstand. It was humble by Arlicia's standards, but for Yatoa it was a luxury. When Yatoa was a child, she didn't even have a bed to sleep in. So, when Arlicia forced her to get out of bed and get ready for the big day ahead of them, Yatoa complained. She loved beds. The squishy mattress supporting her body… the soft fabric of the sheets against her cheek… it was a blissful world away from the courts, jails, legal documents. Out of the bed everything was too hard and cold, and the sensation brought back memories of emotional solitude, of feeling like an illusion in a city obsessed with illusions, of Ghost's letter left on a tabletop early on a winter morning, and-

All these thoughts came to her in a daze as she shifted out of her bed, but they ceased the moment her bare feet touched the cold floor. From there, the morning was a whirlwind.

Arlicia claimed they had a long day ahead of them. She insisted they march to the Saern district, but not before breakfast at a bakery down the street. So, they made their way through the narrow halls of their inn and out into the hot summer air.

They weren't staying in the High Gob District, but rather the Goblin District, home to the working class. Here the buildings were not constructed from marble; instead, they were all massive hollowed out tree trunks. Visionary architects had carved a vast network of corridors and rooms into the monstrous trees like ants in their nest.

They walked through cobbled streets under the shaded canopy of the buildings' branches, and Yatoa couldn't help but stare up. This was the oldest district, yet Yatoa found it much prettier and more comforting than the marble buildings in the High Gob District. The streets were also busier with Goblins hurrying about their business scampering this way and that. It felt as though she was wading through a river of Goblins. As a riverboat fighting the current, she gazed downstream. Red, purple, and green heads all bobbed up and down in waves.

Eventually they came to the bakery and got some sweet buns to go. When Yatoa took a bite into the soft, hot bun, her tongue tingled with spice. The sugary bun had a hint of cinnamon and Goblin powder. An addictive combo. Dangerous.

"So why do you want to head to the Saern District so early in the morning?" Yatoa asked her mentor while still chewing on a piece of her bun. They turned onto a quieter side street, and a weak gust of wind fluttered their capes behind them. "I planned to consult with Dal further."

"Because I promised I'd explain to you exactly why you should get that Goblin acquitted, but I require visual aid." Arlicia took a swig of orange juice from her canteen. "We'll be stopping by the Gob'Alondis household." Yatoa sighed, but she didn't have much of a choice. Once you fell into Arlicia's rhythm you either had to dance or get booed off the dance floor, tomatoes flying in your wake. Tomato juice was not the kind of red Yatoa wanted on her uniform.

"I suppose it's necessary to speak with Dal's family. Building a profile on the Goblin will be helpful for stage two of the trial. It would really help if I could get his family to testify," Yatoa mused as they turned another corner onto a busier street. The din of traffic boomed. Dozens of conversations struck Yatoa's ears at once in an unintelligible hum of high-pitched Goblin squeaks.

"You're assuming Dal's family likes him," Arlicia shouted over the crowd. "They could testify against him. Don't start making assumptions until you have more facts to work from."

It took them a good while to escape the overpopulated bustle of the Goblin district, and by the time they did it was noon. Now Yatoa saw the necessity of waking up so early. The longer the day fermented, the busier the streets became. At the very least the two of them didn't draw many of those big round Goblin eyes like they did in the High Gob district. Foreigners were common here. She had actually seen another Human and two Fairies on the way.

While Yatoa and her mentor didn't excite comment from the crowd, the Fairies enraptured them. The crowd came to a

halt around the Fairies, Goblin children, or goblets colloqui-
ally, cried out with glee. The Fairies fluttered and zipped in
intricate patterns, leaving sparkles in the air. Their long, perfectly straight and absurdly colored hair streamed behind
them. The perfect styling made Yatoa self-conscious of her
own naturally wavy hair, especially since she hadn't had much
time this morning to untangle it.

Yatoa and Arlicia had to push their way through the
crowd. The Fairies didn't interest either of them. For Arlicia's
part, she had defended some in court and claimed the Fairies'
legal system took luster out of them. She lamented to Yatoa
on numerous occasions that Fairy law was a nightmare.

Yatoa on the other hand had spent much of her late teens
in the presence of a Fairies. Eliafa Fa'Natas had been her best
friend when she attended the Three Star Academy in Faestar
Great Tree, and that relationship persisted even when Yatoa
dropped out in favor of the legal academy. Leaving the Fairies
behind, they pressed on and before long found themselves in
a new district.

The Saern district was a far cry from the others. Instead of
intricately carved trees or marble palaces, boxy wooden shacks
held together by nails and prayers populated the streets. The
unpaved streets were so dusty that when Yatoa breathed in she
felt the dust stick to her throat.

The Goblins here dressed in rags. Clothes lines hung between the buildings, and sandy colored garments dominated
the strings.

"Welcome to the real Gobroa," Arlicia said with a grand sweeping gesture of her arms that encompassed the entire scene.

"Everything you've seen up until now was only the top half of the tower. This is its base. Without this district, the whole thing would collapse!"

"You got that right lady!" a purple Goblin yelled from down the street. That was when Yatoa noticed everyone was staring at the two of them. Here in their fancy uniforms and flowing capes they were as beacons. Usually, Yatoa took pride in her attire. Growing up she didn't have nice clothes so she found her uniform empowering. Now she wished she was wearing anything else. This district resembled her home, and she didn't want anyone to think she had grown up with a silver spoon hanging out of her mouth.

"Anyway," Yatoa cut in trying to distract Arlicia from her over-dramatic performance. "Where is the Gob'Alondis residence? You do know where it is, don't you?"

Arlicia stared at her for a moment, then tossed up her cane and snatched it at mid length out of the air. She waved the thin black cane side to side and tsked. "Of course I don't. Figuring it out will be your first practice exercise for the day. Go forth, my apprentice! Ferret out the intel required to defend your helpless client post-haste!"

"Stop shouting and making a scene!" Yatoa hissed. "People are *staring* at us."

Arlicia grinned viciously and spoke in a mock whisper. "The hammer of justice will not wait for your insecurities to resolve themselves my dear. The clock is ticking."

Great. Arlicia had to remind her of her impossible deadline when Yatoa thought she couldn't handle anymore stress. Well, there was nothing for it.

"Excuse me," Yatoa said to the nearest Goblin, a green woman with bright blue eyes and a simple dress. The woman's eyes widened as Yatoa addressed her and she hurried away without a word.

"If you try to catch a fish by hand, Toa, you will find that it will almost always slip from your fingers," Arlicia said. She stood there looking smug with her hands on her hips. Yatoa could feel Arlicia's dark, judgemental eyes on her as she moved on down the street.

Yatoa tried approaching two more Goblins, but each time they saw her towering over them and fled. Arlicia's mocking advice wouldn't cease but Yatoa tried her best to ignore it. Sometimes Yatoa wondered if Arlicia was actually a demon sent to torture her and she had long since died and gone to hell. Well maybe that was a bit harsh. Yatoa did respect her. Arlicia was the closest thing Yatoa had ever had to a caring mother – though she would never tell her that. Despite that, Yatoa wanted nothing more than to rip that cane out of Arlicia's hands and snap it in two.

After a few more inquiries and getting either fright or stony silence in response, an idea struck her. "What if I could offer you something in return?" she said to an old Goblin man who sat on the edge of a porch trying very his best to ignore her. "The rest of my sweet bun perhaps?" The old Goblin's wide, wrinkled face contorted into a grimace.

"Okay, how about money?" The grimace dissipated in an instant and he eyed her with curiosity.

"Five gobbings, and not a penny less," the man grumbled.

"Done," She reached into her pocket and slid out five gobbings. The coins were octagonal and the metal was cool in her hands. She pressed them into his wide palm, careful to avoid his sharp claw-like nails.

"Alright, what do you want to know?" The man asked grudgingly.

"Where can I find the Gob'Alondis residence?" Yatoa asked. The old Goblin's bushy eyebrows raised at that.

"The cobbler Dal? That depends on who's asking."

"His attorney."

The old man shook his head and sighed. "So, the boy really did get snatched up. Thought that was just a rumor. Anyway, if yer his attorney then I suppose I should tell ya. It's around the corner there. First building on the right. There's a big sign that says "Gob'Alondis Cobblers", you can't miss it. The shop is on the first floor but the famIly lives on the second."

Yatoa mentally kicked herself. The shop was just around the corner? She thanked the man then checked herself, and sure enough it was there clear as day. The sign read, "Gob'Alondis Cobblers Est. 4367 A.C."

"You knew it was right here the whole time, didn't you?" Yatoa asked as Arlicia joined her. Arlicia shrugged.

"You should have haggled with him. In Gobroa, never accept the first offer," she said simply. Yatoa rolled her eyes. "It's your loss. I'm not going to reimburse you for it so keep that in mind and let this be a lesson."

With that they stepped into the shop. The main room was small, with a few long tables displaying pairs of simple boots. Dal wasn't being humble when he said he didn't take much pride in his work. These boots looked serviceable, but none of them particularly stood out to Yatoa as quality.

A Goblin woman stood in the doorway that lead to the workshop in the back. It was easy to see the whole of her over the short tables and counter. The small furniture made Yatoa feel as though she were a giant.

The Goblin woman had purple skin, and a round face for a Goblin. She had her boots on, a utilitarian, brown dress, and a bag slung over her shoulder looking as though she was either on her way out, or had just returned from somewhere.

"Sorry we're closed for today," the woman said as she moved around the counter.

"There's no closed sign on the door," Arlicia pointed out.

"Yes, well I haven't put it up yet."

Yatoa closed the gap between them and stood before the woman. "Sorry for bothering you, but are you Dal Gob'Alondis' wife?" The Goblin's round eyes narrowed.

"And what if I am," she replied coolly.

Yatoa gestured to her white suit, then to Arlicia's blood red one. "We're Dal's defense attorneys. Would it be alright with you if we asked you a few questions? We won't keep you long if you're in a hurry."

The woman re-examined them with more inquisitive eyes. "Lawyers, eh? Well, if you're defending my husband in court then I suppose I can spare you the time." She held her hand up to Yatoa. "The name's Garna Gob'Alondis."

"I'm Yatoa Hu'Dectalaciumina. I will be defending your husband. And this is my mentor, Arlicia Sa'Krieglund."

Garna lifted an eyebrow, but she wasn't as shocked to hear the famous name as Dal had been. "The God Lawyer herself and her apprentice are defending my husband?" She shook her head. "What did he offer you? Whatever it is, I regret to inform you that we can't pay it. We couldn't possibly afford-"

"We're taking this case pro bono. You don't have to pay us a single gobbing."

"Sounds fishy," Garna said. "What's in it for you?"

Yatoa spread her arms wide in what she hoped was a disarming manner. "A promotion and peace of mind."

Garna grunted, then exclaimed that it was too dreary down in the shop, so she led to a set of stairs at the back. Once upstairs they entered into a small, cramped sitting room. Though the room likely felt bigger to a Goblin.

At Garna's insistence Yatoa and Arlicia sat next to each other on a small couch. It was too low to the ground. So much so that their knees were higher than their hips.

"Sorry for the uncomfortable seats. We've never gotten a human visitor before."

"It's fine I assure you," Yatoa said. Arlicia seemed content to let Yatoa do all the talking. It made her nervous. It felt as though she was taking a mock assessment at the legal academy – though in a way this all actually was an assessment.

Garna leaned back in an armchair and picked up a half-made scarf comprised of green and yellow yarn with knitting needles poked through it. "You don't mind if I do a little knitting while we talk, do you?" Yatoa shook her head and Garna leaned back in her chair and began clicking her needles together. "So, what do you want to know?"

"I promise we won't take much of your time ma'am. I hope we're not making you late for anything important." Yatoa couldn't help but feel like she was intruding on Garna. Watching Garna knit the small living room was so intimate it felt like reading her diary.

"No, it's fine," Garna said. "I was only going to visit Dal at the jail. He needs company. Poor man. He doesn't do well in stressful situations like this, and always needs some sort of emotional support. He's a sensitive man."

"It's good that he has you to support him. Oftentimes people don't have anyone who will visit them."

"Yes well, I'm sure Dal will have several visitors. He's well-known around here and has a good reputation. He has no dearth of friends."

"That's good for the case. If I can present his good character to the jury, then I may be able to win one of the seven verdicts," Yatoa explained.

"You'll have no trouble with that. I was planning on testifying myself. He's a good father and husband and a pillar of the community. He helps run several major annual community events, and he also teaches kids to read at a night class twice a week." Garna grabbed another spool from a basket; blue to contrast with the yellow she had been working with.

"This is all very good information. I'm sure we'll be able to build a strong case. But all that aside I want to ask you a few questions about the crime itself." Yatoa reached into her suit and pulled out a small red pocket book and a pen. "Were you at all aware of the crime before it took place?"

"Yes, I was. Dal and his crew always plan their heists in the workshop downstairs. I usually bring them drinks late at night. I sometimes even join in on the planning," the small Goblin said with nonchalance.

"Don't mention that last bit in court," Yatoa said.

Garna chuckled in a high-pitched way that only a Goblin woman could. "I don't need legal advice for that Miss Hu'…"

"Hu'Dectalaciumina."

"Mind if I call you Yatoa?" Garna asked apologetically. Yatoa shrugged. She knew her name was hard to pronounce for most people, and she didn't blame them for it. Though sometimes she wished everyone could get it right so she wouldn't have to feel slight embarrassment every time she had to say her name.

"Were you particularly concerned about this heist?"

Garna lifted her chin up in thought for a moment, her large eyes lost in some sea of thoughts, then she sighed. "Sort of? I wasn't concerned about the actual heist itself, but a lot was riding on this particular one. We need money. Our daughter is sick, and there's this One Star Healer in the High Gob District who can cure her, but the price is steep. We just can't afford it."

"Might I ask what your daughter has?"

"The shatter," Garna said solemnly. Yatoa's heart twisted. The shatter was a magical illness that turned the bodies of afflicted into glass over a period of seven months. Yatoa knew it well. She had lost her sister to it. "The girl is only twelve."

Yatoa felt a torrent of hot rage crash into her and sweep away all her thoughts. For a One Star, healing the shatter would be so simple, and yet the healer would charge a fortune for it. That was injustice in its purest form.

"I'm so sorry. I'm sure it must be hard," Arlicia said, breaking her long silence. Her mentor's hard observant expression had softened into something open and vulnerable. Yatoa realized when she spoke that she had been silent for an uncomfortably long time.

"Yes… That's terrible," she added.

"The thing I don't get," Garna said ignoring her pity, "is that Dal was the only one caught, but I haven't seen a single gobbing of the money stolen. It's been weeks. The rules always were that if a member gets caught, incapacitated, or dies, then the crew would send their share directly to their family. Yet it's been weeks and I haven't heard from a single member of the crew.

"At first, I gave them the benefit of the doubt. Perhaps they were having trouble selling it. But then I heard yesterday one of the members had moved to the Goblin district. Clearly, they did sell the jewelry,"

"You think they've all decided to cut you and Dal out?" Yatoa asked.

Garna shook her head. "That's unlikely. The crew usually has one member manage the funds, and she always gets the final say. She is the most loyal to Dal of them all. I would never think this would be her doing."

Yatoa perked up, sitting straighter in her cramped seat and scribbled something into her notebook. Garna frowned. "How big is the crew?"

Taken off guard, Garna knit her brow at that question. "Err yes, I suppose I can tell you that much, but if you think I'll rat out any of their identities think again. The crew is pretty small. There's four members in total. I'm not particularly close to any of them. Most of them are men and they're pretty insufferable."

Yatoa tapped her pen against her notebook for a moment. Something about the whole situation felt off. Yes, Dal *did* commit the crime – that was indisputable fact at this point – but the case didn't seem so cut and dry anymore. Yatoa knew the core of it. The main crucial truth that Dal committed this crime. But she still didn't understand the context.

"Dal told me that his lookout had abandoned him during the heist," Yatoa said, "and that was the reason he got caught. It is clear to me that she betrayed him during the heist. Now you are telling me this same woman is in charge of any funds obtained through sale of stolen goods, and that you have not received your due. To me this is only further evidence that this woman betrayed your husband so she could get a bigger cut."

Garna was silent for a long moment. "I can't imagine she of all people would do such a thing," Garna said with a frown. "But then again… I still haven't received Dal's cut, so there could be some merit to that."

"Dal was also skeptical of the idea of his lookout betraying him. Might you tell us why it seems so implausible?"

At that moment, from around the corner leading into the nearest hallway a small goblet peered into the room. She was very short, only about one and a half feet tall. She had purple skin like her mother, though her eyes resembled Dal's. The little girl's right arm hung stiff at her side. Her arm had completely vitrified, taking on a glossy cast. The girl stared intently at Yatoa and Arlicia with wide eyes.

"Mom, why are there humans in here," the girl said in a shaky squeak. Garna sat up in alarm.

"Darlia! Go back to bed! You shouldn't be moving about!" Garna stood up and Darlia took a step back.

Darlia shook her head emphatically. "It's just my arm, Mom. I can walk fine," she protested.

"I don't care. Go back to your room this instant! I will not have you shattering that arm before we get you healed," Garna's voice was almost hysteric in its insistence.

"But-"

"Now!" Darlia's eyes widened in fright as she jumped back from her mother's screech, then she ran down the hallway she had emerged from and Yatoa heard a door slam. "Don't run Darlia! How many times have I told you!"

"I wish Dad were here, not you!" Darlia yelled back. The high pitched, emotionally charged argument left Yatoa feeling distinctly unsettled.

Garna took a deep breath, then turned back to them. "I'm… sorry you had to see that. Things have been… stressful lately. I know I shouldn't be so forceful with her, but as a mother it's hard to watch your child risk themselves like that. One wrong step and Darlia could lose her arm.

"That's quite alright," Yatoa assured her, though she felt uneasy. Her own mother had never been that hysterical with

Soloa, Yatoa's now deceased sister. Then again, her own mother was... not the best example to look to.

"Anyway, if what you told me is true then it seems I have much to think about," Garna said softly.

Yatoa stood from the couch, signaling Arlicia to follow suit. "I think that it'd be best if we took off and left you to your business, but before we go Mrs. Gob'Alondis may I make a final request?"

"You may," Garna said cautiously.

"Please tell me the name of this woman in the crew. I'd like to speak with her. She could hold some crucial information that would help me with this case, and maybe I can find out why you didn't get your cut."

Garna gripped her chin in thought, then sighed. "Faz Gob'Venicker," she said with a sour twist to her mouth. "But I doubt you'll find her before the trial. I tried getting a hold of her myself, but she's completely evaded me. She's the one that moved to the Goblin District, though I have no idea where."

Yatoa nodded in gratitude, then her and Arlicia excused themselves. Yatoa and Arlicia stepped out of the building into the dry air. It was late afternoon now, and the sun hung low in the sky. They walked in silence for a time back toward the Goblin District. Yatoa felt like she was actually starting to *do* something to prepare for the trial, though what that thing was she wasn't exactly sure yet. Uncertainty hung over her like a thunderstorm poised to strike, and each anticipatory moment was agonizing.

When they reached the bridge marking the end of the Saern District, Arlicia jumped in front of her and spun with a flourish, cape twirling. "Good work Toa!" she said. She had a messy grin on her face and her dark eyes danced. "Now that you have seen some of what this district has to offer, I can explain to you exactly *why* you need to get this man a complete acquittal!"

Yatoa stared at her mentor expectantly. Dust blew past them, riding on the wind. Arlicia wanted her to respond in some manner, to feed the performance, so grudgingly she said, "I've been sitting on the edge of my seat, dear mentor. I am brimming with electric anticipation. Free me from the pains of ignorance if you would!" She finished it with a sweep of her cape, wrapping it around her front. Arlicia's grin widened.

"Very well my apprentice, despair no longer." Arlicia let her smile drop. Her tone sobered to a shocking degree. "I do not defend criminals Yatoa, nor do I defend the innocent."

"Then who do you defend?"

"The weak. Yatoa you've seen the richest district this city has to offer, and you've seen the poorest. Now let me tell you a truth. If someone with fat pockets from the High Gob District committed this crime, then they would get a complete acquittal. Why? Because they have money. Because they can bribe the jury and the judge if they need to. If the city imprisoned them, or crushed them between marble slabs for theft, that would upset a lot of important people in positions of power. No one wants to be on the bad side of someone who has power over them.

"I defend the weak because they need me. I defend the weak because if those in power don't get punished for their crimes, then neither should those they subjugate. I *never* defend the strong."

"Arlicia, didn't you defend a God?" Yatoa asked with keen skepticism. Arlicia's famous defense of the God of wine in God Court was how she had earned the title "God Lawyer" in the first place.

Arlicia smirked. "Power is relative, Yatoa. Even among Gods there are rulers and subjects, but that's not important. What *is* important is the fact that while your client is guilty of a crime, he's only going to die because he wasn't lucky enough to be born on the right side of the river. That's the key difference. He's going to die for something completely out of his control, and that my dear is one of the clearest examples of injustice you could find in this world. And as lawyers… we cannot let injustice stand."

4

Goblona for Three

Yatoa found herself lost in thought as she leaned back against a railing overlooking one of the city's two rivers across the street from the marble jail. It felt… criminal for a jail to look so extravagant. It was ironic that the jail cell Dal was being kept in now likely cost more to construct than his house did.

Next to her Arlicia leaned her elbows on the railing looking down into the river rushing past them below. She had a permanent smile plastered on her face as she watched the waters. To her this was all some elaborate show. To Yatoa it was the most important thing she had ever been a part of. Dal's life rested in her hands. She couldn't afford mistakes.

Yatoa understood the assignment her mentor had given her, but that didn't make it any less stressful. She was still not sure she agreed with her mentor entirely, but she couldn't help but feel drawn in by her charisma like a bee to a sweet flower.

Though for now she didn't have to worry about any of that. It didn't change much. She just had to try her best, as always.

After they had left the Gob'Alondis residence the day prior, they got a late lunch in the Goblin District. Then Yatoa set to formulating a case plan. She didn't have all the information she needed, but the court sent her interrogation transcripts and investigative reports to work from. She had spent most of the evening combing over them on her twin sized bed.

She read until her eyes strained and notated until her hands ached, but she was finally making some good progress on building her case. Only problem was that she was unsure if the way she learned to formulate a case would be effective in Goblin Court. The way Goblin's conducted trials was so alien compared to the trials back home.

There are seven "stages" in a trial. The jury decided a winner and loser at the end of each stage. The winner of a stage earns a verdict. To earn an acquittal a lawyer must win at least four of the seven verdicts after declaring not guilty. The worst part was that each stage was different, and some were so abstract it was hard to prepare for them at all. There was stage six for instance, "the test". In that stage it was possible for Yatoa to lose a limb. Despite the uncertainty, the stages did allow for her to focus on her strengths and pick her battles.

If they plead not guilty, then she could earn the acquittal her mentor wanted. Yet the dilemma persisted. If she plead not guilty and won only three verdicts, then Dal would get the full sentence – death by marble crushing. Yet if she plead guilty, then each verdict she won would lighten Dal's sentence, and in that scenario, it would only take two verdicts to spare his life. Though even if she won all seven Dal would at least face a year in prison for this offence. Much better than dying, but winning all seven verdicts was a pipe dream.

Yatoa glanced at her mentor's wistful face and shuddered as her stress built up inside her.

If Yatoa was being honest with herself, the main reason she didn't want to plead not guilty was because she lacked confidence. As much as she had prepared for her first day in court, she didn't actually know if she'd be a capable lawyer until she actually litigated. She felt this exercise was irresponsible and unfair to Dal. And yet, her master insisted with her tests and ideals. Yatoa had always pegged Arlicia as a realist, though now she was not so certain.

"Dal must have finished his breakfast by now," Yatoa said. They pulled away from the railing and strode back toward the jail behind them. The wet smell of the river filled her nostrils and air caressed the inside of her cape as Yatoa ascended the wide staircase.

"This should be interesting," Arlicia said. That smile was still stuck to her face, and Yatoa thought of letting her know so she could wipe it off.

They met the receptionist Freeda inside. Freeda led them into the same meeting room with the human-sized furniture, and once again Arlicia asked for juice. This time it was three glasses of orange. They waited for a while. Yatoa in her chair with her chin on her fist; Arlicia on the edge of the table fiddling with her cane. Today was a quiet day. Arlicia seemed content to let her contemplate everything in silence. At the very least her mentor was considerate enough to let Yatoa think.

First came the juice, then the client. Dal looked the same as the last time Yatoa saw him. Dejected. It was as if the reaper had already harvested his soul and he was just patiently waiting to lose his body as well.

Dal climbed into his seat, took a sip of orange juice and sighed. Yatoa began, not wanting to waste anymore time. "I spoke with your wife yesterday." Dal perked up. His big brown eyes wide.

"You did? How's she holdin' up? Is she worried about me?" The eagerness to his voice was that of a man starved.

"Has she not visited you? She said she would yesterday."

Dal shook his head. "I was alone all day yesterday. Never got a visit," Dal said.

"Could it be that she didn't want to leave Darlia home alone?" Yatoa put forward. After Darlia tried getting out of bed perhaps Garna had thought better of it.

Dal sighed, resuming his forlorn expression. His ears drooped and his fanged mouth followed suit. "Huh. So, you know about my daughter then." They sat in silence. Yatoa took a long sip of her orange juice. It was quality, and the tang on her tongue was pleasant. Under the tutelage of Arlicia, Yatoa had sampled many juices and developed a refined taste for orange juice. At least they didn't skimp out at the jail.

"Wait!" Dal cried out. "Darlia is still sick? Garna should have gotten the money to heal her by now. Did somethin' go wrong? Did my wife tell you anythin'?"

"The crew cut your family out, Dal. Your wife has received no money, and she hasn't connected with Faz." Dal's eyes widened in alarm at the mention of his accomplice. "Don't worry she only told me Faz's name. She did so because I suspect she has the same suspicions I do. For whatever reason I think Faz sabotaged the heist to make sure you got caught then cut your family out."

Dal shook his head vigorously. "No, that can't be right. Faz is my oldest friend. We've been theivin' off folks since we were goblets. I won't believe it til' I get evidence. That's how you lawyers work right? Evidence?"

"I feel that the evidence I have given you is fairly strong, Dal. The fact is Garna has not received your cut. And before you bring up that maybe the jewelry hasn't sold yet, Faz purchased a new home in the Goblin District. She definitely got her hands on that money, and now your wife has nothing and she can't seem to get into contact with her."

Dal leaned forward and held Yatoa's eyes with his own.

"She could have an important reason not to. I won't believe any of my crew betrayed me without evidence, and I don't give consent to rat on any of my crewmembers. Understand?" Dal's voice was threatening in a way Yatoa had not expected to hear from a Goblin, and his sharp fangs added to the effect.

She nodded. "I give you my word Dal. But I need to ask you a favor."

"And what's that?"

"Do you know of any way I can track down Faz?" Yatoa asked hesitantly. "You said you two are long time friends, right? I want to talk to her and find out why she hasn't given your wife your cut of the money yet. The trial aside, your daughter needs that money. Please let me get to the bottom of this, for your daughter's sake and yours."

Dal stared into her eyes; his lips drawn tight. "Fine. I have no idea where she moved to, but I know a guy who might. On 487 Pal Avenue in the Goblin District there's a restaurant called Geits' Goblona. Ask for a table that's 'too close to the canopy with a view grand enough to impress my mother,' and you'll get a meetin' with one of the best informants in the city. He should be able to help you out."

Yatoa nodded both in thanks and respect, then turned to Arlicia. "I know where we're eating tonight."

"It's a good pick," Arlicia said nonchalantly. "I've been craving Goblona since we arrived."

Yatoa enjoyed traversing the streets of the Goblin District. The massive trees shading her protectively from the sun were comforting. She mused to herself that had she not been so busy with work she may have had a nice vacation in Gobroa.

She did get to experience one part of the vacation though: the walking. She did as much walking as a tourist, only without all the sightseeing. They wended their way through hilly streets for several hours and stopped for directions twice, before finding the place.

Geits' Goblona was a grand establishment. The restaurant shot up six stories into the thick tree it called home, and it served patrons on every floor. From the street Yatoa could see that they had cut away a chunk of the tree, allowing for a portion of the sixth floor to act as a balcony. It was an awe-inspiring structure. Both more aesthetically pleasing and impressive than any building in the High Gob District.

"Shall we?" Arlicia said, holding up her arm for Yatoa.

"If we must," Yatoa said, taking it with reluctance. They stepped up to the front of the restaurant where there were two lines of Goblins. The much shorter line exclusively consisted of couples looking for seats on the sixth floor where one would find a more expensive menu.

When they reached the front of the line a Goblin held out a hand to them. He had green skin and he wore a black suit that bulged with his muscles. If his head at least reached her waist Yatoa might have found him intimidating.

"You two a couple?" the Goblin bouncer asked.

"Just married," Arlicia lied. "We've come to Gobroa on our honeymoon." The bouncer eyed them for a moment. Yatoa was a practiced actor, so she had no trouble giving her mentor a loving smile, though inside she wanted to wring Arlicia's neck. Yatoa was attracted to women, but she would never view her mentor that way, and even though this was all an act it still made her skin crawl.

"Alright, go speak with the hostess about seating. Enjoy your meal and the rest of your honeymoon you two," he said, waving them inside.

"Don't worry we will!" Yatoa said in a bubbly voice she never used. Once inside Yatoa whispered in Arlicia's ear, "We didn't have to do this."

"Ah yes but then we'd be stuck waiting in the other line for over an hour, wouldn't we? And you, my dear, are on a tight schedule." As if Yatoa needed the reminder.

The interior was extravagant. It embraced its natural structure with moss coated bark walls and vines draped over the dining halls. Yet there were touches of civilization abound from soft green carpets to silk bundles of cloth cascading between the tables. Every piece of cloth was carefully arranged, creating a multi-colored bouquet. The pure white table cloths hanging limply over the edge of every circular table gave the restaurant a classy feel.

The host, a short green Goblin woman with small white flowers laced through her brown hair, greeted them with a smile. "Hello and welcome to Geits'. Do you have any seating preferences?"

Yatoa spared a glance for Arlicia and said, "I'd like a table that's too close to the canopy with a view grand enough to impress my mother." The hostess' warm smile didn't falter in the slightest.

"Right this way," she said, leading them to a grand spiral staircase at the back of the room. The green carpet with gold trim that protected the steps felt lush as Yatoa stepped onto it. The softness of the steps eased the effort of the long climb, if only a little. They passed torchlit eaves and occasional windows that let them check their progress. It took only a few minutes to ascend the staircase, and by the time they did Yatoa was about ready to collapse. Her muscles protested that she had done enough walking for one life.

Arlicia looked similarly fatigued, though the hostess seemed unfazed as she glided out onto the sixth-floor balcony. They stepped out into the evening air once more, much closer to the canopy now, and Yatoa could actually see detail on each individual leaf. One branch hung close enough over the balcony that if Yatoa jumped she could actually grab one.

The hostess led them to a small circular table surrounded by three chairs right up against the balcony's railing. They took their seats and before leaving the hostess assured them a server would be with them soon. Then they waited on the comfy chairs. Yatoa felt her leg muscles relax as she stared out over the railing at the forest city. Only the Goblin District was a forest, but it was the largest district, and she could not see the end of it from where she sat. All the massive trees obscured her vision so much she could only see a few trees deep.

It was dark enough now that the windows in the opposing trees glowed warmly with candle light. It was a peaceful sight. Looking at all the windows climbing up each tree she guessed each tree could house one-hundred apartments, maybe more. Yatoa felt unease like physical creature of creep its way over the railing, clutching at her boots onto her boots. In a city this big, what hope did she have of finding one person in only two days?

Yatoa's worries retreated when a Goblin stepped up to their human sized table. He carried a small step ladder with him and used it to step up to eye level with them.

"Good evening, ladies. Would you like a menu or are you only here for our renowned goblona? I assure you it's the best you can find anywhere." His voice was deep for a Goblin and it had a smoothness to it that was quite pleasing to the ear.

"We'll be having the Goblona thank you," Arlicia confirmed. The waiter nodded.

"Wine?"

"Do you have Fae Cabernet illuminion?" Arlicia said.

The waiter nodded. "We have a beautiful bottle from the year 4401."

"That'll do."

"Very well. I shall bring goblona and wine for three. Enjoy your time here." With a bow he stepped down and carted his step ladder away. So, the third chair wasn't just for show. Confirmation came when an old Goblin man strode up to their table with a waiter at his heels. The waiter laid down steps for the man and he stepped up into the human sized seat across from Yatoa. With a wave of his hand the waiter retreated.

The old man had longer ears than most Goblins and gravity dragged them down into a perpetual droop. A gold hoop dangled from his right ear and it shook as he met Yatoa's eyes. Wrinkles edged his eyes and across his face that spoke of an age that did not match the youthful vigor in his gaze.

"To what do I owe the pleasure of meeting the apprentice of the great Arlicia Sa'Krieglund?" the Goblin man asked in a dignified voice.

"I'm here for goblona and good conversation," Yatoa replied. "I've heard this establishment keeps both in fresh supply."

The man smiled. "I'm Geits. Owner and head chef of this establishment. I've heard much about you. Particularly about how you've elected to take on an obviously guilty client with no hope. Pro bono, might I add."

Yatoa bristled at that. "There's hope, Geits. Sometimes a good defense can go a long way."

Geits shrugged. "And sometimes one person isn't enough to eat a plate of Goblona meant for three. No matter how much of a dent they make, Goblona will still remain." As if on cue a trio of waiters brought three plates of steaming Goblona to the table. Yatoa eyed hers with a beastly hunger. Goblona was a simple dish. Easy to learn, hard to master, and yet harder to perfect. And perfect was the only word she could use to describe the sight in front of her. Dozens of sauteed spicy gremlin peppers bathed in an equally spicy, melted cheese sauce, topped with green onions and basil. It came with a small side plate that held half a lime for her to squeeze over the dish.

"Luckily, I only serve plates with enough Goblona for one person. Please, try some." Yatoa did not need the prompt.

She greedily, yet civilly, drenched her food in lime and dug in. Lime and pepper juice kicked her tongue, salty spicy cheese punched it before finally incinerating the remains. It was wonderful.

With tears in her eyes she said, "I've learned recently that nothing is ever quite as simple as it seems." She coughed from the spices and held up a hand imploring Geits to wait a moment. "I need more information if I want to make more than a dent on this particular dish."

"How's the food?" Geits asked, ignoring her comments.

"It is sublime," Arlicia said. "One of the finest things I've ever eaten, and I've eaten a great many things from a greater number of places." Yatoa emphatically expressed her agreement. It was one of the best things she'd ever eaten.

"That is high praise Ms. Sa'Krieglund. Thank you for your kind words." He turned back to Yatoa. His eyes were measuring instruments. "Now that I've shared my dish with you, you must share something in turn with me."

"Like what?"

"Something about you that others don't know. Maybe something you don't want others to know, or something you don't bother sharing." Yatoa figured what he was getting at. It was rude to directly ask someone if they had magical abilities.

"I'm a Three Star," Yatoa confessed.

Geits leaned back in his chair and smiled. "Well now, not quite what I expected. But "illusionist" seems to be an awfully useful credential for your current profession."

"I would never use illusions to tamper with a trial, if that's what you're insinuating." She didn't like talking about this. "Besides they have detectors. Even if I wanted to, I could never get away with it."

"True," Geits conceded. "Yet illusionist training involves more than magic," Geits said with a grin. Guilt gnawed at her. Deep down she knew she was a fraud playing at lawyer. Often, she had wondered if she was actually capable or just a skilled actor. "Either way, you don't need to use your powers dishonestly during a trial for them to give you an advantage."

"What do you mean?"

Geits shoveled some peppers into his mouth and chewed for a long moment. He wiped his mouth on his napkin. "Well, I'll leave you to figure that out for yourself. I'm sure you can think of something."

"I won't," She promised. She had not created an illusion in a long time. She didn't know if she still had the knack for it.

Geits continued eating his Goblona as if it was of no consequence to him. Yatoa did the same. Though it was hard to stay bitter when there was so much spice in your mouth. "So, why did you come here, Ms. Yatoa?"

"It's Ms. Hu'Dectalaciumina," she corrected him in annoyance. Usually she let that slide, but she wasn't feeling so charitable at the moment.

"Ah my apologies Ms. Hu'Dectalaciumina." His effortless pronunciation was somehow even more frustrating.

"I want to send a message to someone by tomorrow night, but I don't know where to find them. I know their name, that they reside in the Goblin District, that they're a friend of Dal Gob'Alondis, but not much else. Can you help me?"

Geits wiped his mouth again. He gestured out to the forest city sprawled before them. It was full night now and bright specks of light from a myriad of windows dotted the thick tree trunks. "There is nothing in this forest that can hide from me Ms. Hu'Dectalaciumina. Of that I assure you. I am confident I can do it. To whom am I sending this message?"

Yatoa licked her lips. She would feel bad telling anyone the name of one of Dal's crew members, but he had practically given her consent. It was also likely that if his network of information was as expansive as it seemed, then he already knew all the members of Dal's crew. "Her name is Faz Gob'Venicker."

"And what would you like this message to say?" he asked, pulling out a small pocketbook and pen.

Yatoa figured he already knew Faz committed the burglary with Dal, but she couldn't be sure. Either way she didn't think Geits was the type to snitch to the authorities. "Give her a written missive that states 'I know you robbed Gob'Franat. If you don't want me to alert the authorities, then meet me and Hreila's Tavern alone at nineteen-hundred hours on the night of the ninth. I will be wearing white." It was the seventh now so setting the meeting for the ninth would allow for some time to get the missive to Faz. The only problem was that the trial started at ten-o'clock on the morning of the tenth. It was cutting it a little close.

Yatoa glanced at Arlicia. It was her fault she was so pressed down to the wire. She barely had any time to prepare.

"I will take care of it." Geits snapped his pocket book closed and stuffed it in his jacket pocket, then waved forward a waiter with their bottle of wine. The waiter had not dared approach the table until the conversation finished. "Now let's enjoy what remains of our evening with some of this fine wine." He eyed the label. "Good pick."

5

The Illusionist

That night Yatoa returned to the hotel feeling some accomplishment. Most of the information on the case was at her disposal, and if things went according to plan a big mystery would clear up. Who was the lookout?

She sat on her bed in her nightgown cross-legged going over her notes and her case plan. All the pieces of the puzzle were fitting together, and she was confident that she'd have a solid case plan ready. Yet… that wasn't enough. She still hadn't decided if she was going to go through with declaring not guilty. If she wanted to pass Arlicia's test and advance in her apprenticeship, then she had to. If she succeeded, then Dal could walk free.

Yet was her apprenticeship worth the risk of Dal's life? With a good case plan, she could at least spare him from death if not maintain his freedom. Her mind had been running in circles on the topic all day. With a sigh she collapsed backward into the soft feather-down mattress.

A headache tormented her. She shut her eyes to the dim wooden room and tried to imagine herself in a place away from Arlicia's watchful gaze.

"How come you never create illusions?" Arlicia asked, breaking Yatoa's mental illusion. "I've always wondered. Usually, most people don't drop out of a Starred University to pursue another career where they don't ever use their magic."

Yatoa left her eyes closed against reality. "I always wanted to be a lawyer. I never wanted to be an illusionist," she said. To her it was simple. She didn't want to talk about any of it. She was a lawyer now and she had left all that behind.

"Well, you are an illusionist whether you like it or not. You can always change your career path, but you can't change who you are, Toa."

Yatoa eased herself onto her side. The fresh sheets felt nice and soft on her cheek. "Think of it this way," she said with her eyes still closed. "I'm retired. I don't have to create illusions anymore. I just retired a little sooner than everyone else. Being a Three Star does not change who I am. Whether I had these powers or not I'd still be here defending Dal. There's no point talking about this."

"I can't stop thinking about what Geits said at dinner. He insinuated he had an idea for how you could use illusions to your advantage in the trial. The idea intrigues me. I've never come across a Starred lawyer before you, and now I'm starting to wonder at what possibilities this opens up."

"It's a waste of time."

"Why are you so against it?" Arlicia asked directly.

Yatoa remained silent with her eyes closed. Candlelight seeped through her eyelids making it hard to completely shut out the room, but she managed. At the Three Star Academy she had spent hundreds of hours training to reject reality and pull herself into imaginary worlds of her choosing. A huge part of being an illusionist was believing in your own illusions.

Everyone who wasn't Starred envied those who were. Many people would dream of magic, and despite the world being full of it few understood what it was like. It was unremarkable. Magic was just something Yatoa could do that others couldn't, sort of like how some people could sculpt or bake. Yatoa could do neither of those things.

Of the four "Stars", or types of mages in simpler terms, that one could be, Three Star had to be the least exciting. Illusions didn't have a daily use case, unlike the magical healing of One Stars or the enhanced physical abilities of Two Stars. Her abilities paled in comparison to the rare, reality bending powers of Four Stars of which only two had ever appeared. Three Stars in contrast were the most common, making her another penny among the many gobbings that filled the victim's bank vault.

However, her mind was open to Arlicia's question. Why was she so against it? The answer took Yatoa somewhere she didn't want to go; home. Yatoa envisioned the room. Her childhood home was only two rooms, and this room was the bigger of the two. She was making ceiling charms out of twine and blue stones she picked out from the beach, while Soloa watched over her shoulder.

Soloa was as Yatoa remembered her. A thin girl, only eight-years-old with curious dark brown eyes. Her hair was straighter than Yatoa's and her skin was slightly darker, both indications that Soloa took more from their mother.

Though one thing stood out. Soloa's left arm was abnormally stiff and had a glossy cast to it. Back then their parents assured them both that Soloa would get healed soon and there was nothing to worry about. So, neither of them worried.

In fact, in the memory they were jovial. Yatoa was showing Soloa how to make the charms, carefully explaining each step and even saying, "when you're healed, I'll walk you through it." To which Soloa replied with an eager nod.

When you're healed… those words stung Yatoa now. She savored every last glimpse of her baby sister in this memory. She would of course never get treatment.

That thought brought her into another time. Yatoa stood in the smaller of the two rooms.

The room had only two beds – one for their parents and one for them. She was staring down at a glass replica of her sister sound asleep in her sheets. Vitrified.

The physical vitrification of her sister mirrored the emotional vitrification within herself.

Her mother clung to the small glass hand and sobbed soundlessly on the floor. Her eyes staring unbelieving through the tears. Yatoa felt nauseous, both in the memory and in the present. This wasn't how it should have happened. There was a healer in town. The healer should have healed her sister and she was going to show her how to make more ceiling charms.

The healer had agreed to do it for free, but on the appointed day a well-known local baker died in the healer's home. The town accused him of murder and took him into custody. In the legal system of Yatoa's home island it was possible to conduct a trial in which the defendant had no attorney representing them. Since the One Star Doctor had been a foreigner the town's only public defender refused to represent him. It was an injustice.

If that doctor had gotten a good defense, then he could have won an acquittal and healed her sister. Instead, he died. Yatoa had thought to herself many times since the day of Soloa's death that it wouldn't have mattered if the man had committed murder or not. If she were the one defending him in court that day, she would have done anything to win a not guilty verdict.

She opened her eyes. Her vision was off-kilter, rotated ninety degrees. Arlicia's bed looked like it was resting on the wall, though Yatoa quickly realized she was lying on her side. Detaching oneself from reality often led to spatial confusion.

Arlicia sat on the edge of her bed staring at Yatoa's face. This case was like the one back then. The moment she saw Darlia, Yatoa's memories dragged her back to those now ancient days. If she could free Dal then the little Goblin girl would stand a better chance. Her mother had no income to speak of, so she needed her father. It was a small hope, but wasn't it worth a shot? Yatoa had finally put two and two together. She had been looking at this trial like it only affected Dal, but Darlia's life rode on this verdict too.

When you defend someone in court you defend their entire life, from their loved ones, to their business, to their dreams.

Dal didn't have the money to heal Darlia, but if he was free then he would at least have the chance to get it.

Cartaneal Gob'Franat may deserve justice for the crime committed against him, but Darlia deserved a chance at life more.

"Yatoa… I'm sorry. I didn't think pressing you would make you cry," Arlicia said. Yatoa started then felt at her face with the back of her hand. It was wet. She shot up straight.

"It's fine. Really," she insisted. "I've made a decision."

Arlicia raised an eyebrow. "And that is?"

"I'm going to declare not guilty at the start of the trial, and I am going to win."

Arlicia grinned then hopped over onto Yatoa's bed, knocking off some of her notes and embracing her in a hug. "Good! Good!" Arlicia shouted in her ear. Reluctantly Yatoa returned the embrace. She hadn't expected such a forceful response, yet she took comfort in the warmth of another.

Abruptly Arlicia pulled away. "Toa. Over the past year you've lamented to me numerous times about your peers ascending to masterhood, while you still wore an apprentice uniform. You always talk about how they must think of you. That you are so far behind them, having never conducted a real trial." Yatoa had said such things on more than one occasion. Those thoughts plagued her every single day.

"You compare yourself to others constantly. To your peers. To me. Over the past few days, I have observed you closely as you have conducted your work and I have seen two things in you. The first is anxiety. You doubt your competence. You think because you haven't defended anyone in court, let alone Goblin court, that you can't do it. You're scared because I am not offering you my assistance when I should. And I should. If you struggle gravely in court to the point of incompetence I will step in and take over, that I promise you. I am not that irresponsible."

It felt good to have Arlicia understand how she felt, and even better to know that she had a safety net should she fall. Though now that she knew it was there, she felt more determined not to fall.

"However, it won't come to that, because the second thing I've seen in you is competence. Yatoa this may be your first trial, but you've been studying under me for two years. That is much longer than any other apprenticeship as you well know. I did that intentionally so that when you took on your first trial, you would not only be ready but also good enough to make waves. I want to paint you to the public as a successful, up and coming attorney. Not just the apprentice of a genius. Imagine the stories it would spark. An apprentice attorney wins her first case without the help of her mentor. A hopeless, indefensible case where she declared not guilty despite the law catching her client red-handed."

Yatoa couldn't help grin Arlicia's enthusiasm. Those dark eyes twinkling in her face were too charismatic. "But do I need to make a big debut?" Yatoa asked, giving in to her skeptical side. "This trial isn't about me. It's about the Gob'Alondis family's livelihood. I don't care if I am respected for it, I just want to help them."

Arlicia placed a hand on Yatoa's shoulder. "And that is admirable of you, Toa, but think of the alternative. I am Arlicia Sa'Krieglund the God Lawyer. If I helped you, then no one would attribute this victory to you. You'd be forever stuck in my shadow. That's the problem with training under a good mentor, Toa. You should've have picked an incompetent one!" Arlicia said with a chuckle.

"Maybe I should have," Yatoa said. She finally let a relaxed smile ease onto her lips.

"No really, I'm not joking. It's what I did back in the day. Intentionally. Sometimes having an example of what not to do can be as helpful as the alternative. And besides, if you're good enough you don't need a good mentor. This whole apprentice-ship phase is just a formality. Nevertheless, you came to me Yatoa, and so I promised I'd do right by you, because innate talent like yours is difficult to come by these days."

Yatoa felt heat rise into her cheeks. "You really think so?" she asked sheepishly.

"I know so," Arlicia replied.

Yatoa spent most of the rest of the evening with her mentor talking about things that had nothing to do with law or courts for once. Laughing and drinking orange juice with Arlicia was the most real moment of the trip, and she figured she would never forget this night. Arlicia made her feel secure in her moments of greatest insecurity. Yatoa distantly wondered if this was what it was like to have a mother who actually cared for you.

After a lull in the conversation Yatoa said, "My sister Soloa was a talented illusionist. She had a knack for it I didn't pos-sess. While we were both illusionists like our mother, my par-ents only saved up money for her to attend the Three Star Academy in Faestar Great Tree."

Yatoa remembered how she had felt at the time when their parents had told them they were choosing to invest in the life of her younger sister over her. It was the first time she had ever felt cheated. Though she didn't harbor any grudge against Soloa, quite the contrary. Her parents on the other hand...

Oh, how disappointed they had been when the shatter left them with only Yatoa.

Yatoa's mother had always loved Soloa more right from the day she had her. She never said it explicitly, but she didn't have to. At first it was understandable since Soloa was just a baby and thus needed more attention. Yet as the years passed and Soloa proved to be more and more like their mother she became the golden child. If Soloa was an angel in their mother's eyes, then Yatoa was a demon. If Soloa knocked over a vase their mother would fret over her, yet if Yatoa did the same thing it would only lead to screaming or no dinner as punishment.

It was frustrating at the time, yet it was still manageable, especially since Yatoa would often be out playing with other kids in the town or looking for crabs on the beach. Yatoa often avoided her home.

However, things took a sharp turn for the worse after Soloa's death. Her mother, who had never harmed her before, turned from verbal to physical punishments. She could barely speak to Yatoa most days, and she almost never looked her in the eye. Every time she was home it felt like broken glass coated the floor and Yatoa was barefoot. There was no right step to take. Only pain.

One of Yatoa's most vivid memories was one of her mid-teen years, shortly before she left. She had been out with some friends goofing off at the beach. Yatoa felt happy for the first time in years, but then she walked into the main room of the house.

She met her mother's gaze. Her mother was standing in their makeshift kitchen holding a knife in her hand. They just stared at each other silently from across the room and the only emotion Yatoa could read in her mother's eyes was resentment. Although her mother did nothing more with the knife that day than hold it still at her side, Yatoa still remembered the visceral fear that her own mother might kill her.

After that day Yatoa was anxious beyond repair. She treated her mother like a dangerous predator by giving her an unreasonably wide berth for the small space. She noticed the same death glare more than once.

"My sister died," Yatoa said after a long pause. "Then my parents reluctantly chose to send me to the Three Star Academy, but I hated it. It felt like they were trying to somehow transform me into Soloa. Being there made me feel sick. Like I was stealing Soloa's future somehow. So, I left and swore off illusions. I took what remained of the tuition money my parents had saved up and entered the legal academy in the capital."

Arlicia was silent for a long time. "Darlia could die," she pointed out perceptively.

"Yes," Yatoa allowed.

"Would you do anything to save her?"

"Yes."

"If you can augment your case with illusions then you should," Arlicia said finally.

"I… don't know," Yatoa said, as she sat up in her bed and crossed her arms. She furrowed her brow. "I associate it with too many painful memories and I haven't produced an illusion in years now."

Arlicia rested as hand on Yatoa's shoulder, her grip firm and reassuring.

"Your sister was a Three Star, sure. But so were you. Your magic isn't something you took from her. It has always been yours. You have the ability to re-contextualize your magic into something wholly your own. Ground your magic in your new life and your future, not your past. I think that there are a few ways you could put it to good use, both in this legal system and others."

Yatoa listened intently. Arlicia's dark eyes and serious expression were so earnest that Yatoa couldn't help but feel them pulling on her emotions.

Yatoa stood. She looked around the small room, taking in every detail from the red curtains that fell nearly to the floor, to the leather straps on the hefty clothing trunks at the end of each bed. With a deep breath she lifted up her right middle and index fingers.

Energy coursed through her chest and into her arm before blossoming into wiry green lines of light that coalesced into flowers around her fingers. Then she got to work, sweeping her fingers through the air as if she were using them to draw. The green floral pattern left faint after images in the air as she molded the light of the room like clay.

In moments an image hung in the air of Darlia sitting in Dal's lap as he read a book to her. It wasn't perfect. There was some shimmering around the edges of the illusion and some of the lines wobbled, though it was more than good enough for her purposes. The more fake it looked the better. She didn't want to trick anyone.

It had been several years since she had created an illusion, and there was something freeing about using it to create something tied to this case. It helped divorce the act from her past life at the academy. However, Yatoa still felt a deep unease staring at the glowing image. Yatoa didn't want to be her sister, yet at the same time she felt a stab of guilt at memories of leaving her friend Eliafa all alone in Faestar, so that she could pursue a legal career. Even if they did stay in touch through the occasional letter.

"I can use it to show the jury what kind of man Dal is, as well as augment my storytelling," Yatoa said. "I'm not sure if this is what Geits had in mind, though the idea has crossed my mind before. I'm not sure what other applications it has but I may be able to think of something."

Arlicia stood grinning like a child. She reached her hand into the illusion and the image scattered away from her like grains of sand, leaving a cloud of color in her wake. "This'll have to do."

6

Trial Fixing

So old Geits was helpful, eh?" Dal mused. They sat in that same old meeting room again, sipping high quality orange juice. "That's good and all, but how are *you* feelin', if you don't mind me askin', Yatoa? How's the case comin' along?" The small red Goblin man laced his fingers together and dipped them in her direction as he said this.

Yatoa shrugged. "It's coming along well Dal. I think my case is strong, though I won't lie to you. We can't know how things will go until we're in court. I know nothing about the prosecutor. They could be much more experienced, or perhaps they're an apprentice like me. There's a lot that could happen in this trial and I want you to be mentally prepared."

Dal nodded grimly in acknowledgement like a headsman given the order to swing. His brown eyes fell into his glass. He swiveled the juice around. Yatoa could tell that Dal was going through a lot, with both the trial and his daughter Darlia. It took a strong Goblin to stay as upbeat and hopeful in conversations as he was, and the more Yatoa learned of him the more her respect for him grew. Dal was a good man all the way down to his tiny bones.

"It'll be alright. We'll get you out of here and then we can make sure Darlia gets the help she needs," Yatoa said in what she thought was a soothing voice.

Dal sighed. "Yatoa I'll be fine. Though... to tell you the honest truth..." He ran a hand through his greasy hair and squeezed his eyes shut. Yatoa could sense a creature inside Dal clawing at his esophagus in a desperate attempt to keep him silent.

"Yes?" she prompted.

"I already resigned myself to my daughter's death a long time ago," he whispered. "The little goblet is tough, but the shatter don't care how tough you are. I never take anything for granted. I always expect the worst and hope for the best, tryin' each day to make my life a little better." He looked up at Arlicia, then over to Yatoa meeting her eyes. His eyes quivered, holding back tears.

"It's hard, Yatoa. When you've spent your whole damn life livin' in the worst dirt imaginable, how could you possibly hope to expect the best? I try anyway, but I'm I' tired. And with this trial I'm worried that this time... this time things will get worse than they ever have and that'll be that." A tear escaped, sliding free down his cheek. "I'm always dealt a rough hand, and I've never folded before, but lemme tell you I've never been so close to foldin'. I'm not sure I can bluff my way through this one."

The injustice made her nauseous. She could not let this stand. Darlia's future was too important to the both of them. "You don't need to play this time," Yatoa said in a soft voice.

"That's why you have me. I'll hope for you and I'll win. Let's play this one last hand together… and go all in."

Dal looked to her in puzzlement for a moment, then understanding blossomed across his face. "You're gonna plead not guilty on my behalf?"

"Not without your consent I'm not," Yatoa said to him, shooting her mentor a disparaging glance. The way Arlicia had disregarded Dal's input in such a cavalier manner was concerning. In the past, Arlicia had always been considerate of such things…

Now that Yatoa thought about it there was a potential explanation. Perhaps her mentor had been testing her. Perhaps she'd been slighting Yatoa's client to entice Yatoa to feel protective over him. At least that's what Yatoa chose to believe. It was in line with the schemes Arlicia pulled in the past, and her mentor would never go back on her own teachings without reason.

With a shake she brought her attention back to the matter at hand. "Listen Dal, more than just your life is at stake. Darlia's is too. You can't do anything to save your daughter if you're in prison. If we win a not guilty verdict we may be able to earn restitution on Darlia's behalf to save her. Such a thing is possible in Goblin law." Yatoa had come to that little revelation in the moment, strengthening her conviction. "We can't fold. We need to win it all while we still have enough chips to make big plays. We have to go all in because if we don't, you'll never have a chance to save Darlia."

"You're right," Dal said, wiping his tears away. He stood tall on his seat. "You're right damn it! The world may not care if I die, but I'll rip the world's heart out if it thinks it can cut my daughter's life short!" His shouts bouncing off the walls of the small chamber.

Yatoa stood. With Dal standing on his chair they stood at eye-level with one another. She held her hand out to him. "Let's play one more round."

Dal gave her a fanged grin and clasped her hand in his smaller one. "We won't be the ones to fold this time," he said.

Yatoa left the jail feeling accomplished and more confident than ever. Whatever happened in the trial she at least had built up the nerve to face it with her head held high.

The morning sun greeted her and its firm presence promised an especially hot day. She was already pulling at her collar to loosen it. With a sigh she descended the front steps of the jail with her mentor in tow.

When they reached the bottom of the steps a horse drawn carriage pulled up in front of them, cutting their strides short. The carriage was stark black with a gold seal of a dragon embroidered on it. The side-door swung wide open and a bald human man in a black suit greeted them with a tight nod from inside the dark carriage. Arlicia took a step back in surprise and brandished her thin cane as a weapon.

The man hopped out of the carriage and stood to his full height. He had over a foot on the both of them. His suit bulged with his muscles that strained the seams to their limits. Whoever had tailored it had not put in much care to his measurements. Regardless, he didn't look like the type of man who should be wearing suits; instead he was the kind of man you'd find in ale drenched clothes at the center of a tavern brawl.

"Cartaneal Gob'Franat is inside. He'd like to have a word with you Ms. Sa'Krieglund," the man said in a gruff voice.

Yatoa deferred to her mentor. Arlicia narrowed her eyes, then met Yatoa's and nodded. Yatoa spared a cautious glance for the big man then climbed into the carriage box. It was more spacious inside than expected.

Though the windows let in little light it was enough to see the Goblin seated on the bench inside. He had green skin and wore a fine black velvet suit with a matching top hat rested on his head. He fiddled with a jewel tipped cane as he watched Yatoa seat herself across from him.

Arlicia clambered in next, and the muscled man closed the door behind her. He stayed outside. Gob'Franat did not want him a party to the conversation.

"He's not the best with words," the man who could only be Cartaneal began. "Human bodyguards are some of the most effective around here. You lot don't seem to have much trouble overpowering Goblins, even if your kind isn't always as well-educated as ours." Yatoa opened her mouth to retort, but Arlicia beat her top the punch.

"It's been… what? Three years? To what do I owe the pleasure, Gob'Franat?" Arlicia said, unbothered by his comment.

The carriage rumbled as the driver urged the horses on, and Yatoa felt a spike of alarm. The way the carriage jumbled over the cobblestones made Yatoa feel as though an earthquake had struck Gobroa.

"Where are you taking us?" Yatoa demanded. Cartaneal ignored her. He didn't even spare her a glance.

"I'll get right down to business, Sa'Krieglund," he said. His accent was posh in the most annoying way. Yatoa had never heard a Goblin speak this way before, even in the High Gob District. "How much do you want?"

"How much what? Juice?" Arlicia said feigning ignorance.

Cartaneal chuckled. "If it's juice you want, then I have a fine bottle of apple resting under your seat."

Arlicia's amused smile expanded into a mischievous grin. "I'll pass, thanks."

Cartaneal shrugged. "You know I'm not talking about juice. How much money do you want to throw the trial of that wastrel?" Alarmed Yatoa gripped the edge of her seat. Her heart raced. He wanted to *bribe* them? Yatoa looked back at Arlicia and for an instant she was afraid Arlicia was going to accept the offer.

"You must be mistaken. I will not be representing Dal Gob'Alondis in court." Cartaneal's eyebrows rose at that.

"My sources are rarely mistaken," he insisted.

"This time they are I'm afraid. You see, it is my apprentice here that will be representing Gob'Alondis, not I."

Cartaneal laughed at this and Yatoa fought the urge to growl like a slighted dog.

"What is the difference?" he asked. "She may be your apprentice, but you'll be assisting her all the same."

Arlicia shook her head. "I'll be doing nothing of the sort. Yatoa will defend Gob'Alondis without my assistance." For a moment the only sounds were that of the carriage jumbling down the street. Finally, Cartaneal turned to Yatoa.

"So. It's you who I should be making my offer to, is it?" Cartaneal said. His body language screamed smug.

"I will never throw a trial, but if you want to give me the money anyway, then I won't complain," Yatoa said with bite. His smile drooped.

"You're only an apprentice. No reputation. No accomplishments. I suppose I don't need to bribe you anyway. I'm sure you'll do a well enough job throwing this trial without my encouragement."

"You're stupid," Yatoa said. Throwing out the basest of insults. It felt good not to think up some clever argument for once. She found that she hated this man. She hated him before she ever met him. Dal had primed her well. This man stood between Darlia and a happy future with her family. "If you were as confident as you pretend to be you wouldn't bribe us."

Cartaneal smacked the carriage door hard with his cane. Yatoa jumped and the carriage pulled to an abrupt stop. "Watch your tongue, wench!" His voice was shrill and as rough as a cheese grater. "You presume too much. I came here to offer the God Lawyer a bribe, not a milkmaid like you. You're the overconfident one if you think you can best the great Breichmar Gob'Stallau in court!"

"Old Breichmar's taking this case? Gods it's been much too long since I've seen him. How is he? Does he still have a broom shoved firmly up his ass?" Arlicia asked playfully. Cartaneal scoffed and scrunched up his face in disgust. "You should know. I figure you'd recognize someone with the same affliction as you."

Yatoa's jaw dropped along with Cartaneal's. Arlicia could be cheeky, but Yatoa had *never* heard her speak to *anyone* this way.

Cartaneal shook with anger and pointed to the door. "Out! Get out!"

Arlicia moved for the door unconcerned, swung it open, then hopped out. Yatoa followed in a hurry. Outside Yatoa found they were in the middle of some wealthy neighborhood in the High Gob District. Marble mansions surrounded them on all sides.

The muscled man stepped down from the driver's bench where he had been chatting with the old Goblin driver. As he stepped back into the carriage with his employer Arlicia called after him. "If you try pulling out the broom, use gloves. It's stuck in there pretty deep." Yatoa gasped. The man give her mentor a frown and scratched his head.

"Come Yatoa, we have more important things to be about. Like deciding where to eat for lunch." With that Arlicia walked off. After a moment Yatoa stumbled after her.

The rest of the day was spent at a restaurant nearby, food long forgotten and a table covered in documents pertaining to the case. Yatoa spent the day sorting through the notes in her pocketbook and reading and rereading official reports and passages from the large leatherbound tome she carried with her everywhere. She knew *Goblin Law* inside and out by now, but there were a few passages that she needed to reconsult. She needed to come at this case from every angle and weed out every single possible path to victory.

The work was tedious and grueling, but it was necessary. Tomorrow she would meet with the judge. The day after she would stand in court and attempt to save Dal's life. She had no time to spare.

It was early evening by the time they returned to their hotel so Yatoa could work on her case plan some more with materials she had left behind in their room.

When they stepped through the front door into the wide, plush carpeted lobby, the concierge hailed Yatoa over to the counter.

"This came for you while you were out Ms. Hu'Dectala… simena," the receptionist said handing her an envelope sealed with wax. Yatoa ignored the fact that the woman pronounced her last name wrong – at least she tried – and took the paper into her hands. The only thing on it aside from the green seal was her name in clean handwriting.

"Thank you," Yatoa said moving back toward her mentor.

"Who's it from, Toa?" Arlicia asked. She leaned over trying to see.

"Not sure." Yatoa broke the green wax seal with expediency and slid out a small sheet of stationary. The border was green and gold and the face held a short message in the same clean handwriting. 'Faz has received the message. You need only wait at the appointed location and time. I believe she will meet with you. – G".

Arlicia tossed her cane up into the air and caught it before it could reach its apex. "Looks like we've got a snag on our line, Toa," Arlicia said. She tilted her head back and expelled a blissful exhale. "What a wonderful feeling. I should have been a fisher instead of a lawyer."

Yatoa excitedly gripped the note tighter. This was the last loose end she could address before the trial. Tomorrow night she would get all the answers and she could go into this trial with a clear mind.

7

Gobroa Superior Courthouse

The Gobroa superior courthouse was much grander than the jail. Its tall domes, marble pillars, and gold spires were enough to intimidate anyone, let alone a greenhorn like Yatoa. Yet as she ascended the many steep steps to the front entrance, she was able to keep her heart rate in check.

She stepped into the spacious entry hall, Arlicia at her side, and gawked at its splendor. Goblins' adoration for architecture was clear. Yatoa could see that passion in the intimate gazes of the nude marble statues of Goblins that towered over them. That sight was also... educational. Yatoa didn't know much about Goblin anatomy. It was her first time seeing nude Goblins, even if they weren't real. But... that level of detail sure made it feel like they were. Yatoa blushed in spite of herself.

The marble floors were inlaid with gold giving the hall an exorbitantly expensive feel even among the mansions of the High Gob District.

Hastening their steps they left the room behind. Yatoa didn't want to be late for her case briefing with the judge.

When they reached the judge's private chambers, they found someone else already standing before the door. It was an older Goblin man in a uniform identical to Arlicia's, cape and all, only instead of blood red it was a pine green. This man was a prosecutor. His green skin was much lighter than the suit and formed almost a gradient. He turned to face them as they approached.

"Ah… Arlicia," The man said in a pleased voice so deep Yatoa almost yelped. "So, you'll be my opponent this time around, eh?"

Arlicia shook her head. "Afraid not, Breichmar. This case belongs to my apprentice here." Breichmar Gob'Stellau looked to Yatoa with mild curiosity.

"It's a pleasure to meet you sir," she said. "I've heard much about you."

Breichmar smiled in amusement. "It appears someone taught your apprentice manners," Breichmar observed, returning his attention back to Arlicia. "Who have you been outsourcing her education to?"

"No one you've trained," Arlicia said.

"Well apprentice. Do put up a good fight in court tomorrow. The last time I stepped into court against an apprentice attorney I won all seven verdicts. A shame really. It was quite a boring victory."

Yatoa seg her jaw. "You needn't worry Mr. Gob'Stellau. I'll be the one with the boring victory tomorrow." Breichmar chuckled, then gestured toward the door.

"It is not good to keep the judge waiting, shall we?" Without waiting for a response Breichmar grabbed the handle and pushed the door out into the room beyond.

Taking a deep breath, Yatoa followed. The Judge's chambers were more than twice again the size of the visitation room in the jail and thirty times as cluttered. Stacks and stacks of papers and folders lined tables on the edges of the room leading to a back wall dominated by a crammed bookcase. The books all had either blood-red or forest-green spines, mirroring her and Breichmar as they seated themselves in the two available leather armchairs in front of the judge's desk.

Arlicia stood with a hand resting on the backrest of Yatoa's throne-like seat. The seat on the other side of the desk however was a throne in truth, and in it sat an elderly purple Goblin woman. A pair of thin spectacles sat on her short stubby nose through which she studied Yatoa.

"I am Yatoa Hu'Dectalaciumina. It is an honor to meet you… err Your Honor," Yatoa said feeling like she had tied her bootlaces together on accident. The judge continued staring for a moment.

"Is this your first trial, Ms. Yatoa?" the judge asked. Yatoa cringed at the avoidance of her last name, but she didn't have the nerve to correct her.

"Yes, Your Honor."

"Hmmmmm. I see…" she said. The judge's eyes still rested on her as if she was observing some painting she didn't understand. "I am very familiar with your mentor. She is a magnificent lawyer. I expect great things from you, Ms. Yatoa." Yatoa nodded vigorously.

"Thank you, Your Honor."

The judge pulled herself up straight then addressed both her and Breichmar. "I am judge Geral Gob'Frey. I will be presiding over this trial. Let us begin with the accusation. The court accuses the defendant, one Dal Gob'Alondis of burglary. He faces a sentence of death by marble crushing. Ms. Yatoa how will the defense plead in tomorrow's trial?" *This meeting is very unlike how they conducted trails back home*, Yatoa mused to herself, but she wasn't worried. She had studied *Goblin Law* so thoroughly she'd had to rebind the pages.

"The defense will be pleading not guilty, Your Honor," she said with confidence. Gob'Frey raised an eyebrow, but she seemed to accept it. Breichmar on the other hand…

"Not guilty? Arlicia it is rather cruel of you to set the girl up for complete disaster," Breichmar said.

Arlicia looked at him and gave him a lame shrug. Yatoa on the other hand wanted to tear a hole in her seat out of anger.

"Your Honor, the defense requests that the prosecution refrain from referring to me as 'girl'," Yatoa said. "I am the defense attorney representing Dal Gob'Alondis in this trial and I demand respect."

Gob'Frey nodded. "Breichmar be civil. I expect more of you than this. Do not make me ask you again. Am I clear?"

Breichmar stiffened. "Yes, Your Honor."

"I will not have this meeting, and especially not the courtroom tomorrow, break down into a children's bickering match. I expect all three of you to be on your best behavior, and yes, I'm looking at you, Arlicia. I know you have a penchant for… making a scene."

Arlicia bowed her head in polite assent. "Of course, Your Honor. I would never dream of it. I intend to be but a mere observer from the defense's circle tomorrow."

"Right. Anyway, I would have a list of witnesses you both intend to bring into the trial tomorrow. I've already received reports from both of you on the details of your respective cases, but I would like confirmation. Breichmar you first."

Breichmar cleared his throat. "Yes well, I intend to call forth the defendant of course. There's also Cartaneal Gob'Franat, the victim in this case, as well as Teran Gob'Jian, the lead investigator and the man who arrested the defendant. And of course, Reg Gob'Gronsa, one of the defendant's accomplices. As you have no doubt heard the watch apprehended him last night."

"What?" Yatoa gritted her teeth, and when she spun toward Breichmar she caught a pleased smile on his lips.

"An accomplice?" Gob'frey asked with curiosity.

"Yes, Your Honor. He struck a plea bargain almost immediately. In exchange for only two years in prison he is willing to testify to the guilt of Dal Gob'Alondis. I have a transcript of his interrogation here to submit to you."

Gob'Frey took a large envelope from Breichmar and tossed it onto a pile of similar envelopes on her desk. "And what about you, Ms. Yatoa?"

"Well, my list hasn't changed from the report I submitted yesterday. I will be calling Dal Gob'Alondis to the stand as well as his wife Garna Gob'Alondis and their daughter Darlia Gob'Alondis. With the opportunity to cross-examine the prosecution's witnesses I believe the list of witnesses in this case to be quite exhaustive, Your Honor."

"And during what stages do you intend to call witnesses Mr. Gob'Stellau?"

"Stages two through four and seven as is standard."

"And you Ms. Yatoa?"

"Um… stages three and seven only, Your Honor." Both Breichmar and Gob'Frey looked surprised to hear this. Stage two was one of the most important stages to call witnesses during. However, Yatoa didn't have any witnesses to call. Stage two was about debating the actual events of the crime. Anyone Breichmar called would be sufficient. The watch caught Dal red-handed, so there wasn't much to debate.

"Very well," Gob'Frey said. Along with your reports I'd like to discuss a few more logistical details with both of you if that's alright. But first, do either of you have any questions?"

"Yes, Your Honor," Yatoa said. "You see I am a Three Star. I have put that information down in my reports to you, so you are most likely already aware. Now this may be unconventional, but I would request leave to use my abilities in stages one and seven of this trial."

Breichmar frowned at this. "Surely you must deny this request, Your Honor. According to case law 'Goblin Night' illusions are not permitted in the courtroom."

Gob'Frey nodded in agreement. "That is true, Mr. Gob'Stellau, though I'm assuming Ms. Yatoa is already aware of that." She turned to Yatoa. "Might I ask what you intend to use these illusions for?"

"I intend to use them to paint pictures, Your Honor. I intend to paint scenes in the air to accompany my story telling, as well as use visual aids for my questioning of witnesses in stage seven. I know the courtroom already has a Three Star detector in it, but that detector could make sure I do not misuse my powers. I do not plan any subterfuge I assure you. I only plan on using my powers in grand, obvious ways that you would be able to grant or deny at a moment's notice."

Breichmar scoffed and waved his hand. "Your Honor, I must object to this foolishness. While she uses big fancy images to distract us, Ms. Yatoa could be doing something sly under our noses. It is a principle for performing illusionists! Distract the audience so they do not perceive your sleight of hand."

Yatoa leaned forward in her seat eager to speak. "Your Honor, if I may, that would not be possible. Well-trained Three Star detectors like the ones that serve in this court would be able to sense any illusion I tried to make no matter how small. There would be no possibility for a slight of hand. If you ask the detectors yourself, I'm sure they will attest to as much."

Gob'Frey sat for a moment considering. She folded her hands atop the desk. "I cannot make a decision on this now, Ms. Yatoa. I will have an answer for you at the start of the trial tomorrow after I confer with the presiding detector. I will say I am curious as to how this use of your powers would work."

Yatoa couldn't keep the smile from her face. She'd take all the small victories she could get. "Though do not count on it," Gob'Frey continued. "Come prepared to perform without illusions if need be."

"Yes, Your Honor."

Breichmar clenched his fists. This irked him for some reason. Perhaps he did believe that she meant to tamper with the trial, or perhaps he didn't want to cede any ground to her. Either way if Breichmar was unhappy, then she was happy.

"Now let's get into the finer details," Gob'Frey said.

When Yatoa stepped out of the courthouse she was mentally drained. "Good luck in the trial tomorrow, Mr. Gob'Stellau. May the best Lawyer win," she said holding her hand out to the man. With his hands stuffed in his pockets he looked up at her with tired eyes and didn't take it.

"Let me give you some advice, kid. I'm sure even your mentor will agree with this too. Sometimes it doesn't matter who the best lawyer is. Some cases are already decided before they even begin, and they just need us to jump through the hoops." Breichmar sighed and shook his head. "Don't get your hopes up. This trial is a formality. There's no doubt whatsoever that your client is guilty, and you should have pleaded that way." With that he turned and walked off.

"He's not very polite," Yatoa observed.

Arlicia ground her cane. "Nope. He's never been very polite. And he's only mostly right."

"What is he wrong about?"

Arlicia frowned as she watched Breichmar's image vanish behind the bend in the street. "Dal may be guilty, but that doesn't mean he deserves punishment."

Yatoa nodded.

They turned and hurried off down the street. They had an appointment to make by evening that Yatoa wouldn't dare miss.

All in all the meeting had gone well save for one significant problem. If this Reg character was willing to turn on Dal, then what was stopping him from turning on the rest of the crew? If he did, then that meant Faz wasn't safe and Yatoa had to warn her before the police caught her as well.

When she explained as much to Arlicia, she said, "It's a possibility, but I'm not worried about it."

"Why not?"

"I'm willing to wager Faz already knows about Reg. If what Dal says is true and they've been at this for a long time, then she'll know how to take care of herself." Yatoa remained unconvinced. She didn't want another Goblin to defend.

By the time they arrived at Hreila's Tavern it was slightly before the scheduled meeting time. They stepped into the low-ceilinged tavern full of patrons crowded around small circular tables. Luckily none of the Goblins were wearing white so Faz was sure to recognize her. She drew the attention of round Goblin eyes as she squeezed her way through the room to an empty table by the back wall. Everything here was Goblin sized, so she felt like a clumsy giant as she tried to pick her way through the tight spaces between loud bunches of Goblins.

When Yatoa took a seat at the table by the wall, tucking her cape underneath her, she found that her knees hit the bottom of the table. She had to scoot her chair back to give herself more room. Once they seated themselves, the attention they had earned wandered back to the patrons' cups.

Right as a tavern maid stepped up to their table, Yatoa noticed a red Goblin woman enter through the front door. Faz's eyes immediately found her.

8

Orange Confusion

Faz hurried over to their table. "What can I get y'all to drink?" the barmaid said with a warm smile.

"I'll have orange juice, thanks," Faz said, taking a seat in the third chair at the table. She had long black hair and black eyes to match. She was as graceful as any lady at court, yet there was a ready athleticism to her movements. Yatoa noticed her lithe muscles when Faz pulled the chair out from the table with one arm. She was more fit than Dal and she dressed nicer than him too. Tonight, she sported a simple orange sundress that complimented her purple skin tone.

"Same for the both of us," Arlicia said with a conspiratorial grin. The orange juice didn't mean anything. It was an Imperial superstition. Despite this, Yatoa felt a chill when Faz ordered orange.

When the Barmaid retreated to get their drinks, Faz leaned forward on the table, first meeting Yatoa's eyes then Arlicia's. Faz's gaze had a cunning edge to it.

"By your attire I'm guessin' your Dal's attorneys." Faz said. Yatoa nodded. Tension spread from Faz's narrow face into the air between them. "You the leader?" she asked Yatoa.

"Yatoa Hu'Dectalaciumina."

"I'm thinkin' you already know who I am, but I'm Faz." The barmaid settled glasses down on the table interrupting them. Three cool glasses of orange juice. After all the walking today Yatoa was absolutely parched, though she was not one to forego table manners. She waited patiently, observing Faz, and only when Faz took a sip did Yatoa in turn raise the glass to her lips. The cool tang of the juice on her tongue was a panacea to her fatigue. She wanted to savor the sensation, but she was too parched for that.

"That's good stuff," Yatoa said, setting down a glass that was already half empty. Faz nodded in agreement but said nothing as laughter and obnoxious shouts from neighboring tables overwhelmed their table.

"I know you said you'd dress in white but still, I expected somethin' at least a little more inconspicuous than a human dressed in an attorney uniform. You're puttin' me at risk here," Faz said.

"I know, but this is worth the risk," Yatoa said before taking another sip of juice.

Faz chuckled without mirth. "Is that what Dal told you when he sold me out? I never would've thought he'd snitch."

Yatoa fought her annoyance as if it were a particularly feisty dog. Once restrained she shook her head. "Dal didn't want to sell you out to me. I had to go to great lengths to convince him. Don't worry though. I am not allowed to report you to the authorities. Everything my client confides in me is confidential, and I would never break that trust. I won't act without Dal's consent. You're safe." *For now*, she thought. She neglected to mention that the authorities had also apprehended Reg Gob'Gronsa. Not yet. Yatoa didn't want to scare Faz off before she could get any answers.

Faz took a sip from her glass and set it down with a hard crack that reminded her of a gavel slamming. Yatoa winced thinking the glass would shatter. "Well good for you. But excuse me if I still don't trust you considerin' many of your peers aren't so honorable."

"Needless squabbling wastes both our time. It is not in my interest to turn you in Faz. You're going to have to trust me on that, because quite frankly you don't have another choice." Yatoa set her elbows on the table and leaned in toward Faz. "Now I'm here because I want to ask you questions."

"And why should I answer them?" Faz shot back.

"Because it is the honorable thing to do."

"Fine," Faz conceded. "What do you want to know?" Yatoa shared a satisfied glance with Arlicia then took another tangy sip before continuing. There was honor among thieves after all.

"Tell me about the night of the crime from your perspective. What happened?" She didn't want to accuse Faz of anything yet. Faz didn't know Yatoa suspected she had betrayed Dal or why, which meant Faz wouldn't know what part of the story to doctor.

Faz glanced about the room. If she saw anything at all that concerned her, she didn't show it. "Alright," she whispered.

"I'll tell you, though it probably won't be much different from what Dal told you."

"That's fine," Yatoa said. "Feel free to take your time."

Faz nodded in contemplation. "The plan was perfect. All plans Dal and I made were. We're the brains of the crew. We spent many sleepless nights preparin' for this one single heist. We had both agreed in private that this heist was our last." That was news to Yatoa. Dal never mentioned anything of the sort.

"May I ask why?"

"We're getting old now. We can't keep this up forever, and we both have bigger aspirations for our lives. For him, he wanted to heal his daughter D'arlia – she has the shatter – and get his family out of Gobroa. Go out into the world and look for something better. For me… I just want to live a quiet life with my girlfriend in the Goblin District. Not the fanciest place mind you, but this part of the city is peaceful enough. She already lived here in a small apartment big enough for only one Goblin. I wanted more for us and I saw this heist as a chance.

"This heist had a big payout. Cartaneal has real fat pockets, and he keeps a lot of his money around as assets like jewelry. Ripe for picking. And so, on the night of the crime we carried out our plan near to perfection. We sneaked into the house through the back garden, picked the lock on the side entrance of the servants' quarters, then slipped in. Our plan was systematic. Hit the jewelry first. He keeps them displayed in a showroom. Then after we send Dal and a lookout to retrieve some real estate documents from Cartaneal's study. Dal would get it done quick and the lookout would keep an eye out for the security patrol. Cartaneal's buff human goons patrol the mansion at all times. Though sneaking around that lot wasn't hard."

"Did you ever meet the person that asked for those documents?" Yatoa asked. She didn't know anything about this mysterious person, but she hoped Faz would let something slip.

Faz disappointingly shook her head. "None of us did. He communicates to us through a middle-man informant. And besides we failed to get the document, so it's kinda irrelevant at this point. I'm not going to lose any sleep over it. Besides, I wasn't the one who had contact."

Faz paused to gulp down some more juice. She polished off the glass then laid it on the table with care this time. After another quick survey of the room, she continued. "Anyway, it's obvious that part of the plan went awry. It shouldn't have, but it did. There was some miscommunication. The person assigned to be Dal's lookout didn't do their job. The rest of us were outside waiting for Dal and the lookout to finish up when we realized that the lookout was actually with us not him. By then it was too late. Only moments later we heard shouts from inside the mansion. We all left and the rest you know."

Faz sat back in her chair and took a deep breath. She looked drained, then disappointed her glass was empty. She gestured to the waitress nearby for a refill.

Faz's story confused Yatoa. The story got a little vague toward the end. Was she claiming she had abandoned Dal by mistake?

"Why do you think you got the plan mixed up?" Yatoa asked, giving her the benefit of the doubt. She wanted to see what Faz would do.

"What do you mean?" Faz asked, sounding confused herself. Before Yatoa could elaborate, the waitress returned with a pitcher of orange juice for refills.

"You are a saint madam," Arlicia said as the waitress tended to her glass.

The waitress grinned. "Why thank you. It's refreshin' havin' customers who appreciate me for once."

Arlicia took a delicate sip of the orange juice, treating it as though it were the finest of wines. "Anyone who bestows upon me nectar this sweet must have descended from heaven above."

"Oh stop! You're making me blush," the waitress said before leaving with a wink for Arlicia. Both Faz and Yatoa stared at Arlicia, conversation momentarily forgotten. Yatoa was trying to have a serious discussion and Arlicia sipped away at her juice and flirted with Goblin girls.

"Don't mind me. Carry on, I'm listening," Arlicia assured.

"Right… Anyway, what I meant to ask is why didn't you act as lookout? What made you deviate from the plan?" Faz stared at her for a moment, her brow knit in consternation as if Yatoa was some unsolvable blacksmith puzzle.

"I wasn't supposed to be the lookout," she said. "It was someone else's job and they messed it up." Yatoa had expected Faz to come up with some excuse or outright deny that anyone betrayed Dal. This was different. She admitted that the lookout didn't do their job, but she insists it wasn't her. But Dal let it slip that the lookout was a 'she' and Garna implied Faz was the only female crew member.

"If it wasn't you then who was it?" Yatoa asked.

Faz shook her head. "I'm sorry, but unless you can already name the person as a member of our crew that's not info I'm willin' or able to divulge." Yatoa clenched her jaw. Faz was blaming someone else yet she refused to name who? Suspicious. If she was guilty of abandoning Dal Yatoa thought she would give a better defense. Yatoa didn't want to believe her. It made things more complicated. Yet Faz's story felt too earnest to be a lie, and the way she talked it seemed she didn't even consider Yatoa suspected her of betrayal.

"Was it Reg?" Yatoa asked, using the only other name she knew. Faz tensed at the mention of the name.

"So, Dal spilled Reg's name too? No. It wasn't Reg."

Yatoa leaned in again, whispering now. "Dal didn't tell me about Reg." This was her shot. If she couldn't get info on the other crew members, then she would at least leverage this vital piece of information to learn what happened with Dal's cut.

"Wait. If it wasn't Dal… then who?" Faz asked. She bit her lip and gripped the table in fear of the answer.

"The answer to that question is one you need to know, trust me," Yatoa said. "But first I want you to tell me what happened with Dal's share of the profits. You bought your place here in the Goblin District, so I'm assuming you sold the jewelry already. I hear that if a member gets caught the money goes to their family."

"That's right," Faz confirmed. "And that's where it went." Yatoa frowned.

"Are you saying you gave Garna the money?"

Faz nodded. "Yup. Last week. Why wouldn't I give it to her? Darlia needs that money, and she's such a sweet little girl. I imagine she's healed by now. If she ends up losing her father's life at least she'll still have her own." But that didn't make sense.

"But-" Yatoa protested, but Faz cut her off.

"How do you know about Reg? Goblin fang for a Goblin fang Yatoa. Tell me." Yatoa sighed.

"The Gobroa city watch apprehended him. He's going to testify against Dal in exchange for a lighter sentence at tomorrow's trial." Faz jumped from her chair.

"I have to go, I'm sorry. I hope I helped- truly I do. Dal is a close friend, so make sure he gets out. But I have to go." She was already stepping away from the table. Yatoa shot up from her seat, slamming her knee against the table.

"Ow! Wait! But what about the money? Garna said you never gave it to her!" Yatoa called out across the bar to Faz who was almost at the door. She spared Yatoa a peak over her shoulder. A look of complete and utter confusion. Then she shook her head and hurried out of the bar.

Everyone in the bar was staring at her now, and Yatoa felt sick. She plopped back down in her seat and leaned her head back against the wall.

"This only leaves me with more questions," she lamented. "I was hoping to clear things up here not muddle them."

Arlicia picked up Faz's half empty glass of orange juice, and swished the contents around. "This is the last lesson you'll learn before the trial, Yatoa."

"What lesson?"

"That the trial always comes whether you're ready or not. It's here now. Time's up. You did well." With her head against the wall Yatoa shut her eyes, purging the room from sight. Not well enough.

9

The Story

Only one word could describe the courtroom: unconventional. Knowing what to expect and actually seeing were two different things. The courtroom was like a miniature arena, a circular bowl of a chamber, seats in rows downhill terminating in a circular shaped space in the center. Within that space rested three concentric circles.

The largest circle was painted on the wood flooring. The circle wasn't a solid color, but instead an intricate pattern of swirls in white against the brown finish of the floor. This circle was the witness circle. The next interior circle was a raised wooden platform. It rose three feet off the ground. The defense circle. The innermost circle, the smallest, was another raised platform twice again as high as the defense circle. This was the prosecution circle.

And finally, the centerpiece inside the prosecution circle was a massive gold cauldron housing an enormous magical bonfire that gave off no heat. The bonfire's flames towered over the court as the sole light source.

Overlooking it all was the judge's stand. Solitary. It was a tall wooden tower with a bench and desk for the Judge to use. In front of the judge's stand, at about half the height, was the jury box.

Yatoa gawked at it all. The flame was imposing, and as the only light source in the room it felt eerie. Only the center of the room was well lit, and as she stepped down the stairs and into the light, she could no longer see the packed crowd. The darkness swallowed the onlookers whole. That was well. Having so many eyes on her could be nerve-wracking.

Dal, who walked at her side, clambered up onto the defense circle. He had his chains removed for the trial so it wasn't difficult for him. Yatoa climbed up after him and stood, her cape falling limply at her side. This was it. The moment she had trained for.

Arlicia hopped up next to her, then gazed out at the crowd as if she could see the faces of the onlookers. She gave Yatoa a reassuring smile, then nodded to Breichmar who already stood atop the prosecution circle. Because the prosecution circle was higher, Breichmar stood at eye-level with Yatoa.

Their eyes met. The edges of his form glowed with the light of the fire. He nodded to her, then looked to Judge Geral Gob'Frey who took her seat atop the judge's tower. From her perch she peered down at them all through her spectacles. Then in one fluid motion she slammed her gavel on its block.

"All rise," she announced in a loud commanding voice. Sounds of shifting emanated from the darkness informing Yatoa that the onlookers stood. "The trial of Dal Gob'Alondis is now in session. The gallery may now be seated." A hushed shuffling erupted from the gallery. Yatoa's heart pounded and she tried to ignore the crowd.

"Is the defense ready?"

"The defense is ready, Your Honor," Yatoa found herself saying. She didn't truly mean the words.

"Is the prosecution ready?"

"The prosecution is ready, Your Honor," Breichmar said smoothly to Yatoa's left.

Gob'Frey nodded. "Very well. Before we begin, I have an announcement to make concerning a request of the defense." Yatoa held her breath and her heart picked up the pace. "After much deliberation we have decided to allow the use of Three Star illusions in this trial for the purposes of providing visual aids exclusively. Ms. Yatoa, you may use your magic in stages one, three, four, and seven. Is this acceptable?"

"Yes, Your Honor," she said. A block of marble eased off her heart. *No marble crushing today.*

"Now then, without further ado let us begin." Yatoa tried taking a deep breath to calm herself, but it barely helped. Everything was happening so fast. She felt lightheaded. "Dal Gob'Alondis faces charges of burglary, particularly theft of items worth more than one-hundred and fifty gobbings. In accordance with the law, he faces a sentence of death by marble crushing. How does the defense plead to these charges?"

Yatoa took another deep breath and stood up straighter. "Not-guilty, Your Honor." There was a lull in the proceedings. First silence, then the void filled with murmurs from the darkness, finally the slam of a gavel.

"Silence!" Gob'Frey commanded. "I shouldn't have to remind the gallery again that the only ones permitted to make a sound in this court are those illuminated by the Fire Demon's light." Gob'Frey let out a dismayed sigh. "At this time, it is crucial that the jury be made aware of the weight of their verdicts. Because the defense has pleaded not guilty the verdict has become a binary. If the defense wins four verdicts at any point in the trial, then Dal Gob'Alondis will walk free. Therefore, it is possible that this trial could not last all seven stages. Conversely, if the prosecution wins four verdicts, then Dal Gob'Alondis will be executed. If you understand say aye, if not then nay."

All ten members of the jury spoke up in unison. "Aye."

"Very well. Now that everyone is on the same page, let us begin with stage one: the story." This time when Yatoa took a breath it shook. "Mr. Gob'Stellau, you may begin."

Breichmar nodded, then turned to face the darkness. "This story is a simple one. All the best stories are." He said, sweeping his arm wide for the audience. "Well-known entrepreneur and philanthropist Cartaneal Gob'Franat was enjoying a fine evening out with friends. A friend invited him to a banquet at the Gob'Kaern estate, and naturally he attended. He hoped to have a pleasant evening and then return home to a fresh bed and a good night's rest. After a social evening like that I'm sure it is not difficult to imagine Cartaneal wanted to decompress in the comfort and security of his own home." At this point Breichmar started to pace, walking along the circle to the other side of the fire. Yatoa followed.

"Now I'm sure you can all understand the dismay and unease Cartaneal felt when he returned home to find his privacy and security violated. Thieves had burglarized his home and made off with most of his extensive jewelry collection. Cartaneal Gob'Franat painstakingly collected his jewelry collection over decades, and it carried both monetary and sentimental value." Gob'Franat grinned a ghoulishly Goblin grin for the audience, then spread his arms wide.

"But it was not all bad. You see one of the thieves got left behind at the scene of the crime! Cartaneal Gob'Franat's own security personnel found the defendant and turned him over to the city watch. The story is simple, and that is the whole of it." That was most certainly *not* the whole of it. Yatoa would prove that without a shadow of a doubt. Breichmar flourished his cape and bowed elegantly toward the jury to signal the end of his story.

It was a surprisingly simple presentation, but Yatoa had to give the man credit. Sometimes simple and straightforward was most effective.

"Thank you Mr. Gob'Stellau," Gob'Frey said. "Ms. Yatoa. Your story if you would."

Yatoa turned to face the darkness. Aside from some faint shapes moving in the front rows she couldn't see the shifting mass of people. Only a void. That void calmed her. She could let all other distractions melt away into it.

"Mr. Gob'Stellau would have you believe this story is a simple one. That couldn't be farther from the truth. This story is far more complex than it may at first appear to be." Yatoa lifted her index and ring fingers tracing a green line through the air. The line blossomed; a floral vine. She whisked her fingers back and forth coalescing light into the form of Darlia.

Yatoa felt so lightheaded she was on the verge of fainting, but she focused all her mental power into staying conscious. The image was a little hazy around the edges, not like what she had been capable of years ago, but still serviceable.

"This is Darlia Gob'Alondis, Dal's daughter. *She* is where our story begins," Yatoa paced around the defense circle. She had to step over Arlicia who sat with her legs dangling over the edge and her cane resting in her lap. As Yatoa paced she dragged the image of Darlia along with her.

"Darlia suffers from the shatter. She only has a few months left to live before the illness claims her life and she vitrifies completely into a glass statue." Yatoa caught Dal's eye. He too was sitting on the circle and his big Goblin eyes gazed mournfully upon the image of his daughter. "In order to cure the shatter, one must seek out the aid of a skilled One Star healer. Unfortunately for Darlia, One Stars cost a fortune in Gobroa – especially for procedure she needs. So, to save the life of his little girl, Dal needed money." Yatoa flicked her hand and the image changed.

The lights strung together forming a miniaturized scene of Dal in a study. Only two walls were visible like a diorama. "An opportunity presented itself. He could rob jewelry off a rich man with too much money on his hands, and he also could steal private real estate documents as well for someone who offered to pay for them. Both would provide enough to not only cure his daughter, but also give her a better life."

Yatoa stopped her pacing when she had rounded the circle again and turned toward the jury. She stood facing them, feeling every single one of their eyes on her. It felt like their stares were physically touching her. She somehow managed to avoid cringing. "But look here," she said, pointing to the diorama. "At the time of his arrest Dal was in possession of no jewels. In fact, he had not taken any at all. Other thieves were responsible for that. Dal on the other hand was here for documents not precious metals. They arrested him before he could even take anything.

"And so, it may seem clear that Dal was trying to burglarize Gob'Franat's home, but he never actually got away with any personal item of Gob'Franat's, and he was only doing this in the first place to save his daughter's life." Yatoa flicked her fingers again. The image changed once more to one of Dal and Darlia in which Darlia sat on Dal's lap with a grin on her face as he read her a bedtime story. Darlia's arm was glassless.

Yatoa stared the jury down. "Goblins of the jury I ask of you today to remember this one thing. Even if at any point you believe without a shadow of a doubt that Dal Gob'Alondis is ultimately responsible for this theft, then please ask yourselves, 'does this man deserve marble crushing for what he's done? Should his daughter suffer his absence and all chance at survival because he tried, and failed, to steal a piece of paper? Over the course of this trial, I *will* prove to you all that the only possible answer to those questions is a definitive no." With her hands shaking, Yatoa dispelled the illusion, grabbed her cape, and bowed elaborately to Gob'Frey.

"Thank you, Ms. Yatoa. At this time, we will take a fifteen-minute recess while the jury discusses their verdict." Her gavel met its block, and Yatoa let out the breath she had been holding. The jury, one by one, stood and filed their way out of the box and into a small side room with a door only big enough for Goblins to enter.

Yatoa hopped down from the defense's circle and Arlicia met her with a grin.

"Very well done, Toa" Arlicia's face was radiant. The way her eyes smiled almost made Yatoa feel as though she really had done well.

"Save the praise for when we hear the first verdict."

Arlicia twirled her cane around a finger. "I don't need to wait. You looked like a full-fledged attorney up there, regardless of the verdict." The sentiment was oddly touching. Yatoa swelled with pride at the genuine praise from her master, then went to find Dal. He was still sitting on the defense's circle, biting his lip.

"This is beyond nerve-wrackin', Yatoa," he said.

"Believe me I know. Try to hang in there, alright Dal? We'll make it through this. I'll show you it's okay to hope." Yatoa didn't feel like she had it in her to comfort anyone right now, and she hoped he didn't see the anxiety in her. Dal nodded.

The next ten minutes were excruciatingly long. Yatoa spent it staring at the great flame in the center of the room, wishing they could start stage two of the trial and get on with it. Occasionally she stole glances at Breichmar, who sat with his legs dangling over the edge of the prosecution circle. His pointy ears were sharp and his eyes focused. He seemed lost in thought, but the whole time he had a self-satisfied smile on his lips.

Orange light bathed his green suit, muting the color. It was interesting seeing a version of her suit, but with radically different proportions. Because of Breichmar's short height the cape was also much shorter, which meant it rested stiffer than Yatoa's did. It flared outward more, whereas Yatoa's draped down toward the floor, hiding her arms.

At the moment she had one side of her cape draped back over her shoulder flashing the red inlay outward. That was intentional. She wanted to remind everyone that while she may be an apprentice, she was still a defense attorney.

Everyone came to attention when the jury came back through their tiny door. As they clambered up into the jury box Yatoa resumed her post on the defense circle. Once in place everyone waited for Gob'Frey to climb the ladder of the Judge's stand and resume her seat. She lifted the gavel and banged it.

"Court is back in session. I trust that the jury was able to come to a decision."

"Yes, Your Honor," the head juror said. She was a matronly looking Goblin woman with her gray hair pinned up in a bun. In a trial back home it would take much longer for a jury to come to a consensus, but this jury didn't have much to discuss. Plus they only needed a seven to three split to decide on a verdict, whereas back home everyone needed to be of one mind. All this made Yatoa feel nervous. Would their deliberations be well thought out? Nevertheless, she held her breath and awaited disappointment.

"Very well," Gob'Frey said. "Would you please announce the verdict to the court?"

"Yes, Your honor. With an eight to two split the jury declares a verdict of not-guilty in stage one of this trial."

Yatoa couldn't believe what she was hearing. Breichmar clearly couldn't either as his smug smile slid from his face.

That'll teach you not to underestimate me, she thought in triumph. Arlicia placed a hand on her shoulder and gave her an encouraging nod, and that made Yatoa's pride swell more than the verdict had. Her mentor approved.

10

The Reasoning

Gob'Frey's voice boomed in the dim chamber vibrating Yatoa's very soul. "The verdicts rest at one to none in favor of the defense. At this time, we will now move on to stage two of this trial: the reasoning. As I'm sure the jury is aware, each side will provide a reason for why they believe the defendant is either guilty or not-guilty. They may do this by any means they see fit. We will begin with the prosecution. Mr. Gob'Stellau I ask you now, for what reason do you believe Dal Gob'Alondis is guilty of this crime?"

Breichmar drew himself up. "Ms. Yatoa brought up an interesting point in stage one. She claimed that since the defendant had not stolen any jewelry, he had not actually committed a theft of items worth over one-hundred and fifty gobbings. This claim does not hold up I'm afraid, as it completely ignores the defendant's intent, as well as the… tools he used to carry out the crime. While he personally did not lay a hand on the jewelry, the fact remains that thieves stole the jewelry. And I assure you he still holds primary responsibility for their theft."

"And what evidence do you have to support this claim, Mr. Gob'Stellau?" Gob'Fray asked peering at him through her spectacles.

Breichmar shot Yatoa a quick glance, but otherwise his face betrayed no emotion. "The prosecution calls Reg Gob'Gronsa to the witness circle to testify to Dal's extensive involvement in this theft." Yatoa felt her gut clench her intestines. So, he was going to call on Reg. She had suspicions of when he would do it, and she had hoped it wouldn't be so early in the trial, but hopes weren't worth much in court.

Gob'Frey nodded. "Reg Gob'Gronsa," She announced out into the chamber in that booming voice of hers. "Approach the witness circle." From Yatoa's right a figure formed out of the darkness coalescing into a green skinned Goblin like Breichmar. He, unlike Dal, was still in chains. Yatoa watched Dal's reaction. She had warned him of this, but disbelief clung to his face as he watched his former crew-mate step onto the painted swirls of the witness circle.

Breichmar stood at the edge of his circle, behind Yatoa. She stepped out of his way so he could get a clear view of the witness, but she stuck close to him. She hoped the close proximity coupled with their now matching heights would make Breichmar uneasy. Breichmar stood with confidence.

"Witness, please state your name and occupation for the court," Breichmar said in a commanding tone. Reg looked up at them with his bright blue eyes, and tried to avoid Dal's accusatory glare.

"The name's Reg Gob'Gronsa and I'm an assistant cobbler at Gob'Alondis Cobblers. Been workin' there for nine years I have," he said pridefully in a high-pitched voice.

Breichmar rubbed at his chin in thought. "Then I suppose that means you are well acquainted with the defendant?"

Reg fidgeted with the chains around his wrist. "Yeah, we go way back. Met when we were just goblets. I was his best man at his weddin', even if I didn't care for his wife much."

Breichmar nodded. "And since you were so close, I imagine you were aware of this crime?"

"Oh yeah. Dal had been plannin' the thing for weeks. I was in on it too you know." Reg held up his wrists to show his chains. "That's why I got these bad boys. Shame really. Thought I was home free I did."

"Can you tell us more about Dal's planning, and your involvement in this crime?" Yatoa dreaded where this was going. At this rate Breichmar would sway the jury in his favor.

"Yeah of course. So, Dal is the real brains of the operation see. He came to me with the idea one day of sneakin' into ol' Gob'Franat's mansion and thievin' some jewels. Being a cobbler don't bring in much in the way of gobbings, especially in the Saern District, so I figured hey why not." Yatoa could think of several reasons why not, chief among them Reg's current position, but she remained silent and tried not to roll her eyes.

"So yeah, anyway Dal set out to plannin'. Every night in the workshop he drew up diagrams and listed off tools we'd need. He went through at least a dozen different plans before he found the perfect one. In that plan I was the jewel nabber while Dal was a document snatcher."

"Was this theft carried out by only the two of you?" Breichmar pushed.

Reg sighed. "No, there was more of us. Five in total to be exact. But I already made my deal. I'm not tellin' ya the name of a single one of em, got that? All that matters here is me and Dal." It was nice that Reg felt such loyalty to his friends that he would keep their identities a secret. If only that loyalty also extended to Dal.

"Of course," Breichmar agreed. "So, the defendant gathered this crew together and orchestrated them in the burglary of Cartaneal Gob'Franat's jewelry?"

"Yup," Reg said without hesitation.

"And he carried out this crime with you?"

"Yup."

Breichmar turned from the witness to Gob'Frey. "As you can see Your Honor, while the defendant may not have laid hands on the jewels himself, the fact remains that he still arranged for Reg to steal them. It is undeniable that the responsibility for the theft lies squarely on the defendant's shoulders." Breichmar lifted a finger and smiled. "But now that I have addressed Ms. Yatoa's concern I would like to provide support for my story. Namely of how the city watch caught the defendant in the act. For that I call Teran Gob'Jian to the witness circle."

The judge nodded then commanded Teran to step forth. Another Goblin emerged from the darkness, this one in full uniform. He was a member of the Gobroa City Watch. His uniform was a bright green and pinned on his chest was a gold shield-shaped badge with the letters 'GCW' inscribed on it. This would be the man that had arrested Dal.

"Witness, please state your name and occupation."

"I am Teran Gob'Jian. I am the lead criminal investigator for the Gobroa City Watch," Teran said in a shockingly high-pitched voice. Reg who was standing next to him actually winced at the sound of it.

"Mr. Gob'Jian," Breichmar said in a much more respectful tone than the one he had used with Reg. "Would you please testify to the court as to your involvement in this case."

"Yes sir!" Teran said shrilly. Teran's large dark eyes flickered to Dal as he said this. "The night of the crime I was on duty at the precinct in the High Gob District when we received a message from a runner at the door. The man told us that a group of thieves robbed Cartaneal Gob'Franat's mansion and that his private security managed to restrain one of the burglars. I made off for the scene immediately with a team of the finest the Gobroa City watch has to offer.

"When we arrived at the scene the mansion was abuzz with activity. Servants were begging details from us as to what was happening and we made sure to put them at ease. I sent some men to check on the jewelry display room while I went to the study. There I found Dal Gob'Alondis restrained by Gob'Franat's Human security guards. He did not resist arrest nor claim innocence. We both knew we caught him red-handed. Afterward, my men confirmed to me that approximately eighty-thousand gobbings worth of jewelry had gone missing. We were able to track down Reg Gob'Gronsa due to his reckless spending of a large sum he logically shouldn't have. I only wish we had caught the rest of the thieves as well."

Yatoa winced. *Eighty-thousand!* That was an unfathomable amount of money. Even split five ways it would be enough to last at least four generations if one managed it with care. Though it seemed that unfortunately for everyone involved Reg had not done that.

"Thank you for your testimony investigator," Breichmar said with his hands clasped behind his back. Once again, he turned toward the judge. "As you can see Your Honor, I have given you not only my reasons for believing the defendant to be responsible for this crime, but I have also illustrated magnitude of it. This is iron-clad eye-witness testimony as to Dal's direct involvement in the theft." Breichmar gave the judge an elaborate bow. "The prosecution rests."

"Thank you Mr. Gob'Stellau," Gob'Frey said. Gob'Frey then inclined her head to toward Yatoa and she gulped. "Ms. Yatoa, I ask you now, for what reason do you believe Dal Gob'Alondis is not-guilty of this crime?"

"Your Honor, I stand by what I said earlier. That Dal Gob'Alondids does not deserve punishment for what he has done. I believe this because Dal Gob'Alondis has not done anything wrong. He is a good man and he only had the best of intentions. I intend to prove this all to you in later stages of this trial." Yatoa said this feeling foolish, but there wasn't much she could do to defend her position in this stage.

She had always planned to take a calculated loss in this stage, but… if she could salvage it somehow. "Your Honor, the defense requests permission to cross-examine the witnesses."

"Permission granted, Ms. Yatoa. Please proceed," Gob'Frey said gesturing toward the two men who still stood on the witness circle. Witnesses were not dismissed from the circle until the end of the stage.

Yatoa turned to face them. The only sound in the room was the crackling of the great fire behind her. "Mr. Gob'Gronsa you said you were very close with the defendant, correct?"

"Yup. He's my best friend. We've stuck by each other through thick and thin." Yatoa took a deep breath then plunged into the hottest burning question.

"If that is the case then may I ask why you agreed to testify against him? Especially when you refuse to divulge the identities of the other members of the thieving crew." Yatoa half expected Breichmar to object to this question, but the prosecutor remained silent. Watching her.

Reg stood still, staring at his feet. Then he looked up at Dal, and finally to Yatoa. She saw what looked like true remorse in his eyes. "The answer is simple. They gave me a choice. Be sentenced to death along with Dal, or live. I never wanted to betray Dal, but when it comes to choosin' between both of us dyin' or just him, then I had to choose just him. I can't die now. I've still got a lot I wanna do and see." Anger surged as Yatoa stared down at the pathetic Goblin. She couldn't help it.

"It never once crossed your mind that maybe he would beat his allegations?" Yatoa blurted out.

"Objection!" Breichmar boomed.

Yatoa nearly jumped out of her uniform. "The defense is badgering the witness, Your Honor."

Gob'Frey nodded. "Ms. Yatoa, now is not the time to express your personal frustrations with the witness. Understand?"

Yatoa swallowed. Despite her frayed nerves she managed a nod. "Yes, Your Honor."

"It's alright I deserve the hostility," Reg said humbly. "It doesn't bother me none."

Yatoa turned back to Reg, feeling ashamed that she had actually thought him pathetic a moment ago. He had made the reasonable choice given his scenario. She had to keep a level head and switch gears fast or she was going to drive the jury further away.

"Mr. Gob'Gronsa, what do you think of my argument? Do you think that Dal deserves punishment for the crime he has committed?"

Reg glanced toward Breichmar. "It's wrong to steal…" He said nervously. "And stealin' should be illegal. Otherwise, nobody'd feel completely secure, but… that doesn't mean it's always wrong to steal neither. And two people stealin' for different reasons shouldn't get the same harsh punishment is what I think."

"Would you care to elaborate on that notion?"

Reg shrugged, then glanced about himself again. Arlicia watched Reg intently and Yatoa wondered what was going through her mentor's brain. Surely, she saw a better way of handling all this than Yatoa. Dal was staring at Reg too, though there was a darkness to his features that made Yatoa uncomfortable. She figured that even if both Dal and Reg survived this ordeal their friendship would not.

Breichmar eyed Yatoa, and Teran stood at attention staring straight ahead at nothing in particular. Either he took his job too seriously or he was actually spacing out.

"Well," Reg began, "what if there's a homeless mother on the street and she can't afford even a single roll of bread to feed her daughter? At that point she's only got two options she does. Either she can let the kid kick the bucket, or she can steal some grub. At that point, stealin' ought to be the right thing to do."

"Would you say that reasoning then applies to Dal and Darlia?" That was probably what Reg was trying to get at in not so many words, but she wanted it spelled out clear for the jury.

"Objection!" Breichmar's voice boomed once more. "The defense is leading the witness."

"Ms. Yatoa, I'll cut you some slack because this is your first trial, but please try to not ask such leading questions in the future," Gob'Frey advised. Yatoa felt a flood of shame. She *really* needed to approach this with care.

Reg held up his hands. "It's fine! I don't mind none. I suppose that's what I was tryin' to say, so she's not far off."

Teran coughed and everyone spared him a glance.

"Now Mr. Gob'Gronsa I-" Another cough from Teran. "Mr. Gob'Jian. Do you need a drink?" She couldn't focus on questioning Reg with that overexaggerated wheezing.

"No ma'am, I'll be fine. But now that we're talking, may I make a comment on something Reg Gob'Gronsa said?"

Yatoa frowned. She wanted to say no, but then she'd come across as rude to everyone in court.

"You may," she said then regretted it immediately.

"His conclusion is absurd. If it was true that there are some times when breaking the law is the right thing to do, then where would you draw the line? Stealing bread for your child, then clothes, then jewelry for money. One thing leads to another and you have people justifying all sorts of crimes. We can't devote energy to discussing which crimes are justified or not, and to what degree. It'd be too much of a burden." Yatoa rubbed her temples at the inanity of Teran's contribution to the discussion.

"Yes, we can devote energy to discussing those things. That is quite literally what trials are for. Mr. Gob'Jian you speak of Reg's scenario as if it's a foreign concept and not an accurate depiction of reality." Yatoa crossed her arms as she met the heavy-set Goblin's eyes.

"But we try street urchins for stealing bread," Teran said as if that proved anything.

Yatoa nodded. "That we do. Reality matches Reg's scenario only the Goblins getting away with crimes they shouldn't aren't homeless. Instead, they live in mansions."

"Your Honor, this philosophizing is irrelevant to the case at hand," Breichmar stated coolly from his perch on the prosecution circle. Yatoa met his round, imperious eyes.

"Your Honor, this subject is vitally important to the trial as the question of the morality of Dal's actions relates to whether the court should punish him," Yatoa countered, not taking her eyes off Breichmar's.

Breichmar smirked and gestured toward Teran. "I believe most sane people would side with Mr. Gob'Jian's point. It is wrong to break the long-upheld laws of our society here in Gobroa. The defense's radical ideas would lead us down a steep slope into chaos." Yatoa gritted her teeth and clenched her fists, making a physical effort to contain her rage from leaking. "Punishment for crime is a deterrent. If everyone thought the way the defense suggests, then we would end up with a society where people would break the law whenever they wish! It is completely absurd. Your Honor, I believe we have heard enough of the defense's argument."

"We already live in that society," Yatoa insisted. "The ones who can get away with crimes are-"

"Upstanding citizens like Cartaneal Gob'Franat?" Breichmar said, cutting her off. She was just a gram from tipping into strangling the little Goblin. His sharp toothed grin was too mocking in a way only a Goblin could manage. "Don't be absurd. Gob'Franat would never commit a crime. Unless the defense feels they can implicate him in one right now. I'll listen, as long as you have the evidence."

Yatoa wanted to retort but she realized too late what all this was. Breichmar was intentionally goading her into floundering in front of the jury and she completely latched onto his bait. This stage was a lost cause and the longer she let it continue the worse it would get. She turned away from Breichmar and faced the judge.

"The defense stands by its claims, and rests at this time."

"Very well," Gob'Frey said after a moment. "We will now take another fifteen-minute recess while the jury discusses their verdict. Witnesses, please return to your seats." With the bang of the gavel on its block everyone followed Gob'Frey's orders.

Yatoa took a deep breath and sat down on her platform to think. She hadn't realized her legs ached until she sat, and she lost herself in massaging them. This one was certainly a loss.

"Calculated losses are necessary at times," Arlicia said, reading her mind as she sat down next to her.

Yatoa never planned to win this stage, but she had still expected to put on a better performance. She had started the trial so strong, but in the end she let her frustration get the better of her.

"By my projections, based on what I've seen of both yours and Breichmar's performance, you will win stage three. You're doing what you can Yatoa, and I want you to know that's enough." Arlicia meant the words to be comforting, but Yatoa didn't want to do just enough. She wanted to do it all. Fix everything. Make it better. "My first trial was in Goblin court too you know."

Yatoa looked up abruptly. "It was?" When Arlicia nodded Yatoa asked, "did you win?"

"Nope! Lost all seven verdicts!" Arlicia said cheerfully. "So, you're already doing better than I did. Better than most. Remember what Breichmar said yesterday?"

"He said a lot of things yesterday."

"He said the last apprentice he faced lost all seven verdicts. Yatoa you're already doing better than most apprentices, and it's not just because you had a good mentor" Arlicia winked.

"Thanks, I mean it." And she did. Yet she still couldn't banish the unease from her heart. This trial consumed every inch of her mind and isolated her from the outside world. Here only illuminated by flame and sitting on the edge of a dark void Yatoa couldn't help but strain against the pressure. She worried she wasn't strong enough to handle it. It would crush her.

Arlicia seemed to think otherwise though, and Yatoa trusted her. So, she would press on.

The door to the jury consultation room opened and the jury spilled out. Once more everyone resumed their places to await the verdict. A gavel sounded.

"Court is back in session," Gob'Frey announced. "Jury your second verdict please."

The head juror stood with her hands clasped in front of her. "Yes, Your honor. With a nine to one split the jury declares a verdict of guilty in stage two of this trial." Yatoa winced, though this was what she had expected. She was a little surprised one member of the jury at least was on her side. To that singular individual Yatoa was winning this trial, and that had to count for something.

11

The Character of the Defendant

A memory flooded into Yatoa's mind as Gob'Frey considered those illuminated by flame. "One of the main functions of Goblin trials is not to prove whether someone did or did not commit a crime, but instead determine the degree of punishment. That's what the seven-verdict system is for, my dear," Arlicia had said to her a few weeks ago during the wagon ride to Gobroa. They were passing through rolling fields of pink flowers used for dye while sitting in a merchant's wagon bed.

"Then what about when you declare not-guilty at the start of a trial? Doesn't the trial become about proving someone's guilt?" she had asked in confusion. Arlicia shook her head.

"Nope. Well sort of, but not necessarily. It's not unheard of for someone who did commit a crime to get a not-guilty verdict if the jury decides they shouldn't punish them. Even if you win some verdicts, if you lose the trial the court hits the defendant with the full verdict, so it's risky and criminals rarely opt for it.

"Instead, they prefer the opportunity to lighten their sentence through winning a few verdicts if they plead guilty." Arlicia had held up her finger. "Declaring not-guilty is a risky move if the defendant did commit the crime. The verdicts have more weight in the eyes of the jurors. The Goblins figure that if someone wins four verdicts, even if they committed the crime, they don't deserve punishment. Only problem is only rich Goblins have managed that. Good lawyers aren't cheap."

The bang of the gavel squashed Yatoa's reverie. "For the jury's benefit I must explain this next section of the trial. Stages three and four change depending on what the charges are. In the case of theft and burglary these stages are about representing the character of the accused and the character of the victim. Therefore, we will now commence stage three of this trial: The Character of the Defendant."

Yatoa drew herself up and rounded the platform to stand at the point closest to the judge, then stood at attention. In this stage only Breichmar was not allowed to interject with any objections. However, afterward Breichmar would have the opportunity to question Dal. Not about the case, but about Dal as a person. As long as you weren't defending a murderous monster then this stage of the trial was supposedly the easiest for the defense.

"Ms. Yatoa, the floor is yours," Gob'Frey said to her.

"The defense calls Dal Gob'Alondis, Garna Gob'Alondis, and Darlia Gob'Alondis to the witness circle," Yatoa said in the most authoritative voice she could manage.

Dal hopped down from the defense circle. Garna materialized from the darkness holding Darlia's good hand and met her husband on the painted lines of the witness circle. Dal gave his wife a tender kiss on the forehead, then bent down to briefly wrap his arms around Darlia. He was careful of her glass arm.

Yatoa gave them a moment to themselves, letting the family have a tender reunion before the jury.

After a time Yatoa cleared her throat and the family turned to face her. "I am going to question you one at a time starting with Dal. Please state your name and occupation."

Dal placed a reassuring hand on his daughter's shoulder. "I'm Dal Gob'Alondis, and I'm a cobbler."

"Tell me about your business," Yatoa said.

"Well, I have my own shop and I mostly make boots see. I don't sell em for much. People in the Saern District can't afford much. So, I don't make much. It's a humble life I lead, Ms. Hu'Dectalaciumina, but as long as it leads to poor folk walkin' comfortably then I don't mind much. Even if my boots aren't anything to brag about at a Saern rodeo." Dal shrugged.

"Do you enjoy your life?"

"I'd say I do. My life is great all things considered. I got a lovely wife and an amazin' little girl, good friends, and my own business. I may not be rich, but my friends and family certainly make me feel rich. Only problem is my daughter's illness."

"Can you tell us more about that?"

Dal's face darkened and his grip on his daughter's shoulder visibly tightened. "The shatter's tough. No one should have to go through it and no one should have to see it happen to family. My daughter got it about four months ago, and with my shop I don't have enough money to pay a One Star to heal her. It's not fair."

"It's most certainly not," Yatoa agreed.

"And so, you have to understand that when a father loves his daughter like I do he'll do anythin' to save her. And I do all I can for her. I love my little girl. I always made time for her, playin' with her, makin' arts and crafts, takin' her for lunch in the Goblin District when I could afford to – you name it. I don't just want Darlia to live, I want her to have a better life than the one I had. I'm not a bad guy, but I want my daughter to be a better person than me. So, to see this happen to her is the cruelest joke the Gods above could have played on me. In Clemency Auto'Reille's name I swore I would do what I could for Darlia."

Invoking the name of the legendary Four Star Clemency Auto'Reille in oaths was loosely binding. Magically. It came from the powers associated with being a Four Star. Clemency, the only Four Star in recent history, was gone from this world now, but her power still draped over it like a blanket over a sleeping child. It had been 4,386 years since Clemency sealed away the God of Darkness, Rainea. This was good for their case. People rarely took such oaths lightly. While the oath wasn't enough to force Dal to steal anything, it did show his conviction.

"Thank you, Dal. I believe that's enough for now." She turned to his wife. "Witness please state your name and occupation for the court."

Garna looked up at Yatoa with a determined expression. "My name is Garna Gob'Alondis and I help with the shop."

"Mrs. Gob'Alondis can you tell us about how your daughter's illness has affected you personally?" It was not the question that Yatoa had originally planned on asking her, but she was feeling… spontaneous at the moment.

"Honestly, it's been emotionally draining. Seeing your little girl like that day in and day out, knowing what's coming, is hard. And I can't say it hasn't put a strain on our relationship-though don't get me wrong! He's a great husband and father. It's just… none of this is what I envisioned for myself."

"What did you envision for yourself?"

Garna shrugged. "I don't know. Something better I suppose. Maybe we'd save up enough money and move to the Goblin District and live happily there. I'm tired of those dusty streets, but now we have to save every penny for our daughter's eventual treatment, and even then, it may not be enough. Dal and I have to work to the bone day in and day out."

Yatoa tapped her chin in thought. Faz had said she'd given Garna the money. Darlia's arm glistened in the firelight, highlighting its smooth finish. Why?

"And so, if all had gone according to plan and Dal had retrieved the documents and the jewelry you would have been able to heal your daughter, yes?" Yatoa asked.

"That's… true," Garna admitted. "Dal only did what he did for Darlia's sake! He's not a bad man. He just wants the best for us. Is that so wrong?"

"I wouldn't say it's wrong Mrs. Gob'Alondis. But I'm curious. Why did Dal even bother with those documents? Wouldn't the money from the jewelry have been enough to pay for the healing?"

Garna opened her mouth but before she could say anything Dal cut in. "Can I say somethin'?" Yatoa considered him imperiously for a moment.

"You may."

"The sum offered for the documents was nothin' to scoff at either. With that money I coulda done more than heal my daughter or move to the Goblin District. I coulda given her the life I've always wanted for her." That made sense, but there was still something else nagging at her. *Who* was going to pay them that money? And why? Both had declined to answer before, and they wouldn't likely answer now in court, but... perhaps someone else would. She shelved the thought for later and decided to move on.

"Garna, how would you describe your husband?"

Garna spared a glance for Dal then her worried mouth cracked into a smile. "He's a kind and caring man. I think it was his empathy that drew me to him. Our parents arranged our marriage as is common in our district, but it was a good match. He's always been sweet to me and our daughter, and he has such a way with people. He's always chatting up customers, asking them about their day, sometimes even giving them advice. He's a man who lives for others. I just wish he'd live for himself sometimes."

"How long have you been together?"

"Fifteen years," Garna said.

"You said earlier that the current situation has put strain on your relationship. Would you expand on that?" Yatoa asked and almost kicked herself for doing so. Not the kind of question she should ask if she wanted to paint Dal in a good light.

Garna hesitated. "Every marriage has its ups and downs. I'd prefer not to talk about the details here in front of Darlia if it's alright with you." Yatoa almost sighed in relief. At least one of them knew what to say.

"Thank you, Garna. I'll now move on to your daughter." Before Yatoa could say a word more she felt a hand fall on her shoulder. Arlicia's hand to be exact.

"Yatoa a word," Arlicia whispered in her ear. Yatoa turned to Arlicia in confusion.

"What is it?"

Arlicia grinned and twiddled her thumbs. Yatoa felt a familiar jolt of despair. Whatever Arlicia was planning this time Yatoa wanted no part in it. "Well, remember when I said I wouldn't help you at all during the trial?"

"Yes, I recall," Yatoa said dryly.

"That was technically a lie. Since this is your first trial, I'm not allowed to let you do everything. I have to contribute meaningfully in at least one way or the judiciary back in the capital will charge me with negligence." Of course. Leave it to Arlicia to omit vital information like this until the last minute. "So, let me question Darlia and I'll be out of your hair."

Yatoa ground her teeth and whispered back furiously, "You couldn't have told me sooner? Do you even know how I wanted to bring Darlia into this, or what questions I wanted to ask her to make Dal look good? If I had known you were going to pull a stunt like this, I would have *planned* for it."

Arlicia shook her head. "My dear, let this be a lesson that trials don't always go as planned. And in terms of the questions, don't worry. I've done this a few times before, I can handle it." Yatoa stared at her mentor for a few moments, then sighed. "Alright."

Arlicia beamed at her then immediately *jumped off the defense platform*. Yatoa groaned. Then Arlicia knelt down in front of Darlia. "Hello little girl!" Arlicia announced. "I will be the one questioning you today. Will you please state your name and occupation?"

Darlia eyed at Arlicia in fear for a moment while clinging to her mother's skirt with her good hand. "Ummm… I'm Darlia and I'm eight-years-old."

"Ah yes. Being eight is such a stressful occupation," Arlicia said with a chuckle. That actually got a laugh out of some of the *jurors* too. "Tell me Darlia, what do you like to do for fun?"

"I… umm… I like to play card games with my dad. He plays them with me every evening. Although he hasn't done that for a few days because he's doing important adult things." Darlia spoke in a shaky quiet voice that made Yatoa want to reach out and hug her tight.

"Yes, he is certainly doing important things, but don't you worry. Ms. Hu'Dectalaciumina is working hard to make sure your dad comes home soon, and she'll succeed I promise."

"Objection, Your Honor!" Breichmar boomed from up on the prosecution circle. "Arlicia-"

"Objection, Your Honor!" Arlicia countered before Breichmar could finish. "I am trying to comfort a sick child, and Breichmar is intentionally undermining me by upsetting my witness with baseless objections. Besides, he should know better than to object during this phase."

"Sustained Ms. Sa'Krieglund," Gob'Frey announced. "Mr. Gob'Stellau please refrain from needless outbursts while the defense questions important, emotionally sensitive witnesses."

"Sorry about that, Ms. Gob'Alondis," Arlicia said with a sweet smile. "No one is mad at you. They're only mad at me I promise. People are always mad at me, because they can't seem to find a way to get over themselves. But I digress, tell me more about you father. Also," Arlicia looked over her shoulder back up at Yatoa. "Ms. Hu'Dectalaciumina would you please supplement Darlia's testimony with some visuals?"

Yatoa sighed readied her magic. Acting as Arlicia's assistant was something Yatoa had ample experience in, but it felt strange to shift into that version of herself when she had been in charge just moments before.

"Well, um… he's a good man. He always compliments me and takes me places when he can. Sometimes we feed ducks together down by the river." Yatoa traced her fingers through the air leaving behind green trails of light that formed themselves into an image of Dal and Darlia down by the river's edge in clothes nicer than ones they likely owned, tossing bread into the water. Yatoa embellished it further by making Darlia look extra cute with her wide eyes and short stubby nose, along with a big grin on her face in spite of the glass arm. "He's also teaching me how to read."

Yatoa created an image of Darlia studying a book at a table with Dal sitting next to her pointing out specific words on the page. The jury watched her illusions in awe as they listened to Darlia and Arlicia converse.

"You don't attend school?" Arlicia asked.

Darlia shook her head.

"And why-ever not?"

"Well, I was, but then I got sick and mommy said I had to stay at home." Yatoa weaved the lights into an image of Darlia snug in bed with Dal sitting at her bedside holding onto her glass hand.

Arlicia nodded, then she flipped her cane elaborately up in the air and caught it without looking, astonishing Darlia.

Arlicia ground the cane before her and stood like an ancient statue of a knight with their hands resting on the pommel of their blade.

"Now Darlia, if a healer cured you today and could go anywhere and do anything with your family, where would you go? What would you do?"

"Hmmm…" Darlia seemed lost in thought for a moment. "I'd want to go to Faestar Great Tree! I've always wanted to play with Fairies!" she said excitedly. A childish delight lit up her face. Yatoa had lived in Faestar Great Tree for a time, so she was able to recreate what a Faestar Street might look like. A winding road carved deep into a thick tree branch spiraling up high above the forest below. Buildings carved into the walls surrounding the road and vines draping overhead. She depicted Darlia playing among some flowers with Eliafa Fa'Natas, Yatoa's old Fairy friend. Eliafa was usually about size of Darlia – like all fairies she could change her size – and she had vibrant aquamarine hair that fell to her waist and almost glowing red eyes.

The Three Star Academy was in Faestar, and while Yatoa had not particularly enjoyed her time in the academy, she did love the city. Darlia's face illuminated by stray lights from the illusion adopted true wonder. She stared entranced at the image of her in that wondrous place. Arm free.

"I hope you get to do that one-day, Ms. Gob'Alondis," Arlicia whispered. "Don't you worry about a thing. This trial will be over before you know it." Arlicia flipped up her hand and reached for Yatoa's. She let her illusion dissipate in into a million green sparkles and helped Arlicia up onto the defense circle.

Darlia no longer clung to her mother's skirt. Instead, she grinned up at Yatoa and Arlicia in a way more adorable than even Yatoa's embellished illusions could manage. The firelight danced in those big, innocent eyes. "One more question for you, Ms. Gob'Alondis," Arlicia's voice boomed loud throughout the court for all to hear. "In your professional capacity as an eight-year-old do you think the defendant Dal Gob'Alondis ought to be punished for this crime?"

"No!" Darlia cried out enthusiastically.

Yatoa looked up from the little girl to Gob'Frey, who was watching the spectacle through her thin glasses. "The defense rests Your Honor."

"Very well, thank you, Ms. Yatoa. Mr. Gob'Stellau, you are now free to cross-examine the defendant if you wish."

Breichmar cleared his throat and boomed in his characteristically deep voice. "Defendant, is it true you are a seasoned thief?" Breichmar said while rubbing his chin.

"Define seasoned," Dal countered.

"Very well, seasoned as in you've stolen before and been tried for it. Albeit it was a minor offense of no more than fifteen gobbings from someone's purse when you were twenty-four, yet still this heist is nothing new to you." Yatoa had found this criminal record early on in her research of the case and she knew Breichmar would bring it up. She didn't think it was overly important though.

"Then yeah I'm seasoned," Dal said calmly. "But I was a stupid kid who needed a good lickin' back then. Haven't done it since. I've grown a lot."

"Clearly not," Breichmar said with a smile. "Because here you are fourteen-years later in court for theft once more, only this time on a bigger scale. If you've done any growing defendant, it's been into a more skilled and ambitious thief. You even have a crew this time. This seems to indicate to me that you've indeed done this kind of thing a few times since you were twenty-five."

"Objection, Your Honor!" Yatoa shouted eagerly drawing the attention from everyone in the room on her. "The defense requests that the prosecution refrain from baseless accusations. Mr. Gob'Stellau is accusing him of yet more crimes, yet has no evidence these crimes took place or that Dal was even involved."

"Sustained. Mr. Gob'Stellau please refrain from any more accusations unless you can provide some incriminating evidence, testimony, or connection to the court."

Breichmar took this in stride. While Yatoa's objection was a victory for the defense it was a small one. He had already done damage. The jury heard what Gob'Stellau implied and that would color their perception of Dal. Breichmar likely expected the objection.

"Defendant, was your family aware this crime was going to take place before hand, or did you hide it from them?" Breichmar asked then waited with his hands behind his back.

From his perch he looked awfully cocky. He was literally looking down upon Dal.

"I didn't tell them," Dal lied.

"And when you succeeded, what lie would you have told them to explain the sudden fortune you gained?" Yatoa saw Dal clench his jaw, and she prayed he would have the sense to stay calm.

"I was planning on tellin' them the truth after the fact."

"And would your wife approve of what you had done?"

"That's irrelevant," Dal shot back. "No matter what my wife thinks I did this for my daughter. Even if my wife ended up resentin' me for it, which I doubt, it would all be worth it to see Darlia cured."

Breichmar smiled again ghoulishly. "I see, though you failed. And now your family has to go through yet more hardship with this trial."

"It was worth the risk!"

"Perhaps, though don't you think you should have consulted with your wife first before deciding for your family what ought to be? Your selfishness has only made things worse for them."

"Objection!" Yatoa cried out. "The prosecution is badgering the defendant."

"Sustained. Mr. Gob'Stellau please refrain from personal attacks." Though once again, the damage had been done.

"There's no need for that, Your Honor," Breichmar said with a flippant hand gesture. "The prosecution rests."

"It is time then for another short recess," Gob'Frey announced. The jury exited the room in a manner that already felt rote and Yatoa was once again left alone with her thoughts. The witnesses left the circle.

Yatoa took a seat next to Dal on the defense platform and together they waited, taking comfort in each other's silence. They both knew the same thing. It would be a grim prognosis if the Jury landed on a guilty verdict regarding Dal's character. Convincing the Jury he deserved to walk would become as Goblins flying through the air without wings; impossible.

Anxiety built in Yatoa. She felt confident in their performance, but Breichmar's digs concerned her. She felt he had done too much damage. Well, she'd soon find out.

"Thank you," Dal said. "For bein' here for me. Not even my closest friend is here to support me, but you are and we barely know each other."

"I'm just doing my job," Yatoa said.

"You're doin' more than that. Even if things don't work out, I won't resent you for it. You're doin' your best and that's what counts." That touched a vein deep in Yatoa's heart.

She thought of a man with no one to defend him, and a girl whose fate rested on the verdict. This situation was so eerily similar that one from her distant past, but this time Dal did have someone to defend him. This time Yatoa wasn't powerless.

"I'll get you acquitted," Yatoa stated. *That's a fact, right?* She thought while trying to avoid glancing into the dark depths of her anxiety's gaping maw.

The jury finally finished and everyone stood.

"Court is back in session," Gob'Frey announced after a slam of the gavel. "Jury your verdict."

The matronly head juror stood once more and said, "Yes, Your Honor. With a seven to three split the jury declares a verdict of not guilty in stage three of this trial." *Seven to three?* Yatoa grimaced, but she would take what she could get.

"Very well. This means that currently the verdict rests at two to one in favor of the defense. At this time, we will progress to stage four of this trial: The Character of the Victim.

12

The Character of the Victim

Yatoa half-listened as Breichmar called Cartaneal Gob'Franat to the stand. She knew she would lose this stage no matter what she tried. Despite her basic research into the man and the one conversation Yatoa had with him, she hardly knew anything about the money-grubbing Goblin.

He stood there now looking distinguished in his blue, silk suit and his slicked-back hair. His ears drooped and his smile ominously displayed his razor-sharp teeth.

Breichmar stood tall looking down on Cartaneal with a too pleasant smile.

"Victim please state your name and occupation for the court record."

"I am Cartaneal Gob'Franat. I am a property owner, jewelry collector, and philanthropist," Gob'Franat said in his squeaky, obnoxious voice.

"Can you elaborate on what you mean by philanthropist?" Breichmar asked.

"Well, I donate monthly to several charities, I fund a major public school, and I run several homeless shelters. As a matter of fact, last month I organized a fundraiser that raised three-thousand gobbings for shatter research. They're trying to find ways to treat the illness without the aid of a One Star healer."

Yatoa wanted to wring Gob'Franat's neck. How dare he say that with Darlia watching. Testifying against her father; trying to kill the only Goblin who would save her. It made her sick.

"I see, that is very noble of you."

"It is what it is. I just want to do everything I can to make Gobroa a better and safer place for all."

Breichmar nodded. "I'm sure that is a sentiment everyone in this room can appreciate. I personally thank you for your efforts in that regard Mr. Gob'Franat. You are an inspiration to us all." Yatoa desperately fought the urge to roll her eyes in front of everyone.

"Now about the robbery. How did you feel when you returned to find that thieves had burglarized your home?"

Cartaneal tugged at his cravat which looked much too tight around his thick neck. The short man looked uncomfortable standing in the witness circle, looking up at them. He usually looked down. "Well, to be honest I felt violated. It's hard to walk around your own home after someone has broken in. Usually, your home feels like a sanctuary, but once that's violated you start checking over your shoulder at every little noise. I tell you the other day I saw a shadow shift in my bedroom and I jumped out of my bed screaming."

Cartaneal cleared his throat. Listening to this testimony made Yatoa feel like she was being punished in some deep circle of hell. It was bad for her case, but that was the point.

Unless Breichmar stepped out of line somehow Yatoa would have to bear it.

"I have a deep fondness for my jewelry. That jewelry collection has been carefully built up over the last three decades. All of the pieces are one of a kind, hand-crafted masterworks. Many of those stolen were from foreign nations, and some even belonged to monarchs. It held an immense sentimental value to me. In this theft I lost much of my assets as well as my treasure. It is irreplaceable and I will never forgive those who have wronged me."

Breichmar nodded sympathetically. "Tell me, is there any piece that you particularly miss?"

"Two pieces in fact," Cartaneal said. He held up two fingers excitedly to emphasize the point. "The first was a necklace with a green jewel shaped like a four-pointed star. It used to belong to Clemency herself. At least I have the certificate of authenticity still…" Cartaneal sighed. His shoulders slumped.

"The second piece was a blue and gold floral brooch that used to belong to my mother. Now *that* was irreplaceable. It's been in my life since I was a babe. Never in my life have I gone so long without seeing it." Yatoa cringed. Despite the fact that she didn't believe Dal deserved punishment, the gravity of the crime he committed was hitting her at full force. The estimated value of the goods stolen alone was enough to make her cringe.

"I still have a lot of money," Cartaneal continued, "so it's not as though this has ruined me, thankfully, but this is a huge blow to my finances. It could limit my capacity to help the public I'm afraid."

"That would be a loss for us all," Breichmar said in a defeated tone.

"Yes, a loss that is no fault of my own, but that of miscreants," Cartaneal said in a huff.

Breichmar nodded in agreement. "I'm sure everyone in this room is aware of the Gob'Franat Academy of Higher Learning. Mr. Gob'Franat can you tell us a bit about this institution?"

Cartaneal puffed his chest out and grinned in a way that made him look like an over-powdered jester. "Why it would be my pleasure. The Gob'Franat Academy of High Learning is the most prestigious institution in all of Gobroa, churning out our society's finest minds each year. My late father started it and I have inherited the duty of seeing to the school's needs. I make sure it runs smoothly and I keep it afloat through my investments. The school has flourished. It has also granted opportunities to even some of the least fortunate members of the Goblin District."

But not the Saern District, Yatoa thought bitterly.

"What of your family?" Breichmar asked.

Cartaneal chuckled. "They're the light of my life! I have two daughters and one son. The former two are attending the academy as well. One of them is studying to be a prosecutor like you, Mr. Gob'Stellau."

A smile crept onto Breichmar's face like a snake stalking a bird; cold, sinuous, and calculated. "A noble profession."

"That it is! I eat dinner with them every night, you know. Jolly good kids. And their mother… Ha! Fantastic woman!

She's drop dead gorgeous too. I love them all! My love for them isn't even rivaled by my jewelry collection. I'm thankful they only stole my assets and not my family."

"You are truly an inspiration to us all. If only our society had more true gentlemen like you Mr. Gob'Franat." With that Breichmar turned to the judge and swept a deep bow. "That'll be enough. The prosecution rests, Your Honor."

"Thank you Mr. Gob'Stellau," she said. "Ms. Yatoa, the floor is yours." Finally. Yatoa didn't have much to say to Cartaneal about his character, but there was still one thing nagging at her.

"Mr. Gob'Franat is it alright if I ask you about some details of the case?" she asked as courteously as she could manage. It was hard to look at him and not think of how he had tried to bribe her.

"That is what I am here for," he pointed out lamely. Yatoa bit back her annoyance and pressed on.

"Mr. Gob'Franat. It has come to the attention of the court that the defendant was trying to steal some documents from your office. Would you be willing to give us a basic explanation of what they contained? Or at the very least what one could stand to gain from seeing their contents?"

Cartaneal considered her for a moment, and Yatoa thought he'd refuse. "That detail has been bothering me actually," Cartaneal said finally. *It was bothering* him? Yatoa thought with a frown.

"Elaborate," she commanded.

"Well, the documents were a real estate landscape report. The report concerned the land I have recently purchased in the Saern District. You see I plan to liven up that part of town with a brand-new high-end market. It would help bring in more affluent members of the city." *And push out the poor ones.*

"But what gets me is that there's nothing important in those documents, and furthermore their contents are generally public knowledge. In fact, much of what is in them was recently published in the Gobroa Times. If you aren't familiar Ms. Yatoa, it is a new craze called a newspaper! It's sort of like a written report on recent events within the city that everyone can read so they can keep in touch with current events." Yatoa had heard of newspapers before. Admittedly she had never actually seen one. "Anyway, they were not important documents. I have no idea why someone would steal them let alone pay someone a significant amount to do so."

That… was strange. "You're absolutely sure there are no business rivals who could stand to gain from stealing these documents from you?"

Gob'Franat rubbed his chin in thought for a moment. "I'm certain. Especially when it comes to the Saern district. A lot of my rivals spurned the idea of trying to buy land there. They said I was foolish for doing so, but they shall see soon enough."

Standing there, gripping the edge of her cape, Yatoa came to a conclusion. Someone set Dal up. Whoever it was, they wanted Dal in that room, separated from his crew. It wasn't actually about the worthless documents. No other explanation made sense. And if that was the case, then the lookout had to have been in on it. Could it have really been Faz? Had she lied?

An image of Faz drinking orange juice came unbidden to Yatoa's mind. That was just a silly superstition. She couldn't make any meaningful decisions based on juice... right?

The juice she had brought with her to the trial in her bag for the final stage betrayed her desperate attempt at citrus atheism. Yet, Faz could have lied about not being the lookout, especially if she wanted Dal to get caught. The only question that remained was: why? For now though, Yatoa had to grill a rich Goblin.

"How many students from the Saern District does your institution admit each year, Mr. Gob'Franat?" She asked, veering in a different direction.

Cartaneal frowned. "None."

"And whyever not? I thought helping the unfortunate was a passion of yours. Don't you want to provide them with equal opportunities?"

Cartaneal scoffed. "I want to provide the less fortunate with opportunities, not uncultured bottom-feeders that contribute nothing to our society!" he snapped. Yatoa paused to let his words sink in with the jury.

"Is that how you'd describe Darlia Gob'Alondis?" Yatoa asked softly.

"I can't be worrying about every sick child in the city," Cartaneal said. "Truly her situation is pitiable, but that doesn't change what her father is. A dirty thief! One who steals both money and one's sense of security. He's no member of our society. He's a leech!"

Yatoa shrugged and tossed one side of her cape over her shoulder. "Don't you think that maybe if Goblins had more equal opportunities they wouldn't have to 'leech' off others so to speak."

"Of course not!" Cartaneal said sounding scandalized. "It is not their circumstances that make them this way, but their very nature! Thieves like Dal Gob'Alondis don't stop after they take others' money. They continue to leech more, and if one does not rip a leech off, then death from blood loss becomes inevitable. These are not the types of people we should be supporting as a society."

"Yet they live here, amongst you all in Gobroa. Just because you choose not to see them doesn't mean they're not actually there," Yatoa said. She hated this man. "Open your eyes, see clearly, are they leeches or are they simply making a place for themselves? They don't have the power to legally take money like you do, so they steal it. Regardless of the details, both those with and without money leech. It's the way society is set up." Cartaneal opened his mouth to respond, but Yatoa didn't want to let him have the final word. "The defense rests, Your Honor."

Cartaneal tensed and glared violently at Yatoa, but she did her best to ignore it. "Very well. At this time, we will undergo another recess."

This left Yatoa with yet more time for contemplation, and this recess no one interrupted her. Though Arlicia stared her down. It made her feel like a zoo animal. Yatoa could only guess at the mental notes Arlicia had been making. What had Yatoa missed? Could Arlicia have done a better job? Was it possible to have three verdicts at this point instead of two?

Of course it was possible. Of course she could be doing a better job. Yet she had to tell herself that none of that mattered right now. All Yatoa needed to do was keep calm and take each moment as they came.

She gazed into the dark void that was the audience as she thought, and it occurred to her that she was probably staring down some poor soul in the gallery. She averted her eyes to the flame. The flame was not hot. Instead, it undulated in on itself as if alive.

There were three mysteries to this case. The first, why was Dal set up? That one she was unsure of, and there was no way to know unless she knew who had done it. Which led to the second mystery, who was the lookout? Again, she'd need to learn more before she could say for sure. The third and most important, where was Dal's share of the money? If she could figure that out somehow, then she could save Darlia.

Returning to the first mystery, even if she found who set Dal up, how would it affect the trial? Could she use it to get the jury to sympathize with him? Either way it wasn't something she could count on.

She rested her elbows up on the prosecution circle and analyzed the flame. Despite illuminating her immediate surroundings this flame also consumed everything beyond it, hiding it from view. Its light felt unnatural. Everything in its illumination radius was more brightly lit than it should be for a flame this size. The illumination ended too abruptly at the gallery as well. Almost as if the light refused to travel beyond the edge of the litigation area.

Then Yatoa realized what it was she had been staring at all this time. This wasn't a flame at all.

The jury returned though Yatoa didn't notice until they shut the door behind them. She spun, heart beating. She prayed she had done enough. Hopefully she had left them with a bad enough taste in their mouths.

The gavel slammed, stimulating Yatoa's nerves. "Court is back in session. Jury your verdict."

The head juror stood and Yatoa crossed her fingers behind her back. A win here would put her a breath away from winning this trial. "Yes, Your Honor. With a seven to three split the jury declares a verdict of guilty in stage three of this trial." Yatoa's heart sank.

She hadn't swayed enough of them. Perhaps she had swayed a fourth or a fifth juror, but not strongly enough to survive the jury's deliberations.

"That leaves us at a tie of two verdicts to two verdicts," Gob'Frey announced. "With that we will move on to stage five of this trial: The Flame Demon's Judgment."

13

Piriel

Jury, you should already be aware of this, but just in case know that your judgment will not be required for this stage nor the next as external factors determine both verdicts," Gob'Frey explained. "Without further ado I surrender all judgment and authority to the Flame Demon." Gob'Frey pressed her fists together and held them up to her forehead. For a moment nothing happened.

The whole room shook with a sudden violence that knocked Yatoa's shoulder against the prosecution circle. The Goblins with their lower centers of gravity fared better, and Arlicia, who had clearly expected this, was already seated. The flame in the center of the court exploded upward, climbing all the way to the ceiling. Streams of fire spiraled out of the central column and gripped the edges of the defense and prosecution platforms as if they were the arms of some giant beast. Yatoa realized a moment later that was exactly what they were.

The fire concentrated, flames collapsing in on themselves like paper folding again and again, until it formed one central humanoid mass.

Then the flames extinguished plunging the room into darkness.

The room no longer trembled, but Yatoa still did. She glanced around in a panic. Yatoa hadn't known what to expect despite reading about this stage in detail and how unconventional it was. This was *certainly* unconventional.

A deep, grating voice punctured the darkness with a single question. "Would you care to go first, little Goblin?" Its intonation unkind.

"Yes, My Lord." Breichmar's voice.

At once light abounded. No fire illuminated the court. Light just seemed to exist in the air around them without a source. In the center of the room, standing atop a platform of purple crystal that filled in the hole of the prosecution circle was the Flame Demon.

It did not at all look like what Yatoa had expected. She had expected fangs, horns, sharp claws, glowing red eyes, and fire everywhere. What she saw was a nine-foot-tall humanoid figure standing in the middle of the room. Its skin red. It wore an elaborate robe that draped over only one shoulder, then gathered around its waist and fell down to its ankles. The materials of the cloak were of the finest quality. It was a myriad of warm colors with flame like patterns woven into the fabric and it sparkled as the demon moved. With only one shoulder exposed the demon bared a single breast out to the open. While the demon did have breasts, for whatever reason Yatoa still felt as though it had no gender. Its smooth face that was at once hard and soft in an impossible combination looked neither masculine nor feminine, but something else entirely. Its long, blood-red hair cascading down its back brought only one word to mind: wild. Yatoa could see flames reflected in its eyes, though there were no flames in the room.

"I am Piriel, the Flame Demon," Piriel said in that harsh voice. When it spoke, it revealed that it did in fact have fangs, so Yatoa's original mental image wasn't completely off.

Piriel looked massive standing on the platform above Yatoa, and even larger still when standing next to Breichmar. The Goblin had to crane his head all the way to meet Piriel's eyes. "I am Breichmar Gob'Stellau My Lord. The prosecutor in this case."

With an eye-blink, Piriel was standing in a different spot. It was on the defense platform now, right next to Yatoa. In spite of herself Yatoa screamed. Piriel paid her no mind.

"Breichmar. I have observed the entire trial up until this point," Piriel said. It still towered over Breichmar even on the defense platform. It rested its hand next to Breichmar and crouched down. "Tell me. Do you believe Dal deserves to die for what he did?"

Breichmar stared into those flaming eyes unflinching. There was no wind in the room, yet his cape blew gently away from Piriel. "Yes. I believe Dal should have his body crushed between two slabs of marble, so that it may not even his own family will recognize him" Horror seized Yatoa. How could anyone say such a thing in a courtroom?

"Objection!" she cried out. But Piriel lifted a hand and flicked a finger through the air, sealing Yatoa's mouth shut.

Yatoa panicked. She tried to pull her lips apart to release her screams, but her body refused to listen. Horror settled in, making itself at home.

"Do not speak unless spoken to. You will have respect for Ancient Ones such as I, or I shall burn you alive," Piriel said this while still staring at Breichmar. "Breichmar. Would you kill Dal with your own hands for committing this crime?"

"If the law permitted me to My Lord, then I would," Breichmar said with a bow of respect.

Piriel smirked, ignoring Yatoa's muffled screams. Then Piriel placed its large hand over Yatoa's shoulder in an almost comforting gesture. At least it would have been comforting if its hand wasn't unnaturally huge. Warmth radiated from Piriel's hand into Yatoa. Yatoa ceased her scream attempts out of fear of what Piriel might do should she continue.

"Would you kill Dal if I told you to do so?" Piriel asked, leaning in close to Breichmar. Breichmar to his credit did not move a muscle.

"No," Breichmar said.

"Even if I would kill you otherwise?" Piriel was frowning now. For a moment, Yatoa felt true fear for Breichmar's life.

"I would never break such a sacred law as the law not to kill. Not even for one so great as you, My Lord."

Piriel stood to its full height, taking its hand off Yatoa's shoulder then in an instant it was seated next to Yatoa on her other side, facing out toward the gallery. Piriel sat between her and Dal she realized. Yatoa could not see Dal over its large form. Piriel smiled as if in fond remembrance.

"You stay true to what you believe in Breichmar. I respect that. But tell me. Why should Dal be punished?"

Breichmar looked at the back of Piriel's head. "Because he violated the sacred laws of our society, created by your kind so that we may live in peace and harmony. If I allowed people to do such things then our then society would be impossible."

"Very well said, Breichmar. Seat yourself." Breichmar did as asked, sitting with his legs over the edge of the prosecution platform. "Close your eyes." Breichmar complied once again. He grew stiff. His jaw clenched. It lasted only a few moments, but then he relaxed, opened his eyes, and released a shaky breath. "The prosecution will now rest," Piriel said. "Defense it is your turn."

Yatoa blinked then found herself in a completely different position. She was sitting in Piriel's lap like a child. It took all her willpower to force herself into staying calm. Hesitantly she looked up at Piriel. Piriel smiled warmly down at her, but the fire in its eyes singed Yatoa's already frayed nerves.

"Should I kill Dal?" Piriel asked in a too pleasant tone. Yatoa swallowed.

"No, you should not," Yatoa said, then belatedly added, "My Lord." Piriel chuckled. The sounds were disturbing. Too much like a crackling fire for a humanoid mouth to make.

"And why shouldn't I? He has committed a grave crime."

Yatoa took a deep breath, grasping for any mental tricks that would help herself retain control. "We have not finished trying Dal yet. A sentence cannot pass until this trial concludes. If we executed people on the spot without giving them the chance to defend themselves, then as Breichmar said earlier, society wouldn't be possible."

"And yet he did commit the crime. What more is there to discuss? If all we need is a verdict then why shouldn't we go ahead and pass it? It'll save everyone's time." Yatoa didn't like the sickly smile on Piriel's face.

"That would be wrong. Just because a man commits a crime doesn't mean he deserves to die. Dal deserves to live," Yatoa said forcefully.

Yatoa was in a different place. She was standing on the purple crystalline platform. Piriel stood on the defense circle below with its arms resting on her platform. "You would dare dispute the sacred laws my kind worked so hard together with the Goblins to create? You are a human. What could you possibly know of our ways?"

"I am an attorney," Yatoa corrected. "I live to interpret laws. Laws should change. Sometimes laws should be overlooked. Laws are not final. Society has no need for laws that function only to keep down the weak." Yatoa believed in what she was saying, but before those firey eyes her voice faltered a bit. It was hard to speak.

"Why do you think Dal doesn't deserve to die?" Piriel asked. It seemed to ignore Yatoa's previous answer. Yatoa did not think it even listened.

"Dal is a good man who stole an apple from an apple orchard so to speak. Gob'Franat does not need so much wealth. That wealth could be put to better use improving the lives of the less fortunate. Dal's daughter Darlia for instance. Dal could cure Darlia with that money."

Piriel shook her head. "Cartaneal needs the money in order to help the less fortunate. It is the law that dictates who has money and how they can use it. It was not Dal's place to go outside the law. I find your argument distasteful and insulting. You would suggest the very nature of this law be the result of a lapse in judgment on my part."

"That's not what I-"

"Silence!" Piriel roared. Yatoa was back on the defense platform now and Piriel stood on the platform above her looking down on her in every sense of the word. "Laws are absolute in this world. Only those who have the power to bend them deserve to. All others must be bound, else what world will there be? One of beasts, not one of men. One of stagnation, not one of progress. I should kill Dal right now." Piriel held up a palm in Dal's direction.

Not even knowing if it would help or not Yatoa flung herself in the way. "Don't you dare," she spat at Piriel. "By the same laws you claim to uphold, Dal is innocent until proven guilty in a court of law, which hasn't happened. I declared *not-guilty* at the start of this trial. If you killed him now, then you would be stepping outside of what the law requires of you."

Piriel waved a hand in dismissal. "Flame Demons are not bound by the laws of Goblins. We may kill if we wish."

"Not on my watch," Yatoa snapped.

"Such a tone! Very well, Yatoa. If that is what you wish I will respect it. There but remains one more step to this little exercise," Piriel said. "Close your eyes."

Yatoa did as instructed.

She was no longer in the courtroom. Instead, she was in an endless purple tunnel, floating in its center. She could see through its transparent walls into the violet star-filled space beyond. Fear and anger battled within her chest like two violent storms clashing. Why? Why did she feel this way? What was she doing again?

She felt wind rush past her, or perhaps it was her rushing past the wind. She was flying down the tunnel. Everything was some shade of purple and at these speeds they blended into a gradient of streaks. Then she hit it. The ground.

She was in a house. Her childhood home. A safe place. A dangerous place. A paradox. She moved. The house wouldn't let her. She screamed. Her mother answered.

"My dear what brings you home so early?" Her mother was older, lines streaked her face. Her skin was as dark as Yatoa's and her hair just as wavy. Her nose was more pronounced though. Just like Soloa's had been.

"I came home for a break from my studies," Yatoa answered truthfully. "I needed… a break. Bad. Because it was getting too stressful."

Her mother guided her to the kitchen table. The same table she had carved animals into the underside of with her sister. When her mother seated her, Yatoa felt at the dog carving underneath the lip. It was familiar. It was home.

Yatoa lifted her arm up onto the table. Why did it feel so stiff all of the sudden?

"How is the Three Star Academy treating you?" Her mother asked, seated across from her. Her smile was genuine. Her mother had not smiled at her that way in years.

"It's fine," Yatoa lied. She didn't feel bad for lying. It felt natural. Like putting on a well-worn coat. "How is father?"

Her mother clasped her hands together in delight. "I am *so* proud of you, Soloa," she said gleefully. Soloa was not here though. Why would she say that?

"Why would you say that?"

"Because you are my beloved daughter, and you are here with me again. I am so happy." Tears leaked from her mother's eyes and she grinned. That expression felt wrong.

"I am not Soloa," Yatoa said.

Her mother leaned in so far her eyes almost touched Yatoa's face. She wanted to move back but she couldn't. "You could be, Yatoa. All you have to do is try for me. Won't you try for mommy? Won't you be a good girl for once?"

"No… nonononono NO!" Yatoa panted. She couldn't take her eyes off her mother.

Her mother cupped her cheek with her cold hand. "But my darling, you're already doing such a good job! You've even got the hand right." Yatoa was free to move her eyes once more, but now she was too afraid to. "Go on, look."

Yatoa looked.

Her arm was glass.

Yatoa screamed into the courtroom and only stopped when Arlicia gripped her shoulder.

"Pathetic," Piriel said, its tongue dripping with disdain. Yatoa was back on the defense platform, with Piriel looming tall from its crystal above. "Do you even care about Dal Gob'Alondis at all? You defend him, but in your heart, you're making this trial entirely about yourself, aren't you? A wretched, self-centered little girl like you doesn't belong in the sacred Goblin courts."

She *was* selfish. The words imprisoned her in her mind. This *was* about her. This was some weird second chance to avenge her sister, but only in her head. This trial wouldn't bring

Soloa back. This trial wouldn't make Yatoa feel like her own person. She was just playing pretend using someone else's life. Her sister's life. She wasn't supposed to have any of thIs. She Wasn't supposed to be here. If her sister was alive their parents would have married Yatoa off and she'd have been a housewife to some fisherman on her home island, not an apprentice to the God Lawyer.

She wasn't supposed to have any of this. This was wrong. Did she even care about Dal? About Darlia? Or was this all about Soloa?

Piriel raised a hand and snapped its fingers. The sound was the sharp crack of a whip. "My judgment is set. I, Piriel the Flame Demon, declare the defendant Dal Gob'Alondis guilty in stage five of this trial."

Yatoa saw the future play out before her. She would lose this trial and Arlicia would cast her aside like a child that had grown bored of a new toy. Then Dal would die. Then Darlia would die. Garna would grieve her family, all alone...

Selfish...

She gasped suddenly, oxygen filling her lungs and shocking her from her spiraling mental descent. The hairs on the back of her neck stood, but she dared not give voice to her new thoughts before they were fully formed. She knew the truth of this trial now.

And it was horrible.

Piriel's fist clenched and the room went dark.

14

Yatoa Hu'Dectalaciumina

A flame exploded forth in the center of the room bathing everything in a warm glow. Piriel was gone.

"That concludes stage five of this trial," Gob'Frey announced. "The verdicts stand in favor of the prosecution at three to two. I would like to remind everyone that should the prosecution win this next stage the defendant, Gob'Alondis, shall be declared guilty immediately and the trial shall end. Ms. Yatoa, do you understand this?"

Yatoa just stared at the judge dumbly for a moment.

"Do you *understand* this?" she repeated impatiently.

"I understand, Your Honor," Yatoa forced herself to say. She wasn't a lawyer, but if she didn't stop pretending to be one what would she have left? Breichmar cleared his throat and raised an arm. "Yes Mr. Gob'Stellau, what is it?"

"Your Honor, this is the defense's first trial in a court of law and so it would be cruel for things to end so terribly because the defense was overconfident, naïve, and unprepared causing them to declare not guilty at the start of this trial. Dal Gob'Alondis will die if I win this next stage, and so I have an offer to make to the defense. The prosecution is willing to accept an admission of guilt now through appealing to civil court rule 14-5: special accommodations of guilt.

"If the defense chooses to plead guilty at this point in time the trial will end immediately and Dal Gob'Alondis will get the reduced sentence that two won verdicts would have awarded him had the defense pleaded guilty at the start. That would reduce his sentence from marble crushing to a minimum of fifteen years in prison."

Yatoa chewed over the words in her brain, analyzing their taste. She didn't hate the taste. It was appealing. If the trial continued, she'd get Dal killed. There was no way she could be certain that she'd win the next two verdicts, especially after losing the last two.

A hand on her shoulder. "Yatoa, if you need, I can take over for you. I can handle this and you can rest alright?" Arlicia said to her soothingly. "No need to plead guilty."

That was also attractive. If she could let a real lawyer handle this then she could stop pretending and no one would judge her. Arlicia might even be able to save Dal's life.

Arlicia's eyes were tense with concern. The crinkles at the edges were tell-tale signs. Did Yatoa look that distressed? That shaken? If everyone could see it in her, then what chance did she have? Even the jury probably saw her as an inexperienced apprentice in over her head. The judge didn't even have the decency to use her last name.

"Ms. Yatoa, what would you like to do?" Gob'Frey asked. "Will you plead guilty on the behalf of your defendant, or will you defer to Ms. Sa'Krieglund?" That was the choice.

Which one was better? She didn't know. Whichever one got her out of this courtroom quickest perhaps.

Yatoa was about to speak when she caught the eye of the only person in the room who mattered. Dal's large Goblin-sized brown eyes held confidence. Faith. He didn't look at her the way everyone else did.

At that moment Yatoa knew what he saw. He didn't see some silly apprentice, nor did he see some pale imitation of her perfect sister. Instead, he saw the one person who through all of this was willing to stand up for him and fight. Someone who had his best interests at heart. Someone to defend him.

Yatoa wanted that for herself. She wanted someone to defend her, to hide her from the pain. But she knew that it was not the job of a shield to hide from pain. Shields bore pain. Shields *defended.* And so would she.

"The defense will continue as is, Your Honor," Yatoa said, not taking her eyes away from Dal lest she lose the strength she needed to say it. "I will continue to represent Dal Gob'Alondis until the end and I refuse to plead guilty."

Gob'Frey nodded. "Very well. Then we shall commence stage six of this trial: The Test. Bailiff bring forth the Honest Blade." A purple Goblin man in a blue uniform approached the defense circle with a sheathed longsword. "At this time, I ask that both the defense and the prosecution step down form their platforms and stand before the jury."

"Yatoa… Are you sure about this? If you have any doubt in your heart the blade will know," Arlicia said with a hand on Yatoa's shoulder.

"I know the risk, and I'm willing to take it." Yatoa stepped off the platform and dropped to the ground, her cape trailing behind her. She strode confidently then stood before the jury with her hands folded behind her back. Breichmar joined her, standing up straight at her side, though only coming up to her waist. The Bailiff stood between them and the jury box with a hand on the hilt of the Honest Blade.

"As you know, the blade decides the verdict in this stage of the trial. Just so the jury is aware the Honest Blade will not slice clean through if a person stays true to their convictions. First, I will ask them a question as to what verdict they truly believe the defendant deserves. They will give their answers. Then they will wager a part of their body on their answer. The blade will swing an if they have even the slightest doubt then it will cut straight through. If they are firm in their beliefs then the blade will stop short, just giving them a scratch."

A juror raised a hand.

"Yes? Juror number three?" Gob'Frey said.

"Um well," the juror began, "what happens if the blade slices through neither of them, or even both of them?"

"A good question. At that point the victor is determined by the significance of the body part wagered. Usually, this stage is easier for the prosecution to pass the test of conviction, so the defense gets to go second giving them the advantage of upping the ante. Any more questions?"

The jury remained silent and a few of them were already covering their eyes. Yatoa didn't blame them. If either her or Breichmar failed in their convictions this would become a gruesome display.

"Mr. Gob'Stellau. Do you believe the victim ought to be punished with the full weight of the guilty verdict, and crushed to death by marble?" Gob'Frey asked quite morbidly.

"Yes, I do," Breichmar said with no hesitation.

"What will you wager for your belief?"

Breichmar raised his hand into the air. "I wager my left hand, and I do so with the utmost confidence." He held his hand out before him and pulled up the sleeve of his suit revealing his bare, green wrist.

The bailiff drew the Honest Blade. Its blade was unlike any blade Yatoa had ever seen. It was jade green all throughout, with words engraved into it. The characters were of an ancient language, unfamiliar to Yatoa, but it shared a vaguely similar writing style to how Goblins wrote the Stellarian language in modern day.

"Are you ready Mr. Gob'Stellau?" The bailiff asked with some concern in his voice. Breichmar was far from young, and so Yatoa could understand the bailiff's reservations of slicing into an old man, even if the bailiff was seasoned in this particular activity.

"As ready as I'll ever be," Breichmar replied. "Do it and marvel at my conviction."

The bailiff nodded then raised the sword high over his head. He brought the blade down in a savage chop on Breichmar's wrist. Yatoa forced herself to watch.

The blade stopped mid swing. Unnaturally so. It was as if it had struck an invisible stone. The bailiff pulled the blade away revealing Breichmar's hand intact. The only sign the blade had struck him was a tiny cut that leaked a single droplet of blood. Breichmar lifted the wound to his mouth and licked it clean.

"Simple," he said. He sounded far too pleased with himself.

Yatoa gulped in spite of herself. This was a true test. This whole trial had been a test from the beginning, but this was the moment where she passed or failed. If she succeeded, she would prove to everyone that she was what Dal saw in her… If she failed… she'd only prove what she herself had always suspected. That she was a child playing grown up.

Piriel was right. This trial had always been about her, not Dal. In a way she had been the one on trial the whole time. Desperately fighting to prove that she was her own person – that she had a right to exist. Only she played with someone else's life. There had been no real stakes for her. Only her ego had been on the line.

Until now.

She would fix that. If she was to be on trial with Dal then she would give herself the same stakes.

"Ms. Yatoa. Do you believe the victim ought to be punished with the full weight of the guilty verdict, and crushed to death by marble?" Gob'Frey asked her. Yatoa took a deep breath. Even if this trial was actually about herself, she still wanted to defend Dal. It was about him too. She would do so to the bitter end.

"No, I do not," Yatoa answered. Her heart raced. Palms slick with sweat she counted every moment until the next question.

"What will you wager for your belief?"

"My head."

That brought gasps from beyond the darkness and the once silent courtroom flooded with murmurs. The members of the jury all stared at her as if she was insane. Even Gob'Frey looked taken aback with her spectacles nearly falling off her nose. The first to cut through the noise was Arlicia.

"Yatoa," she said sternly.

Yatoa turned to face her mentor and looked up into her face. Arlicia towered above her on the defense platform. "Yes?"

"Are you absolutely sure? If you have even a shadow of a doubt then…"

"I'll die," Yatoa finished for her. Something gripped Yatoa's wrist and she turned to find Breichmar's hand. He had genuine concern on his face.

"Listen kid, I know this trial is important to you and you've been trying your best, but this really isn't worth throwing away your life over. I promise I'm not saying this because I want to win." Yatoa ripped her arm away. How *dare* he.

"Yatoa for once I agree with the guy," Dal said from up above. "I'm happy you're defendin' me, but I don't want ya to die on my behalf."

"Um, Ms. Yatoa, I think you should listen to them," the bailiff added. A gavel slammed against the block three times. Causing everyone but Yatoa to give their attention to Gob'Frey.

"Ms. Yatoa this is a grave-"

"*Stop* calling me that!" Yatoa roared over the judge. That stole all the attention back to her. She knew she was violating court decorum, but quite frankly she did not care anymore.

"Do not call me *kid*. Do not call me *Ms. Yatoa*," she said through gritted teeth into the otherwise silent room. "My name is Ms. Hu'Dectalaciumina and I wager my head. Now cut it off!"

Yatoa sank to her knees before the jury and angled her chin up, exposing her neck. Then she waited patiently.

Everyone in the room remained silent.

"Your Honor," Yatoa said, looking straight into Gob'Frey's eyes with her neck bared. "The defense requests that the bailiff does his job."

Gob'Frey sighed, then waved a hand toward the bailiff. "You heard Ms. Hu'Dectalaciumina. Let's get this over with."

The bailiff reluctantly took his place in front of her. On her knees she was the same height as him. Perfect for a decapitation. He lifted the sword, the whole time staring into her eyes with a nervous trepidation.

"I won't blame you if I die," she said to him. "If I die here then it's my own fault, but I'll promise you this: if you swing that sword, it will stop, and I will live. You needn't worry. Only a droplet of blood will spill."

The bailiff cleared his throat nervously. "A-are you ready Ms. Hu'Dac- Hu'Dectalaciumina?"

"I will never be more ready." It was the only thing to say.

They stared into each other's eyes for a long moment. It was an intimate thing to stare into her potential killer's eyes moments before she would possibly lose her life. There was something shared between them. A sort of fatalistic understanding mixed with a morbid curiosity. They both knew that either way this event would be one of the most important of either of their lives. It was the heaviest few seconds Yatoa had ever experienced.

The bailiff raised the jade-colored blade and readied to strike. Yatoa clenched her jaw as an instinctual attempt to make her neck stronger. It was foolish, but she couldn't think straight with her heart trying to beat her chest open from the inside.

The bailiff swung and Yatoa refused to cringe or shut her eyes. The edge met her neck.

And stopped.

Heat blossomed on the right side of her neck and she felt something wet drip onto her suit. Yatoa glanced down in fear to see three coin-sized bloodstains blossom on the white fabric of the right side of her chest.

The bailiff drew the sword away immediately away and as fast as he swung, he applied something to her wound. Yatoa gasped in disbelief as he worked. She was alive. Her cut was worse than Breichmar's but that was only because of its location.

The bailiff was the only person who moved in the room. Everyone just watched. After the bailiff had applied a sticky leaf as a bandage over the wound, Yatoa stood. The leaf radiated a soothing coolness that repressed the sting of the cut and distantly her mind wondered what the leaf was.

Yatoa looked Gob'Frey in the eyes. All she could hear was the crackling of the flame.

"The verdict in stage six has been decided," Gob'Frey announced. "Not-guilty."

Yatoa grinned. Maybe she was a lawyer after all. With that thought in mind she climbed back onto the defense platform. As Yatoa stood, Arlicia pointed to the bloodstains on her chest.

"Seems you've finally got some red. Happened sooner than I thought it would," Arlicia said, swelling with pride. Yatoa could see it in her body language. In her smile. In her eyes.

"Thank you for being proud of me," Yatoa said, wanting to cry. Arlicia shook her head in dismissal.

"No. Thank you for being an apprentice I can truly be proud of." Still not caring for the propriety of court, Yatoa embraced her mentor.

"It's not over yet," she whispered into Arlicia's shoulder.

15

The Family

The verdicts stand at a tie, so we will be moving on to the seventh and final stage," Gob'Frey said as Yatoa released Arlicia from her embrace. Dal tugged on Yatoa's sleeve and held his hand up to his mouth to hide his words from all the onlookers.

"No matter what happens in this next stage I wanted ya to know that you're the best lawyer I could've ever asked for. I'll remember that for the rest of my life, no matter how long I got left in this world."

"Again Dal, I'm just doing my job," she explained. She couldn't help but feel heat rise to her cheeks though.

Dal chuckled. "It ain't your job to die for me," he pointed out. It wasn't, but that wasn't what she had done either. She had absorbed the blow. She defended.

"Don't worry I'll win this one too."

"Ms. Hu'Dectalaciumina, please pay attention."

Yatoa straightened. "Yes, Your Honor," she said, feeling like a cuffed child. *Careful with the overconfidence Yatoa.*

"As I was saying, we will now begin stage seven of the trial: The Family. In this final stage we will call all witnesses to the witness stand and the prosecution and the defense will have the opportunity to question them all. And so, I call all witnesses to the witness circle."

From the darkness all the players emerged. On one side of the circle Cartaneal, Reg, and Teran stood on the the curved, painted line equidistant from one another. Mirroring them on the other side stood the Gob'Alondis family, each spaced ten feet apart from each other with Darlia in the middle and Dal closest to the jury box. Yatoa surveyed the Gob'Alondis'. Darlia looked nervous but Dal and Garna looked... focused. If they were ready, then that was a good sign.

"Mr. Gob'Stellau the court is yours to do with as you will," Gob'Frey informed from her podium.

Cartaneal nodded in silent acknowledgment. He turned to face the jury first. "Goblins of the jury, we've put on quite the spectacle today I must admit. This trial has certainly taken some turns, but through it all there has been one consistent theme. And that is the defendant's guilt. The defense pleads not guilty, but what have we learned so far?

"An upstanding citizen of our society was violated. A large portion of his wealth stolen. A known criminal carried out this crime with an organized criminal group, and he has the nerve to try and get away with it. The Flame Demon itself sided against the defendant. And despite the fact I did not wager a body part more substantial than the defense in the last stage, I must remind you that I did indeed stay true to my convictions. The blade did not cut. The defendant deserves punishment for what he has done, make no mistake. And I sense you agree with me."

Yatoa seethed listening to Breichmar's drivel. In this stage she couldn't interject unless Breichmar started badgering the witnesses. Anything else was fair game. That was a blessing and a curse, for it also meant that when her turn came the rules of the court would restrict him in turn.

Breichmar paced along the prosecution circle, rounding the great flame. He stopped in front of Cartaneal. "Mr. Gob'Franat. How do you feel about the defendant?" That was a dangerous question. Yatoa rounded the fire to get a good look at the old Goblin's face as he answered.

"I pity the fellow somewhat. No father should have to see their daughter go through pain like that. Not ever. Having said that I cannot forgive him for what he has done to me. Those jewelry pieces were mine by rights. How *dare* he violate our city's most sacred laws and steal from me!" Cartaneal boomed.

"So you believe the defendant deserves punishment?" Breichmar asked.

Cartaneal nodded. "Of course I do, dear sir. This trial is the perfect opportunity to show the masses that we will not tolerate this kind of behavior."

"Can you explain further?" Breichmar pressed.

"If the jury passes a not-guilty verdict, then what kind of message does that send? That we're willing to let thieves walk free on the streets of Gobroa without any form of punishment whatsoever? That is unacceptable. The citizens of Gobroa have a right to feel secure. It's politics! This case will send a message whether we want it to or not, so I encourage the jury to think wisely before they declare their next verdict."

Breichmar smiled, obviously pleased with his witness' answer. He rounded his platform to Teran. "Mr. Gob'Jian, please give us your thoughts on the matter."

"Yes sir! I agree with Mr. Gob'Franat. This case is about much more than Dal Gob'Alondis. Everyone here is watching the verdict closely, and after what we've seen today you can bet that no matter the outcome word will spread of the events taking place right now in this room. It will influence the thoughts of the populace; of that I assure you."

Teran stood tall as he spoke. The perfect model of a member of the city watch. Yatoa found that she didn't disagree with the sentiment. The verdict of the trial would have larger implications for Gobroa's future – but she was no politician. All she cared about now was winning this case and getting Dal out of this courtroom.

"And do you think the verdict ought to be guilty?"

"Of course! Like Mr. Gob'Franat said, we'd be sending exactly the wrong message to the populace, and furthermore it would only embolden the criminals out there. The streets would likely grow more dangerous." Teran cleared his throat. "If that does happen though I would like to personally assure everyone here that the city watch will do its very best to protect you all."

"Thank you Mr. Gob'Jian," Breichmar said as he stepped in front of Reg. "Mr. Gob'Gronsa, do you think we should punish Dal for what he's done?"

Reg shook his head. "Listen Mr. Gob'Stellau, I don't think Dal should die at all. Though don't get me wrong, I still think what we did was wrong, I just don't like the idea of my best friend dyin' much yenno?" He raised his cuffs into the air. "He should be goin' to the same place I'm headed."

Breichmar raised a finger. "Ah but I'm afraid the defense has given up this option. And now we find ourselves in this unfortunate position. Dal must die now for the greater good. We cannot let him get away with this."

Reg shrugged. "I mean sure, I guess. He did something wrong and now he's got to pay the consequences. We all knew the consequences goin' in. We knew it could come to this. I only wish he would plead guilty. I hate to see him go." Reg's voice had an edge to it, like… he was holding back tears. She could see it in his eyes. They may have known the consequences, but Reg at the very least didn't think they'd ever have to face them. This was the harshest reality check a Goblin could get.

"Thank you Mr. Gob'Gronsa," Breichmar said, continuing his round until he came to stand in front of Garna. "And what do you think, Mrs. Gob'Alondis?"

Garna glared at him with eyes that could have frozen the Flame Demon solid. "If you're asking me if I think my *husband* should die, then I'm afraid I have to disappoint you."

"I wouldn't expect that of you," Breichmar said in a civil tone. "But tell me, how does it make you feel to know that your husband did not consult you about his little plan before carrying it out? He put your family in an even worse position, didn't he?" Garna spared a hesitant glance for her husband who watched intently.

"It did frustrate me." Yatoa stiffened. *What?* What was she *doing?* "I would have liked to have known about all this beforehand, and now we're in this situation… It's… hard."

Yatoa's brain scrambled. Garna was lying. She knew about the crime, she had told Yatoa as much. But she was doubling down on Breichmar's narrative. Had she given up on Dal? Did she not believe Yatoa could win? Maybe she was trying to throw all suspicion off of her as a potential collaborator. So many justifications ran through Yatoa's mind, but they all rang hollow, because deep down she already knew why.

"I see," Breichmar said. He seemed as taken aback by her answer as Yatoa did. He moved on from her, not giving her another chance to speak. He likely didn't want her saying anything unexpected that could potentially be bad for his case.

Breichmar skipped Darlia entirely, and almost completing his circle at Dal. "Mr. Gob'Alondis, was this all worth it?"

Dal stared at him silently. The fire crackled. Yatoa swallowed. The entire room waited for something to happen. They waited for *someone* to just say something. "I hate guys like you," Dal said finally.

Breichmar chuckled. "Whatever do you mean?" Yatoa tried to motion for him to stop talking but Dal ignored her.

"People in the boat," Dal said. "You hold our heads under the water. You look down on us from up high." Dal stepped a little closer as he spoke so his neck had to crane to look up at Breichmar. "You pick on us. You treat us like dirt. You bully us because we can't fight back. So of course it was worth it. Gob'Franat doesn't deserve what he has. He never actually *earned* any of it. I would do it all again in a heartbeat, especially if there was a chance of saving my daughter. I'd even hide it from my wife if I had to."

Breichmar opened his mouth to speak but Dal held up a hand. "You're right, Mr. Gob'Stellau. This trial will send a message to the people. Regardless of whether the verdict is guilty or not-guilty it'll show the folk like me back home in the Saern District that we can fight back, and we will. A verdict isn't stoppin' it. This is just the beginnin'."

Breichmar stared at Dal for a moment, considering his words. Then he turned and completed his circle standing in front of the jury once more. "And we end on a threat from the defendant," he shook his head. "Goblins of the jury I know you see the truth. This man is too dangerous let walk free on the streets of Gobroa. The only verdict you can declare now is a guilty verdict. For the good of all." Breichmar grabbed his green cape and swept a flourished bow. Then he raised his eyes up to the judge. "The prosecution rests, Your Honor."

"Very well," Gob'Frey said. She turned her attention to Yatoa. "Ms. Hu'Dectalaciumina the court is yours."

Yatoa took a deep breath. This was it. Her final performance. She had an idea of what she needed to prove, though she didn't know if she could. If she was right though, then it was the best chance Darlia had at getting healed. Unless Yatoa did everything right in this stage Darlia would follow Dal to the grave, and she could *not* allow that.

So, she faced the jury directly. Yatoa met each of the jurors' eyes in turn. All of them unique, yet all of them expectant. They watched hungrily, her gravitational pull drawing them in, waiting to see what she might do next.

"I've shown you the kind of person Dal is. I've explained to you why I think he shouldn't die. Now I will convince you that a not-guilty verdict is not only right, but necessary. To do that we need to solve three mysteries."

Yatoa held up a finger. "First, *why* was Dal hired to steal those documents?" She held up another finger. "Second, *why* did Dal's lookout abandon him?" she held up a third. "And finally, *where* is Dal's share of the money now?"

Yatoa dragged her three fingers through the air creating an image of Dal meeting with a hooded stranger in his living room. "You see… it just doesn't make sense to me."

She rounded the platform to stand in front of Cartaneal. She stared the old man down. His wide mouth twitched in discomfort at the silence. "Why would anyone want those documents? Surely there must be a reason?"

Cartaneal creased his brow. "I assure you Ms. Hu'Dectalaciumina I have no idea. I cannot think of anyone who would want those documents."

Yatoa turned to the jury to include them in the conversation. "We have two options," she said. "Either we can believe Mr. Gob'Franat, or we can decide that he must be lying to us." Yatoa changed the illusion to a single sheet of paper. The unreal sheet fluttered in the air as if carried on an imaginary breeze. It trailed lazy loops through the courtroom.

"I elect to believe him, since we have no reason not to. That paper is unimportant." With a judicial swipe of her hand the paper blew into the darkness of the gallery, out of view. "And if that is true, then there must be another reason why someone hired Dal to steal it."

Yatoa strode further along the defense circle, stepping past Arlicia who watched Yatoa as intently as the jury. "Lead investigator," Yatoa said to Teran. "If the person who hired Dal didn't want the document, then why would they hire him to sneak into that room to steal it? I imagine you have experience with such conundrums." Teran nodded then rubbed at his chin for a moment.

"Well… If they didn't actually care whether Dal Gob'-Alondis stole the documents, then they must have wanted something else…" His pointy ears twitched in alarm and he stared up at Yatoa wide-eyed.

"I see you've come to the correct conclusion," Yatoa said to him. "Mind sharing with the court?"

"The person who hired him only did it because they wanted him in that room," Teran said in a revelatory tone.

Yatoa nodded then swished her hand through the air, drawing light together and forming an image of the room for the jury. It was not to scale and was missing two walls, but Dal stood in the center looking at papers on a desk. "And what happened when he entered that room?" Yatoa asked the jury. She flicked her fingers a few times and the room's door burst open. Security guards, two human men in black suits, rushed into the room. Yatoa paused the scene.

"He got caught. Exactly as the person who hired him wanted," Yatoa said.

"Wait," Teran interjected. "But if that's the case, then how did this person know he would get caught? Dal testified that he had a lookout with him. If the lookout did their job then this mysterious employer's plan wouldn't have worked."

Yatoa smiled. "Yes, but the lookout didn't do their job and Dal got caught. Which brings us to question two. Why did Dal's lookout abandon him? It might just be so this secret benefactor's plan would work. The lookout was in on it. Whoever it was, they betrayed Dal."

Yatoa erased the scene once more and replaced it with the silhouette of a mysterious Goblin. "I propose that this mysterious lookout was either working for this employer… or they *are* the employer. The latter would make the most sense as I find it hard to believe any third party could have known Dal was going to carry out this crime. Not unless a member of the crew told them. I propose that this lookout wanted Dal gone for some reason."

With a sharp swipe Teran raised his hand in the air, clearly indicating he wanted to speak.

"Yes Mr. Gob'Jian?"

"Could it have been so that they get a larger cut of the score? If there's less people to split it between, then everyone would get a bigger cut."

Yatoa shook her head. "I do not believe that is the case, but to explain why I must appeal to Mr. Gob'Gronsa." She turned to Reg and met his curious expression. "Mr. Gob'-Gronsa. Is it true that your thieving crew has a rule that should the city watch catch any member that the crew would distribute their share of the money to their family?"

Reg considered her with obvious surprise that she even knew that. "Yeah, it's true."

"Therefore, this mysterious traitor couldn't have done it for a bigger cut, as they would still split the money the same.

This makes the third question important. What happened to Dal's share of the money?"

Yatoa positioned herself in front of Reg. "First Mr. Gob'Gronsa, I must ask an important question of you. I understand if you don't want to answer it, however this question is crucial. If you give me a truthful response, then depending on the answer... Dal could walk away from this trial a free man."

"Ask away," Reg said cheerfully. "If it'll really help my buddy, I'll answer."

This was it. No turning back. It was time to make her final plays in this game. She had to set down her hand on the table for all to see. "Is there more than one woman in your crew?"

Reg stood still. He was thinking over the question. Likely he had not expected it. "Hmmm... I suppose that's safe enough info to let slip. Yeah. There's more than one."

Yatoa felt a chill. Her hunch had been dead on the mark. "One more question. How many members were in this crew in total?" Again, Reg took his time to think it over.

"Five," he said reluctantly.

"Thank you. Now let's move on to that third mystery, shall we? I'm assuming you were present when the crew divvied up the money between all the members?"

Reg nodded. "Yup! If I had never got that money, then I wouldn't be in this mess to begin with."

"And when you were there, was someone there to collect Dal's share of the money?" she asked carefully.

"Yup," Reg said, then his eyes widened and he cupped a hand over his mouth. "I mean... um. I didn't mean to-"

Yatoa wasn't going to let him weasel his way out of this massive slip up. "According to your rule it must have been a member of his family. No one else could accept the money on his behalf."

"No!" Reg shouted at her. She didn't startle at the outburst. "It was *me!* I collected that money! I got double the share." Yatoa sighed.

"Mr. Gob'Jian, how much was the jewelry stolen worth in total?" she asked. Teran reached into the inside pocket of his uniform jacket and pulled out a small pocket book, then flipped to a marked page in the middle.

"It was worth around eighty-thousand gobbings," Teran said.

"And how many gobbings did Reg have in his possession, or spend in total by the time you caught him?" Teran flipped to another page in his book.

"Well, including the gobbings he obviously spent, then it should be around twenty-thousand gobbings in total." Yatoa turned back to Reg.

"That's one-fourth of eighty-thousand," she said to Reg.

Reg waved his shackled hands at her in dismissal. "See? If I had just gotten my share, it would have been a fifth! I got more than that because I got all of Dal's share too."

"Mr. Gob'Gronsa, that is not how math works," Yatoa said with a smirk. "If you had gotten Dal's share you would have had double sixteen-thousand. Thirty-two-thousand gobbings. How do you explain the missing twelve-thousand?"

Reg held up a finger. "Whoa there! How do you explain my extra four-thousand?"

"That's simple," Yatoa said. "It's because the money was only ever supposed to be divvied up four ways, not five, despite there being five of you." Teran's hand shot up again. "Yes Mr. Gob'Jian?"

"But why? That doesn't make sense unless they were always planning on cutting Dal out of the equation." It was a good point.

"Ah but there is another explanation," Yatoa said. It was time to reveal another card from her hand. "When I first met Dal, he told me something interesting. I wrote the quote down here in my notebook," Yatoa said holding up the little pocket book for all to see. She flipped open to the bookmarked page.

"Dal said, and I quote, 'I wanna be clear, I only get half a share of the dough. You see I'm an upstandin' guy. Real moral. I don't take more than I need, so that way everyone else on the crew gets more.'" She snapped the notebook shut. "That would mean that Dal's share was only ten-thousand gobbings. Yet if there were five members of the crew, and Reg got twenty thousand, then that leads us to another potential conclusion: that the fifth member of the crew also received half a share. So, they split the money five ways, with three members getting twenty-thousand, and two members getting only ten. Otherwise, it's impossible for the other members to all have gotten a full share."

Yatoa tucked the notebook away allowed a smile to creep onto her face. "But why would two members willingly take only half? They should have split it more evenly, especially if Dal needed the money to cure his daughter's illness. He couldn't have done so with only ten-thousand gobbings.

Which leads me to my alternative explanation: two members of the crew shared twenty-thousand, rather than getting paid ten each separately"

Teran screwed up his face in disbelief. "That's a complicated explanation. Why would they share twenty-thousand?"

"Perhaps they're a couple," Yatoa pointed out. "Couples often share assets and expenses. Regardless of the reason, all this information illuminates something far more important. Reg made a slip up. He claimed that someone did in fact accept Dal's share and it couldn't have been Reg himself." Yatoa pointed toward an illusory Goblin silhouette floating in the air.

"I propose whoever received Dal's share was the lookout. If Dal was to share twenty-thousand with someone, it would only have been natural for them to accept on his behalf. With Dal out of the picture they don't necessarily get more money, but they do get an absolute say in how it's spent. The person who betrayed Dal wanted to control the funds entirely."

"I would like to move on to the next witness to help this along, but first I am sure our witnesses must be parched by this point in the trial. I wouldn't want a dry throat to hinder each witness' ability to speak. Luckily, I thought ahead and I brought two bottles of juice with me." Yatoa turned to Gob'Frey. "Your Honor the defense requests permission to provide the witnesses with refreshments."

Gob'Frey considered her. With her mouth drawn in a thin line indicating exactly how much patience she had, she nodded. "You may, but be quick about it." Yatoa retrieved two bottles from her satchel which she had stowed under the defense circle before the trial started. She didn't know if these bottles would come in handy, but it felt right to put them to use now.

She offered Reg the choice first. "Apple juice or orange?" With that comical frown on his face it was clear he was angry with her and declined both. Teran accepted the orange, and Gob'Franat the apple. That last one was unsurprising to her. Yatoa didn't know if she bought Arlicia's superstition, but there was something to it that she couldn't explain with words. It felt… right.

She rounded the circle to the Gob'Alondis side. "Garna, would you care for a glass of orange or apple juice?" Garna hesitated for a moment, looking up into Yatoa's eyes. Garna blinked.

"I'll take a glass of apple thank you."

"Of course," Yatoa said smoothly as she poured the Goblin a glass. Then she moved on to Darlia. "Orange or apple Darlia?"

"Orange!" she said enthusiastically and Yatoa obliged. Finally, Yatoa came to Dal and gave him no choice. She poured him orange without asking.

"I'm sorry about what I have to do, Dal. But Darlia's life depends on this." Dal's face betrayed no emotion. He accepted the glass and said nothing as Yatoa climbed back atop the defense circle. This time she arranged herself in front of the jury with the fire to her back.

"All of this brings us to a fourth and final mystery: who is the lookout?" Yatoa said. "And for that, Goblins of the jury, we turn to Darlia Gob'Alondis."

Yatoa stepped in front of Darlia. "Hello sweetie. I just need to ask you one question alright? And it's an important one, so please answer as best you can, okay? It'll help your dad come home."

"O-okay," Darlia said.

"On the night your father was arrested and didn't come home, was your mother at home with you?" Her entire hand was on the table now. She only needed to see how everything would play out from here.

"Darlia was sick, she probably can't remember that night clearly," Garna cut in from the side.

"Mrs. Gob'Alondis do not speak out of turn," Yatoa commanded. "I am currently questioning another witness."

"Um… no she wasn't. She was out until late and I was home alone," Darlia said. "I can remember mom! My arm is turning to glass, not my brain." And there it was. The answer Yatoa was looking for.

"Thank you, Darlia," Yatoa said. With that she hopped down from the defense circle and strode over to meet Garna. She stood four-feet away from the Goblin woman and looked down on her. "I propose," Yatoa announced to the court, "that Garna Gob'Alondis was the lookout."

16

The Lookout

Murmurs filled the court's dead air, and Garna's eyes widened in outrage. Yatoa swept her cape back over her shoulder, freeing her right arm from its shelter, and permanently exposing the blood-red inlay. The gavel sounded, cutting everyone's voices down in one slice.

"Order in the court!" Gob'Frey boomed. "Ms. Hu'Dectalaciumina, this is a very serious claim. Do you have evidence?" Physically she didn't unfortunately. But she just needed a little more information for this to work. Especially if she could get Dal to say something incriminating in her favor, but she wasn't counting on it.

"I do not, and while I can't prove it right at this moment it is still vital to this case that we discuss this possibility further, Your Honor," Yatoa said. "We have learned from Reg that someone did in fact receive Dal's share on his behalf."

Yatoa needed to find out what had happened to that money. Twenty-thousand gobbings unaccounted for. A girl still sick. And Yatoa felt she was so close to the truth, only she didn't know the answer to a crucial question. Why? What would Garna's motive have been? Why did Garna want complete control of the money? What would Dal have prevented her from doing?

That last question struck a chord. While she didn't know exactly what it was Garna wanted to do, she did know how Dal would have gotten in Garna's way. Dal would have used the money to heal Darlia.

"Dal had a lookout," Yatoa said to Garna. "Someone he apparently trusted with his life. And only that person could have set him up. The crew split the money four ways, and there were four other members besides Dal. We know Dal wasn't cut out because someone received his share. Furthermore, it mustn't have been suspicious for this person to do so, or the rest of the crew would have caught them in their treachery."

Garna clenched her teeth.

Her glare stood Yatoa's hairs on end. The sheer malice in it was unexpected, especially so from this small Goblin woman. "So what? I had nothing to do with this crime. I said as much. I didn't even know it was happening. Maybe he planned on sharing the money with one of his thieving buddies."

Yatoa paced. She moved lazily back and forth in front of Garna, thinking for a moment. "I'm afraid that's not likely," Yatoa said. "Dal's closest friend got his own share, and the only person he would trust more than his closest friend would be you." It also didn't make sense financially. It would bleed a large portion of their profits dry to heal Darlia. That wouldn't make for a good arrangement unless both parties wanted Darlia healed.

"I'm telling you I wasn't involved," Garna asserted once more.

"Then where were you that night? Your daughter says you weren't at home."

Garna froze. Her tongue wet her lips and she watched Yatoa like prey eying a potential predator. "I was home," she said a little too late. "That girl is so sick she can't tell up from down."

Yatoa strode away from Garna. She knelt in front of Darlia instead. "Is that true?"

Darlia shook her head. "Mom always treats me like I can't do anythin' myself. I said before that my brain isn't glass. I can remember that night fine. My mom and dad left the house together in the late evening and told me to be a good girl and stay in bed. I don't know why my mom is lying about this."

"Do you remember when I came to your house?" Yatoa asked.

"Yup."

"Were you eavesdropping on my conversation with your mother?" Garna's ears drooped slightly in shame. "No, no it's okay. You can tell us anything here in court. Do you remember what your mother said to us?"

"Ummmm she was talking about the crew. Telling you things about them. Like when they all planned together in the shop downstairs. My mom and dad would never let me in the room durin' those conversations," Daria said with a pout. "They treat me like I'm entirely made of glass already. Don't they realize that it's just my arm?"

"Stop this!" Garna demanded. "Darlia don't say another word or I'll lock you in that room when we get home! You shouldn't lie to these fine people in court."

"I know I shouldn't lie, but you're the one whose-"

"My daughter is *sick*," Garna said, striding over herself. She positioned herself protectively in front of her daughter, trying to shield her from Yatoa. "She isn't fit to testify in court."

Yatoa looked down at this stubborn woman. Yatoa already had enough to convince the jury that Garna was at least part of the thieving crew, but it still wasn't enough. She had built the arch, but she was missing the keystone. Yatoa glimpsed Dal's troubled red face and the color sparked an idea in her head.

"Very well Mrs. Gob'Alondis," Yatoa said. "If you insist." Then she turned to the judge. "Your Honor, the defense would like to add one more witness. Is this possible?"

"It's possible," Gob'Frey said. She watched Yatoa with an avid curiosity. Even Breichmar was eying her attentively. She had the whole court enthralled. "The defense calls Arlicia Sa'Krieglund to the stand."

"Objection!" Breichmar said. "The defense cannot stand as a witness! It is absurd."

"Ms. Sa'Krieglund is not the defense today," Yatoa said. "She's just overseeing this trial. I am the only lawyer officially representing Dal Gob'Alondis, and Ms. Sa'Krieglund has important testimony.

"Denied Mr. Gob'Stellau," Gob'Frey announced with a bang of her gavel. "Ms. Sa'Krieglund please step down onto the witness circle."

Arlicia jumped from the defense circle, flipped through the air, and stuck the landing right next to Yatoa. Her cape made it look as though she was nothing more than a shifting ball of fabric as she flew. Yatoa grinned. Leave it to her mentor to make a scene. Arlicia winked at Yatoa then took her place at the witness circle with her hands clasped behind her back.

In response, Yatoa climbed back up onto the defense platform, towering over her mentor.

"Witness, please state your name and occupation," Yatoa commanded.

Arlicia's face straightened, though her eyes still smiled. "Arlicia Sa'Krieglund, attorney at law."

"You were present for the conversation I had with Garna. Is Darlia telling the truth? You likely remember it."

"Darlia spoke honestly," Arlicia said. "Garna told us that she knew all about the plan. She told us that she was present for the meetings, though she didn't get too detailed. In my expert opinion Garna is lying to this court."

"What else did she say," Yatoa prompted.

"She said…" Arlicia took a moment to think, but Yatoa suspected that moment was just for dramatic effect. She already knew what to say. "She said that there was only one member of the crew that was a woman. She told us the name of that member, so that we might meet with them, but she expressed doubt that we'd ever find them."

"Another lie then," Yatoa pointed out. "It must be. For earlier in the trial, I asked Reg if there was more than one woman in the crew. To which he replied yes, and we have no reason to believe that he is lying about that."

Breichmar raised his arm in the air. "Mr. Gob'Stellau," Gob'Frey addressed him. "Did you have something you wanted to say?"

"Does the defense mean to imply that they met with yet another member of the thieving crew?" he asked. Yatoa nodded. "Who?"

"I'm afraid I cannot say." She wanted to keep Faz's identity a secret. The less Goblins accused of theft the better in Yatoa's book. "But Ms. Sa'Krieglund can testify as to what was said in that meeting. Is this acceptable Mr. Gob'Stellau, or do you object?"

Breichmar visibly warred with the choice. Yatoa had never seen him so shaken up. "I accept this testimony," Breichmar said grudgingly. Yatoa thanked the Gods that his curiosity won.

"Well then Ms. Sa'Krieglund would you testify as to what this woman said to us?" Yatoa asked. Arlicia obliged with a deferential curtsy that almost felt mocking. Yatoa blushed in spite of herself.

"It was a simple meeting really. We learned two things. First, that this woman was *not* the lookout. I'm sure Reg and Dal would even testify to that. And the second thing we learned, perhaps more important, was that she was in charge of distributing the shares. She claimed that she had given Dal's share to Garna last week. That is all." Arlicia quieted. Yatoa waited a long moment to let the new information sink in, and naturally all eyes fell on Garna. Her throat bobbed. The pressure was breaking her, but it still wouldn't be enough.

It was time for Yatoa's final gambit. She rounded the defense circle until she was face to face with the jury.

"Goblins of the jury, there is a lot of information to keep track of here, but to make things easier for you I shall arrange all the pieces of the puzzle.

"We know that they split the money four ways, but there were five crew members. We deduced that two of these members must have jointly taken a share. We learned that someone received Dal's share. This someone being Garna Gob'Alondis. We also learned that the lookout for Dal Gob'Alondis had betrayed him. Likely setting up a fake job for him to carry out in order to get him caught. They did this so they likely could get full control of the funds. We also learned from Reg that there was more than one woman on the crew, and from Darlia that her mother was directly involved in the planning of the crime. But you may be asking yourself why the lookout has to be a woman. Well, Dal Gob'Alondis has previously let slip that the lookout was a "she".

"All signs point to Garna being the lookout. There's only one piece of the puzzle missing. *Why?*" Yatoa preemptively turned to Garna, expecting her to butt in.

"I would never betray my husband!" Garna said firmly. "I love him more than anything."

Yatoa stared Garna right in the eyes and held it. She could see it. The fear. Yatoa imagined her own eyes looked similar not too long ago. Though now she felt an unnatural calm resting its weight on her like a thick blanket. She felt focused. Sharp. Confident.

Without breaking eye-contact she said, "to help us find out why we must first ask another question. If it's true that Garna has the money, then why isn't Darlia healed yet? If she really did want to heal her daughter then she would have done so at the soonest opportunity. Twenty-thousand gobbings is more than enough to treat the shatter in Gobroa. The rate is only fifteen-thousand gobbings."

"That's right!" Garna cried out. "I would have healed my baby." She turned to Dal. "You believe me don't you honey? I would have healed her, I would have!" Dal kept his eyes focused on Yatoa and still he said nothing. His muscles were tense, but those eyes spoke of trust. Even now he still believed in Yatoa.

Yatoa lifted her head to the judge once more. "Your Honor, the defense requests that Darlia Gob'Alondis be removed from the courtroom." Gob'Frey considered. She pushed up her spectacles, then banged the gavel and ordered the bailiff to escort Darlia out of the room. She left after a few protests, and Yatoa waited for the sound of the doors closing before saying anything else.

"Yes Mrs. Gob'Alondis you would have healed Darlia… if you loved her. But you didn't, because it would be so much more convenient for you if she died, wouldn't it?" Yatoa accused angrily. Garna's eyes widened in outrage.

"You claim that I don't love my own baby goblet? How dare you!"

"No…" Yatoa said softly. "Not just that. I also accuse you of not loving your husband."

"I LOVE THEM *BOTH!*" Garna roared. It was a shrill shriek of a pitch only a Goblin could reach. It sounded like it tore at Garna's throat. The silence that followed felt all-consuming by contrast. Yatoa stood watching. She was patient. She would do this right. It was time for the last play.

Yatoa hopped down from the defense platform again, then strode out of the light of the fire and into the darkness beyond. She headed toward where the bailiff would normally sit, venturing far enough into the darkness to obscure herself from view.

Then she enacted her plan. With two fingers she created an illusion. That of a jade-colored blade. The Honest Blade. It weighed nothing in her hand. It was a fake after all.

With her fake blade in tow, she stepped back into the light, eliciting gasps. Garna especially looked gaunt at the sight. As Yatoa expected she watched a Goblin man emerge from the shadows next to her. He wore a blue robe with three gold stars embroidered into the breast. He said nothing, but moved for the judge's stand, climbed the ladder, then whispered into the judge's ear.

He was the Three Star detector. He would be telling Gob'Frey now that the illusion Yatoa held was not in fact the real thing. Garna hopefully wouldn't know that.

Yatoa held Garna's eyes. "Would you wager a hand on that conviction?"

Yatoa then looked to Gob'Frey. She didn't dare risk another action without the judge's assent. Unfortunately, Breichmar spoke first.

"Your Honor! This is unacceptable! No one has ever used the Honest Blade on a witness. This is unprecedented, and I am not convinced that is a precedent we should set." He sounded panicked. Well for one thing Yatoa agreed with him, that *wasn't* a precedent they should set. Yet she couldn't tip her hand.

"I think…" Gob'Frey said, "I would normally not allow it… but I will allow it this once. Defense, proceed."

"But-"

"No buts Mr. Gob'Stellau. You must accept my rulings." Yatoa didn't wait for any further discussion on the matter. She approached Garna.

"If you truly love your family Garna, then hold out your hand and this blade will stop short. You should have nothing to fear." Garna hesitated. Her stance wavered for a moment and Yatoa thought she might faint, but Garna held strong. She clenched her jaw and slowly brought her hand up in front of her.

Yatoa nodded, then made a show of hefting up the weightless illusion and readying it to strike. "Are you ready Mrs. Gob'Alondis?"

"Y-yes," Garna said with a wince. Yatoa panicked for a moment. Garna was calling her bluff. There was nothing for it. Yatoa swung down.

Garna pulled her hand away at the last second and Yatoa's fake blade whizzed by.

"Alright! Alright dammit you win, okay? Just let me keep my hand!" Garna was crying. Yatoa let the illusion dissipate and the sword scattered into light. Garna cried harder.

"Why did you betray me? Betray us?" Dal asked. He was right there, standing next to Yatoa. Tears clung to his cheeks as well.

Garna wept. Her wails were loud, but the court was patient. Eventually she calmed down enough to answer. "This life… it's not what I envisioned for myself. I never thought I'd be stuck in the Saern District forever with a man I didn't even love and a daughter who was so sick I had to watch her every waking moment. I wanted something better."

"If you didn't betray me, we would have gotten somethin' better Garna," Dal said.

Garna turned away from his pain.

"The time for me wanting to be a wife and mother has long come and gone. I saw an opportunity. If I could get that money for myself, and get you out of the picture as well, then all I would have to do is wait for the shatter to run its course." Garna took a deep breath in a vain attempt to calm her shaky, sorrowful voice. "Then I'd be free. Alone with twenty-thousand gobbings. I could restart and have a brand-new life. A much better one."

"How could you even *think* of doin' that to *my* daughter?" Dal asked in a voice that made Yatoa want to weep right along with him.

"I don't love your daughter," Garna said, looking away from him into the void beyond. That settled it for Dal. He walked away, back to his designated spot, and refused to look back in Garna's direction. Yatoa hated to put Dal through this pain, but it was necessary.

Yatoa left Garna where she was, then climbed back atop the defense platform and stood before the jury. "Goblins of the jury I ask you today to consider more than this case. More than the man Dal Gob'Alondis. I ask you to consider a little girl who is turning into a glass sculpture of herself in real time. If you declare a verdict of guilty today, then that girl will have no one. But I implore you. Please let Darlia keep her father. Dal and Darlia have undergone enough punishment, and he doesn't deserve a guilty verdict on top of this." Yatoa grabbed the edge of her cape and swept a final bow. "The defense rests."

The slam of a gavel commanded all attention. "At this time, we will take a final thirty-minute recess, during which the jury will have to come to their final verdict in this case. Goblins of the jury your verdict here decides the defendant's fate. Choose wisely."

Yatoa exhaled and felt every last bit of energy flee her body, riding on that breath. She sank to her knees and shut her eyes. For better or worse, it was done. The trial was over. She had defended Dal Gob'Alondis to the best of her current ability, and all that remained was to see if that was enough.

"I'm impressed," Breichmar said from behind her. Yatoa cracked open an eye and looked back over her shoulder at the Goblin silhouetted by flames. "You're much more sensible than your mentor, and you show a lot of promise. You're easily the most impressive novice I've seen, and I've seen my fair share. No matter how this trial turns out you should be proud of yourself."

Yatoa couldn't believe the words she was hearing. Such high praise from Breichmar of all people? She must have really made an impression these last few stages to earn his respect. "Thank you," she said not knowing what else to say. To his credit he nodded and left her alone.

Arlicia was next to approach her.

"Toa!" she practically yelled to Yatoa's embarrassment. "Now *that* was a performance! Wow! I knew I was onto something when you chose orange juice two years ago."

"I'm allergic to apples," Yatoa confessed. Arlicia's expression grew blank. Then she burst out laughing.

"That's *perfect!* That just means you're bodily incapable of ever disobeying my trust! Ha! *Allergic* she says." Arlicia shook her head with a chuckle and grabbed Yatoa's hand. She gave a tight, reassuring squeeze. "No matter what the verdict is, I'm proud of you Yatoa. You did everything I wanted you to and then some. Perfect marks."

Yatoa didn't feel like she deserved perfect marks. If she had gotten perfect marks then this trial would have ended in stage four, not seven. "Thanks for sticking by me through all this."

Arlicia waved her hand in dismissal. "I did nothing." With that Arlicia picked up her cane and trotted off. Yatoa was once again left alone with her thoughts. As was Dal. He was back on the defense platform now, and he sat nearby staring at his hands in his lap. Yatoa felt guilt for having exposed the truth to him, but there was nothing she could do about that now. It was what both he and Darlia needed. Yatoa wasn't going to sit by and let Garna kill them both.

She suspected Garna the night before the trial, after the conversation with Faz, but at the time there were too many missing pieces and nothing fit together right. But the longer the trial went on the more certain she became.

She hoped it was enough to convince the jury.

As if on cue the jury came out early. Eighteen minutes early in fact. They all lined up inside the jury box, and everyone in the courtroom stood at attention. Then the gavel.

"Court is back in session. At this time the jury may announce their final verdict. All stand at attention," Gob'Frey's voice boomed.

The head juror stood. "With a unanimous vote the jury finds the defendant Dal Gob'Alondis…"

17

Not Guilty

Not guilty."

Yatoa couldn't believe what she was hearing. It felt like a dream. She didn't move until Dal barreled into her, wrapping his arms around her waist.

"Thank you… Thank you so much…" he said into her stomach. "Thank you so much from the bottom of my heart."

"The verdicts stand at four to three in favor of the defense," Gob'Frey intoned. "Thus, the court declares the defendant not-guilty on all charges." A smooth motion of the gavel brought the trial to a close. "Court is adjourned!"

The next day Yatoa did not wear her uniform. Arlicia sent it to the cleaners. She couldn't walk around with blood-stained clothes after all. Instead, she wore a simple blue sundress. It was light and refreshingly cool in the hot summer air. That was well, as the walk from their hotel to the Gob'Alondis residence was long.

It took them all morning, and while they did admittedly stop for something to eat, that only delayed them about twenty-minutes. It was noon by the time they reached the dusty street in front of Gob'Alondis Cobblers.

It felt strange not to wear work attire after so long, but it helped her relax as she opened the front door of the business despite the closed sign. She called out her arrival as she wended her way through the display tables of the empty shop, and the sound of footsteps beating down the stairs answered her. When Dal saw her, he beamed brightly with those sharp teeth.

"Yatoa! And Arlicia too! It's good to see you both. How do you feel after winnin' your first case?" Dal said. "Let's talk upstairs."

"I feel exhausted," Yatoa said as they ascended the steps. "I've had enough excitement for now I think." They went into the same sitting room they had questioned Garna in a few days ago and Yatoa felt a chill. It was Garna's sitting room. You could see her touch in the style of the furniture, the knitted blankets, and the patterned rug. Garna was the Goblin in a jail cell now.

"Take a seat," Dal said plopping down into the same armchair Garna had sat in. Yatoa and Arlicia sat on the couch. Despite them not having a case to work on, Arlicia almost always wore one of her suits, though this one was a light cream color rather than the usual red. It was a suit reserved strictly for business outside of the courtroom. Arlicia tucked her cape carefully underneath her as she sat. "What brings ya both out here so soon? Is there somethin' I can help ya with?"

"No," Arlicia said before taking a sip of orange juice from her canteen. "But *we* can help *you*."

Dal scoffed. "I already owe ya more than I could ever repay."

"Nonsense!" Arlicia said. "You owe us nothing, and especially myself in particular. If there's anyone that you're in debt to it is Yatoa, but this comes as a favor from me personally."

Before getting to that subject though, Yatoa preferred to get the difficult part of the conversation over with. "You're getting ahead of yourself Arlicia. First, I'd just like to ask how you're holding up Dal. Are you and Darlia alright?"

Dal's smile dropped in an instant. He looked more forlorn in that moment than he had when he was facing a death sentence. "I keep wishin' I could live on in ignorance yenno? No man wants to hear that his wife doesn't love him, though I suppose it's better than pretendin'. The part that really hurts though was that we coulda cured Darlia and gotten out of this place, then she coulda left me. But instead, she tried to kill us. It's… scary." He gripped the armrest.

They sat in silence. A clock on the wall ticked away the seconds and Yatoa counted each one as she thought about the tragic situation. It was hard for her to parse it, even if the facts were clear to her. She couldn't imagine what it was like for Dal. Yatoa did not know how much Dal had told Darlia of the situation, but since he was speaking so openly, she figured that Darlia already knew everything. Poor girl. Yatoa knew what it was like to have a mother that wanted you dead. She felt her hairs stand as she thought on that.

"Do you think she'll get the death sentence?" Dal asked.

"That depends on her lawyer," Arlicia answered. "Breichmar is litigating this case, and it's not a hopeful one. This has a pretty good chance of being a sweep. At best I expect she'll be in prison for the rest of her life…" Arlicia let out a long sigh. "The Goblin legal system is strange and flawed in surprising ways sometimes. Look at this one crime. You're walking free, Reg is getting three-years for his cooperation, and Garna is likely going to get a severe sentence. Yet you all committed the same crime."

Yatoa was inclined to agree. It was far from consistent, and not entirely based on legality. It was a fairly lax system all things considered. Though it did have its merits. Dal being here with them in his home was testament to that. Yet there was one thing Arlicia left out. They were also trying Garna for attempted murder, though that charge might not stick.

"The Goblin legal system is heavily dependent on the quality of the lawyers. A lot of systems are, but this one is more dependent upon that than almost any other legal system. That's why I tested you on it, Yatoa," Arlicia explained.

That made sense. If the trial was in anyone else's hands Yatoa was not sure that Dal would have gotten the verdict he did. She supposed the same was true for Breichmar as well. If the wrong prosecutor presided over this case, then Yatoa would have won the verdict with much less grief. Likely before she would have gotten the chance to expose Garna. In a way, Breichmar's competence which she originally found so annoying brought about this outcome as much as she did.

"I see…" Dal said. "I'll still mourn her. We both will. Isn't that right Darlia." Dal looked over his shoulder at the open mouth of the hallway. A little purple Goblin head poked out. Darlia's eyes were swollen from crying, but now she looked alert.

"Come in sweetheart," Arlicia said, beckoning Darlia forth with her hand. Darlia hesitantly stepped into the room and went to stand by her father. Dal rested a hand on her shoulder to comfort her. Yatoa's eyes fell on Darlia's glass arm and her heart seized up. The court forced Garna to turn over the money so now there was nothing left.

"So, onto more hopeful news," Arlicia said with a smile for Darlia. "We're going to sue for restitution on the basis of emotional distress and hopefully get you some money to put toward Darlia's treatment. We should be able to get at least half of the cost covered I think."

Dal smiled wanly. "More time in court, eh? I guess I can't exactly afford to rest given the situation. At least it's a start," he said, making an effort to sound hopeful. When he was a prisoner, he had seemed dejected, but there was still vigor in his attitude. Now though, grief smothered that vigor.

"It's not a start," Arlicia said. "It's the solution. Once we win the restitution, and we will win because I will be the one representing you this time, I will cover the other half of the treatment. Darlia my dear you'll be normal again within a matter of weeks."

Darlia gasped and Dal sat up straight. The disbelief on their faces was plain. Dal moved his mouth but no words came out. Finally, a tear streaked down his cheek. "Thank you," he said. "That's not an offer I can refuse"

"And you won't have to stand trial again," Yatoa said. "This'll happen in a Judge's office."

Dal chuckled through the tears. "Yeah, I… don't wanna set foot in a courtroom more than I have to. It's traumatizin'."

They ended up staying over until the late afternoon, by which time Yatoa and Arlicia decided it'd be best if they left Dal and Darlia alone. They needed time to mourn the loss of Garna, though not her life necessarily, but their idea of her as she had been in their minds. They mourned a mother and a wife. It was not an easy thing to have your entire perception of someone you loved upended.

The early evening air was hot and the sun hung low. Though the summer days were at their longest now so the sky clung to its blue cloak still. They walked in silence for a long time, far into the Goblin District, and it wasn't until they sat in some small, homey restaurant near their hotel that Yatoa finally said something to her mentor. "I guess we'll be staying in Gobroa a few weeks then?"

"Yeah, I need to get this restitution sorted," Arlicia explained while picking up a menu. "There's also Garna's trial. I'm sure it would mean a lot to Dal if we were both there for the emotional support. It'll also be a good chance to study up more on Goblin trials so you'd better be taking notes." She set the menu down, likely having decided what she wanted. "After we get all that sorted and Darlia healed, we'll take our leave of Gobroa."

"Where are we headed next?" Yatoa asked, but Arlicia ignored the question and called over a waiter to order orange juice with a side of pasta. Yatoa did the opposite. For her the juice would be the side because she wasn't a juice obsessed freak.

The dinner was nice and for once they discussed trivial things. It felt good to unwind with her mentor. It was like soaking in a hot bath, letting all her stress just float away, only it was the pasta that warmed her and set her heart at ease. Things may have ended in a messy fashion, but they would be alright. Things always turned out alright for Yatoa with time. That sentiment brought her ex, Ghost Dra'Vein, to mind and Yatoa winced. Well, most things anyway.

The next week was a whirlwind. During much of it Yatoa had entirely too much time on her hands, so she looked for ways to fill it. While her mentor went to work in the court-house, Yatoa had leave to peruse the city as she saw fit. Finally, there was time for her to be a tourist.

She walked the streets of Gobroa with a sense of finality. She was unsure when she would see these tree towers again, maybe not for a long time, but she knew for certain that she did want to visit Gobroa again. When she had first arrived, the massive city had seemed overwhelming with its impressive structures and swarms of tiny creatures milling past her, but now she had grown accustomed to the chaos.

Wading through Goblins she found her way to a massive park in the center of the Goblin District. Monstrous tree tow-ers surrounded it on all sides, some of the biggest in the city, yet the sky above the park was clear of branches.

Trees in the park were small and few and far between. It was mostly populated by flowers, insects and families enjoying an afternoon outing. Yatoa sat on a bench for a time.

Goblin watching.

Some cute goblets ran by holding kites. Their large eyes brimmed with excitement as one of the kites caught the wind and soared up high above the park. Free.

Yatoa had set Dal free, and it was the most fulfilling feeling in all the world. She smiled, and that smile remained with her for the rest of the day as she strolled the shaded streets from noon until late in the evening when she met her mentor for another dinner out. They went for more Goblona at Geits' restaurant. This time they didn't bother meeting with the man himself, but Yatoa made sure the waiter knew to give him their regards as they left. Arlicia had tipped well.

The next day wiped the smile clean off Yatoa's face. Garna's trial was a dark affair. Even Breichmar, who had been brimming with confidence a few days earlier carried out the trial with a more somber, reserved tone. He was harsh in his cross-examinations of Garna though, and it was hard to watch let alone take notes on. Sitting in the extremely dark gallery also made it difficult to take notes, and no doubt by the time she could scrutinize them in the light they'd be an illegible mess.

Breichmar was surprisingly respectful and considerate when questioning Dal. That alone was enough to drastically improve her opinion of him. The only reason she had been so annoyed with him before was because he was doing his job well.

Garna's defense was competent, but there wasn't much they could do to defend her. They plead guilty at the start of the trial, so they would conduct all seven stages, and then proceeded to lose every single verdict.

When it came time for the fifth stage and Piriel emerged from the flame Yatoa couldn't help but shake in fear. She still had not overcome her trauma, not completely, and seeing the demon's massive form brought back vivid memories not only of Piriel's horrible illusion, but also real memories of physical and verbal abuse suffered at the hands of her actual mother. On that damn island. Yatoa would never return. That she swore.

The vision had been embellished to a nightmarish degree, but in essence it hadn't been far from reality. Yatoa was glad when Piriel disappeared.

The trial concluded with Garna earning a sentence of life in prison. In a way Garna had gotten what she wanted. A life away from her family. Though despite how Yatoa felt about the woman, she felt the sentence was too harsh. Yatoa found a new dislike for her textbook, *Goblin Law*.

After the trial Dal muttered to her in the hallway, "she'll never have to worry about us again. I just hope she can find peace with herself someday. Though that may be a little hard when she's behind bars." Yatoa didn't respond.

It was only a few more days later that Dal's restitution came through. It turned out that Arlicia had actually fought for restitution on Darlia's behalf, not Dal's. "It would have been difficult to beg for restitution on Dal's behalf considering he stole eighty-thousand gobbings," Arlicia explained one night in their room. "Darlia on the other hand has suffered a great deal, and she deserves recompense."

18

Darlia's Future

It was early morning by the time Yatoa, Arlicia, Dal, and Darlia all arrived at the office of a One Star healer in the High Gob District. It was a thin marble building on a street corner a short walk from the river. Two thick columns sandwiched the building's entryway and there was only enough room for two people to stand in front of the door. Arlicia and Dal took point, while Yatoa hung back holding Darlia's tiny hand in her own. That hand felt so fragile and it wasn't even her glass one.

After a few knocks the door opened and an Elf woman poked her head out. Her hair was black and pulled up into a messy bun revealing ears pointier than Dal's. Her face thin, and her eyes squinted through her large, thick lensed spectacles at Arlicia and then Dal in turn. "Arlicia? What do *you* want?" the woman asked discourteously.

"We're here for a healing Lynne," Arlicia said, stepping aside to reveal Darlia and her glass arm behind her. The woman, Lynne apparently, squinted down at Darlia.

"The shatter? It won't be cheap you know, not even for you Arlicia. This is my whole day booked right here."

Arlicia grinned wide. "I know the price well enough and I'm prepared to pay it," she said handing her a check. Lynne frowned at it, then she looked up again and scanned them all. She really took them in. She stared at Yatoa in particular for an uncomfortably long time. Then she swung her door wide open to reveal that she was still wearing her nightgown. Their knocking had likely woken her.

"Inside. Move it. Haven't got all day," she said, herding them in with her hands. Once inside, Lynne escorted them past the entry hall into a small, but extravagant marble kitchen. Gold trim accompanied each white surface and massive windows let in ample light. It was an impressively bright for a room.

"How do you know this woman?" Yatoa whispered to Arlicia.

Arlicia's signature mischievous smirk lit up her face. "She's my ex-girlfriend." Astonished, Yatoa stared at Lynne again bug-eyed and reevaluated the woman. She *was* very pretty. Though what surprised her was that Arlicia had an ex-girlfriend that Yatoa had never even heard of before. She made a mental note to grill her mentor about all the details later and watched as Lynne led Darlia to a large, messy kitchen table draped with a checkered tablecloth. Without much care she grabbed the cloth and ripped everything off the table. A large steel candle holder and several forks clattered to the marble floor. Lynne then bent over and scooped Darlia up with ease.

"Hey, careful with her!" Dal cried out in alarm.

"Relax Goblin man," Lynne said as she set down a giggling Darlia on the table. "Lay down child. I want to get this over with as soon as possible so I can get back to my book."

"What are you reading?" Darlia asked as she lay down on the kitchen table.

"None of your business. Keep quiet and try to stay still while I save your life." Then, the rest of them forgotten, Lynne traced a line of light through the air. Unlike Yatoa's green lights, Lynne's were a bright blue. The lights coiled into vines that wrapped themselves around Darlia's glass arm. Arlicia pulled up some chairs for them to sit and watch.

The procedure lasted hours. At first the blue healing magic mesmerized Yatoa. This is what it would have been like had her sister been healed all those years ago. She was interested in the process, though most of it was non-visual and Lynne did not suffer questions from the gallery. After the first hour the magical luster of the procedure wore off and grew boring. Yatoa let her mind wander, though she noticed Dal watched the whole thing intently. He never took his eyes off the procedure for even a moment. Arlicia had the foresight to bring a book with her which made Yatoa very jealous.

When Lynne pulled away from the table and dismissed the magical vines, Yatoa could see that it was already evening through the windows. Lynne, still in her nightgown, collapsed into a nearby chair. "Alright, take her and get out of here. Office is closed," Lynne said while panting.

"Is she healed?" Dal asked as he shot up from his chair. Lynne glared at him.

The answer to the question came as Darlia sat up on the table and flexed her newly healed hand. In a flash Dal leapt across the room, gathered his daughter up in his arms, and wept into her shoulder. Darlia grinned in an adorable way that only a goblet could and hugged her father back.

"Thanks. Thanks, from the bottom of my heart," Dal said to Lynne once he was finally able to pull away from his daughter.

Lynne stood and shrugged. "Your check is thanks enough. I'm more interested in your bank account than the bottom of your heart. Now will you people please get out of my house?" They gladly took her up on her invitation to leave.

Once outside they all walked together to a nearby restaurant for dinner. Neither of the Goblins had ever eaten in the High Gob District, so Arlicia thought it would be a nice treat after the long day.

"We're takin' a trip. We need it," Dal said before shoving a piece of tender steak in his mouth.

"Where are you going?" Yatoa asked.

Dal smiled a shared conspiratorial smile with Darlia. "Faestar Great Tree. We're leaving tomorrow. I figure it'd be good to get away from Gobroa. Maybe find something better for Darlia."

"I want to see Fairies!" Darlia shouted as she viscously cut into her steak using her freed arm. Yatoa couldn't help but grin whenever she saw the wondrous sight. It was a miracle. This was the happiest she had ever seen Darlia. "But what about you guys? Where are you goin' next?"

Arlicia rubbed her chin in thought. "I haven't decided that yet."

Yatoa frowned. There was no way Arlicia didn't already know. She was just being coy. Yatoa hoped it was Stellaar, the capital of the Five Star Empire. Home.

After dinner they said their goodbyes. They would see each other again tomorrow as Arlicia and Yatoa were also set to leave around the same time. Yatoa felt sad to have to say good-bye to the two of them, but it was time she moved on to the next stage of her apprenticeship.

The next morning, Arlicia left Yatoa to pack up their things in the hotel room while she fetched Yatoa's uniform from the cleaners. It was only then, in a quiet room by herself, that Yatoa actually allowed herself to feel proud. It was a first.

"I am my own person," she said to herself as she tucked some dress shirts into her trunk. "I am not a replacement for my sister. I am me." It felt good to say that out loud. Spite the Flame Demon. To spite her mother. It also felt a little silly.

She startled upright when the door opened. "Ah! Toa my dear! I got those bloodstains off your uniform. Take a look." Arlicia flung the uniform over her head and it flipped in the air, landing in a heap atop the bed.

"You couldn't set it down like a normal person?"

"That would be boring, Toa. Besides this only adds to the tension. Go on, unfurl the uniform and take a look for your-self." Yatoa rolled her eyes but did as Arlicia asked and spread the white fabric out over the bed. The bloodstains were gone, but there were still three marks there. Three bright red stars sewn into the fabric. Three stars…

"What is this? This isn't standard regulation for apprentice attire," Yatoa protested. Arlicia laughed at that.

"You, my dear, are not a standard apprentice. You're something more now, if not a full lawyer. You've earned at least some red I would say." Arlicia flicked up her cane and pressed the tip into Yatoa's sternum. "You can't become a full attorney until you've litigated at least five cases, but I want people to recognize you as something more than an apprentice. You are already superior to many of your former classmates. Take heart Yatoa."

Yatoa didn't know what to say.

"You can say thank you," Arlicia said with a smirk.

"Thank you…" She forced herself not to cry now in front of her mentor, but she couldn't hold herself back from giving her a hug.

They took a little longer than they should have getting ready, but they managed to make it out of the hotel before the designated check out time. Yatoa donned her new uniform and she could feel the stars burning bright on her breast as she strode down the street.

Yatoa felt no anxiety walking through these streets now. She felt confident and strong. Pride propelled her onward toward her new future, and that future lay beyond the gates of Gobroa.

Once outside the gates they found the wagon they had hired to take them to their next destination. A destination which, until seeing the wagon, had been a complete mystery to Yatoa.

Yatoa halted the moment she saw Dal and Darlia in the wagon.

"Hello there! Come to see us off, have you?" Dal called out to them. Arlicia confirmed Yatoa's suspicions by tossing her trunk into the wagon bed, and climbing up into it.

"I thought we were going to go *home*," Yatoa said in an accusatory tone. Arlicia stood in the wagon and looked down upon her apprentice. She spread her arms wide with a smile. "We're not going home for a long time yet my dear. For now, we're headed straight for Fae Star Great Tree with our good friends Dal and Darlia."

"I'm so excited!" Darlia yelled. "I get to spend more time with Auntie Yatoa!" *Auntie?* Yatoa sighed and climbed into the wagon, once again roped in with Arlicia's shenanigans. "You're so cool Auntie! When I grow up, I'm gonna be a lawyer like you!" Yatoa blinked in surprise. This little girl wanted to be like *her?* Really? Was she sure? Not like Arlicia Sa'Krieglund the God Lawyer, but like…

"Just like Yatoa the Three Star Lawyer, eh?" Arlicia said with a lazy amused grin. She was leaning back against the wagon railing without a care in the world.

"The Three Star Lawyer?" Yatoa said skeptically.

"Well, you do have three stars on your suit," Dal pointed out. That was certainly true. In short order the wagon was off and rolling down the road. The driver was a human man who was chewing on some nuts as he steered. They rolled away from the city of Gobroa. It struck an imposing figure in the distance with its high walls, and even higher tree-buildings. They all watched it in silence until the horizon demolished it.

She left behind the experience of her first case and washed her hands of it now. She glanced toward Darlia. Well not completely. Yatoa figured that she never would wash her hands of any case. She touched one of the stars on her suit jacket. She would always take a bit of each case with her.

She imagined watching the city disappear impacted Dal and Darlia with much more finality. Dal had dreamed of leaving this city one day with his family, but now he was leaving both it and Garna behind.

Their destination, Fae Star Great Tree, was a city Yatoa had meant to return to for four years now, but she never had the chance. She resigned herself to her fate, figuring a visit to her old friend Eliafa Fa'Natas was long overdue. Although studying to be a Three Star in Faestar Great Tree had was not for her, she did find herself missing the city on occasion. Cautiously, she allowed herself to get excited.

"Give me *Goblin Law*," Arlicia commanded. At first Yatoa was confused by the request, but then she remembered the giant tome in her satchel. She reached into it and brought it out. It was a thick, black, leather-bound book with gold lettering on the front that read "Goblin Law". She handed the tome to Arlicia.

"Thank the Gods I don't have to study that infernal thing anymore. That made the last trip a headache inducing nightmare," Yatoa lamented as she leaned back against the railing and looked out over rolling fields fat with crops.

"I wouldn't thank those Gods so soon if I were you, Toa," Arlicia said reaching into her own satchel and pulling out an even thicker tome.

Yatoa took the tome with dread. She turned over the smooth leather tome in her hands and read the words inscribed on the cover in shiny pink lettering.

They read, "Fairy Law".
"You're joking."
"Nope."

About The Author

Alexander Pappas was born in 1998 in Vancouver, British Columbia. He spends his days working as a financial regulation consultant in the DC area, and his nights partying with his puppy and Fiancée. Without the escape and challenge of writing, he would not be where, what, or who he is today. He loves orange juice, fantasy, role-playing video games, spacing out, melting toasters, flooding apartments, leaving his bag on the train, and, well, writing.

www.ingramcontent.com/pod-product-compliance
Lightning Source LLC
Chambersburg PA
CBHW030139010826
48973CB00002B/638